THE
INCUBUS
TAPES

ALEX CONNOR

First published in Great Britain in 2024 by Merisi Publishing. https://www.merisipublishing.com

Copyright © 2024 Alex Connor

A CIP catalogue record for this book is available from the British Library.

ISBN 978-1-7385363-4-4 (PB)

ABOUT THE AUTHOR

ALEX CONNOR writes thrillers, often with an art theme. She has been published in many countries and translated into many different languages. She had a world No 1 with THE CARAVAGGIO SAGA and won the Rome Prize for THE ISLE of the DEAD. She is also a professional artist, an historian and a FRSA.

THE INCUBUS TAPES is the 8th in her series of art thrillers. She lives in the UK.

Also by Alex Connor

THE REMBRANDT SECRET
LEGACY OF BLOOD
THE MEMORY OF BONES
THE CARAVAGGIO CONSPIRACY
THE BOSCH DECEPTION
ISLE OF THE DEAD
A WREATH of SERPENTS

Incubus: A spirit that, in heathen mythology, was believed to torment or to suffocate sleepers. Morbid oppression in the night resembling the pressure of weight upon the breast.
Samuel Johnson
(A Dictionary of the English Language 1775)

'Emulation embalms the dead; envy, the vampire, blasts the living.'
(Henry Fuseli)

'The scariest monsters are the ones that lurk within our souls.'
(Edgar Allan Poe)

WEEK ONE

Letter from Henry Fuseli to Johann Lavater.
London 1782

My dear friend

How I miss your counsel and long for your steady company. I do not sleep well, and what little rest I do achieve does not refresh my senses. The painting entitled 'The Nightmare,' I named rightly. Its exhibition has created an outcry! Its display at the Royal Academy has caused women to faint, men to demand it be removed, and others to insist on my genius - or insipient madness. There are psychiatrists who seek interviews with me - which I do not grant - to press me on my inspiration. Where did the image spring from? Was it based on any experience I had undergone? Was it an hallucination? Some unsteadiness of my mind? Or was it dreamed? And if so, what had caused me to dream this creation?

Regarded as mad or sane, I am still feted in London, invited to all manner of events and dinners, my Swiss self, isolated, a perplexed island in a sea of bobbing admirers.... Dear Johann, you would find much to laugh at here! And for now, I am amused. Yet for how long, I do not know. There are bizarre stories beginning to circulate about the painting. And they make me wonder if, perhaps, the work - borne out of a troubled mind - holds some dark energy. I know too well my feelings when I painted it - did they impregnate the canvas? Do they reach out to those that view it? .... I pray they do not, yet wonder. Thank God, you are the only person alive who knows the origin of this painting.

Write as soon as you are able, loyal friend.

With affection,
Henry

PROLOGUE

1941 - Psychiatrist Addison Franckel opened a sleep clinic investigating shell shock. Many of the patients' histories were filmed. What the tapes revealed was so disturbing the government had them suppressed. Amongst accounts of sleep paralysis and night terrors, there were intimations of unexplained paranormal activity. Accusations of medical abuse and rumours of missing patients followed, and in 1945 Addison Franckel disappeared.

2024 - Researcher Gus Egan begins work for Louis Willes, a historian writing a biography about Henry Fuseli, painter of 'The Nightmare.' Willes's property was once part of the Franckel clinic and as soon as Gus arrives an anonymous contact tells him there are copies of the infamous tapes hidden there.

Hindered by the secretive art world, watched by authorities unwilling to have the past resurrected, Gus risks his own life to expose the link between a notorious painting created in 1782 and the harrowing Incubus Tapes.

ONE

Royal Academy of Arts
The Strand, London,
1782

Raising the lantern to shoulder height, the nightwatch-man walked passed the paintings slowly, studying each to ensure that nothing had been disturbed or dam-aged, that no thief had managed to avoid the guards on front duty, or the dogs at the back. The Strand at night was pitted with opportunists, as many drunks as theatre goers; as many wealthy aesthetes as vicious yobs. For every member of a private gentleman's club there was a slack jawed pimp or pick pocket; for every noblewoman in a carriage there was a whore selling her wares against an alley wall. King George III might earn himself the sobriquet 'Farmer George' for his love of the land, but his bouts of instability were rumoured to be worsening, England anxious, St Paul's holding services to beg God for the sovereign's deliverance.

Yawning, and longing to end his shift, the watchman continued his progress. Still using the lantern to light his way, he moved from the ground floor up the grand staircase - steep and winding as a coil of hair - which lead to The Exhibition Room above. At the top of the steps he paused to allow his eyes to adjust to the darkness. All lights inside the gallery had been extinguished, the candles snuffed out, the lanterns quenched, except for the great glass orbs that flanked the front entrance of the imposing stone façade. The illumination was limited, yet strong enough to travel through the upper windows and make its way over the wooden floor. It slid across panels, crept over walls, and nuzzled against the gilded frames, finally coming to rest on the picture hanging on the far wall, the painting directly facing anyone who entered the gallery as it loomed out of the darkness.

Startled, the night watchman stepped back, dropping the lantern, the light immediately extinguished. He could not see clearly, but had caught a glimpse of a dark shape scuttle across the floor. Instinctively he reached for the nightstick in his belt, the metal Billy club weighty in his hand as he waited for another movement to indicate where the intruder was hiding. A burglar, the watchman thought, some sneak thief or drunk looking to find a place to bed down. For weren't there enough of his type on Piccadilly?

"Oi," he called "whoever you are, come out."

There was no response.

"Come on, I'll not take any of your mischief."

Irritated, he moved forward, peering into the far off, darkened corners, his eyes scanning the gallery. An ex-pugilist, he wasn't afraid of anyone that he could stop with his fists, or his baton, his boots sounding loud on the wooden floor as he struggled to relight the lantern. Mumbling to himself, the watchman suddenly sensed another movement in the room and an ominous feeling overcame him as he heard a soft shuffling. Unnerved, his gaze turned in the direction of the sound, but he could only make out a humped shadow, crouching, its attention seeming to be fixed on him.

"Who's there?" he asked, backing away, his progress stopped as he walked into a closed door. The same door by which he had entered, the door he had left open. The door someone else had closed.

As his hand reached behind him, scrambling to turn the door handle, the watchman's gaze moved round the gallery. Whoever had broken in was not going to be scared off; or intimidated. Whoever was hiding had locked the door and trapped the watchman inside... With his free hand, he clenched the baton. If they attacked, he had something with which to defend himself; but there was not another sound, just a pulsing, ominous silence.

The light from the outside lamps did not reach the far corners of the gallery. They remained in darkness as the guard's nervous gaze moved over to the painting that faced him, Fuseli's depiction of *The Nightmare*. The picture that had transfixed London, the painting that had drawn crowds to gaze on the sleeping woman, and the malignant figure of the Incubus crouching on her breast.

But he wasn't crouching there now.

He had moved.

The watchman could see the blank space on the canvas, could hear the muted thud as something landed on the floor.

The terrified guard's mouth opened, but no sound came from it, his eyes widening as he stared at the transformed painting. It was only feet away from him as he turned to the door and began to drum on the wood frantically, calling out for help. Too afraid to turn and see what was behind him, the watchman continued to struggle with the handle, twisting it desperately as something moved across the floor *towards* him.

Unnerved. sobbing with terror, the guard continued to beat his fists on the wooden door, staggering and losing his balance as a heavy weight landed on his back. As his legs gave way he could smell the putrid breath, feel the saliva against his neck, and flinched as the coarse fur brushed against his cheek. Horrified, screaming for help, the watchman crawled forwards inch by inch on his belly - the creature still clinging to his back - finally wrenching open the door and staggering towards the staircase. Only as he descended the first step could he feel the creature fall away from him, and then ran down the staircase without looking back, barely coherent as he burst out of the building and into the London street beyond.

When the watchman reported to his colleagues what he had seen, they mocked him, then went to investigate. They found nothing amiss. Fuseli's painting of *'Nightmare'* was still in place, undamaged, intact, the Incubus gazing out from the painting unchanged. In the dim light at first no one noticed the imprint of feet at the base of the easel.

Small feet, barely larger than a dog's.

By morning they had disappeared.

TWO

Soft land, cushion-backed hills of chalk, scarps and moist green valleys running along downlands to the sea. Further inland, the green is computer screen highlighted on an autumn afternoon, Gus Egan driving through a dip in a sensuous open valley. The Sat Nav had told him with precise directions to turn right, which he did, only to discover that the address he was looking for was not what he found.

Graybrooke Lodge was in semi ruins, a workman pausing, hand shielding his eyes from the late low sun as Gus entered the drive.

"Hello there," he called out "can you help? I'm looking for Graybrooke Lodge."

"Well, this ain't it." The accent was pure East End of London. "You want to go further along, 'bout hundred yards, that's Graybrooke Lodge. This is Graybrooke Cottages. Or it used to be."

13

Gus could tell that the man welcomed the diversion, two other men sitting against a wall in the shade, all of them glancing over to him as he gestured to the building.

"Are you renovating the place?"

"Trying to, but every time we think we're getting somewhere we find more woodworm." The builder shrugged. "The cottages were never treated for it. You stand on a beam at your own risk... You visiting?"

"If I can find the place, yes." Gus said drily.

"So you know old man Willes?"

There was a frisson of dislike as he said the name.

"Not really, I'm going to be working here. What's he like?"

"Funny bastard. You can't get a handle on him. One day he'll wave, smile, nice as anything, the next he'll ignore you or curse, saying your van's taking up too much road and how could an ambulance get by?"

Gus looked down the lane and shrugged. "There's a sharp bend, but an ambulance could get past."

"That's what we said" the builder continued, wiping the sweat off his forehead with the back of his arm. "We heard he's in the art world. Must have money, or valuable stuff at his place anyway. The alarm system he has there isn't for show... Does he sell paintings?"

"No, he writes about art." Gus replied, "He's hired me to help with the research."

"Sounds dull." The builder lost interest, turning to go, then added. "Just a word of warning - watch his driving."

"In what way?"

"It's too fast. If Willes hasn't killed someone already, he will do."

THREE

It sometimes happens in October, that when the sun sets the dusk arrives like a gatecrasher, coming in unexpected and fast. Within minutes the lane had shaded over, the iron gates of Graybrooke Lodge standing open, a battered Volvo in the drive, a Jaguar with a dented bumper outside the front door. Remembering what the builder had said, Gus parked his car at a safe distance under a tree, then looked around.

The Lodge had once served as an introduction to a larger estate, but that had long since disappeared, leaving it a deserted testimony to a grand past, its mullioned windows armoured with bars on the ground floor, the upper floors guarded by a prominent alarm system blinking its bloodshot eyes at all intruders.

At first glance it was impressive, but many of the wooden window surrounds were rotted and patched, the fresh putty gurning out from the gums of its faded neighbours. A few centuries had not felled the chimneys, iron supports now crutches for towering stacks, the roof lichen-furred over rusted gutters. It seemed at once intimidating and fragile, and as Gus studied it a tall, stooped man snatched open the front door and beckoned for him.

"You're late." Louis Willes said impatiently. "I don't like people who are poor timekeepers." He regarded his visitor with mistrust; Gus Egan, mid-forties, burly physique, dark hair and a self-assured manner.

Smiling, Gus put out his hand, Willes backing away. "No, I don't shake hands. We had an epidemic, you know."

"I heard." Gus replied evenly, glancing around. "Your home's beautiful."

"You think I don't know that?" Willes responded. He was wearing a tweed jacket long out of shape, leather patches on the elbows, a knitted tie with an overtight knot. "I have security, so don't get any ideas." He studied Gus for several seconds. "To be honest, I don't know if you'll fit in here."

"Well, maybe I will and maybe I won't." Gus replied.

Surprised that he was neither cowed nor apologetic, Willes gestured for Gus to follow him into the house. A moment later the dimness of the hall was transformed, the historian turning on the lights to reveal a life size statue of the *Dying Gaul* placed centrally under a weighty Dutch chandelier. It was an obvious trick to catch visitors off guard, the pieces designed to impress and say more readily than words that Louis Willes had both finances. And taste.

Eyes narrowed, he watched Gus for a reaction, and seeing none, was compelled to speak. "Are you qualified for this job?" he snorted, his head balding, his scalp liver-spotted, the surrounding hair a web of quivering activity. "Because I need an expert."

"You know my work, Mr. Willes, that's why you asked me to come." Calmly Gus walked over to the massive marble copy of The *Dying Gaul*, then glanced at a small painting on the wall beside him. "Gerrit Dou?"

"Don't try to impress me with your knowledge, Mr. Egan."

"I wouldn't dare. I don't claim to be an authority."

"Yet you were dealer in Dutch 16th century paintings."

"I *was* a dealer, but left the business. Didn't like the people."

"You still give lectures."

"Where I want to, and when I choose." Gus replied.

"Do you still write?"

"Good God, no," Gus smiled, "there are too many books in the world, and I have nothing to say that someone else hasn't said already - or will do."

Willes clicked his tongue. "A man *should* know the extent of his abilities."

"Or his place. Or are the two things the same? You need a researcher, Mr. Willes, and that's something I do supremely well. We both know that you will have checked out my references and no doubt spoken to people who have hired me before to reassure yourself that I am more than capable. So why the interrogation? Are we shadow boxing for any particular reason?"

"You're a smug bugger."

"No, it's just that if you want to throw me out please do it now, it's a long drive home and it gets dark early." Gus replied, watching as Louis Willes opened another door and ushered him into a library.

It smelt, not unnaturally, of old books, a damp Yorkshire terrier sitting on a window ledge. Taxidermy trophies hung high above the book shelves, horns and antlers holding eternal sparring matches, their glass eyes reflecting the artefacts and furniture below. Chairs, windows, rugs, and side tables sporting opened books and half emptied mugs, a bag of Cheese and Onion crisps discarded in the iron grill of an antique grate.

"As I explained over the phone, I'm writing a biography on Henry Fuseli, and the psychology and paranormal aspects of his work." Willes gestured to a large reproduction of *The Nightmare* hanging above his writing desk. "Everyone knows this painting, everyone *think* they know what it means. But it's not obvious. There are many meanings, just as Fuseli painted many versions… D'you like it?"

"Yes, I always have done. Freud had a copy in his consulting room --"

"Which copy?"

Gus frowned. "Does it matter?"

"More than you know," Willes replied, becoming suddenly businesslike, his voice quickening. "We have some serious work to do, Mr. Egan. Are you up to the task?"

"Why wouldn't I be?"

"It might not be what you expect."

"What is?" Gus countered. "Just what d'you want me to do."

Willes paused, then finally continued. "You've heard about the newly discovered Fuseli painting?"

"Hasn't everyone? The Lavery Foundation have announced that the last version of *The Nightmare*

18

painted by Henry Fuseli has been found in Germany - but all enquiries are being directed to Zurich." Gus paused. "Have you seen it?"

"Only in reproduction." Willes grumbled. "What about you?"

"Not yet. But I could get to see it."

"Really?" Willes queried, his tone mocking. "The anonymous owner has a go between, the dealer, John Cummings."

"John Cummings?" Gus asked, raising his eyebrows. "He has excellent contacts. His father's a lawyer in New York and his brother's practice is in London. Not much has been heard about Cummings for the last year or so, but then again, he's always been very discreet."

"Well, he's back in the limelight now."

"And he's handling all information and PR about the Fuseli in Switzerland?" Gus considered the news. "Why not Berlin if the painting's there?"

Willes was growing impatient. "I don't know! All I know is that John Cummings is not forthcoming. In fact, he's very secretive."

"Everyone with something to hide is secretive."

Gus's frankness caught the historian off guard, but Willes was beginning to warm to him. It was true, he *had* investigated Gus Egan before he had offered him the job, and had been more than satisfied with what he had discovered. Respected and methodical, he had a reputation for uncovering research that had been overlooked or hidden. Such talent should have made him the ideal working partner, but Willes was unsure of Gus Egan. His confidence was daunting for a man who liked to bully, and his self-assurance was unexpected.

Restless, Willes moved about the library, his hands thrust deep into his pockets. He paced in silence, sat down, then moved over to the curtains and drew them closed, the terrier ignoring him. Willes knew his nervousness would seem obvious, his blustering manner suddenly replaced by a frenzied urgency.

"Can I trust you, Mr. Egan?"

"What do you expect me to say to that?" Gus answered. "If I'm genuine, I'll say yes. If I'm a fraud, I'll also say yes."

"You're blunt."

"You're asking me the impossible. It's for *you* to judge if you can trust me."

Leaning on the arm of a wing backed chair, Willes rubbed his forehead, the thin white skin crinkling like sand after the tide goes out. "What if the job proved too difficult?"

"In what way?"

"Demanding, possibly even dangerous." Willes, shook his head, the dandelion hair floating like waterweed.

"Dangerous?"

"Possibly! *Maybe.*" As though decided, Willes rushed on. "I'll be open with you. I'm coming to the end of my life and I'm eager to settle old scores before I die. But for now, I want to keep my intentions hidden." He gave Gus a penetrating look. "The book on Fuseli must be written in total secret. I need you to sign an NDA, a Non-Disclosure --"

"Agreement. Yes, I know, I've signed them before."

" -- only after that can we begin work. Whatever I tell you *must* remain between us. This house is huge, some rooms are closed off but there's more than

20

enough space to accommodate you, even if the plumbing *is* shit. You'll work here full time --"

"No," Gus interrupted him. "I'll work here Monday to Friday, weekends I go back to London."

After a pause, Willes nodded. "Alright."

"You agree to cover all expenses incurred?"

"Within reason. And I want receipts, my accountant likes order."

"If I have to travel, you agree to cover those expenses too?"

Irritable, Willes slammed his fist down on the arm of the chair. "*Yes, yes*! Just let's get on with it. I'm old and my health appears to be in a race with my longevity." He stared at Gus, his expression combative. "I've been told that I've got only a few weeks to live. *Now* do understand why I can't waste time?"

FOUR

In fact Gus understood better than Louis Willes could ever have imagined. Three years earlier he had been diagnosed with leukemia and given his own death sentence. But the cancer had gone into remission. The all clear had sounded. He didn't know if it would return like a hungry mongrel looking for another feed, or if it had found a more compliant host and moved in permanently. So when Willes had confided that he was dying he understood the old man's urgency. Gus had also learned that life was finite and he wasn't prepared to squander any of it. The possibility of some danger - which would have been daunting in the past - was now almost welcomed.

Having returned to his flat in London, Gus had carefully considered his conversation with Willes, only one phrase causing him any unease. The historian's talk of '*settling old scores.*'

Willes had said it in a voice without emotion, but his face had an expression Gus knew only too well - the venal combination of self-pity and malice.

His thoughts were interrupted when his mobile rang, the name Ziva flashing up. "Hi, I was just going to call you --"

She interrupted immediately. Like she always did. "Did you go and see the historian?"

"I did."

"What was he like?"

"A windmill."

"What?"

"The whole interview was like trying to put a ski suit on the sails of a windmill."

"I've never tried to do that." She said dryly.

"Don't bother, it's difficult." He replied, moving over to the table by the window and glanced at a weary palm tree in a chipped pot. Picking up a half empty glass of water from the day before, he dribbled some water onto the parched soil. "I don't think it's a good idea."

"The ski suit?"

"No. I don't think it's a good idea for us to have another child."

There was a pause at the other end, Gus imagining Ziva blowing out her cheeks, her dark eyes closing for an instant, then reopening widely. "I would take full responsibility --"

"We already have a son that we take care of together. You can't expect me to father a child and then step back. It doesn't work that way. You know how involved I was with Mark when he was a baby; how much time I spent with him. My life has changed, I don't have the time now. I couldn't be around enough for another child. It wouldn't be fair, Ziva. It's impossible, and you know it."

"Why?"

"*Because we're divorced.*" He said, sighing.

He had overwatered the plant and the excess was trickling out of the bottom of the pot and onto his desk, sneaking towards his laptop. Grabbing a cloth from the kitchen, he mopped up the spillage, Ziva unusually silent. He knew full well that the proposition would seem reasonable to her, and her enthusiasm had, for an shuddering instant, made it seem viable to him. But the moment had passed and now he was vehemently against the idea.

Their divorce had not been due to any bitterness between them. It had not been the result of an affair or exhaustive arguments. They had simply reverted back to the friendship they had had before marriage, both agreeing that neither wanted to be the other's life partner. They had always been friends. They had remained friends - and yet Ziva now wanted Gus to father another child *without* reuniting as a couple and *without* any other commitment. Or so she claimed.

"I'm sorry" he said when she had remained silent for too long, "but it wouldn't be right, Ziva, and it wouldn't be good for Mark."

"Mark is twelve now."

"You'll meet someone and marry again."

"*Jesus Christ!*" she snapped. He could hear her slam her hand down on the table at the other end of the line. "Why is that always your response?"

"Look in the mirror, Ziva. Wherever you go you get attention --"

"Attention isn't a relationship!"

"You've just not found a man you want to settle down with." Gus paused, walking back into the kitchen and tossing the wet cloth into the sink. "I haven't married again either."

"But you *could*. I have limited time left to get pregnant - you have years to make a whole new family." Her tone was plaintive. "Are you still seeing Madelaine?"

"Yes. But we're not going to get married."

"You've been together two years."

"No," he corrected her "we've been together for about three months. That's the time we've *spent* together; you know how much she travels, and I've been busy too. It's not serious, Ziva, and besides she don't want to have children." He wondered why he was suddenly downplaying his relationship and if, subconsciously, he was giving his ex-wife hope.

"It seems such a small thing to ask." She replied. "I make enough money to provide for another child, and I'd have support from my parents if I needed it. I wouldn't have to ask you for help -"

"But I'd want to *give* it!" He countered. "Can't you understand that?"

"Is it because of the cancer?" She asked. "It's over. You're well again now. You had the all clear -"

"Can we just let it drop, please!" His voice rose, then he steadied himself. "Look, I don't want to quarrel with you, Ziva. We're too close to have any bad feeling come between us."

"I know, I know..." She agreed, changing tack. "So tell me about Louis Willes, are you going to take the job?"

"He's paying well and it could be interesting." Gus replied. "Willes mentioned the Fuseli painting at the Lavery Foundation. He even intimated that he had some secret, dangerous, information about it."

"Dangerous?"

"It's bullshit. There's always some conspiracy in the art world and he was probably just trying hook me in." Gus said dismissively. "The business runs on rumours, you know that. Whispers, finds of Old Masters that pop up like bloody mushrooms every few years. Everyone's in a fever about this newly discovered Fuseli. Apparently it's the last version of *The Nightmare* he painted." Gus laughed. "Or some *forger* painted. Either way, the art world will be slavering over it, the dealers sizing each other up, phoning their Dubai collectors and trying to keep Sotheby's out of the loop." He thought of the historian. "Willes has picked a good time to release his Fuseli book. But he's a cantankerous bastard and I suspect he's unpredictable too."

"You don't have to take the job, Gus."

"He's throwing money at me."

She was surprised. "Money isn't usually the deciding factor for you."

"True, and it certainly wouldn't be easy to work for him. Besides writing the book on Fuseli, Louis Willes is also intent on getting revenge."

"On who?"

"God knows."

"So why are you even thinking of working for him?"

"He's dying."

Ziva's response was muted. "Oh…"

"Willes is eighty four, he's got cancer. And before you ask, I didn't tell him my medical history, but knowing what he's going through made me more sympathetic." Gus paused, hearing his laptop ping to tell him that he had a message. "I should go now. I'll see you at the weekend, Ziva. Look after yourself, and give Mark my love."

There were, in fact, seventeen messages waiting to be opened, many junk mail, most of the others replies from universities and libraries that Gus had approached asking for research material. There were also a couple of messages from the bank, one from his garage, and a reminder from Mark that he was playing in a football match a week on Saturday. Scrolling down, Gus paused, seeing at an unknown e mail address.

It read:

> *So Louis Willes is working on his Fuseli biography and getting you to do the research.*
> *Make sure he tells you everything. Especially about Addison Franckel's Sleep Clinic. Five patients died there and the journalist investigating the place committed suicide.*
> *Have I got your attention, Mr. Egan?*

Gus read the message twice before he replied:

> *I'm not a journalist or a detective.*
> *Contact the police if you have evidence of murder.*
> *It's not my field.*

There was a minute's delay before another message came up in Gus's inbox.

It read simply:

> *It became your field the moment you took the job.*

FIVE

Dover Street
London W1

Slumped in an over-stuffed leather chair, Edward Leigh stared out from an upper window in the flat situated above the gallery below. He was thinking that he could call his PA for her to bring him a coffee, but knew she would do it with an ill grace and slop some of it into the saucer deliberately. If she had not been a relative of his partner he would have fired her long ago, but any criticism drew a droll response from Anthony Hallett, followed by some nuanced reminder that he had the larger stake in the gallery. And the larger profits.

His attention moved back to the online article written by a dealer in Switzerland, a man Edward knew well. A man who weighed every word he spoke as a diamond merchant weighed the carats of a stone. In his middle forties John Cummings was slightly built, extremely short, dressed with lethal exactness, and had a reputation for secrecy. Because of it, rumours abounded that he was involved with some disreputable clients, from countries as diverse as Russia, USA and Holland; but Cummings was clever in his dealings and slid through the rumours intact. His confidence was well supported by his family connections, his father and brother, both lawyers, his parent in New York, his sibling in London.

Turning his laptop away from the window so he could see the screen more clearly, Edward scanned the article for the third time that morning. An unknown version of *The Nightmare* had been discovered, allegedly the last Henry Fuseli ever painted.

"It's a fake!" Edward muttered to himself "and where's it come from all of a sudden?" He read on. "So it was found in Germany…but as the Lavery Foundation is giving out all the information I bet it's stored in Zurich for an 'anonymous owner'. Lucky that Cummings is based in Switzerland."

He glanced up as someone entered, a striking middle aged, mixed raced woman bearing a Costa coffee in a polystyrene cup. Raising one eyebrow, she handed it to Edward. "I don't suppose the harpy downstairs has watered you, has she?"

"I daren't dare ask her." He admitted shamefaced, "I'm old, she terrifies me."

"You're fifty six, Edward, don't play the ancient just yet." She pointed to the laptop screen. "So you're reading about the Fuseli?" Ronnie continued, sitting down in a chair beside him and crossing her legs. Shapely legs in Louboutin shoes, never seen in trainers, never seen in jeans, Ronnie Gilchrist was a complete, unabridged woman, and ensured that every one noticed. "So, what do you think of it?"

"Fake."

"Maybe." She agreed, "but Fuseli painted many different versions of *The Nightmare*, so it could be genuine."

"Or it could be a copy. The picture was so popular in its time he would have had followers churning out reproductions. There are bound to be copies and remember, Fuseli had pupils."

"Constable and William Blake --"

Edward cut her off. "Never liked Blake, he was a nudist, weird. He and his wife used to sunbathe naked in their garden. In full view of their neighbours."

"You're such a puritan," Ronnie replied, amused, her American accent less pronounced when she was in London. In New York, she sounded like a native. "Naked or clothed, Blake, or his fellow apprentice, Constable, *could* have copied Fuseli's picture. But if it's original, it'll fetch a big price at auction. And an even bigger price if it's sold anonymously."

"Is that why you're in London, Ronnie, sniffing around for clues?"

"You are so suspicious! It's just a fleeting visit, I'm going home tomorrow." She directed his attention back to the computer screen. "So, what d'you reckon about the Fuseli? Real or fake?"

Leaning forward, Edward studied the painting's image on screen. There was the same familiar figure of the recumbent, sleeping woman, the same Incubus ghoul squatting on her chest, but instead of a horse peering out from between the bed curtains there was an indistinct figure. Whether man or woman it was impossible to tell, the person blurred, their head bowed and face lost in shadow.

"Expand the image," Ronnie said, leaning closer, then impatiently taking the mouse away from Edward. Adeptly, she honed into the painting, scanning every inch in closeup, then paused, pointing to the screen. "Look at that."

"What?"

"Doesn't that look like a hand to you?"

Edward reached for his reading glasses, his eyes magnified through the lens. "A hand?"

"Well, *doesn't* it look like a hand?"

He grimaced. "I can't tell, the image isn't clear enough. It could be, or it could be a shadow. You'd have to see the actual painting to be sure."

"Fat chance of that! The Lavery Foundation won't tell anyone where the painting is. Just that it's in Berlin somewhere. When I asked to have a meeting with the Press Department at the Lavery I was stone walled," Ronnie folded her arms with a look of weary impatience. "I tried to get information, but was told that all details about the painting were suppressed until it was exhibited --"

"Where?"

"I dunno! No one knows."

Edward twirled his glasses around his index finger. "Know anything about the owner?"

"Not yet."

"Do they want to sell?"

"Now if I knew that, Edward," she said, her tone teasing "why would I tell you and give you a head start?"

"You'd rather tell my partner," he replied, dryly. "Are you and Anthony still an item?"

"Are you and your wife?"

Edward winced. "Low blow, Ronnie." Stung, he turned back to the laptop. "I bet you know more than you're letting on. In fact, I'd put money on it."

His placid face, with its trimmed grey beard, was aimable, but his mind was pitted with trip wires to unman the naïve, or the innocent fooled by his urbanity. No one maintain a strong presence in the art world without being shrewd, and Edward Leigh had been prominent for over thirty years.

"I've heard something very interesting." Ronnie smoothed the hem of her skirt, then looked back to Edward, her gaze searching. "Did *you* know that Louis Willes is writing a book on Fuseli?"

"He's been writing that bloody opus for years. He'll never finish it, he's lost his motivation."

"He's dying."

Edward raised his eyebrows: *"Dying?"*

"Cancer. He's only got a few weeks left, or so the rumour goes, which has certainly motivated him and made him very keen to finish the book." She continued hurriedly, her voice speeding up. "There's another rumour going the rounds, that he's out to settle old scores."

Edward flushed, his face blotchy around the neck where his beard couldn't disguise it. "Willes is always fighting with someone! The old bugger's paranoid. You know that as well as I do, he's always imaging that he's been ripped off. Or someone's plotting against him."

"Oh come on, Edward! He has reason to hate the art world, and if he's dying he'll want to get his revenge before he goes. You should watch your back -"

"It was a business transaction, no more!" Edward replied unnerved. "I believed the painting was by Turner. It's all down to attribution in this business. It wasn't my fault that Willes discovered it was a fake after I sold it to him."

"Shame he didn't see it that way. Willes thought you took advantage of him. After all, he's a historian, not a dealer."

"Then he should have got professional advice --"

"So you *did* cheat him?"

"No!" Edward shook his head. "I didn't say that, Ronnie! Don't put words in my mouth. The truth is that I didn't know it was a forgery when I purchased it. Or when I sold it to him. I'm not a cheat! Remember that I lost money too."

"Not as much as Willes." She retorted slyly. "You've gone very red faced, Edward, you should learn to lie better... Anyway, I wouldn't worry too much, you're not the only one Willes has a beef with."

"Indeed I'm not." Edward agreed. "What about you? You accused him of plagiarism when he wrote his book on Goya --"

"It was *review*. Anyway, I didn't used the word plagiarism. I merely said he 'borrowed' from some established writers. Who doesn't? Besides, it was nothing to what others did to Willes. I've heard there are people that have crossed far sharper swords with him."

"He's been around a long time, no one can expect to survive in the art world without getting some cuts. Besides, his old rivals and competitors are mostly dead now –"

"Yeah, but we aren't." She smiled conspiratorially. "It'll be interesting to see how much revenge Mr. Willes can accomplish before he meets his Maker. After all, he has help now."

Edward jerked up his head, suspicious. *"Help?* What kind of help?"

"I'm surprised you haven't heard. Willes has hired Gus Egan to do research for the Fuseli book."

"Egan?" Edward thought of the researcher who had refused to work for him.

"I had a feeling that would interest you." Ronnie said, amused. Standing up, she tucked her hair behind her ears and smiled down at the agent. "Gus Egan's going to stay with Willes in Hampshire. I don't envy him. The old bully is difficult to handle, but it will be interesting to see what comes out of it."

Edward's voice was wary. "Does Egan know what happened to Louis Willes's wife?"

She clicked her tongue. "Hey, Edward, that's a long time ago, people will have forgotten all about it."

"People never forget bad news, my dear. They have long memories for scandal. *You* remembered easily enough."

Shrugging, she replied. "But nothing was ever proved. It was supposed to be an accident."

"Tragic, wouldn't you say?" Edward raised his eyebrows. "Maybe it *was* an accident, but I wouldn't want to move in with Louis Willes, albeit temporarily. He may be old and dying, but --"

Impatient, she cut him off. "Who knows *what* happened in the past? Who cares? Today is what matters. Just imagine how much the old man will confide in Gus Egan in the weeks to come. When they're working together, under pressure, holed up in that creaking mausoleum. Just think of all the memories and grievances Willes will want to get off his chest." She paused to let the words have effect, knowing that Edward was listening. "He's dying, he needs a confidante. Willes is an atheist, he's not going to turn to God, and he has no family or close friends to confide in. He *needs* someone to listen and we both know that Egan is a clever man, with his own reasons to loathe the art world." She planted the next thought carefully. "In fact, I would say that in Gus Egan poor old Willes has found himself a very willing listener."

SIX

Lavery Foundation
Zurich, Switzerland

October, high skies and jay blue horizon, the top points of the mountains bleakly grey, with just the beginning promise of white, the wooden chalets indolent before the noisome impact of the season. Standing on the balcony of his house, John Cummings turned and moved back into his bedroom, staring at the dry cleaning his butler had just brought to him.

"Don't pay them."

"Very good, sir."

"Tell them I will not be using their services again and will advise the people I had previously recommended to do likewise." He liked the feel of the words. Petty spite was always piquant, his own irritation temporarily assuaged by the infliction of pain on another.

Expressionless, Cummings continued to study his valet. "Hire someone to dry clean my clothes privately. If you can't find someone in Switzerland, fly

37

the items to London or Paris." He turned away, then turned back. "My secretary is unwell and I've sent her home. You may leave early also - after you have organised the laundry issue. It's Friday, make sure that the dry cleaner gets my message before close of business, will you?"

The impact would destroy the man's weekend and a large chunk of his livelihood; but Cummings felt no remorse, his attention taken by his mobile phone vibrating. There was no number displayed, but he knew there wouldn't be, the voice altered mechanically. As ever, the secrecy amused him.

"Mr. Cummings?"

"Yes."

"I'm calling as we arranged, to talk about the painting. My client is interested to know if the owner of the Fuseli is willing to sell."

"They are not decided."

"But have not refused to consider it?"

Watching through the window, Cummings could see his valet, an ex SAS soldier, his arms ladened with the rejected clothes, bound for the dry cleaners and a surfeit of garbled excuses. It was wise to have a butler who could also act as a bodyguard because Cummings didn't want too many members of staff on his property. They might come with implacable references, but Turner was the only one he trusted, and besides, Turner owed his employer an old favour.

"Mr. Cummings?"

"Yes, I'm listening. I was considering your question" he lied "perhaps the absence of a definite refusal might be considered - tentatively - the possibility of some consideration." The words might have been uttered by his father or his brother, the barrage of syllables falling on the listener like plaster from a stuccoed ceiling.

"Can you press them for an answer. Mr. Cummings?"

"This is a matter which requires delicacy."

"We will match, or exceed, any offer for the Fuseli." The caller replied, sensing an opening. "And we would also be willing to offer a generous retainer to ensure that we would be notified exclusively when the painting is up for sale."

"*Exclusively?*" Cummings rubbed the side of his nose. "That would not be possible I'm afraid. If, or *when*, the Fuseli is available for purchase it would be at the owner's discretion and on his terms. It is not a matter on which I am qualified to make any agreement at present."

"Then I'll wait to hear from you, Mr. Cummings." The caller replied tersely. "I'll call on Thursday at the same time --"

"Sadly that will not be convenient. Would you be kind enough to telephone later, around ten?" John replied, suspecting that the caller was ringing from New York and would be inconvenienced to have to phone in the early hours of the morning.

Inflicting another little irritation pleased him, fattened up his peevish streak, soothed his malcontent, made him feel powerful, even tall. An illness in infancy had stunted John Cummings's development, his height never exceeding five feet two inches. Another man might have come to terms with it, but the presence of a father and brother both over six feet only underlined what he thought of as a handicap. In an attempt to convince the world he was unconcerned, John occasionally dated models who were always a head taller than him. He meant it as a defiant two fingers to his detractors, whilst inside he ached with insecurity, a little man tip toeing about a lofty world.

In business he had no insecurity. Secrecy and skill had allowed John Cummings to attract an exclusive bevy of clients; collectors from every continent and creed. As he would say grandly *'art is not racist.'* He was correct, but what he failed to mention was that art was also at times immoral, conveniently blind to the reputations of its collectors. Paintings were currency, the export and import of many works of art held in massive storage holds at airports and docks; in a twilight zone where an Old Master was equivalent to a savings account.

Others works – although Cummings was careful to avoid any involvement - were stolen to order, or pilfered from countries at war, the Arab Spring breaking open borders and the vaults of abandoned museums. Although regarded as a gentleman's business, the dregs of the art world survived in a wasp's nest of activity and hustle. In an endless jostling for position and power amongst other ruthless and rapacious characters who had also learned to manipulate the swarm.

No one more so than the tiny and devious Cummings, shuffling his clients like a croupier, whilst making sure that no one at the table could see what cards he dealt.

SEVEN

Graybrooke Lodge
Hampshire

Having arrived for work early, Gus was greeted by
two men who appeared to be waiting for him on the
drive. One was a doctor holding his mobile phone, his
medical bag under his left arm, whilst the other was
a younger man, Asian in appearance, who nodded a
greeting to Gus.

"Good Morning. My name is Je-Yun and I am Mr.
Willes's private assistant." He spoke carefully, with
only a suggestion of an accent, Gus judging him to be
around thirty. His clothes were simple, a dark shirt and
black trousers, his hair long enough to cover his ears.
"Unfortunately Mr. Willes will not be available until
later today and has asked me to ensure that you are
made comfortable in the meantime."

"Is he ill?"

"He slept badly and suffered some pain, so I called
for Dr Richards," Je-Yun gestured towards the medic

who had obviously overheard. He nodded in agreement, his manner pre-occupied as he continued to talk on his mobile. "Mr. Willes wants me to pass on his apologies --"

"There's no need to apologise," Gus reassured him. "I'll take the chance to look around and get to know the place. I have access to all Mr. Willes's books, don't I?"

"All but a selection which are stored under lock and key. They must be kept at a certain temperature to avoid deterioration. In fact, Mr. Willes had a chamber specially built for them two years ago." Je-Yun explained, moving towards the house, Gus following. "Apart from those, you are welcome to view anything in the library."

At the front door he turned and bowed to the doctor. "Thank you for calling."

"Let me know how Mr. Willes is later, will you? Ring me after surgery, about six." He frowned, thin faced, distracted. "No, better make it seven. But then I might be out on calls..." Still talking, he moved over to his car. "I'll tell you what, call me at seven and if I don't answer leave a message." Tossing the medical bag onto the passenger seat, he climbed into the car. "Or you could text me. Yes, better text me!" He called out, before finally reversing and driving off.

"Does Dr Richards come every day?" Gus asked, following Je-Yun into the dimly lit hallway.

"Mr. Willes only calls him out when he feels it necessary. Some days he does not like people to fuss him, other times he can be demanding." He glanced at Gus, his dark eyes unreadable. "You will soon learn to judge his moods. I mean no disrespect, just offering advice to make your stay here easier."

Pausing, he then pushed open the heavy swing doors which led into a spacious, old fashioned kitchen with a massive iron range, the oven lighted, two copper pans releasing aromatic vapours on the hob above.

"This must be an antique" Gus said, surprised. "How old is it?"

"Apparently over a hundred and twenty years, but it's been reconditioned and updated to keep its original appearance."

"And you cook for Mr. Willes using it?"

Je-Yun inclined his head slightly. "I was trained to cook in Seoul, before I came to London."

"You were recommended to Mr. Willes?"

"I was."

"By people in the art world?"

"No," Je-Yun replied, "I have no connection to the business. My brother does, but not myself."

"Does he work in London?"

"Germany."

Gus was walking around, noticing the heavy butcher's block with myriad notches made by myriad blows from myriad knives, some of the marks deep and blackened with age, the iron hinges the colour of wet peat. With surprise he then spotted a huge, ultra-modern fridge at the back of the kitchen, both his and Je-Yun's reflections mirrored in its sterile, stainless steel doors

"Family sized fridge. A *big* family sized fridge." Gus said, gesturing to it.

"Mr. Willes likes to keep everything fresh and he doesn't like to be short of produce so it's always kept filled. Please feel free to take anything you wish."

"I will, thanks." Gus smiled. "Have you been with Mr. Willes long?"

"Three years."

"And you live here?"

"Oh yes," Je-Yun replied, "should Mr. Willes need me at any time I must be available."

"Twenty four hours a day? Surely you have some time off?"

"The gardener stays in the house then. Mr. Parker is devoted and has been with Mr. Willes for many years. He was here when Mrs. Willes was alive." Je-Yun paused, then added. "My employer does not really require a bodyguard, but at night he fears a burglary."

"Have there been many break ins?"

"Not recently."

"But there have been in the past?"

"Apparently when Mr. Willes first moved here from London there were a couple, but nothing since. Although we've had some strange phone calls and unexpected visitors over the last twelve months. Then again, people do get lost out here, it's a long way from town and the property is very remote."

He was standing to attention as if expecting orders, Gus moving back into the hallway and picking up his case. The Korean immediately put out his hand to take it, Gus stepping back. The action reminded him of the time he'd had cancer, too weak to lift anything, even a plate. He had found his fragility belittling, old age coming in the guise of sickness; and after his recovery any reminder of frailty had become intolerable.

"I'm fine, I can manage" Gus said curtly, "but if you could show me to my room, I'd be grateful."

-o0o-

"Why are you phoning me?" Louis Willes asked, secreted in his bedroom, keeping his voice lowered so that he wouldn't be overheard. "I haven't had contact from you in over a year."

"I heard you were ill --"

"Dying."

" -- and thought I'd come and pay you a visit. Would you like that?"

Propping himself up against the pillows, Louis Willes stared at the bedspread covering his long, sparsely fleshed legs, the old fashioned crewelwork meticulously crafted. It had been inherited from his mother, handmade over a hundred years earlier, and still beautiful. No one made anything to last anymore, Willes thought disgruntled, his attention reluctantly returning to Ronnie Gilchrist.

"I don't want any guests."

"It would do you good."

"Piss off, Ronnie!" He snorted, infuriated. "I don't have time for games."

"I imagine all your time is taken up with writing your Fuseli book," she purred, ignoring his animosity. "You need to get it published fast whilst there's all the interest in this newly discovered painting --"

Willes cut straight across her. "I don't have any influence, Ronnie. Don't look to me, I can't pull any strings for you, because that's what you're angling for, isn't it? I'm not a dealer and I'm not in London anymore."

"But no one knows more about Fuseli than you--"

"And what I know I'll keep to myself! You want to know if it's coming up for sale, don't you? You want to know if it's genuine? Well, find out for yourself. Or you could ask that midget Cummings for information - *but don't bother me!"*

Irritated, he cut the connection and clambered out of bed, pulling a shabby tartan dressing gown over his shirt and trousers and looking for his slippers. Unable to find them, he moved to the door, shouting for Je-Yun, the Korean running down the corridor towards him.

"Mr. Willes, what is it?"

"This!" he shouted, flinging the mobile at the man and just missing the side of his head. "When did I ask you to get me a bloody mobile?"

"Last month, sir."

"Well, I was out of my mind and I don't want it now. Ringing and ringing. Demanding to be answered. I am not a slave to a piece of fucking plastic!" He paused, catching sight of Gus coming down the stairs from the upper floor. "Give it to him."

Je-Yun turned to Gus and then looked back to his employer. "You want me to give the phone to Mr. Egan?"

Willes nodded, smiling, all anger gone as he beckoned for Gus to approach. "We're going to be working together from now on, so *you* can answer my calls, can't you? Hardly anyone has the number and those that do are exactly the people I don't want to talk to." He was suddenly all conviviality, patting Gus on the shoulder. "It's good to have you here. You've met Je-Yun? Tremendous help. He can cook like a demon. We have a cleaner than comes in daily, so the place is looked after – but you'll have to make your own bed, she doesn't do beds. It's a thing with her, probably some religious idiocy. You can manage to make your own bed, can't you?"

Gus smiled. "Yes, I can manage that."

"Good," Willes said, wrapping the dressing down around him and fastening the cord tightly about his waist. "We can't waste any more time talking, Mr. Egan, let's start work."

He moved quickly, more steadily than before, Gus suspecting that he had taken his medication and was out of pain. The routine was familiar to him: you feel re-invigorated, fool yourself into believing you're recovering, until the effect winds down. He guessed that by afternoon Louis Willes would be struggling again.

With Gus following the historian, they moved into the library, a brass inlaid secretaire placed close to the door, Willes's monumental desk glowering at him from the bay window twelve feet away.

"You have your laptop with you?"

Gus nodded. "Of course." He looked around the room. "I don't need anything except a Wi-Fi connection. How is it out here?"

"Mobile connection and the internet's reasonable during the day, but it wavers at night, don't ask me why, and the weather can affect it." Willes glanced towards the window. "Remember, we're out in the sticks here. And if you work late the signal drops around one or two in the morning," He sat down at the desk with his back to the light. His hair was thin, sun shining through it, a gloriole around his domed skull. "The pile of notes on your left are my jottings, I've forwarded all my research to your laptop."

"Yes, I just received it."

"The bibliography is particularly important for this book --"

"The Fuseli?"

"Who else am I bloody writing about?"

"I wondered if you wanted to refer to any of his pupils or contemporaries." Gus replied, "I mean, this newly discovered painting could have been done by one of his pupils, so perhaps we should look into Constable and William Blake?"

Willes narrowed his eyes. "You're more interested in the painting than the book?"

"I didn't day that," Gus replied. "I just wondered, that's all."

"Well, stop wondering. I want you to concentrate on Fuseli, to follow up on, and check, the queries in my notes."

"That's fine, tell me what you want and I'll do it."

"I should think you will, charging what you do."

Inwardly amused, Gus leaned back in his chair. "I've been meaning to ask you something - what's your connection to Addison Franckel?"

He could see Willes flinch.

"Addison Franckel?" He repeated, jumping to his feet and moving over to Gus. "What the fuck are you up to!" Angry, he leaned across the desk. "Who are you? What are you after?"

Surprised, Gus answered him. "Last night I was contacted by someone who knew I was doing research on your book –"

"Who?"

"I don't know. They simply said that I should ask you about Addison Franckel and his Clinic."

He could see Willes wavering, his hands tightening the dressing gown cord around his waist. "You said you were contacted, *how*?"

"Email."

"Who sent it?"

"I don't know, it was anonymous. An email address I didn't recognise," Gus replied, keeping his voice calm. "Look, I'd never heard of Addison Franckel before last night –"

Willes interrupted him. "What did the message say?"

"That five patients had died at Franckel's clinic."

"*Who* said that?"

"I told you, the person that contacted me was *anonymous*." Gus repeated, irritated. "They also said that a journalist who had been investigating the clinic committed suicide."

"Bullshit!" Willes looked aggravated. *"Five dead patients and a dead journalist?* I don't suppose they gave you any names, did they? No clues to this massacre?" His anger had passed, amusement taking its place. "It's a hoax! Some nutter!"

"Look, I'm just repeating what they said. They told me to ask you about it, that's all I know."

Without replying, Willes moved back to his desk and pressed a buzzer. Moments later, Je-Yun entered, moving over to Willes, listening, nodding, then leaving the room.

Curious, Gus looked at the old man. "Why do I feel that I'm being left out of something, Mr. Willes?"

"Why do think someone contacted *you* with this ridiculous story?"

"I wouldn't know. Nothing like this has never happened to me before. But you did say that the work might be dangerous --"

"I was teasing you!" Willes replied, waving his left arm airily. "I exaggerate sometimes. It's a failing of mine. You'll get used to it."

"But what *do* you know about Addison Franckel?" Gus persisted. "And what about his Sleep Clinic?"

"I don't doubt you looked up it on the Internet." Willes replied, his voice tart. "So what did *you* discover?"

"Hardly a thing. Only that Franckel was a psychiatrist who specialised in sleep disorders. He set up a clinic in England somewhere."

"Here."

"What?"

"Graybrooke Lodge was his clinic, but it was called Reid Hall then. There were a few outbuildings - wards and such like - tacked on in the 1930 and 40's, but they were all demolished." He spoke casually, as though eager to appear nonchalant. "Rumour was that Franckel had some strange methods and he was struck off the medical register."

"Struck off?"

Willes shrugged. "Apparently so. His name became something of a disgrace and so all trace of his treatments and his clinic were suppressed."

"They weren't suppressed, they were *obliterated*," Gus retorted. "The man's been wiped off the face of the earth. How's that possible? Apart from what I've mentioned, I can't find anything else about Addison Franckel, and, believe me, I know where to look."

"Why are you so curious?"

Gus ignored the question, asking one of his own. "When did you move here?"

"In 1970, with my wife. We were both in our early thirties and wanted to renovate the place, which was falling apart. My wife couldn't have children, so this place became our legacy."

It sounded plausible, but didn't convince, Gus uncertain as to whether he should pursue the matter or let it drop. His curiosity won out.

"So what *was* your connection to Addison Franckel?"

"We don't have a bloody connection!" Willes's rheumy eyes fixed on him. "I just own the building that was once his clinic."

"No more than that?"

"What more *could* there be, Mr. Egan!" he snapped. "When you buy a house – any house – you're not responsible for its previous owner. Or what they did. When he was disgraced in the 1940's Franckel was middle aged, he's long dead."

"And you don't know anything about his medical treatments?"

"No!"

"There were no notes, no records left here?"

"No!"

"The person who contacted me stated that five patients died." Gus continued. "Later, when a journalist started to investigate, he committed suicide. And you're saying that the clinic was here and you don't know anything about it?"

Willes' tone became wheedling, plaintive. "Mr. Egan, I have no connection with Addison Franckel other than owning this building. It was stripped to the bone when I bought it, no files, no records. The outbuildings that had been used as wards were flattened long before 1970, the ground levelled. Nothing remained. I can't tell you what I don't know…Why don't you ask your anonymous pen pal why he's contacting you." Willes moved back to his desk, dropping into his chair, his voice childlike. "Why are you asking all these questions? Why can't we just get on with the work I hired you for, and forget some idiot acting like a bloody clown?"

"You're right, let's forget it –"

Sighing, Willes stared at Gus. "You should be *helping* me."

"And I will. It was obviously just someone's idea of a joke." Gus reached for the imposing stack of papers beside him, some in spiral note books, others pinned together with staples, many highlighted in places with a marker pen. "Just tell me what you want me to do first."

"I need help…"

"And you've got it." Gus reassured him. "Where d'you want me to start?"

Willes paused before replying. "Find out where Fuseli stayed when he went to Germany."

"Ok."

"He was there for a time before he came to London and always retained a fondness for the country. He said he thought and wrote in German." Willes was back in control, his voice strong again, giving our orders. "Find out where he lived."

"Right, I can do that."

"I want to know. I *need* to know." Willes said, his tone becoming sly. "You see, I don't think it's a coincidence that Fuseli's newly discovered painting suddenly turned up in Berlin."

EIGHT

London

Jimmy Gold was sitting at a bar in Beak Street, Soho, trying to make a connection with an attractive young woman on the stool next to his. She was staring ahead, ignoring him, her glass of wine untouched, the fingers of her right hand wrapped around the stem. Every few moments she would brush away her hair from her eyes, the dyed streaks cupping her face. He had wondered about it as soon as he had seen her; why she had done it, why she had chosen a red the colour of crushed raspberries. It was crazy, he'd thought, no one had hair that colour.

"I've never seen you here before." He began "Are you waiting for someone?"

A muscle in her upper arm flinched, Jimmy anticipating that at any moment the glass of wine would be thrown over him.

"If you want to chuck it at me, go ahead. I've had a fucking awful day, it would be the perfect ending."

He paused, adding. "Has anyone told you that you look like Natalie Portman?"

"No."

"They wouldn't, because you don't."

She turned to him, her expression cold. "Fuck off."

"Now?"

"What d'you mean, '*now?* '"

Jimmy raised his eyebrows. "If I fuck off now, you'd never get to know me. Never know if you'd missed something special."

Her eyes raked up and down his thin frame. "If you're something special, I *do* look like Natalie Portman."

They both laughed, Jimmy just getting into his stride when his mobile rang. Seeing the caller's ID he smiled apologetically at his companion, then answered.

"Gus, I'm in the middle of something. I'll call you back."

The girl sighed, getting off the stool, Jimmy catching hold of her wrist. "It won't take a minute, please don't go." His large, brown eyes took on a pleading look, then he smiled as she sat down again, reluctantly turning his attention back to the call. "Gus, what is it?"

"Are you free to do some research for me?"

"What kind?"

"I'm working for someone writing a book on Fuseli. Thing is, we're really short of time, and I need some help. Fast."

Jimmy paused, he had often worked with Gus Egan, knew him and Ziva well, the latter inspiring a devoted - but unspoken - admiration. Years earlier, when Gus had been a dealer in London, Jimmy had tracked the shaky provenances of paintings that had been offered to Gus for sale; thereby ensuring that nothing suspicious tarnished Gus's reputation. In return, Jimmy Gold became Gus's right hand man. It didn't hurt that having once been jailed for fraud, Jimmy had kept some of his connections; the runners and low lives who worked around the periphery of the art world.

Unwilling to continue with his own criminal activities, Jimmy had changed tack and become respectable, maintaining his contacts and turning to them for information that he could pass on to the dealers who hired him. It was a profitable business for everyone, and when Gus finished working as a dealer, he had continued to use Jimmy when he needed information that wasn't available to anyone without a criminal background.

"Can you help me out?"

"About Fuseli?" Jimmy asked, his interest ignited, "is this about the painting that's just been found?"

"Up to a point." Gus replied. "I need to know where Fuseli travelled after he left Switzerland around 1771. He went to Germany, but which city? Where was he living before he came to London in 1779 and settled here?"

"Doesn't sound too difficult. I can do that."

"Also can you find out where the painting is now? Apparently the work is in Berlin, but The Lavery Foundation in Zurich are answering all queries, which seems odd if they don't have it in their possession. Like I say, I don't have much time. Can you work on it right away?"

Jimmy was listening, but smiling at the girl at the same time, anxious to get off the phone. "Yeah, I'll do it. Usual fee?"

"Usual fee." Gus agreed. "There's one other thing. Can you look into a man called Addison Franckel." He spelt out the surname. "A-D-D-I-S-O-N F-R-A-N-C-K-E-L, he was active around 1930's - 40's."

"Art dealer?"

"Psychiatrist."

Having got his full attention, Jimmy laughed. *"Psychiatrist?* What's he done?"

"He's disappeared, wiped from history. Apparently he ran a Sleep Clinic and was struck off the medical register - after which everything about him and his work was obliterated. Can't find *anything*, apart from his name and mention of the clinic, nothing else." Gus was speaking from his flat, relieved that he was away from Graybrooke Lodge and couldn't be overheard. "The historian I'm working for is Louis Willes and when I asked him about Addison Franckel he said knew nothing about him --"

"Why should he?

"Because he owns what used to be Addison's clinic, Graybrooke Lodge, in Hampshire. That's where I'm working. And as soon as I took this job I got contacted – anonymously - by someone who told me to ask Willes about Addison Franckel."

Angered at being ignored, the girl had slid off her stool and left the bar, Jimmy interested in what he was hearing and oblivious to her departure as he continued to talk to Gus. "Anonymous contact out of the blue?"

"Yes, I asked an IT colleague if he could track the sender's address, but no luck."

"Could be a gag" Jimmy replied thoughtfully. "But then again, how would they know you were going to work with Louis Willes unless someone told them?"

"Come on, Jimmy, we both know how much people gossip. Everyone finds out what everyone else is doing. Louis Willes is well known -"

"Only in the art world." Jimmy said dismissively. "Which means that it has to be someone in the business. Someone that knows you, or this Willes fella. I mean, people don't send anonymous messages randomly. Unless it's a joke, Gus, unless someone's playing a trick on you."

"That's what I thought at first, but they seemed serious, especially when they said that five patients had *died* at Franckel's Clinic."

"You're joking."

"No, that's what I was told. They also said that the journalist who was investigating the place committed suicide."

"Bloody hell."

"So if it's true that patients *did* die at Franckel's clinic, it would be dangerous for anyone digging around. Which makes me wonder if the journalist actually did commit suicide" Gus concluded "or if he was murdered."

Jimmy snorted down the line. "You're taking a bit of leap there!"

"Am I? If five patients died it was bloody convenient for someone noseying around to kill himself before he found the evidence that everyone else was trying to suppress. All the information about Franckel was wiped. The authorities certainly wouldn't want it all dug up again. A journalist would have been a real threat."

Jimmy will still unconvinced. "But even if the authorities tried to keep a lid on it, people talk. They can't help it, especially if there are rumours of murder. It would have been a scandal."

"It was wartime, people had other things on their mind."

"Maybe." he changed tack. "Or maybe people were *threatened* into keeping quiet."

"That's what I'm wondering."

Moving out of the bar onto the street outside, Jimmy pulled out his vapouriser, his thin frame huddled into a doorway. "The 1940's are a long time ago." He paused, inhaled. "Why does it matter now?"

"If people died, it matters. I want to know why it was all hidden, what Addison Franckel did, and why *I'm* being dragged into it."

"You told me why - because you're working in what used to be the shrink's clinic." Jimmy's inhaled, then let out the smoke slowly. "What's the place like anyway? I hate bloody hospitals."

"It's a private home now. The old wards and out-buildings have been flattened, there's nothing left. Seriously, *nothing*. Like it was never there." Gus paused, then added. "Thing is, I don't believe Louis Willes. I think he knows about the scandal. I mean, how likely is it that he *wouldn't* know? Who buys a place and knows nothing about its history?"

"Where is it?"

"In the countryside, with no close neighbours and remote from any town. But having said that a psychiatrist setting up a clinic and then being struck off would cause *some* comment. The scandal had to be known." Gus thought for a moment. "Then again, if people were afraid to speak out, maybe it *would* remain a secret. Time passed, people died, and perhaps the 'suicide' of the journalist sent out a warning to anyone else who got curious."

Jimmy whistled softly. "The deaths of five patients and a suicide is a *big* secret to keep hidden."

"Which makes you wonder" Gus replied deftly, "why someone wants to dig it up."

NINE

Dover Street,
London

To Edward's surprise, his partner seemed genuinely moved. Anthony Hallett sitting in the easy chair in Edward's office, his tailored form immaculate in a three piece suit, his pugnacious face crestfallen. Although unattractive, even bordering ugly, he was inescapably masculine, something almost Simian in his features. Perhaps, Edward thought, that was why women were attracted to him; the promise of some hint of Neanderthal under the Saville Row mohair.

"*Cancer…*" Anthony said, shaking his head. "How old is he now?"

"In his eighties."

Anthony sighed, the sound unexpected and poignant. "You never know, do you? Louis Willes seemed like he would go on forever. He's always been a good historian, but when he was younger he had a great turn of phrase, incisive, biting. Hannah and I used to stay at

Graybrooke Lodge, the Willes held impressive dinner parties in the 90's. Once they had the garden ringed off, put up this massive tent and held a circus for their guests. Not clowns, nothing so vulgar, but they had Russian acrobats and gymnasts brought in. Louis always said how inventive Ava was, what an incredible hostess."

He trailed off, Edward imagining the Russian acrobats and thanking God he hadn't been invited. He was tempted to bring up the subject of Ava Willes's death, but resisted, turning the conversation round to another subject.

"Willes will be under even more pressure to finish his book on Fuseli. And now he's got Gus Egan helping him… Stroppy bastard refused to work for me, thinks I had a hand in that forgery scam."

"I heard he wasn't keen on being your employee."

"But even with help" Edward said, hurrying on, "if Willes gets that book completed it will be a miracle."

"He'll want to get it done, to leave his legacy." Anthony replied, blowing his nose and dabbing at his eyes. Was he really moved by Louis Willes' plight, or enjoying the drama, Edward wondered.

"Apparently the old man is looking into the paranormal aspects of Fuseli's work."

"That doesn't surprise me" Anthony said, nodding. "Louis always had a fascination with the occult."

This was news, Edward leaning forward in his seat. "I didn't know that."

"You weren't a close friend."

"Neither were you, or you would have known about his cancer."

Ignoring the barb, Anthony continued.

"When Louis Willes left London and went to live in the country he distanced himself from the business, and when Ava died he just withdrew from everyone. There were all kinds of rumours that he was involved with the paranormal, mediums, and such like --"

"He wanted to contact his dead wife?"

"I imagine so. That's what grieving people do, or I'm told. And of course Willes was always banging on about the Fuseli book. I never thought he would actually finish it." Anthony paused, remembering. "I wonder if he'll tell the story of *The Nightmare* in his book? About the first time it was shown in London. It was a good yarn, he used to recount it well at his parties.

"What was the story?"

Anthony settled back in his chair, always ready for audience. "Fuseli's greatest friend, Johann Lavater, was forced to leave Switzerland due to a run in with some politician, and Fuseli left with him. After a while they split up, but remained in contact by letter. Fuseli spoke several languages, but preferred writing in German."

Edward nodded, feigning interest, although he was already bored, Anthony's bass tones rising and falling as he created the atmosphere. Was *that* another reason women liked him? Edward wondered. Perhaps he told them stories in bed or in the throes of orgasm? Something *had* to account for his success with women.

"You see…" Anthony was easing himself into the tale "…. when Fuseli came to London he was soon accepted into the influential salons of the day…"

Like being invited to Louis Willes's private circuses, Edward thought grudgingly.

"…. and he found a champion in Sir Joshua Reynolds, founder of the Royal Academy. Encouraged by his support, and inspired by the enthusiastic response to his work, Fuseli turned his attention to the paranormal, selecting aspects of Shakespeare that he could illustrate, like the Witches from Macbeth. They were hugely popular, because London was very eager to accept Romanticism."

"I didn't know you were so knowledgeable about Fuseli."

Anthony smiled modestly. "I don't pretend to know much, but there was one particular story about the painter that stuck in my mind."

"Really?" Edward said, sneaking a look at his watch.

"Rumours began to circle that Fuseli was an opium addict."

"*Opium?*" Edward replied, now genuinely interested. "Like de Quincy and Coleridge?"

"They came after Fuseli. In their time it had become commonplace, artists believed the drug inspired them." Anthony explained grandly, moving on. "As for Fuseli, perhaps - if he *did* indulge - opium flung open the gate to his imagination." He extended his own arms to demonstrate, Edward wincing. "Yet he kept his addiction a secret, even though it *was* suspected as the bizarre and supernatural became more and more obvious in his work." Leaning forward with his elbows resting on his knees, Anthony continued, the afternoon dimming into evening, a desk lamp offering the only illumination in the room. "Apparently, in one letter to Lavater, Fuseli describes his painting of *The Nightmare*. He said he had based it on folk lore and a *dream* he had personally experienced. A terrible dream in which he had awoken to find himself paralysed, unable to move, with a demon squatting on his chest, its eyes fixed on his, its breath hot on his face. He said he could feel its fur on his bare skin, and its claws puncturing his flesh, but couldn't move to defend himself..."

Edward was listening, transfixed, as the light dimmed further and rain began to fall in the street outside.

"... Fuseli described the creature's black, stunted body, its back humped, its legs bent at the knees, the pads of its feet burning hot against his chest. He wrote that he had never felt such fear, the ghoul's bestial features repugnant, its size that of a hideous child as it peered down at him. Fighting for breath, Fuseli said the horror nearly overcame him."

Outside a car backfired, Edward startled and turning to look towards the window. The afternoon had faded into darkness, his reflection gazing back at him in the glass pane. And for an instant - just one instant - he saw not his partner, but the outline of a dark humped figure sitting in Anthony Hallett's place.

"What the hell!" Shaken, he spun round, only to find Anthony smiling at him.

"It's a good story, hey? But that's not the end of it. You know that when it was first exhibited at the Royal Academy there were rumours it was haunted?"

For reasons he couldn't fully understand Edward was sweating, the room overheated, his voice remote. "I never heard anything about that."

"A night watchman saw something. He swore that the Incubus came out of the painting!" Anthony laughed. "It was his imagination, of course, but the man would never return to the Royal Academy, and several of the other guards reported odd sounds and seeing things. Some visitor to the gallery insisted that she saw footprints on the floor, and another reported having nightmares for weeks afterwards. It was probably just a way to drum up interest, a clever PR ploy. They did have them, even in 1782, and it worked astonishingly well. The picture's still famous, reproduced endlessly."

Edward was finding it hard to form words. "Do you believe a painting can be haunted?"

"I believe that people enjoy a lurid tale, the more eerie the better." Sighing, Anthony rose to his feet, gazing out of the window into the city street below. "Perhaps there *is* some truth in it, because the night-watchman never recovered. He went mad and roamed London telling his story and was finally committed to Bedlam. A couple of years later he was found dead in his bed, suffocated."

"Suffocated?"

"There were bruise marks on his face. As though something had been pressed over his nose and mouth to smother him…" Turning back to his partner, Anthony shrugged. "All nonsense, of course. But a good story – unlike the watchman - never dies."

TEN

The mobile vibrating on the bedside table woke Gus with a start, his hand reaching out as he squinted to focus on the text message.

> *Have you asked Louis Willes about Addison Franckel yet? Perhaps you have, or perhaps you'd rather just dismiss my messages.*
>
> *Don't do that. If you want proof, talk to Ella Fairchild, I'll send her contact details later. Her grandfather was a soldier in the 2nd World War, he died at Addison Franckel's Clinic.*
>
> *She knows all about the place. She knows what was done there and she knows about the Incubus Tapes. They did experiments at the Clinic - next to the very building where you're now working. They made notes and filmed what was done, and what they saw. It was claimed that the old*

*tapes disintegrated or were destroyed, but
one set of tapes survived.
They must be found.*

Irritated, Gus replied:

*Why don't **you** find them?
Take them to the police.
Why involve me?*

The reply was immediate:

*The police and the authorities suppressed
them before and would again. You ask why
I involve you? You're on site, Mr Egan, you
have access to the building and grounds -
and access to Louis Willes.*

Gus replied shortly:

*You think I believe all this?
Try out your fantasy on someone else,
or do your own detective work.
But leave me out of it.*

The reply was brief:

*Your maternal grandfather was a soldier
admitted to the Addison Franckel Clinic. He
was one of the five that died there.
Now do you understand?*

An address followed for Ella Fairchild and then the connection ended, Gus throwing his mobile to one side and moving into the kitchen. The water hadn't been run long enough, and wasn't cold when he took a drink, its taste tepid and almost musty. The mention of his maternal grandfather had come as a shock. Both his parents deceased, Gus knew little about his relative and had no means of checking the information. Frowning, he leaned against the fridge door, trying to recall any memory his mother had shared with him.

All he could recall was that his grandfather had been a widower and had violently objected to his mother's choice of husband. If he had hoped to change her mind he had been bitterly disappointed, the couple marrying and severing any connection with him. That was all he knew.

So how did the *contact* know about his grandfather?... The thought irked him. He was being used, dragged into something he had no desire to investigate. And there was the word - *investigate* - the one activity he abhorred. There *had* been times in the past, more than once, when he had investigated paintings; when he had been a dealer, eager to ensure that the detritus of the art world's under current did not sully his reputation. But it had cost him money, nearly resulted in a prison sentence, and almost ruined his health, Gus finally forced to step back from the bear pit of the galleries.

He knew he could back off, tell Louis Willes to get another researcher, but although the idea appealed momentarily it was dismissed. The communication had excited something inside Gus; something far more absorbing than uncovering the provenance of a painting. And he realised then that he was bored. Safe, paid handsomely, his health fully restored, his life in balance and yet, and yet...

He moved from the kitchen back into the living room, slumping onto the sofa and picking up his mobile.

Slowly he re-read the text he been sent. Someone had researched him, researched his life and family, someone who was watching him, and guiding him - but why? And where?

Irritated, he punched out a number and waited for the familiar voice to answer, Jimmy Gold launching in without preamble.

"Got some stuff about Fuseli in Germany --"

"Great, send it to me, will you?" Gus interrupted him, changing the subject. "I need you do something else. Find out about a member of my family, my maternal grandfather."

"Name?"

Gus raised his eyebrows. "George something --"

"You don't know? He was your bloody grandfather!"

"My mother was estranged from him. There was bad feeling between them. My parents never talked about him, and they're deceased so I can't ask them." Gus thought back to his childhood. He had been happy, enough love offered to easily compensate for any estranged grandfather. But now that forgotten grandfather had been resurrected, dragged into Gus's field of vision as a victim, a patient who had died in the very place where he was now working.

The thought was chilling.

"Are you still there?" Jimmy asked, reaching for his vapouriser and inhaling noisily.

"Yes, I'm here. All I know is that my grandfather was a soldier in the 2nd World War and he ended up under the care of Addison Franckel --"

"Whoa! The same Addison Franckel?"

"Yes, the same. He was allegedly one of the five patients who died."

"*If* they died," Jimmy countered. "You don't know if the stuff you've been told is even true."

"The contact knows about my grandfather --"

"Does he?" Jimmy replied, "or is a hoax? *You* can't even remember Grandpa's name, so they could being telling you a right tale and you'd never know. I reckon it's a bleeding con."

"What kind of con could it possibly be?" Gus asked. "Someone wants me to look into Addison Franckel and his Clinic. The fact that one of my relatives was murdered at Graybrooke puts me in *exactly* the right place to find out what went on."

Jimmy snorted with irritation. "Don't be an fucking ass! You can't let someone mug you around, Gus. This joker's using *you* to do the hard work. If they're smart enough to uncover your grandfather's history, why can't they find out about Addison Franckel? And why don't you hand this over to the police?"

"I've already told you, the police and the authorities suppressed everything about Franckel. That's what he told me --"

"He?"

"What?"

"You said '*he told me*' - how d'you know it's a man? It could be a woman. Never underestimate a female." Jimmy said dryly, inhaling again. "I'd be careful. Gus. You're being paid as a researcher, not a detective. And you don't have to do it. So back off --"

"It's too late. I've just been sent details about a woman called Ella Fairchild; apparently she knows what went on…"

"And?"

"…what I didn't tell you before was that the patients at the Clinic were filmed --"

"Filmed?"

" – they were called *The Incubus Tapes*. And along with everything else to do with the clinic they were destroyed. But apparently some survived."

Jimmy was frowning at the other end of the line. "What's an Incubus?"

"That 'newly discovered' Fuseli painting shows an Incubus --"

"Oh yeah," Jimmy replied, "some woman with a gnome sitting on her boobs."

" -- yes, and that gnome thing is called an Incubus."

"So you think this Fuseli painting is the connection between Louis Willes, Addison Franckel, and you?"

"Could be." Gus considered his next words for several seconds before voicing them. "What if these films show real Incubus activity?"

"What?"

"Bear with me. It sounds incredible, but what if they did?"

"They're not real." Jimmy said, his voice a mixture of incredulity and amusement. "It's bullshit, fairy tales, folk lore --"

"But what if Franckel discovered they *were* real? What if he had evidence that proved it?"

"Now you've lost me."

"Addison ran a Sleep Clinic, he was treating insomnia, night terrors, and sleep paralysis. As a psychiatrist, he would have used drugs that could have caused hallucinations. Remember, he was dealing with soldiers suffering from shell shock - how did he treat that? No one would have known what Addison Franckel was doing at Graybrooke. It was during the war, people were intent on their own survival, not interested in a doctor running a remote clinic. He could have done anything in secret --"

"Until he was found out."

"Exactly! Was that why Franckel and his work disappeared?" Gus paused, feeling his way along. "Don't you wonder what those tapes showed? Something dangerous? Something unethical?"

"Something illegal?"

"Or lethal? *Five patients died.* Apparently my grandfather was one of them." Gus said, hurrying on. "Willes is expecting me back at Graybrooke tonight - but on the way I'm going to take a detour. Let's see if my contact was bluffing, or if Ella Fairchild really does know what went on."

ELEVEN

The needle was being inserted into the raised vein of the forearm, Louis Willes closing his eyes, the lids mottled purple, the lashes feather white. He mewled like a cat, once, then relaxed, Dr Richards emptying the vial, his gaze fixed on the old man's face. From his pocket came the sound of his mobile phone ringing, then silence as voice mail clicked in. He looked exhausted, puffy eyed, his cheeks as concave as ice cream scoops.

"You should have called me earlier," he said, his tone fretful as he turned to Je-Yun who was standing beside his employer's bed. "I supposed he stopped you?

"Mr Willes believed he could manage the pain."

"He's stubborn and puts his body through more than it needs." The doctor replied, weary already, even at eight fifteen in the morning. "Is he still writing that book?"

"Mr Willes is determined to complete the manuscript, and works all day and into the evening - until he can't go on any longer," the Korean replied, dressed in his usual dark sweater and trousers, as immaculate as a cut out. "He is dedicated."

"He is also dying," the doctor said, concerned. "Has he much more to do to finish the damned thing?"

"It's faster now that he has a researcher working with him. Mr Egan will be back today and stay until the weekend."

"Shame he isn't here full time." Dr Richards replied, glancing back to his patient. Willes was breathing evenly, the doctor gesturing to the scatter of books on his bed. "Move those, will you? Put them out of his sight and hopefully out of his mind."

Picking up the volumes, Je-Yun looked from the patient to the doctor. "Is Mr Willes's condition worsening?"

"He's holding steady at present, but I don't know how much longer he can. If he'd rest more… but he won't." Resigned, Dr Richards clicked his bag closed, his mobile ringing again. "Let me know how he is later, will you?"

Nodding, Je-Yun escorted the doctor downstairs, watching him answer his phone as he climbed into his car. With a half-hearted wave, he finally drove off, Je-Yun closing the front door and walking into the library. His steps were muffled in soft soled trainers, his shadow moving along the wall as he passed the sunlit windows, turning at the far door, unlocking it, and entering a small ante chamber. Inside many books were housed, all meticulously labelled, kept in a controlled temperature, a few rare volumes protected inside an ebonised cabinet. Je-Yun tipped his head tipped to one side as he counted the row of documents. Satisfied, he then drew out a heavy drawer from under the cabinet and studied the contents for several minutes. Finally, with some effort, he slid the drawer closed, locked the cabinet, and left the antechamber, ensuring the door was secured.

The weak sun followed him as he passed the windows again, the light from an arched casement on the landing tracing his progress as he mounted the stairs to Louis Willes's bedroom. Inside the light was dimmed, the old man breathing rhythmically as the silent Je-Yun moved over to the chair beside the bed. Carefully he then dropped the key he had used to open the anteroom into Louis Willes's dressing gown pocket. That completed, he took a seat at his employer's bedside and sat in silence, hands together, watching the steady rising and falling of the old man's chest.

Maida Vale
London

"I wasn't at all sure if you would come, people say all kinds of things but don't follow through. It's very strange, but then much of life is strange, is it not?" Ella Fairchild glanced at Gus like an inquisitor, her gaze intelligent. "He said you were a researcher."

"Who said?"

She raised her eyebrows. "What *are* you talking about?"

"I'd like to know who you've been dealing with."

"'*Dealing with*?'"

Gus tried again. "I was sent your details anonymously, Miss Fairchild --"

"*Mrs.*"

" -- excuse me, *Mrs* Fairchild, and I wondered *who* sent them. Who's been in contact with you?" Gus could see she was suspicious and hurried on. "I've been getting messages for nearly a week -- "

"Good God!" She said imperiously. "You don't know anything, do you?" Her voice was cold, her tall frame rounded at the shoulders, her expression autocratic. "Mr Egan, please come in, I don't like standing and talking in the hallway. It's drafty."

Suitably chastened, Gus followed her down the narrow passageway into a sunlit room which looked out through a grille of painted black railings towards the street beyond. Tall ash trees were throwing shade onto the pavement, the leaves restless like children fidgeting in church, a man parking his car on the third attempt. Curious, Gus looked around him, expecting old photographs and artefacts, but Ella Fairchild's surroundings were unexpectedly modern, with only one nod to the past - a vintage portrait hanging over the fireplace.

"That was me, many years ago." She said, gesturing for Gus to take a seat. "I was rather beautiful, wasn't I?" She carried on without giving him time to reply, her movements cautious, as though she had suffered a fall and dreaded another. "I don't know who contacted you. And I don't know who contacted me, it was all done anonymously."

"By email?" Gus asked, catching the look in her eyes.

"Yes, I *can* use e mail," she retorted. "Old people are very adept these days, even if sometimes it's beneficial to pretend otherwise."

"I only asked because I'm being contacted through email and text."

"I detest mobile phones!" She said. "Not because I can't understand how they work – the principle is not difficult – but because they are so intrusive." Gus thought of Louis Willes's irritation with his phone and watched as Ella Fairchild continued. "No doubt, if I applied myself, I could send and receive texts, but why bother?" She smiled to herself. "It's interesting though, isn't it?"

"What is?"

"That our mutual contact only uses email to get in touch with me. It's as though he knows my personal preference... Would you like a drink?"

"A drink?"

"You're not very bright, are you, Mr Egan?" She responded, then smiled, Gus relaxing, just as she intended him to do. "Come on, have a gin and tonic with me! You'll feel so much better if you do. And don't tell me it's too early, who will judge us?" Slowly, she moved over to a cabinet and made the drinks, the quick fizz of the tonic water following on from the chinking of ice cubes.

Outside the temperature was falling to Autumn, but the smell of juniper reminded Gus of heat and long forgotten holidays, his attention reluctantly turning back to the woman who was watching him, amused.

"Nothing like gin, is there? Memory in a glass." She took a long sip of her drink, her hands disfigured with arthritis although the nails were manicured and painted coral. "Now tell me everything you know, Mr Egan --"

"Gus."

She nodded, but he was doubtful she would accept the familiarity. "You really have no idea why you were contacted?"

"None. I'm working for a historian who's writing a biography about Fuseli" he paused, seeing her expression flicker. "Does that mean something to you?"

"Oh, yes," she replied, holding the glass with two hands because they had begun to shake, the drink as unsteady as a dingy on a rough sea. "Fuseli has had quite an impact - albeit indirectly - on my life. I read that another version of *The Nightmare* has just been discovered."

"In Germany, yes."

"The first one should be have been burnt. They should *all* have been destroyed." She said, her voice becoming hard. "Addison Franckel had a copy of *The Nightmare* in his consulting room. You know the work - it's unsettling, to say the least." Gus thought of the reproduction hanging in Louis Willes's study as she continued. "I've always hated it, but apparently Franckel loved it. They all do, all these psychiatrists, like Freud, they read something into it. But somethings aren't in a language we are *meant* to understand." Taking a deep breath she composed herself, then began to speak again. "My grandfather suffered from shell shock and was invalided home during the Second World War and sent to Addison Franckel's Clinic." She paused, checked herself. "I must make it clear that my grandfather never confided in me about what happened, he only spoke to my father. It was my *father* who told me the story - and only at the end of his life." She stood up warily, and moved to a small desk, taking out a batch of papers, tied with old string. "Please look at this."

Taking the bundle from her hand, Gus selected one and began to read.

Patient – Ernest Shore

Age – 48

Occupation –London banker

Condition – sleep paralysis

Duration of time in clinic – 2 weeks.

Under the care of Dr Addison Franck - Patient's narrative recorded exactly as he related it to me.

"I reached out for the light, but I couldn't move my arm. Or any of my limbs. I said - 'Wake up, you're dreaming!' But I couldn't, I was paralysed...."

(Patient at this point is very distressed. Given a glass of water and asked to continue.)

"...There were noises coming from the next room, but the nurse said it was empty. They were only faint at first, the sound of whispering. There were two voices, then a third, and they started to laugh..."

(Mr. Shore is sweating profusely, and I have to wait for him to continue. He is also clenching his hands together. The effects of the sedation have worn off.)

"....the room was only feet from where I was lying, only a wall separating me from whoever was on the other side."

(I tell him it was not real; that he was hallucinating.)

"No! It was real. And I was paralysed, unable to defend myself... How you any idea how that feels, doctor? Have you?"

(I reassure him and ask him to continue.)

"The whispering went on, then I heard the creak of my door opening... I could hardly breathe, sweating, straining to move. Oh God, I thought, just let me move. Please let me move...."

(The patient is too distressed to continue. I wait for a while as he sips at a glass of water before he finally carries on.)

"Then there was silence, not a sound coming from the room next door... And I wondered if they'd heard me. Had I cried out as I struggled to move? Did they know I was there? Would they come for me?... I stared at the door, waiting... Only my eyes could move. Only my eyes! And then I watched as slowly, unbearably slowly, the door opened. And I couldn't look away because I couldn't close my eyes!... The door swung back on its hinges! It banged on the wall behind..."

(Mr. Shore has stopped talking, his terror acute.)

"... Then I saw a movement. Something scurrying through the door, jumping onto the bed, then looming over me... I felt its weight crushing my chest, and then – Christ help me – I saw a face, pressing down towards mine."

(Patient collapses, taken back to his room and sedated. He has had another attack of sleep paralysis and the usual accompanying hallucinations. There has been no progress over the last two weeks, his medication ineffective. Alternative methods must be employed.)

Will begin filming Mr. Shore tonight.

Signed: Dr Addison Franckel
Hampshire, UK

Gus looked back to Ella Fairchild, then glanced at the other notes in her hands. "Where did you get these?"

"Is that your first question, Mr. Egan?"

He turned the medical report over in his hands. "There's no date on this. It would seem that Addison Franckel was very particular about recording his patient's words accurately, yet there's no date."

"There is on the others."

"May I read them?"

She hesitated, wary. "So you need to see more before you can give an opinion? *This* is evidence of what went on in the Franckel Clinic. Isn't that what you want to investigate?"

"It is, but I'd still like to see more - and I'd like to know *how* these papers came into your possession."

She sat down, the notes on her lap, impatient, shaking her head. "We are on the same side!"

"Against what?"

"*Whom.*" She said firmly. "The authorities, all the people who tried - and succeeded - in obliterating Franckel and hiding what he did. My father gave me these notes just before he died."

"When was that?"

"1984."

Gus picked his next words carefully. "So why didn't you want to talk about until now?"

"Because I had a family," she retorted, taking another sip of her drink. "I had a husband and a daughter, both of whom I wanted to protect."

"You were afraid?"

"We were *all* afraid."

He was surprised by the admission, taking out his mobile phone. "Do you mind if I record our conversation? It would only be for my personal use."

"Why?"

"For accuracy. I need to have everything recounted in your own words. It's important that I get the truth."

"You want the truth?" Ella countered, suddenly uncertain. "We all want that, but it seems rather elusive... I suppose the first thing I should have asked is this - *why* were you contacted. Why you, Mr Egan?"

"Perhaps because I'm working for the owner of the house that was part of Franckel's Clinic."

"I thought it was destroyed."

"The wards and outer buildings were, but the original house remains. It was rechristened Graybrooke Lodge."

"It used to be Reid House... What about the operating theatre? What happened to the theatre?"

"I didn't know there was one." Gus replied. "It's not there now, there are no outbuildings. But then again, I haven't had chance to search the grounds."

She leaned back, folding her arms. "I'm rather confused. How much *do* you know?"

"Very little. All I was told came from this anonymous contact. As soon as I started working with Louis Willes they got in touch and told me to ask him about Addison Franckel."

"Did you ask him?"

"Yes, Willes said he knew nothing about Franckel and that their only connection was the house."

"You believe him?" she asked.

"No, not entirely."

"What else were you told?"

"That everything about Franckel was suppressed by the authorities. I was also told that five patients died and that the journalist who tried to investigate the clinic committed suicide."

"I didn't know that." She said, glancing away.

"About the deaths?"

"About the journalist. Of course I knew about the deaths! We all knew about the deaths."

"You keep mentioning 'we' - who d'you mean?"

"Some of the nurses were on the patients' side, others supported Franckel. There were German and

Swiss mostly, the English nurses were the ones who tried to help. That's what I was told anyway. Miriam Levy was the Sister in charge - until she suddenly left."

"And no one heard from her again?"

"It was wartime, Mr Egan, people were mobile, their lives were unsettled. They went home on leave and often didn't come back. Sometimes they were killed by the bombing. I heard of two cases where they left England and went to serve overseas. You wonder how the information was suppressed so easily? Why people lost touch? I'll tell you why - a private clinic in Hampshire might not have seemed that important when there was a war on."

"But Addison Franckel was doing war work. He was investigating shell shock."

Her eyes fixed on him. "*Was he*? Some say he was using the soldiers for his experiments."

"Is that why Franckel disappeared? He was struck off - and yet there's no record of *why*. I can't even find a listing for when Franckel qualified as a doctor."

"Is there a record of his death?"

"No, but if he died in another country it would explain why there's no record here. Same if he qualified abroad." Gus glanced at his mobile, checking it was still recording. "It takes a lot of effort and power to erase someone's entire existence."

"The medical profession, the police, and the Government had a lot of power in the 1940's."

"You're saying they were all involved? Working together?"

"After my father told me what had happened, I approached my MP about Franckel - and was warned off in no uncertain terms. Told to 'mind my own business' and that 'the situation had been dealt with' and that for the good of everyone, it should be forgotten."

"That sounds draconian."

"Especially as it was forty years after the events had taken place."

"But people *must* have gossiped when Franckel was disgraced," Gus persisted, "how could it have been kept quiet?"

"Don't be naïve, Mr Egan. As I said before, it was wartime. The clinic was private, remote, perhaps the people that knew about it believed that Franckel was *helping* the soldiers; all those broken minds getting the care they needed." She paused, staring into her drink. "My grandfather was sick when he went to that place, and they destroyed what was left of him."

"I'm sorry." Gus hesitated, reluctant to dig deeper, but knowing he had to. "Can you tell me what Franckel did?"

"What they are *still* doing!"

"Are you saying his methods are in use again?"

"Why do you think I'm willing to get involved!" She snapped. "We have to stop it. No one's going to scare me off this time. And I'm not the only one. There are other people that lost relatives to that maniac. You asked about his nurses - look into them. They must have talked, or left some record. Franckel's treatments were inhuman. And now there are rumours that his work is being resurrected, that he has followers. They probably believe that enough time has passed for people to forget Addison Franckel -- but no one forgets the Nazis, do they?" her voice became defiant. "I won't die without bearing witness to what was done."

"Then tell me what *was* done." Gus could see her stiffen in her chair. "I know that Franckel kept records on the patients and filmed them, *The Incubus Tapes*." He tapped the notes in his hand. "The filming is mentioned here."

Her head shot up. "Why are you involved?"

Wrong footed, Gus shrugged; "I told you, I'm working in Franckel's old clinic --"

"No! That's *not* the reason, is it? Don't lie to me, Mr Egan, I'm too old and too angry."

"You're right," he agreed "it's not the reason. The truth is that my maternal grandfather was one of the patients that died."

"Oh, I see." She paused before speaking again. "Are you married?"

"Divorced, but I'm close to my ex-wife and we have son together." Gus leaned towards her, changing tack. "Whether it turns out to be true about my grandfather, or a lie, I'm involved. And I'll be honest with you, until it became personal I didn't want to be. But now I *need* to know what happened. People died, including my relative. And the facts have been buried with them."

"You could still walk away."

Impatient, he pressed her. "*Do* the films exist?"

"You should leave --"

"*Are* there copies of the *Incubus Tapes?*"

"Stop!"

"Oh, but I can't, can I?" Gus replied, infuriated. "And now I'm beginning to wonder if you and my anonymous contact are one and the same person."

"*Are you mad!*"

"Well, as you said, you can use a computer and could easily have sent me the emails."

"For what reason?"

"To get me involved. Perhaps *you* want to recover the *Incubus Tapes* and need someone to do it for you. You talk about your grandfather, and my contact talks about *my* grandfather, both of whom apparently died at the Addison Franckel clinic." He pressurised her. "Is it true? There seem to be a lot of deceased grandfathers involved."

Her voice was steely. "I don't like your manner, Mr Egan."

"No? Well, I don't like being dragged into this mess. And frankly, it's hard to believe."

"Yes, it is! It's hard to believe that you and I were contacted anonymously by someone who wanted to get us both involved. Nevertheless, we were, and we must make up our own minds as to how we respond." Her expression was contemptuous as she stared at him. "Let it go, Mr Egan. You don't *have* to do anything if you don't want to. Delete the messages, forget it."

"Just like that?"

"Why not?" she responded. "I'm old, I've had my life, I can take a risk - but you're not willing to. Fair enough. Perhaps if you'd continued, you might have come to regret it. At present you don't know enough to be in danger. Or for your family to be threatened."

"Why didn't you warn me off at the start?" he retorted. "Admit it, you *wanted* to get me involved --"

"And I was wrong. Please, forgive me, and don't give it another thought. Walk away, Mr Egan, no one would blame you."

"It's too late." Gus replied coldly. "We should never have met up, but we did. I should never have listened, but I did. I can't back out now - and you know it."

WEEK TWO

Zurich,
Switzerland
1779

Henry Fuseli pulled a fresh sheet of notepaper towards him, eager to write. Although proficient in three languages he preferred German, as he always thought more lucidly in the language. In his urgency he found the ink from his nib spluttered and smeared the paper, mocking his clumsiness, his own lack of grace, as he chased down the words.

His old school friend, Johann Kaspar Lavater, would be the first to know because they had shared much, being confidantes since boyhood. Although an artist himself, Johann Heidrich Fuseli had intended his son for the church, ignoring Henry's artistic skill in favour of a classical education at the Caroline College in Zurich. Obedient, Henry had attended the College and there met Johann, the two forming an unbreakable friendship. So unbreakable that when they took orders in 1761 Henry was embroiled in the scandal Johann instigated when together they exposed a corrupt magistrate. It had been a reckless move, and one that would change their lives forever.

Pausing, Henry thought back. The politician's family had not taken kindly to their relative's loss of status and wanted revenge. Having assisted Johann in the exposure of the politician both were forced to flee Switzerland and move to Germany, their escape intensifying their bound. From then onwards - whether together or apart - their lives had remained intertwined. So when Henry became infatuated with Anna Landolt, a tall, blonde twenty year old, it was in Johann he confided. He had fallen in love with her, he wrote, with the kind of love that was overheated, sweaty, eating into his thoughts, a love that impregnated every waking and sleeping instant.

'....Last night I had her in bed with me, tossed my bedclothes hugger-mugger, wound my heart and tight clasped hands about her, fused her body and soul together with my own, poured into her my spirit, breath and strength. Anyone who touches her now commits adultery and incest. She is mine, and I am hers, and have her I will....'

Embarrassed, but amused by his own ardour, Henry continued the letter, moving onto another subject, one that absorbed him almost as much as Anna Landolt.

'...As you know when we were last together, I am painting and hoping to take a trip to Italy - how I long to see the great masters, Titian, Michelangelo and Raphael. Do I leave out Leonardo da Vinci? You see what treasures are there? And all for these longing eyes to relish. In the meantime I am working, yet find myself reluctant to slavishly follow academic discipline. I long to see imagination in art. Passion over precision... Greece and Rome is to be admired, yet it

is contrived, and I long for something invigorating, unsettling perhaps. '

'I have been remembering our time in Germany and recalling the folk lore and how the Germans believe that demons and witches possess people who sleep alone. Just as they believe that a woman lying on her back encourages nightmares. I am reminded of the fable of the 'Mara' the demon of death and desire. (Are they not connected? I feel sometimes I could die willingly just to hold Anna Landolt in my arms.) Do you know, that in the 24th century BC the Mesopotamians wrote of a creature, 'Lilu,' who disturbs and seduces women in their sleep? And in the Northern countries they believe in another version of 'mara' a mythological spirit which torments and suffocates sleepers in its lust. Such are the fables that gave credence to the Incubus.

Perhaps I am becoming such a creature, my dear Johann! For I am thinking of Anna again, of her face and body. Do I shock you? Perhaps, yet in this madness I am inspired. I have made myself a promise that I will paint her portrait, but in the meantime I am supporting myself with a variety of writings for which I am reasonably paid. Please send me more of your insightful work on physiognomy. If I am able I will do my best to see this published in English.

Goodbye for now, my friend, write to me with your news, as I will with mine.

With affection,
Henry

TWELVE

Dover Street
London

"Why?" Edward Leigh asked simply, tucking his mobile under his chin and fumbling with a hand towel. It used to be a matter of hygiene that he never took his phone into the cloakroom, but after being caught out by two important clients mid-pee he had decided that he and his iPhone were never to be parted again.

"Can't you hear me?" Ronnie said, her American voice strident over the line.

"Yes, of course I can hear you! I just don't understand why you're visiting Louis Willes." He hadn't dried his hands thoroughly and couldn't get a grip on the door knob, the brass slippery as an oyster.

"I need to know about this Fuseli and I think Willes knows more than he's letting on."

Finally opening the door, Edward moved into his office, his PA throwing a caustic look in his direction before she left the room.

"Why are you telling me?" He asked. "I mean, let's be frank here, we're rivals and both of us are interested if the Fuseli comes up for sale, so why are you letting me know about your plans? This is not like you, Ronnie, not at all."

"You think I have an ulterior motive?"

Edward remembered their previous dealings. "You *always* have an ulterior motive, Ronnie. I have seldom endured your 'unusual' and at times aggressive methods, but I have watched from the side lines as you have fed your victims through a meat grinder."

She laughed.

"That wasn't meant as a compliment," he retorted, his tone suspicious as he thought of his partner. "Have you spoken to Anthony?"

"Anthony is not the right person for this." Ronnie replied, her tone soothing. "I need *your* expertise, *your* experience."

"For what?"

"An alliance."

Reaching into his office drawer, Edward took out a pair of nail scissors and a small magnifying mirror, setting the mirror before him and laying his mobile on the desk so he could continue with the conversation. As he considered his reply, his attention turned to the mirror, picking up the nail scissors and beginning to trim the hairs of his moustache above his top lip. They had caught his tongue once or twice, a sensation he had found singularly unpleasant.

"*'An alliance*?'" He mused. "What does that mean?"

"If the Fuseli came up for sale it would fetch a fortune, but only if it was sold to a private collector. We don't want it going to public auction."

"It might not even be coming up for sale --"

"True, it might not, but we should be prepared if it does. Any auction concerning the Fuseli should be a *private* one." She called out to someone at her end, her voice unexpectedly honeyed, then continued. "You have clients who would want it, and pay well to get it. So do I. If we got them bidding *against* each other we could drive up the price. And our commission."

"Only if we had the painting."

"That's my point," Ronnie replied. "We would need the funds to buy it first, then sell it on."

Pausing with the scissors in his hand, Edward stared at his reflection thoughtfully. "I don't have enough money for that --"

"Neither do I, but if we pooled our resources, we could manage it. Of course we'd have to do it anonymously, but that not a problem."

"And what about my partner? Am I supposed to leave Anthony in the dark about all of this?"

"I didn't know you were so sentimental, Edward. How often have you griped about him having more shares in the gallery?" She tweaked the old wound. "I mean, it used to be the other way round, didn't it? You used to have the whip hand."

Edward laid down the scissors and leaned back in his seat. "So you're coming back to the UK to see Louis Willes because you think he might have some knowledge that would benefit you?"

"Yeah… Well, not just me, you too."

"And if he had information *why* would he confide in you, Ronnie? He's dying, I would think business matters are the last thing on his mind."

"Oh, you're wrong there! Think about it, Edward - he's desperate to finish his fucking tome about Fuseli.

Louis Willes wants to leave a legacy, he wants to be remembered, like every other art historian. But now he's in luck - a lost Fuseli painting has turned up and presented him with the opportunity of a lifetime."

"But *does* Willes know anything?" Edward queried. "He's been out of the business for a long time."

"Don't kid yourself," Ronnie retorted, "I know a few people here in New York that have always kept in touch with him."

"Really?"

She laughed down the line. "You are such an innocent, Edward! I'm giving you good advice - don't write Willes off because he's old. He's also crafty and clever - and he's dying. He wants revenge on the art world and the dealers, eager to settle scores before he pegs out."

Uneasy, Edward returned the magnifying mirror to his desk drawer. "Do you *really* think Louis Willes is planning something?"

"I don't know, but that's what I'm going to find out." She replied crisply. "It's a long slog from New York to Hampshire, but it might be worth it. For *both* of us."

Graybrooke Lodge
Hampshire.

When Gus entered the house it was unexpectedly quiet, his footsteps resonating on the wooden floor. Usually Willes was playing music, speakers planted throughout the property, from the bedrooms to the library, and even the kitchen. Gus had wondered if Willes had adopted the habit that many solitary people employ; music masking the loneliness of silence; but when he spoke to Je-Yun the Korean explained that Willes believed he could preserve his hearing by having music playing constantly.

Gus had soon become used to the background noise of Stravinsky or The Beach Boys, Willes's taste surprisingly catholic. Which was why the present silence unnerved him, the lengthening October day dimming the light, the *Dying Gaul* a cold white body washed ashore.

"Who the fuck's in here?" A voice called out, Willes coming into the hall and flicking on the light switch. He was wearing his tartan dressing gown and a pair of Wellington boots encrusted with soil.

"It's me, Gus, Gus Egan. Your researcher."

"Researcher? Oh, yes…" It was obvious Willes was drunk, unsteady, grasping pieces of furniture to hold himself upright as he made staccato progress towards Gus.

"You look different." Willes said, his tone accusing. "I thought you were shorter."

Momentarily Gus wondered if Willes had lost his mind, but then old man began laughing and clapping him on the back. "Just a joke! I know you! Of course I know you! My researcher, Guy --"

"Gus."

"I know, I know!" An attempt to stand upright unaided proved too much for Willes, Gus supporting his employer as they moved back into the library. "I've been working and thinking… it doesn't pay, you know. Thinking and remembering is for fucking losers."

Lowering Willes into an armchair, Gus glanced round. The desk was mottled with papers, doodles, open books with numerous turned down edges, reference notes, and a lap top, the screen saver displaying an image of *The Nightmare*. Beside it was a glass, and beside that two empty wine bottles, one tipped over and leaking the last remnants of a Bordeaux onto the leather desk top. Righting it, Gus watched as Willes leaned forward and grabbed another glass off a side table beside him.

"You've had enough --"

"**Bugger off!**" Willes replied, but in reaching for the glass knocked it out of Gus's hand instead. They both watched as it smashed on the wooden floor, Willes slumping into an armchair, his voice breaking. "Why can't it be over and done with?"

"What?"

"*My life,*" the old man said plaintively, "the cancer is chewing away at me, bit by bit. I can't think straight --"

"If you sobered up, it would help" Gus replied.

He wanted to confide, to say that he had also suffered from cancer and knew exactly what Willes was feeling. But how could he? His disease had been expunged, obliterated by chemotherapy; he was healthy again, whilst the historian, obviously terrified, was facing the end.

"*I don't want to go...* The doctor says I have only weeks to live." Willes paused, struggling to stop the tears. "He says it with no emotion, just like a bloody potentate passing the death sentence... I should have done more with my life."

"You've achieved more than most."

"I didn't achieve what I should have done! I've done a lot of harm too." He reached for the glass and realising it wasn't there, grabbed hold of the carafe and took a long gulp of wine from it. As he did some dribbled out of the sides of his mouth, running down the shirt he was wearing under his dressing gown. Pausing, clinging tightly onto the carafe, he stared at Gus. "I want revenge."

"Most people do."

"You too?"

"Yes, I want to get my own back on people that cheated me, but it's wasted effort. It's the past, think of the now --"

"What do I have *now*?"

" -- the book. The Fuseli book that you've been working on for decades. Finish it," Gus urged him. "Don't let people say you failed. Write the best book you can, make it your legacy."

"Are you married?"

"I was. I'm divorced now."

"D'you have children?" Willes asked, his head tilted to one side, his eyes struggling to focus.

"I have a son, Mark."

"We never had children. My wife... well, she didn't think she would have made a good mother. Or perhaps I wouldn't have made a good father," he paused, rubbed his left eye with his index finger, the lid reddening as he continued to talk. "He thinks I don't know, but I do. I knew he was sleeping with my wife."

After turning on the desk lamp and banking up the fire with logs, Gus had taken a seat, the little terrier padding over to its place on the rug before the hearth. The flames began slow, then grew in strength, the heat reaching out as Willes glanced over to Gus, his expression shifting between maudlin and sly.

"Don't you want to know who I'm talking about?"

"D'you want to tell me?"

"I'm talking about Anthony Hallett," Willes said with contempt. "D'you know him?"

"I knew him a little when I was working as a dealer."

"He fucked my wife." Willes said curtly. "He used to visit us, here at Graybrooke, him and his wife. And all the time he was after Ava." He took another swig from the carafe. "You know, they were married once?"

Gus found the revelation fascinating. "So you married Hallett's ex-wife?"

"Yes, they divorced because Hallett fell in love with someone else; the dreary woman he's married to now. He picked her after he *dumped* Ava. Left Ava for that colourless drab." Willes glared at Gus. "Have you seen my wife?"

"No."

Abruptly, Willes waved his hand towards a sofa table. "That photograph, there. That one, look! The woman standing under the tree, that's Ava."

Gus moved over to the table and picked up the image. The woman was smiling, dark haired, fine bodied, arrow slim. Refined, almost aesthetic. "She was very elegant --"

"*And that snout faced dealer left her*! D'you know what a bastard is?"

"Yes," Gus nodded. "I've met plenty."

"Anthony Hallett is a bastard, a smarmy bastard with a pug's face and the oily charm of a Victorian poet. Seems that the women go for that sentimental crap..." He coughed hoarsely, his body shaking, Gus looking towards the hallway.

"Where's Je-Yun?"

"Why?"

"I wondered where your medicine was. If he was going to bring it, or I should get it for you. You should rest --"

"I don't want to rest!" Willes shouted, coughing again, Gus moving into the kitchen. He returned with a glass of water to find Willes hovering over his desk and throwing papers around. **"He thinks I don't know!** But I knew all along. Just like I knew about Ronnie Gilchrist." He paused, exhausted, drunk, leaning against the desk, the terrier moving over to him and lying at his feet. "Move her. Move her! *Please!"* Willes gestured to the animal. "I don't want to step on her. I don't want to hurt her…"

Picking up the terrier, Gus put the dog in the kitchen, her whimpering accompanying him as he moved back to the library. In the time he had been gone Willes had found another bottle of wine and was grappling with a corkscrew.

"You don't need that," Gus said, taking it from him, the palm of Willes's hand cut and bleeding profusely. "Have you eaten today?"

"What fucking difference does that make! Eat or starve, who cares?" Shaking off Gus's hand, he blundered back to the fire, dragging the armchair closer, his gaze fixed on the flames.

"Where's Je-Yun?" Gus asked again.

Willes didn't even seem to hear the question and continued talking. "As for that American cow, Ronnie Gilchrist. She wrote a review about my Goya book. The bitch said I'd copied someone else's work. I hadn't, but when she wrote it and everyone read it, they believed her. Lying bitch…" Willes's head had slumped down, his chin on his chest as he mumbled. "I wanted to, I *really* wanted to, but I'm so tired. And now it's too late to get my own back…"

"Not if you finish the book," Gus replied. "You're paying me a lot of money to babysit you. Why don't you put my skills to better use?"

Willes wasn't listening. "Ava never slept well when we lived here. Never… she had all kinds of dreams…" Willes was staring into the fire, unblinking. "She used to scream so loudly she would wake herself up… Terrible nightmares, that made her so afraid." He riddled the logs with a poker, blue flames amongst the yellow. "We used to have wonderful parties here, madly extravagant, the driveway and gardens torchlit, with the staff holding name tags above their heads, sculptured in gilded fretwork, so the guests would follow them to their allotted seats." He sniggered to himself drunkenly. "So bloody silly, so bloody pompous, and so much bloody fun. We had themed parties, and famous people here - not film people, not like that, we had *real* talent, musicians, artists, even mediums. Many of them religious people, some of them immoral …"

"You were interested in the paranormal?"

Willes nodded. "Everyone is. They deny it, but if money could buy the answer to the meaning of life there would be a lot of penniless billionaires." His voice wavered. "Ava dabbled, not in black magic, too crude for a woman who was so refined. Besides, she was already aware that the Devil existed. He does, I know that… He comes here sometimes. The last few months he's been coming here a lot. You can hear him, those cloven hooves, tap,tap,tap on the floors --"

"I'll call for your assistant." Gus interrupted, Willes reaching out and gripping his arm.

"Don't you feel anything in this house?"

Gus shook his head. "No."

"You will, in time you will. You might even see something. I do… Ask Je-Yun. He does, though he won't admit it, tries to make me believes it's just my imagination."

"You 'see things'? What kind of things?"

"Old ground holds more than earth...Graybrooke Lodge was once Reid Hall ..." He paused, voice wavering. "Ava would go, you see. I told her not to, but she insisted. Women do that, they *insist*... And I gave way, because I loved her. You see what love can do? Squeeze your brain, burst the vessels of your heart, until there's only memory and lies remaining..." He was rambling, his words jagged. "I never thought she would leave me, but she did... And she *would* insist, she *would* know, asked so many things, things that weren't good for her."

"Like what?" Gus asked, curious.

Willes continued as though he was alone, talking to himself.

"She comes to see me when I sleep. At first it was a comfort, I liked it..." Willes's voice was slurred, mumbled. "Now she frightens me. She wants to take me with her - and I don't want to go!" his voice rose, high pitched as he turned to Gus. "She always loved the garden. ... I would have liked to keep her nearby, close to me. I would have liked to know she walked the grounds and the house at night." He shook his head. "But that was then - now she's *too* close. Like the others..."

"What others?"

"Others... a few others... I can see them at the head of the stairs, or in the garden. Ava would have kept them away from the house." He stared at Gus. "Yet she never really thought it was *our* house... Not really... she said it was his."

"Who d'you mean?"

Willes's voice had relapsed into a semi wail. "My wife couldn't handle the world on her own. But together we could. It was only later that she became afraid, couldn't sleep. And now *I'm* afraid... I deserve to be, but Ava didn't. She tried everything **not** to fall asleep... I should have listened. I s*hould* have allowed her to find out what he did." Willes was nodding to himself, rocking backwards and forwards. "I promised I would, I said I'd find out. I *promised* her --"

"Mr Willes," a voice said quietly, interrupting him. "You must take your medication now."

Not having heard the Korean enter, Gus turned, startled, and then watched as Je-Yun moved over to his employer, bending down and offering Louis Willes his medication and a small glass. It obviously wasn't water, but something the colour of pomegranates. The intervention seemed suspiciously timely, the historian snapped back into sobriety.

"Yes...yes, thank you." Willes said after a moment, taking the medicine and then allowing his assistant to help him to his feet. "I'm afraid I was rather foolish, Mr Egan, you must make allowances. I know better than to drink when I was warned not to."

"It wasn't wise," the Korean chastened him. "You know the medication is not safe to take with alcohol, Mr Willes."

"Perhaps I was attempting suicide?"

The joke fell on deaf ears.

"You will feel much better after you have had a sleep." Je-Yun continued. "Your head will clear --"

The historian frowned, unsettled. "Was I talking nonsense?"

"It was the wine."

"Did I say anything foolish?"

Je-Yun guided his employer to the door then turned to Gus. "I think Mr Willes needs to rest now," he said calmly. "Dinner will be ready at seven."

THIRTEEN

"You know when people say, 'what d'you want to hear first? The good news or the bad?' --"

"Yes, and it's always irritating," Gus replied, straining to hear over the bad mobile connection. Ringing from Berlin, it sounded as though Jimmy was in a bar, then Gus realised that he was in a train station, a tannoy announcement drowning him out for several seconds.

"Did you hear that?"

"Every word - but I don't speak German." Gus replied dryly, Jimmy hurrying on.

"I've been digging around a bit and discovered something very tasty about Addison Franckel. You're going to like this."

Gus leaned forward in his seat, glancing upwards and hearing Je-Yun's muffled footsteps overhead. He had helped Willes to his bedroom, silence following after a short exchange of words. A very short exchange, Willes's voice remarkably strong after it had been so plaintive before. In fact, Gus thought, the historian had sounded angry.

"Go on, I'm listening," he urged Jimmy "tell me what you found out."

"Addison Franckel worked as a doctor in Berlin, using the name *Otto Weiner*."

"He qualified in Berlin?"

"Nah, just practised. As a psychiatrist."

"So where did he qualify?"

"Don't know. Can find a listing anywhere."

"So where did he practice in Berlin?"

"I knew you'd ask me that, and I found out" Jimmy paused, then added "but the building was destroyed in the war."

"Let me guess - and all the patients notes were destroyed at the same time?"

"Yeah." Jimmy agreed, "but I found out something else, Otto Weiner was married to a woman called Elise. She's dead, but they had a son, born in 1943. His name is" there was a shuffling of notes before Jimmy continued, "Fritz Weiner. Thing is, I can't find anything out about him, but then I discovered he'd changed his name."

Hearing further noises from above, Gus moved to the door and glanced up the stairwell. The soft padding of Je-Yun's steps crossed the landing and then entered another part of the house where he had his own bedroom and sitting room. Closing the door quietly, Gus heard Jimmy calling his name down the line.

"Gus! You still there?"

"Yes."

"Why are you whispering?"

"I'll explain later. So what about the son, is still alive?"

"Otto Weiner's son changed his name to Freddy Wilson --"

"Same initials as Fritz Weiner."

" -- yeah. He's eighty and living - guess where?"

"Surprise me."

"Last recorded in London. Don't know exactly where, but he's still alive, even though it seems like he's dropped off the radar."

"Happens a lot in that family."

"And there's something else. I've found out about your grandfather."

Gus took in a breath. "I never knew his full name... what was it?"

"George Lyman, he was a soldier invalided home from the front in 1944. He came to the UK and was admitted to St Edward's Hospital in London, but his condition was so bad he was transferred to Spike Island-"

" 'Spike Island?' "

"The Royal Military hospital at Netley. Massive place on the banks of Southampton Water, where they treated shell shock patients. All the poor sods sent home with symptoms of hysterical paralysis, amnesia. You heard of someone called Wilfred Owen?"

"He was a war poet."

Jimmy wasn't impressed. "Well, whatever, Wilfred Own was treated at Spike Island." He paused, relishing the next piece of news, "but this will *really* get you thinking - Netley was doing experiments with LSD in the 1950's."

Gus raised his eyebrows. "Did Addison Franckel work there?"

"It's not recorded if he did, but there's something else, at Netley the patients from the First World War were *filmed*. They called shell shock *'war neuroses'* then and made a documentary to show the patients before and after treatment. Sometimes using hypnosis. It's on YouTube, I'll send you the link --"

Gus interrupted him. "Yes, do that, thanks. But what about my grandfather?"

"He was transferred from Spike Island --"

"Transferred *again?*"

"Yeah, but there's no record of *where* he was sent."

Rising to his feet, Gus moved into the garden. He didn't want to be overheard and needed to speak freely. It was coming up to dusk, the lights from the library throwing honeyed illumination onto the lawn. Light also came from several of the upstairs windows, the arched casement of Willes's bedroom lit dimly, only one lamp burning inside. A moment later Gus saw a shape moving across the window, then pause to draw the curtains, Je-Yun's silhouette as black as an ink drawing.

"Hang on a minute, Jimmy, will you?" Quickly Gus crossed the lawn and descended down a slope he had seen from the house; a gentle slant of grass leading to a copse of trees. He had been looking for a place where he could talk undisturbed and paused there, leaning against a stone wall. "Sorry about that, I didn't want to be overheard."

"Why? What's going on there?"

"I don't know," Gus admitted, "but something's wrong. When I got back today Louis Willes was drunk. He was talking *way* too much, and when he said about his wife having nightmares and how he hadn't helped her, his assistant suddenly materialised out of nowhere. He acted as though he was looking after him, but it was a deliberate interruption. Je-Yun didn't want the old man to talk."

"Why not?"

"I don't know, but nothing's what it seems. Willes is lying, I can sense it." Gus paused, looking up to the house, the lights coming on in the back passageway leading to the kitchen. "I went to see Ella Fairchild."

"You did? And what did she have to say?"

"She knew what was going on at the clinic, but wasn't forthcoming. She showed me a file, medical notes on one of the patients. It was bizarre what Franckel was up to, but nothing damning, except that it did mention that the patient would be filmed. Nothing more, nothing explicit. Thing is, she wouldn't let me take the notes, but I recorded our conversation. One thing's for certain, she was *not* going to be drawn on the subject of the Incubus Tapes."

"You think they're real?"

"Judging from her response, I think they are. She confirmed the anonymous messages I've been getting --"

Jimmy snorted down the line "How trustworthy is an *anonymous* contact?"

"He put me onto Ella Fairchild, and she's real enough." Gus countered. "And you've just told me about the films done at Spike Island, so why shouldn't there be films from Franckel's Clinic? He was a psychiatrist, he obviously he wanted to keep a record --"

"But he was struck off, so his methods can't have been kosher. It's rumoured some doctors are using Franckel's methods again."

"How did you find that out?"

"I'm in Berlin, aren't I?" Jimmy countered "And due to German efficiency, newspapers are kept, dating way back. I looked at some around the time of the 2nd World War and found a reference to Otto Weiner, and then another in 1969."

Gus frowned. "But Weiner had adopted the name Franckel in the 1940's, and by 1969 he'd disappeared --"

"*Let me finish!* He was just mentioned in an article about two psychiatrists using '*Franckel's methods*' to get addicts off drugs."

"So the treatments didn't stop?"

"Exactly." Jimmy agreed. "And who's to say they aren't going on now?"

Gus took a moment before replying. "Ella Fairchild said she'd been warned off by the authorities when she started asking questions. She made it sound like a conspiracy, that it was dangerous to pry. But now she wants to expose what went on."

"Why?"

"Exactly. I don't trust her." Gus said. "She *could* have set all this up. She could have been the one who contacted me."

"She's an old woman!"

"Yes, old like Louis Willes. And just like Willes, she's clever. Bragged about using a computer. Almost like she *wanted* me to know. Or perhaps she wanted me to suspect her."

Jimmy exhaled down the phone. "Pah! Sounds farfetched."

"Everything about this sounds farfetched" Gus replied. "And after she'd drawn me in she told me to back off. Just like you tell a fish to spit out the hook when its already swallowed it."

"You *could* walk away, tell her to find someone else --"

"Whose grandfather was a patient at the Franckel clinic?" Gus replied drily. "You know something? I didn't even believe the story about my grandfather until you just confirmed it."

"I confirmed he was ill, but not that he was treated by Addison Franckel."

"No, but Ella Fairchild told me he was at the Franckel Clinic." Gus reminded him. "There *must* be data about my grandfather somewhere. What about his death certificate?"

"Nothing recorded."

"He can't have disappeared." Gus replied. "You said Franckel went under the name of Otto Weiner in Berlin?"

"Yeah, but before you ask that's a dead end too. All references to Otto Weiner stopped in 1942."

Gus changed tack. "There must be other living relatives of Franckel's patients. People who were afraid to speak, or been warned off. Ella Fairchild and I can't be the only ones, there are others out there."

"You want me to find them?"

"I think" Gus replied thoughtfully "they may well come to me."

FOURTEEN

Passing through the underground, interlocking passages, John Cummings's short form moved purposefully towards the archway, unlocking the last, leather-fronted door. The chamber that opened out before him was secret, unknown to all except his brother, father and lawyer, the steel walls and regulated temperature ensuring that the priceless objects held there would be protected and preserved.

Over the previous years three Impressionists pictures, an Artemisia Gentileschi portrait, an Epstein sculpture and several Durer engravings had visited the Swiss vault, following the likes of Titian and a relief by Giovanni Bernini. All had been worth considerable amounts of money, all had been sold to private - often anonymous - buyers, and all sales had been accompanied by an eye watering commission fee. The payment was well earned. Every detail, every negotiation, and every payment completed in absolute secrecy. Why? Because Public Relations were an anathema to John Cummings. He found the idea of promotion daunting, and even the suggestion of being photographed - his stunted, unappealing form set up as an Aunt Sally for the masses - frightening. To stay remote and unseen allowed people to imagine some aesthetic demi-god, some genius dealer before whom kings grovelled and Hollywood came begging.

Few people ever met John Cummings, even fewer were friends, his family offering the only closeness he desired. His few forays into society in the company of models and had been noticeably brief. There *had* been a wife in the past, but she had returned to Italy, or Spain, or Germany, no one was certain because the story changed every time it was told. She had been a model, a scientist, a singer, and music teacher - she had been all professions in the twelve years since she had exited his life, leaving behind a plethora of options, like a stained glass window changing colours with the daylight. John Cummings never expressed regret for losing her, nor did he want to replace her. If she entered his mind at all it was merely fleeting, as insubstantial as a sneeze.

Thoughtful, John stood before the easel, scrutinising the Fuseli painting, the last version of *The Nightmare*. If pressed, Cummings would admit that he was not a lover of Romanticism, his taste leaning more to Poussin; but he would never utter such publicly. Better to let his clients believe he was enthralled by the work, its value lauded as catnip to avaricious and competitive collectors. London, New York and Dubai had interested parties, and all had been notified that the 'discovered' Fuseli might be coming up for sale. *Might* being the operative word.

No one knew how it had come into the hands of John Cummings. Just like the vault, the provenance of the Fuseli painting was guarded, steel-fenced and temperature controlled; a modern day mummy in its Swiss sarcophagus.

Highgate,
London

"Aren't we meeting up this weekend?" Ziva asked, flicking her mobile onto loud speaker as she diced some vegetables in the kitchen, a window opened to let the steam escape from the bubbling pans on the stove. "Mark's playing football on Saturday. He's looking forward to seeing you."

"I'll be there," Gus reassured her "and if you like the three of us could go for a meal afterwards."

She paused, knife poised above a half sliced tomato. "That would be great. Incidentally, his teacher called me --"

"Problem?"

" -- no, she just said that Mark wasn't interested in mixing with his friends. Not as much as he used to. She said he was keeping his distance, still loving sports, but otherwise not hanging out with others."

"He's twelve," Gus said reflectively, "and he's starting to mature early. He's taller than everyone else in his class - that makes a kid stand out."

"He doesn't like to stand out."

"That's what I mean, Mark's never been an extrovert." Gus replied, "I'll have a chat with him at the weekend, just the two of us, see if he's worried about anything. But I've got to go now. See you Saturday, around one."

And that was the moment that Ziva wanted to scream with frustration. Ask - *why is it that are you such a good father, so willing to listen and empathise, and yet you won't even consider our having another child?* She didn't say it, because if there was even a scintilla of hope, she didn't want her impatience, her eagerness, to crush it. But every time they spoke Ziva remembered how it had been when they were married. How Gus had been as a father, remembering his euphoria when their son was born. He had been fighting tears, a burly man picking up an infant weighing eight pounds, holding him protectively to his chest. The love had never wavered, it had intensified, and as Mark had grown Gus had taken him to school and to football matches; attempting to make a treehouse which he didn't finish because it fell down during a storm. Good memories - until Ziva remembered the cancer.

He had told her with absolute calm. And she knew he had been practising, probably at the bathroom mirror, making sure the killer diagnosis sounded something merely inconvenient, something they could overcome.

"We don't need to tell Mark --"

"Surely he should know?" Ziva had replied gently. "He's nine, old enough to know."

Gus had been emphatic. "No child is old enough to think their father might die. We would have to lie. To say that everything would be alright; that Dad has good doctors and it would work out fine. And Mark would - because he's a good kid - pretend that he believed us. But he wouldn't, because that fear, that

116

anxiety, would have been planted in him as soon as we said the word *cancer.*"

She had tried to remonstrate, loathing her next words. "Even if you don't tell him, he'll *see* it, Gus. Our son will see you change with the chemotherapy, and then he'll think that you didn't trust him to handle it --"

"Are you sure that he can?

"Yes, because he's your son and he needs to be included in this." Ziva had replied with certainty. "Exclude him and he will resent it…. You can't hide the cancer, however much you long to. You can't protect him, Gus, I know you want to, but you can't. Think about it. Please, think."

Then she had realised that the truth, the raw facts, had escaped him. That he would lose his hair, suffer crippling nausea, and be unable to keep down his food. He would become thinner, and tired, and the strapping, handsome Gus Egan would become reduced to a stranger - unless Mark was prepared for the change, for what was going to happen to his father. That he wasn't a stranger, just a different kind of Dad.

Sighing, Ziva put down the kitchen knife, her right hand going to her stomach, resting there. In the end it was a battle Gus lost. Mark *was* told that his father, his beloved father, had cancer. And as the situation was explained to him he had listened, grey eyes steady, looking from his father to his mother and then back to Gus, as though - perhaps - one of them would deny it, or claim it a joke. But he knew, and later that night, around eleven, he had come to their bedroom and sat on Gus's side of the bed and told them all about a boy at school; how his mother had suffered from cancer and how she had got better. He told the story like an ancient scribe, placid as a monk, then returned to his bedroom. When Gus heard his door close and silence fall again, he had wept.

In the end, it had been worse than they had imagined. Perhaps, because of Gus's physical strength, they had fooled themselves into believing that he would escape the worst of the side effects; but he didn't. As his hair fell out he would make light of it, but the vomiting after the chemotherapy exhausted him. Despite all his determination, the weight evaporated, his clothes becoming loose, and at times Ziva would catch him staring at the grey faced, bald headed interloper in their home.

The cancer became real to Gus. He thought of it as a personality, and gave it a face; some demon/CGI creation, by turns omnipotent and cringing. And when he confided in Mark they bonded over it, his son finding relief in having a creature to hate. Even making drawings which Ziva would keep, a child's depiction of the evil that threatened to kill his father.

Weeks passed, the chemotherapy finally coming to a grinding end. The result was positive, the demon trodden under the feet of Gus and Mark Egan, Ziva watching, alert, wary. And she *continued* watching, on guard, as Gus restored his strength, his bulk, and his hair - albeit now scuffed with grey. The cancer lost.

As did their marriage. The disease took her husband, but left behind her best friend, her ally, the one person she trusted, the father of their child. And as Ziva remembered the past, and the divorce, she wondered if her longing for another child was her subconscious craving for her husband's return.

And if she would ever admit it.

FIFTEEN

The next message woke Gus at six in the morning, his mobile vibrating on the bedside table until he reached for it. He expected another anonymous email, but this was from Madelaine. His girlfriend, of sorts.

> *Back from Saudi, but not staying over in*
> *London except for one night. Will be home in*
> *two weeks. Too much work, awkward people,*
> *and not enough of you. Want you big time.*
> *Love M xxx*

He rolled onto his back and thought of her. Yes, he wanted her too; liked her energy; liked her ambition and quick mind, but knew he could never spend more than a week with her. Maybe not even a week. A night here a there, a weekend, even a long weekend, but no more. Besides, neither of them wanted a committed relationship, Gus's attention suddenly taken by the mobile ringing again.

This time it was an email. No heading.

*So you met up with Ella Fairchild. She's very
old, but sharp. She was impressed with you,
Mr Egan, although she felt you didn't trust
her. But now you have the fly Jimmy Gold
helping, you'll know more about Addison
Franckel. And your grandfather, George
Lyman. He was at the Franckel Clinic. He
died there.
As did a woman called Elizabeth Shore.
Some servicewomen also suffered from shell
shock, and Elizabeth Shore was one of them.
Her grandson - Paul Shore - will contact
you. He wants to know what happened to his
grandmother.
He'll be in touch.*

Gus typed a response:

Stop pissing about. Tell me who you are.

The reply came back immediately.

*I'm an interested party, that's all. I need your
help and you need mine to find out what
really happened to your grandfather, and
what went on a Graybrooke Lodge.*

Gus replied:

*Not good enough.
Any more e mails will be deleted, unread.*

Several moments passed before the answer came:

*Your co-operation would be appreciated,
Mr Egan. Working for Louis Willes and
residing at Graybrooke Lodge makes you
ideally placed. Besides, you're an ex-dealer
in the art world - who better to investigate
this newly discovered Fuseli? Or are you
still stinging from the matter of the Vermeer
painting? ...*

Gus winced, reading on.

> *... You were absolved, but no longer acted as a dealer. Perhaps your illness forced you to step back? Or were you just eager to avoid further complications? I really would appreciate your co-operation in this matter. It might be less dangerous for you.*

Enraged, Gus typed his response:

> *Are you threatening me?*

Reply:

> *Is there something I can threaten you with?*

The exchange had taken an unpleasant turn for Gus, the reminder of the Vermeer situation as unnerving as the reference to his illness. Someone had been watching him, following his career and private life, and he remembered how he had been watched before. How the strain had precipitated his illness, his life under a double sided attack from cancer and the art world.

Finally he replied:

> *Perhaps I should show these emails to the police and see what they have to say.*

Reply:

> *And you think they will find me? I know you'll have tried, but it's impossible. And if you **do** go to the police they'll look into the Vermeer affair. Once a liar, always a liar... Isn't that right, Mr Egan? Just help me and everything will be fine. There's no reason to be afraid, your family's perfectly safe.*

It was the 'reassurance' that unnerved Gus. The '*your family is perfectly safe*' - then why had he mentioned them? Why bring them into it? Gus could feel his breathing speed up as the thought back.

The Vermeer incident had happened years earlier, when Gus was working as a dealer on Albemarle Street. He had found the environment unwelcoming to a man who had inherited a gallery from his father's partner. To the other dealers, Gus had done nothing to earn the largesse; he had been disinterested in dealing before, and never appeared at the exclusive social gatherings where many deals, and even more gossip, was exchanged. Instead he had come into the business by default, honouring his late father's wishes.

His beginner's luck had incensed the established dealers. His background also counted against him; Gus had lived abroad, had been a researcher, a profession deemed lowly by the standards of the dealer grandees. And worse, he was an outsider, his closest ally, Jimmy Gold, an ex-convict with a record for fraud.

Two stuttering and largely frustrating years had passed, a time in which Gus found himself ostracised, his attempts at making alliances within the auction houses met with rebuttals. They wanted him out and closed ranks. And when he didn't pack up his tent and leave, he was forced out.

The inevitable happened. Gus would never know *who* had organised the switch, but a small interior by Vermeer was brought to him for sale, via the lawyer of the Dutch owner. It had come with a full provenance, to prove its authenticity, and the owner - via their lawyer/agent - had agreed to pay a commission fee of 25% on the sale. The fee was high, higher than most of the other dealers, but Gus didn't intend to leave the art world empty handed.

When he looked back, his naivety was embarrassing. The Vermeer had excited much interest and although it was first intended to be sold at auction, it ended up being caught in a private bidding war between two collectors: one in Milan, the other in St Petersburg. The Russian finally succeeded, the owner's agent delivering the painting personally. And somewhere between London and St Petersburg - whether at the airport, or on the plane, or in the cars transporting it - the Vermeer was stolen and a fake took its place.

Gus had insisted to the police in London that the *original* painting had been sent to Russia. In St Petersburg the authorities insisted it was a fake and demanded full recompense, threatening a jail sentence. Gus had known all along that the painting was genuine and that he was being victimised, his reputation destroyed overnight by his rivals. Demanding that he see the picture claimed to be a fake, he was told that it had been destroyed; that the Russian collector, incensed at being cheated, had burned it. The lie was obvious, but could never be proved. The Russian magnanimously declared that he would not press criminal charges, reluctantly accepting that Gus could have been duped, the Dutch agent having disappeared overnight.

And with the agent went Gus's commission fee. As for the Vermeer, it could never be proved, but Gus knew it was in St Petersburg, just as he knew the art world had rid itself of an unwelcome dealer. For a while afterwards Gus wondered if the whole episode had been laid to rest, or if it would re-emerge, some Russian coming to London looking for him, or the dealer who had framed him reigniting the charade.

The peevish coup had driven him out of the art world, but that was no loss to Gus - who had already prepared himself to leave. What he *had* minded losing was his reputation. That had truly burned, creating a blister of revenge. Over time the blister burst and scarred over, but the wound was still there, and now it was being picked open.

Realising he was cornered, Gus typed:

What do you want from me?

The reply was immediate:

Co-operation. You're a researcher, find out about Addison Franckel and the dead patients. Find out about Louis Willes and discover where this version of The Nightmare came from. And most of all, Mr Egan, find the Incubus Tapes.

Gus hesitated before replying.

What if I can't?

Answer:

You have to.

London,
1781

My dear Johann,

*I am writing to tell you I have been a fool, a blind,
ignorant ass of a man, driven by dreams and visions
of a life and love that were never within my grasp. You
know I write of Anna Landolt? I loved her. And, I tell
you honestly, I still do - yet she now assures me that
she has never seen me as anything other than a friend!
Why is that word so cruel? So bitter, so wounding?*

*Is there another word in the English language
which causes such pain? Even in German it sounds
vicious - 'Freund' - see how I write it with a capital letter as though it were a person? How I wish it **were** some
malignant competitor I could crush and tear apart.*

*My stupidity embarrasses me, humiliates me, and
I wonder how she might have mocked me for offering my
heart. Perhaps she enjoyed toying with it for some time,
batting it about like a shuttlecock before returning it to
me in bloodied pieces... Maybe I am not being fair to her;
she never promised me love, yet I made it real in my mind.
I made a ghost of her affection, a cherub of her sweetness,
when in reality, it was a goblin sweating from lust.*

*Forgive my frankness, dear friend, I fear I am becoming a little mad, and only writing to you keeps me from leaving London and all my ambitions behind. She is to marry. Yes, Anna is to **marry** someone else. How stupid, how myopic I have been! And yet - even with this damming evidence - she haunts me.*

I dream of her, as I did before. I lust after her, I long and ache for her, and she belongs to another man. And in my insanity I am painting her portrait! There is a theory that to paint a person is to exorcise their hold. Are you aware of this old wives tale? God forgive me, I want to hate her, become her tormentor, but I cannot. I cannot hate what she made me feel, how she unhinged my senses by desiring her.

Strangely my imagination is drawn even more readily towards the unreal, the unknown. Academia bores me; I wish to drive a chisel into the holy sepulchre of Michelangelo and Titian. Not to destroy them, nor to minimise their genius, yet to challenge - nay, honour - another form of painting. One without strictures, except those of the imagination.

*Did I not **imagine** a life with Anna Landolt? Was it not real to me? Do I not regard the desire I feel for her as tangible as a person, some creature of darkness, of misplaced hope, of lust unexpressed?...*

Pardon these absurd ramblings, Johann, take them as an expression of your friend's foolishness and embarrassment. The love I felt now mocks me, yet in doing so sets free all manner of images. I will work, yes, I will work, and in doing so see what my imagination - awake or asleep - will bring to me.

Your troubled, disturbed, and fanciful friend,
Henry

SIXTEEN

Graybrooke Lodge,
Hampshire

Je-Yun was in the kitchen when Gus walked in, the
Korean smiling and inclining his head slightly in greeting. "Mr Willes is resting now. Dr Richards sedated
him an hour ago."

"*Sedated him*?"

"He has been restless and distressed, and has not
been sleeping as he should." Je-Yun moved over to
the cooker and opened the oven door, a blast of steam
entering the kitchen. "Mr Willes was looking forward
to your return, he wants to continue with the book as
quickly as possible." Je-Yun pierced the skin of the
chicken breast with a fork, the metal prongs jabbing
into the yielding flesh, juice seeping out from the
puncture. "May I ask a favour of you, Mr Egan?"

"What d'you want?"

"I need to do some errands. Mr Willes will sleep for at least a couple of hours, and needs nothing, but I don't want him to be left alone."

Gus nodded. "Fine. Go ahead and do what you need to do. I'll be working in the library."

"Thank you, I shouldn't be much more than an hour, perhaps an hour and a half. The cooker's on a timer. It will turn off when the chicken's done." Je-Yun explained, sliding the roast back into the oven. "Only Mr Willes needs watching."

Returning to his room, Gus put his jacket and bag on the bed and glanced out of the window, watching as the Korean's car moved down the driveway. At the gates he paused, then turned into the narrow road, his headlights marking the bend ahead. In contrast to London streets, the dark byways of Hampshire could be treacherous, the turns sudden, a tractor or a van forcing right of way. Curious, Gus wondered where Je-Yun was going; surely not for provisions as the nearest supermarket was over ten miles away. And more than likely to be closed after six pm.

But what did it matter? He now had an hour and a half alone and unsupervised at Graybrooke. The opportunity was his for the taking, Gus moving to Willes's room and glancing in. The same dim lamp was turned on beside the bed, the historian's face in profile as he lay on his back, his hands resting one upon the other like an effigy. For several instants Gus watched, and when he was sure Willes was deeply asleep, made his way down the stairs and headed for the back door, locking it after him and pocketing the key. The November dusk had fallen headlong into darkness, the garden a black abstract of trees and hedges, leaves shuffling underfoot as he moved down the back lawn towards the land beyond.

Willes had been defensive about the history of the house and emphatic that nothing remained of the clinic. But his insistence had been unconvincing, and under his employer and Je-Yun's scrutiny, Gus had not had an chance to explore the grounds. But now he did, Ella Fairchild's remark coming back to him.

"....*What about the operating theatre?...*"

Had it been destroyed? Gus wondered. Or if there were any remnants left? Using the torch on his mobile, he illuminated the slope before him that led into the copse beyond, a startled fox darting across his path into the shadows. The darkness as he moved into the trees increased, the branches overhead interlocking, the torch illuminating only ten feet ahead. The Graybrooke gardens might have been well maintained, but the outer grounds had been left to nature, the plot extending further than Gus had expected, without fences or walls to mark any boundary.

Purposefully he moved on, finally coming across a building almost absorbed into the landscape, a roping of brambles and ivy overhanging it, the door secured with a rusted padlock. Curious, Gus tried to open it, feeling the wet coldness of the stone as he pushed against the entrance. When it held fast, Gus shone the torch over the roof and then walked to the back of the building. There was no other entrance, merely rubble, old bricks and portions of masonry, scattered like mushrooms amongst the brambles and long grass.

There was no immediate evidence of an operating theatre, no partitions, walls, nor obvious foundations, Gus aware of the limited time he had to search. Yet even if the authorities had closed the clinic and suppressed all mention of the place and its owner, there had to be some residue or fragment that had survived. Buildings with wards, secretarial records, and medical equipment could not disappear without leaving some imprint. An oxygen cannister, a surgical instrument, the broken spool of a typewriter ribbon, or even a name tag of a long dead patient - and yet Gus could find nothing. Like a thief wiping away his fingerprints, the authorities had obliterated all trace of what had once been.

Disappointed, Gus checked the time. He had been searching for over an hour and was eager to get back to the house before Je-Yun returned. Moving quickly he tried to retrace his steps through the trees, but couldn't recognise the path he had taken only minutes before. He knew he had passed a fallen elm, the trunk eaten by rot and ant burrows - but the tree was no longer there. Obviously he had lost his way, and what he had believed was a spinney was actually a wood, far denser than he had first thought. Irritated, and aware of the time passing, he shone the torch around; but it gave him no clues to his whereabouts, only lighted more trees, the branches above him meshed tightly, the darkness absolute.

And then he heard something behind him. At first he thought it was another fox, some night animal prowling, but the sound was distorted and unnatural. It was more of a mewl, a noise low pitched and unsettling. Wary, Gus scanned the light around, then heard the sound again, this time closer. And with it came the soft snapping of twigs and the unmistakable sound of footsteps.

"Who's there?"

Silence.

He called out again, scanning the trees and thicket with the torchlight. "Is anyone there? *Je-Yun?*"

Again, no answer.

The silence was threatening, the hairs on the back of Gus's neck rising as he realised he was being watched. By an animal? Or a human? Another noise followed, then further silence, not even a leaf stirring or a sigh of wind. Unnerved, Gus moved rapidly in what he thought was the direction of the house. But instead of moving *away*, he realised that he was moving further *into* the wood, and that with every step he was becoming more enmeshed within the trees.

Disorientated, he heard the mewling again, spinning round and pointing the light directly towards the sound.

The woman was standing under a tree.

Still. Silent.

And in her hand she held a set of keys.

Transfixed, Gus stared at her, and in the same instant the torch flickered and went out. Panicked, he shook it, the beam finally reviving as he turned the light back towards the woman.

But there was no woman. Only a keyring lying on the ground under the tree where she had stood. The metal was rusted with age, the label faded, but clear enough to read the name *Addison Franckel.*

SEVENTEEN

Graybrooke Lodge
Hampshire

"How the hell do I know why he won't see me!" Ronnie Gilchrist snapped over the phone, Edward Leigh wincing at the other end. "He's got some Asian guy here and he says that Louis Willes '*is resting and will not be available until tomorrow.*'" She snorted with irritation, glancing over to the taxi driver, sitting with the engine running whilst he read the local paper.

Tapping on the plastic panel with separated them, she asked. "Hey, is there a good hotel nearby?"

The man found her American accent barely decipherable, rerunning the words in his mind slowly before replying. "We've got no hotels near here."

"You must have! Where do people stay when they come to this place?"

He glanced in the rear view mirror at the angry woman in his cab, his voice resigned. "Well, to be honest, people don't generally come here."

Irritated, Ronnie climbed out of the taxi, walking to the entry of Graybrooke Lodge and leaning against one of the gates, her attention turning back to Edward Leigh in London. "I didn't come all this way to give up! I'll have to stay here overnight." She glanced over to the taxi driver, who was still reading his paper. "Apparently there are no hotels. Willes said I could stay with him, but who knows if he meant it."

"So what's the problem? Insist --"

"*Insist?*" she replied meanly. "How can I do that? I can't get passed his fucking carer!"

"Isn't Gus Egan there?" Edward asked, secretly amused. "He's supposed to be working with Willes. Ask to talk to Egan, he might be able to sort it out."

"Yeah, I will. I'd forgotten he was here," Ronnie replied, glancing through the gates to the house. "I'll call you back."

Telling the taxi driver to wait in case she needed him, Ronnie walked back up the gravel drive, the leather heels of her stilettos scuffed by the time she reached the front door. Having pressed the bell and hearing it sound inside, she waited. No one came. Then she pressed it again, this time keeping her index finger on the button until the door was opened, Je-Yun expressionless.

"As I said before, madam, Mr Willes is not able to see you at present."

"Yeah, you told me. I want to speak to Gus Egan," Ronnie interrupted. "Tell him I'm here. My name is --"

"Ms Gilchrist," Je-Yun said quietly. "Yes, I remember, madam. If you would like to wait in the drawing room, I will try and find Mr Egan for you."

"'*Try to find him*'? Isn't he here?"

"He was here earlier," the Korean replied. "However I'm not sure where Mr Egan is now. I did expect him to be working in the library. That was where he said he would be" he shrugged, the action barely noticeable "but perhaps he was called away."

The news was unwelcome. "Please can't you find him for me? I have a cab running." When Je-Yun didn't reply, she was forced to continue. "Is he staying here overnight?"

"I do not know Mr Egan's plans --"

"*You must know if he's working here!*" Ronnie snapped. "I don't understand what all the mystery's about. And who are you anyway? Louis Willes's nurse?"

"Assistant."

"Well, if you'd be kind enough to *assist* me and find Mr Egan, I'd appreciate it."

Having decided to stay, Ronnie took a seat on the nearest sofa and unbuttoned her coat, her gaze settling on a magazine lying on the coffee table before her. Curious, she scanned the title - *Fuseli, Last Version of The Nightmare* - and the sub title - *The Haunting of An Artist*. Idly, she read the first paragraph, the author drawing a tortuous connection between Fuseli and Freud, Ronnie glancing up as Je-Yun re-entered.

"Did you find him?"

"Mr Egan is not here --"

"You told me that before," she retorted. "Well, it seems I have, or rather *you* have, a problem. Mr Willes invited me here, including an invitation to stay overnight, and that is what I'm gonna do." Her gaze scrutinised the Korean triumphantly as she handed him some money. "If you'd get my bag from the cab and pay him off, then we can relax and wait until Mr Egan returns. Or Mr Willes feels up to seeing me."

Berlin

It happened every evening in every hotel bar. Men and women on their own, travelling for work, disappointed or jubilant as to how the day had gone, but whatever the outcome each of them wanting someone to talk to. The pretty, petite woman had been the first one to start the conversation and seemed ready to accept a drink - and the others that followed - from Jimmy Gold. She was British, called Lily, on some unexpected jaunt. She had never visited Germany before, she told him, an actress auditioning for a part in a Sci-Fi movie. She was also lonely and nervous of travelling alone, Jimmy sympathising and wondering if it was worth asking for her number, but then again, if they spent the night together did he *want* to meet up again in London? Didn't that feel a bit too much like a relationship?

"You're pretty." He told her. You'll get the part."

"I dunno, there were some good looking girls there, with more experience."

"Yeah, but was that for acting?" Jimmy asked, Lily laughing and nudging his arm. He liked the gesture, felt familiar and friendly at the same time.

"So why are you in Berlin?"

"Investigating something." He replied, making it sound mysterious and knowing at the same time that it made *him* sound mysterious too. If a man wasn't tall, well-muscled, or particularly handsome, an interesting line of work helped.

"I knew you were into something like that!" Lily replied, apparently overjoyed. "You can always tell when people do something out of the ordinary. It gives them a kind of special *aura*."

"You mean like in a religious painting?"

"That's a halo!" she replied, sipping her wine and leaning towards him, the dark dress underlining her pink and white pallour. An orchid, Jimmy thought, that was what she reminded him of, an orchid.

"So what are you investigating?"

Jimmy shrugged nonchalantly. "Nothing much."

"Oh, come on, tell me! I've told you all about why I'm here." She smiled, encouraging, her eyes watching him over the rim of her wine glass. "Is it a secret? You can tell me. You *have* to tell me! I've had a lousy day and I need to take my mind off things. Tell me, Jimmy, *please*."

"I've just been looking into some wartime doctor. A shrink who got struck off --"

"A *Nazi?*"

He laughed, but had wondered momentarily if he should add Nazi to Franckel's repertoire, resisting the impulse as he continued.

"No, he wasn't a Nazi, but then again he did disappear just after the war." Relaxed, with some wine in him, he forget how much his feet hurt, even in trainers. All the walking he'd been doing and his feet ached. He wasn't even old, Jimmy thought, but his feet... Jesus, his aching feet.

"Is it dangerous?" she asked, urging him on.

Jimmy laughed dismissively. "Nah."

"Oh..." Disappointed, she pulled a face, Jimmy suddenly realising he had lost ground.

"But he was a right bastard."

"In what way?"

"Medical experiments." Jimmy said, then hesitated.

Sharing a bit didn't matter, he reassured himself. She was an actress, they were both tipsy, talking in a bar, like thousands of others in Berlin. Tomorrow - *if* they slept together - they would wake and barely remember the conversation. And if they didn't spend the night together they would part without recall of their talk; because people talked all the time. They talked to avoid being alone, they talked to get laid, they talked to feel important, or forget that in the morning they would wake up in a hotel bedroom with thin curtains and processed milk in cartons by the kettle.

His eyes widened as she slipped her arm through his and leaned into him. "Are you sure he wasn't a Nazi? They did medical experiments, didn't they?"

"His experiments weren't torture," Jimmy paused again. He didn't really know that for sure, did he? What he *had* heard about Addison Franckel's Clinic sounded sinister, and there been five deaths…but he wouldn't tell her that, even if the information tickled his tongue. No, he wouldn't confide that much.

Lily was staring at him, transfixed. "So what *were* these experiments?"

Musing, Jimmy finished his wine and ordered refills for both of them. She was looking prettier by the moment, the weather was bad outside, and if the hotel wasn't one he would recommend to someone he liked, they were in the same place and both looking for company. Anyway, what was the problem? He wouldn't mention any names, no details, but he could tell her the juicy bits.

"He ran a sleep clinic…"

"A *what?*" she asked, drinking half the wine in her glass and gazing at him.

"… investigating sleep problems."

Her interest waned; Jimmy could see it, a light turned off, her face lapsing into disappointment. *"Sleep problems?"*

"Yeah, but not your usual stuff. Not insomnia, or restless legs, more the psychological stuff. Like night terrors or sleep paralysis." This was what she wanted, Jimmy thought, she was leaning towards him again, excited.

"Is it true?"

"Is *what* true?"

"That people get paralysed when they sleep."

"Yeah, sometimes," Jimmy agreed, warming to his theme and determined to keep her interest. "People wake up and can't move. Something's on their chest, pushing down on them, and they can't even scream..."

"Jesus," she said, crossing herself. "You mean like in that Japanese film, The Ring?"

He frowned. "That was about a woman crawling out of a well."

"Yeah," she agreed, "but there's a part when one of the characters wakes up and there's this thing crouching on them." She shuddered, unnerved. "It was so scary."

"You're not kidding." Jimmy replied. "A person could lose their mind waking up to that."

Her voice was urgent, a mixture of excitement and fear. "But this thing - *what's it doing?"*

"It's called an Incubus...." Jimmy replied grandly, although he had hadn't known the word a week before.

"Incubus?"

".... The male *Incubus* seduces women in their sleep. He impregnates them." Jimmy paused, knowing her had her full attention. "... And the female Incubus, called a *Succubus,* squats on men's chests and seduces them...."

They stared at each other in silence, both thinking exactly the same thing at the same instant, Jimmy leaning forward and kissing her on the lips. She laughed, slipping off the stool and picking up her bag.

Then she handed him her hotel key: "Your room," she said, "or mine?"

EIGHTEEN

Graybrooke Lodge,
Hampshire.

Growing impatient as she waited for Gus to re-emerge, Ronnie Gilchrist wandered out into the hallway, standing before the life size replica of *The Dying Gaul* and wondering why Louis Willes had chosen it. In her experience it was an erotic choice, favoured by gay men, although the sinuous curves of the stone was more than a little appealing to her taste. Why was it that real men never looked like statues? She wondered, circling the sculpture and imaging the stone becoming flesh. There were no human counterparts in London or New York, no idealised, living beings working in galleries or auction houses. Only the lots themselves were beautiful, taunting, demanding admiration, crooning from private screenings or glossy brochures.

"I've made up a room for you." Je-Yun said behind her, Ronnie startled.

"Jesus, I didn't hear you!" she said, automatically glancing down at his feet in their soft, padded slippers. Dark grey, matching his shirt and trousers, Ronnie wondering how long he had been watching her. "Don't creep up on me like that, its unnerving."

"Excuse me, madam, but Mr. Willes doesn't like noise and wishes me to wear these shoes."

She composed herself quickly. "Still no sign of Gus Egan?"

"No, not yet." He replied, smiling. "No doubt he will return shortly. Dinner is at seven, and naturally you would be welcome."

"I'm vegan."

"I will see to it," the Korean replied, unfazed.

"So you cook for Louis Willes, do you?"

"Amongst other duties, and I drive him wherever he wishes to go."

"Thank God for that!" She snorted. "I remember hearing all about his driving, reckless wasn't the word." Amused, she studied the man. "What else do you do here?"

"I run the house and garden. We have an excellent gardener and handyman, but the property is substantial and the grounds extensive. Mr. Willes regards me as his assistant and manager. And of course I take care of the dog."

"The dog?" Ronnie echoed. "I haven't seen any dog."

"She's a little terrier, and becomes very nervous around guests, particularly women. You may not see her at all during your stay."

Ronnie wondered at his precise speech; he sounded like he was giving a guided tour. Was that because English wasn't his first language? Yet he was obviously fluent with the merest accent. Who would have imagined Louis Willes to have a male housekeeper? Back in the day he had admired women, indeed he had married a beauty. But then that had been a long time ago, Ronnie mused, the front door opening and Gus Egan walking in.

"Well, here you are!" She said, eyeing him with pleasure. Oh yes, Gus Egan had always been an attractive man, she thought, just a shame that he had failed in the art world. "I was waiting for you."

He nodded and walked past her, mounting the stairs.

"Hey! Don't you remember me? Ronnie Gilchrist --"

"I know who you are," Gus replied, turning on the landing and looking over the bannister rail. "But let's not pretend we like each other."

Angry, Ronnie moved towards the stairs, staring up at him. "You have some fucking nerve talking to me like that!"

"Why are you here?" Gus countered. "Not to see how Louis Willes is doing. More likely you want to pick his brains about the Fuseli painting, see if he knows something you could use to your advantage --"

"Oh, for God's Sake, you know the business! I'm a dealer, why not share what we know?"

Gus laughed drily. "*Share?* You don't share, Ronnie, you hit and run. You think that because Willes is a specialist on Fuseli he'll have some information you might use. Well, he hasn't."

"And you'd know that, would you?" she sneered. "You're just his lackey, his hired help --"

"You know something, Ronnie? I was forced out of the art world - my reputation ruined - by people like you. In fact, you *were* one of those people. I can't prove it, but one day I will. And now I'll tell you something you *don't* expect - you did me a favour, because I hated the business and the scum that inhabits it." He turned to Je-Yun. "Is Ms. Gilchrist supposed to be seeing Mr. Willes?"

"My employer is not available at present," he replied, taking care not to look in the American's direction. "If he feels well enough they might have a meeting tomorrow morning."

Gus nodded. "Well, when he's ready, let me know and I'll make sure I'm there."

"You're not his fucking watch dog!" Ronnie snapped. "I don't want you there --"

"If you can't agree to it, get out now." Gus retorted coldly. "Because there's no way you're seeing Louis Willes on your own."

Leaving an infuriated Ronnie in the hallway Gus made his way to his room, shutting the bedroom door behind him and locking it. He had no wish for anyone to disturb him, his hands shaking as he took the keys out of his back pocket and looked at the label - *Addison Franckel.* There were three keys on the ring, two door keys, and one for a smaller lock.

Sitting down on the side of the bed, he thought of what he had seen. Or *thought* he had seen. A woman who had materialised out of nowhere and then disappeared into nothingness. But that wasn't possible, was it?... Gus stared at the keys, turning them over in his hand. The woman had been wearing dark clothing, her hair also dark, but she hadn't been close enough to make out her features, just an impression of a tall woman in her forties.

The ringing of his mobile broke into his thoughts, Ziva's voice cheerful. "So how are things going in deepest darkest Hampshire?"

"Fine."

"Yes, I can hear the excitement in your voice," she replied wryly. "What's up?"

"Nothing."

"Try again."

"I don't believe in the paranormal."

"No, you never did. *But*?"

"Something happened" he looked at the keys in his hand, disturbed. "Would you say I was a gullible man?"

"In which particular area?"

"Seriously, Ziva, would you say I was easily duped?..." he laughed to himself "...asks the man who was accused of dealing in fakes and nearly ended up in jail."

"You were framed --"

"Like the fakes," he replied, trying to sound light hearted, but failing.

"What's going on, Gus?"

"I had a bit time of my own and I was exploring the grounds, looking round the place," he was picking his words carefully, not wanting to alarm her. "There's a wood here, and it was stupid of me, but I lost my way. It got dark and I thought I was heading back for the house, but I was actually going further away."

"And?"

"Suddenly there was a woman standing in front of me. She just appeared. From out of nowhere. My torch failed and when it came on again, she'd gone."

"Perhaps it was someone trespassing?"

"I wanted to think that, but there were sounds *before* she appeared, weird noises. And she was there one instant and gone the next." He hurried on, giving Ziva no time to interrupt. "A human being can't do that. She was standing in front of me, and then she wasn't. My torch had failed and when it came on again, she'd gone." He shook his head, bewildered. "Perhaps she *was* a trespasser - but I don't think so, because whilst I was fiddling with the torch I'd have heard her footsteps moving away. And when the torch came back on – only seconds later - I would have seen her walking off. But I didn't. *Because she'd vanished."*

He could hear Ziva take in a breath. "Why were you exploring the grounds in the dark?"

"I was curious –"

"Is it to do with the moron sending you those anonymous messages?"

He realised at once he had said too much. "Forget it. It was dark, I just imagined it --"

"**Gus!**" she snapped "don't start confiding, and then back off. You *told* me about the messages you'd been getting. You also said that working for Louis Willes could be dangerous."

"I shouldn't have said that --"

"But you did! So *are* you in trouble?"

"No," he reassured her "I'm just tied into something I don't want to be."

"So walk away."

"I can't, it's about a member of my family."

"Your family?" Ziva said, surprised. "Who?"

"My maternal grandfather, George Lyman, the one who was estranged."

"How's he involved in this?"

Gus wondered how much to confide. "Louis Willes's house was once a clinic run by a doctor called Addison Franckel. He was struck off for misconduct. My grandfather was one of his patients..."

Her voice was steady. "Go on."

"... and he died here."

"*He died?*" She repeated. "How? Why?"

"I don't know, that's what I want to find out. There were four other patients who died. In all, three men and two women --"

"When was this?"

"Wartime," Gus looked towards the door, hearing footsteps pausing outside. "Sorry, Ziva, I'll have to I call you later. I can't talk now."

As he ended the connection he could see the shadow of feet blocking the light coming under the door. For a few instants the feet didn't move, then they walked on, the firm footsteps fading into the distance. Not Je-Yun's soft slippers, Gus thought, so it had to be Ronnie Gilchrist, or Louis Willes. Perhaps the old man was feeling better and pottering around?... Again Gus looked at the keys in his hand and wondered where to hide them. Could he hide them safely in Graybrooke amongst his belongings? He decided against it. Who knew if Willes or Je-Yun would find them. Who knew if his possessions had already been searched?

Gus hesitated, he had assumed that his contact was an outsider – but what if he wasn't? What if it was someone working *with* Louis Willes? And what if the sighting of the woman had been a clever trick? Some plan to unnerve him?

But *why*? For what purpose?... Gus jingled the keys in his hand, whatever the woman had been, *they* were real. They were metal, hard, cold on his palm, and he decided to keep them with him. If he had been meant to find them, he was meant to use them.

They had belonged a man powerful or dangerous enough to unnerve the authorities, Franckel's life buried, his work expunged. And Gus wanted to know why; why he had been drawn to Graybrooke Lodge; and if his grandfather had died on the land where he now stood.

He slid the keys into his pocket. When the right time came he would use them to discover *exactly* which doors they had opened for Addison Franckel.

NINETEEN

Ealing,
London

It had been an impulse - didn't everyone want to know about their family and where they came from? It was natural to want to understand your roots; and so Caroline Lever had signed up for an online Heritage Site and paid her fee and started to track down her descendants and cousins, half cousins, half brothers and sisters, and all the other voluminous family members she was certain were out there.

They weren't. What she discovered was what she *didn't* want to know. She had no family - her parents were dead, that much she already knew - but she had no living aunts and uncles and no siblings either. So she wrote to the Heritage Site and asked for her money back, and they replied that it wasn't their job to find a family that didn't exist. Caroline wrote again, threatening exposure in the papers and citing sharp practice, and then she received a reply from a solicitor who pointed out - in an archaic and stilted manner - that her family had died out. She was alone. Without issue. Without the fee she had paid. And wasn't getting back.

As a woman who resented losing money, and as a woman with an obdurate nature, Caroline Lever decided that she would re-read the information she had paid for and find out *something* about her relatives. Even if they were her dead relatives. She wouldn't have the joyous reunions, the tearful meetings, the promises of shared Christmases and birthday messages from those with whom she shared blood, but she *would* get to know them. Even dead. And that was something.

Certainly not something she would have admitted to her friends, fearing the ridicule which would follow. People with family didn't understand that yearning to belong, and besides Caroline was regarded as a tough minded, independent thirty four year old, with one marriage and divorce under her belt, and a PR job promoting alternative medicine. It didn't matter that Caroline didn't believe in it, it mattered that she could sell it, and get paid well for the privilege.

The 'lost relative' pickings had turned out to be drearily slim until Caroline came across one name, Miriam Levy, her late father's half-sister, who had been considerably older than him. A woman Caroline had known nothing about. The details stated that Miriam had worked as a nurse during the war. What caught Caroline's attention was not the poor dry bones of Miriam's story, but the note - *Missing. Presumed dead, 1945.*

Caroline leaned her head back against the sofa, thinking, imagining Miriam Levy. Her father had not been a devout Jew, not really a Jew at all, hence the family's name change to Lever, but Miriam had kept her the original name, which said something about her. And surely there had to be a death record for her. Perhaps for Miriam Lever? Or Miriam Levy?

The records said that she had been presumed dead in 1945, but Caroline had read of a number of people who had turned up after the war was over, people who had been declared dead in error. And there were cases of others who had gone abroad, or married. Perhaps Miriam could have done the same.

Caroline liked the idea. It appealed to her that her relative could be resurrected. Another thought followed, an old memory about something she had once read. Wasn't there a record of nurses who had qualified? Even long ago, decades earlier, in the last century. She wasn't sure where she had read it, but was certain that somewhere there were records. And if there were, she needed to see them.

Turning to her laptop, Caroline scanned a list of entries, most irrelevant, then finally coming upon a listing:

> **Ancestors - UK**
> and the words:
> **'....we have a record of over 1.5 million nurses who trained and worked in the UK between 1921 - 1968. These are available online....**

Smiling, Caroline stared at the entry. It was just a matter of time before Miriam Levy was no longer Missing. Dead certainly, but no longer Missing.

Discontented, Ronnie Gilchrist pushed the vegetables around her plate, her expression sour. She had
changed her clothes, her dark skin enhanced by a
cream silk dress, her make up precise, but out of place
in rural Hampshire. In New York she would have fitted
like an arrow to bow, in Hampshire her exotic appearance jarred, like a geisha in a monastery.

Sitting silent opposite her, Gus looked up with
surprise as Louis Willes entered and was helped to his
seat, his ubiquitous tartan dressing gown over a shirt
and crumpled trousers.

"Louis!" Ronnie cried, leaping to her feet and
bending down to kiss his cheek. "How lovely to see
you! I've been --"

"Get off me! Bloody woman," Willes muttered,
glancing at Je-Yun. "I thought you said she'd gone."

"No, sir, I told you Ms. Gilchrist was staying the
night. She was waiting until you felt ready to see her."

"Well, I don't feel ready to see her!" Willes countered. "What's she doing here anyway? Come to spy,
pick my brains --"

Ronnie hid her embarrassment well. "I came to
see how you were, Louis. It's been so long since we
met up" she oozed on relentlessly. "We're all so worried about you."

"Pah!" Willes snorted, turning to Gus. "How
much work did you get done today?"

"Plenty, and I found out the dates you needed...
as well as some other interesting things." He replied
enigmatically.

Unimpressed, Willes glanced back to Ronnie. "I suppose you came all the way from New York to check on my health? Probably wondering if I was dead yet."

"Louis, how can you even think it!"

"I know the art world. You know them too, don't you?" He asked, turning back to Gus. "Screwed you over good and proper once. Don't look so surprised, I said I'd checked your background and it wasn't a secret what they'd done. To be frank, it convinced me to hire you. Made me think we had something in common - our mutual dislike of dealers."

Discomforted, Ronnie pushed away her plate, her smile forced. "Sure as hell I had nothing to do with Mr. Egan's *downfall*."

"Just like you had nothing to do with that review you wrote for my Goya book?"

She shrugged her shoulders. "It wasn't *my* review! You know what editors are like, they're always changing the wording --"

"The wording was '*plagiarism*'" Willes reminded her, beckoning for Je-Yun to approach. "I hope you're not going to serve me that crap," He said, pointing to Ronnie's sautéed vegetables. "I'm prepared to die of cancer, not malnutrition."

"I will bring you some chicken, Mr. Willes. The same as I prepared for Mr. Egan." He inclined his head briefly as he moved away, returning within minutes and laying down a meal in front of Louis Willes.

"Now *this* is food. Not great food, but food," Willes smiled at his assistant, Gus noticing a surprising, but fleeting, warmth between them, before the historian turned his attention back to Ronnie. "Have you got the painting yet?"

Her eyes opened wide. "**No!** Have you?"

"We've had it here all week, haven't we, Gus?" Willes asked, then laughed, wheezing and coughing with the effort, his mouth covered by a napkin. "Christ, you should have seen your face, Ronnie! You bloody believed me!"

"I wouldn't put it past you," she replied, churlishly. "We all know it's with John Cummings, locked away in his little fortress in Zurich. He tried to make everyone believe it was with the Lavery Foundation, but I bet that little blow fly has it. I just want to know if Cummings is gonna sell it. He must have got a client already --"

"You don't know that."

"-- on the last count he had three collectors in Dubai and a displaced Russian oligarch on his books."

Gus shrugged. "Doesn't mean he has a definite buyer."

"Of course he has! And he'll be acting as agent, getting a huge cut in commission." She reached across the table to rest her fingers on Willes's veiny hand. "But sadly, even with all this mystery and PR, we both know it's gonna be hard to shift."

Willes's paused, fork half way to his mouth. "Why's that?"

"You don't know?" She said dramatically. "It's cursed."

"Jesus," Gus replied, "who thought that one up?"

"It's true! If you did your research more thoroughly, you'd know." She snarled. "Since the painting was found there have been hundreds of incidents."

"Hundreds?" Gus repeated wryly. "It was only found two months ago.*"

"Ok, not hundreds, but there have been plenty." She persisted. "The driver who transported the picture had an accident the day after."

"Where was he transporting it to?"

"BER --"

Willes looked at her. "*What?*"

"BET - Berlin Brandenburg Airport."

"Strange" Gus interrupted. "I heard a murmur that was where - allegedly - it been stored in Berlin."

"Who knows? Who cares?" she retorted. "What matters is that the driver had an accident."

"After he'd got the painting?" Gus asked drily. "Or before?"

"After, or course! And after the painting was loaded the plane nearly crashed." She dabbed at the sides of her mouth with a napkin, leaving lipstick stains on the starched linen. "Well, not crashed, but there was a problem with one of the engines and they had to bring it off the runway to have it checked out."

"That's two, Ronnie."

"*Huh?*"

"That's just two incidents out of the 'plenty' you claimed."

"What about when it arrived in at the Lavery Foundation? The man on night duty there said it moved."

Willes laughed. "He probably bloody dropped it!"

Angry, she turned on him. "*It's true!* The painting shifted its position."

"That," Gus said pointedly "is a very old story, Ronnie. It dates back to 1782 when the first *Nightmare* was exhibited and the watchman swore it came alive. The story was reported everywhere and still is." He jerked his head towards the library. "In fact, there's a

155

magazine in there which you were probably reading earlier. All about Fuseli, the *Haunted Painter.*"

Ronnie drummed her fingers on the table, Willes watching the exchange, amused, and waiting for her to speak again. He admired her blind ignorance, her holding court about a painter on whom *he* was the leading authority. Was that because she was female? American? Or stupid?

"Fuseli *was* haunted!" Ronnie repeated, her voice strident. "It's well known, the first painting made women faint when they saw it. The Incubus terrified London, people coming from everywhere to view it, doctors and psychiatrists all fascinated." She looked from one man to the other, warming to her theme. "Of course it was indicative of the times, psychology coming into its own and people investigating dreams and such like. Psychiatrists and philosophers of the day talked about it nonstop, like it had some insight into the meaning of dreams." Whether she realised it or not, she had Gus's attention. "They say Fuseli based it on one of his own nightmares --"

"Utter tripe! Women's magazine stuff." Willes snorted, Ronnie continuing.

"-- he'd lost the woman he loved and painted her lying there, on the bed, stretched out waiting for him. But it wasn't him that came to her, but a ghoul, a hideous creature squatting on her breasts and impregnating her."

"*Through her breasts*?" Gus asked. "You should brush up on your biology, Ronnie."

She ignored the comment, continuing. "I'm just saying, this new picture's got a bad vibe about it. It's unlucky, and that'll make it hard to sell. And anyway, judging from the reproductions I've seen, it's nowhere near as good as the first version."

"It doesn't have to be," Willes said, "it just has to be by Fuseli. And I don't agree with you, I've seen a photograph the Lavery Foundation sent to me, and it looks impressive, I like the figure in the background instead of the horse. That bloody horse never rang true."

"Fuseli based it on folklore --"

"We know!" Gus said, an exasperated Willes nodding in agreement. *"Everyone* knows about it, Ronnie, and your feeble attempt at making this version undesirable is just that, feeble. It'll sell on the Fuseli name, despite how good or bad it's considered - or if it's even genuine."

"It's genuine all right. It's been checked out."

Gus laughed. "So have a quarter of works in galleries around the world, and yet the forgeries keep getting through."

"Well, you'd know all about that."

Immediately the atmosphere chilled, Gus leaning over the table towards her, his voice warning. "Don't push your luck *or* my patience, Ronnie. I haven't forgotten the past. Or the part you played in it. You owe me - and on the day you least expect it, I'll collect."

TWENTY

Zurich,
Switzerland

It was past midnight when John Cummings's butler, Ted Turner, completed his initial search of the property. His employer, who suffered from intermittent insomnia, was not in his bedroom, nor in his study. Knowing that he often went for a swim to encourage sleep, Turner made his way to the indoor swimming pool. All the lights were turned on, even those under the water, as were the outside lamps that illuminated the patio and gardens beyond. Surprised that there was no sign of his employer, he walked around, but nothing seemed out of place. As ever, palms trees in metal urns stood silent guardians of the pool house, a couple of wet towels thrown onto a divan beside an open magazine.

So his employer *had* been swimming, Turner thought, moving into the changing room and finding a discarded suit, shirt, and shoes. But no John Cummings. Uneasy, Turner walked back, looking down into the pool, the snow white tiles unmarked, steam rising from the water set to blood heat. His gaze moved along the sides of the pool, looking for any disturbance, any sign of a fall, any mark of blood. Perhaps his employer had slipped and was unconscious somewhere, wearing only swimming trunks.

Anxious, he phoned Cummings's secretary. "Miss Birch?"

The woman was obviously woken from sleep. "Yes… Is that you, Turner? What's the problem?"

"Did Mr. Cummings have an engagement tonight? One that was made at the last minute?"

"No," she yawned. "Not that I know of."

"No visitors?"

"Why?" she asked, now awake. "What's the matter?"

"I found his clothes in the pool house where he'd had a swim, but I can't locate him."

"You found his clothes?" She frowned. "Well, maybe he just left them there, went back into the house and put on something else --"

"He isn't in the house." Turner interrupted, "that's why I'm ringing you."

She was sitting up in bed now, turning on the lamp beside her. "I spoke to Mr. Cummings at five o clock and I haven't heard from him since… Perhaps he had some secret business meeting. Or maybe someone flew into Zurich unexpectedly and wanted to see him. We both know he has plenty of those *discreet* visits."

"He would have notified me." Turner said firmly. "Mr. Cummings is very precise and careful to make sure that I know all his movements."

She could tell he wasn't going to let the matter drop. "So when did you last see him?"

"At lunch, he was pre-occupied, and seemed irritated after a short altercation over the phone."

"With whom?"

Turner sighed, his ex SAS bulk impressive, his voice curt. "I don't know. I was hoping that you knew more than I did, which you don't. Forgive me for troubling you."

By this time growing concerned, Turner wondered if his employer had left the property in a hurry and forgotten to inform him. But in checking the garage, the car - one of many - was still there and the chauffeur had not been called out. In fact, none of the maids or gardeners had seen their employer. To all intents and purposes the last time anyone had seen John Cummings was at lunch. The last phone call had been at five o'clock, and since then, nothing.

Alarmed, Turner crossed the garden, traversing the underground passages and moving towards an archway, finally unlocking the last, steel-framed door. Having been in service to John Cummings for over fifteen years - and bound by loyalty and an old favour - Turner knew of the secret chamber. He did not advertise the fact, and Cummings's father and brother did not know of their relative's rare example of trust, but Turner *had* been trusted. He had also been told that should his employer be killed, or kidnapped, he was obliged to enter. Cummings had then explained that any disastrous event was to be reported to the police, his lawyer, then his family, and that the instructions for entry and exit to his private gallery must be observed meticulously.

You must understand that the temperature
at which the paintings are kept must be sta-

ble. Do not allow the entry and exit doors to be left open for longer than one minute and thirty seconds or irreparable harm may occur. No one is to be allowed to remain inside unattended. You, my father, or my brother, must accompany anyone who enters.

Remembering the instructions, Turner unlocked the door, ensuring that he closed it after he had entered. Once inside, he turned on the subdued lighting – as carefully monitored as the temperature - and moved into the room beyond, employing the key entrusted to him several years earlier. Although he had never used the key before, it slid into the lock and turned, rotating smoothly.

Turner's first impression as he pushed open the weighted door was heat. It was well over eighty degrees, and more than that the lights were blazing, every overhead bulb, every picture light turned up to the maximum. Moving fast, Turner lowered the thermostat and flicked off the wall lights one after then other, then hurried towards the central, secret chamber - the inner sanctum of John Cummings, the hidden area where he had kept, and enjoyed, some of the most valuable paintings ever traded. With a growing sense of dread, Turner entered the chamber then stopped in the doorway, staring at the antique easel before him, the skylight above spotlighting the image below.

The Fuseli painting that had been there only hours earlier had gone. In its place was his employer, John Cummings bloodied and spread eagled, tied with ropes, his mouth gaping open in a final scream.

TWENTY ONE

Graybrooke Lodge
Hampshire

The e mail came through short and to the point.

Have you heard, Mr. Egan?

John Cummings has been murdered...

Stunned, Gus re-read the message, glancing over to Ronnie Gilchrist who was still regaling Willes with some tedious anecdote. The historian looked bored, pushing away his meal and calling for Je-Yun.

"Have we got any ice cream?"

"We have, sir. Would you like some?"

"I would like you to pour some over her head," he replied, pointing to Ronnie.

She jerked back in her seat, her expression pained, Willes ambling into the sitting room, Ronnie scurrying after him. In the hallway Gus watched them as he read the next part of the message on his mobile.

It's a shock, isn't it? His body was naked, bloody, hung up on an easel - the same one that had held the Fuseli.

Which is now missing...
So who do you think has it?

Taking care not to be overheard, Gus moved out into the garden beyond. Near to the house the lawn was illuminated by the lights from the sitting room, Gus turning up the collar of his jacket against the chill. He was thinking about his reply when his mobile rang, a voice - obviously mechanically distorted - greeting him.

"I thought it was time we spoke in person --"

"Who are you?"

"Why do you keep asking me that, Mr. Egan!

Do you really think I'm going to tell you? And then what, you'd tell the police? No, that's not going to happen."

There was a pause on the line, but when Gus didn't reply, the caller continued.

"The Fuseli painting has been stolen."

"Yes, I read your message. Why are you telling me?"

"So you can tell Louis Willes, see what his reaction is. If he looks like he might have something to do with it."

"The man's in his eighties, terminally ill!"

"I'm not suggesting he got off his death bed and flew to Zurich, but Willes has contacts that he's built up over the years --"

"I thought you wanted me to find the Tapes." Gus said sharply. "Don't tell me you now want me to find a bloody painting."

"If anyone could, you could."

"No! I'm involved with the Addison Franckel business because of my grandfather. I don't give a shit about the painting."

There was a hesitation on the line before the voice spoke again.

"Have you heard from Franckel's son,

Freddy Wilson?"

"Not a word."

"You will."

"Maybe, maybe not. Why would he want to dig up the scandal about his father?"

"Money! To sell the story to the papers.

He's an addict, he's old, and he'll do anything for money."

"Yet you - and Ella Fairchild - went to great pains to tell me that as soon as anyone starts digging they get threatened."

"No one's threatened you, have they?"

"Not yet."

"What about the crafty Jimmy Gold?

He's in Berlin, isn't he? To be honest, he might be better off looking closer to home, Germany's not got much to offer, and they never like anyone resurrecting the past."

"You know about the doctors in Switzerland and Germany who are apparently using Franckel's methods?"

"There are rumours."

"This is *all* rumour." Gus responded. "Or perhaps this a personal vendetta. Was a relative of yours a Franckel patient? Or are you a doctor yourself? Perhaps you want the Tapes to pick up some tips --"

"The Tapes are no joking matter!

Patients suffered --"

"So you say, but I don't see any evidence. I keep being given hints, innuendos, but nothing concrete. Tell me, how bad are these Tapes? Why did they need to be destroyed? Why were the authorities determined to bury Franckel?" Gus took in a breath. "And if I *did* find the Tapes would I be in danger?"

"Perhaps."

"And perhaps I'd end up like the journalist who tried to investigate? He committed suicide, didn't he?"

"Maybe."

"What was his name?"

"Ted MacNeice."

"Why was he involved?"

"He was young, ambitious, wanted to make head-lines. He did that actually, throwing himself off Battersea Bridge. But did he fall, or was he pushed?"

"You think he was killed?"

"His family did. They protested and demanded answers, and then Ted MacNeice's flat was broken into and all his possessions and papers were taken. It was supposed to be a burglary, but no one believed that."

"Did MacNeice have the Incubus Tapes?"

"Who knows."

"But even if the tapes survived, what good are they to anyone?" Gus asked, deliberately provoking him. "It's a fool's errand. Why don't you just let the matter rest?"

"Because the Tapes should be found!"

"To what end?"

"To expose them --"

"It's nearly eighty years ago! It's dead and buried."

"You don't understand!"

"No, I don't." Gus agreed.

"People died --"

"Did they?" Gus retorted. "Did they *really?* Well, I need to know more than that, and I'm going to finish this call now unless you answer one question."

"Which is?"

"Have you seen the tapes?"

And then the line went dead.

166

TWENTY TWO

Taking the medication offered by Je-Yun, Louis Willes studied Ronnie Gilchrist, the American positioning herself on the sofa as though she was waiting for a photographer. He noted the gym-honed arms - the heat of the sitting room a welcome contrast to the cold outside - and he marvelled at her hypocrisy, her utter lack of intelligence. Did she really believe that her feigned concern would lead to some confession or confidence? Perhaps she hoped he might peg out in his chair, his dying words heard only by her, a final declaration about the Fuseli painting.

He had to admit that although he was in pain and weary to the spine, her machinations amused him, his memory reviving the sting of plagiarism. How she had damned his Goya book! How she had nit-picked, declared that he had creamed off other peoples' work and re-written it so it would enmesh seamlessly with his own. As if he needed to! Even in the jealous hub of the art world Louis Willes was recognised as an authority.

"So when are you leaving?"

Ronnie sulked. "I've only just arrived, Louis, and you're asking when I'm leaving! What kind of a welcome is that?"

"More of a goodbye than a welcome," he replied, deliciously malicious and thinking of the heated exchange over dinner. "So what's the argument with Gus Egan?"

"He's never gotten over being rejected by the dealers. Poor Gus, he just wasn't fitting in."

"No, he was 'fitted up,'" Willes replied deftly, Je-Yun tucking a rug around his employer's legs. Intuitively he was looking for a sign, some intimation that Willes wanted Ronnie Gilchrist removed, but there wasn't any. Instead there was an expression of mischief. "You know," Willes continued "I'm getting to like Gus Egan, he's doing a good job."

"So he should. I was told how much he charges - and he refused to work for Edward Leigh!"

"I like him even more now." Willes said, amused. "Is Leigh still trimming that ludicrous beard of his? Someone should tell him that he looks like a drunk that forgot to wipe off the shaving foam. I remember him when he was just starting out. He cheated me, you know. Swore blind he didn't, but he did. His wife's money covered all his losses for years. Poor cow, imagine marriage to Edward Leigh being your life's work."

Bored, Ronnie changed the subject. "So how long before you finish this book?" She asked, reaching into her bag and taking out a lipstick. Deftly, she applied it without using a mirror, Willes watching her.

"Why bother with the make-up, Ronnie? I'm too old, and Gus Egan isn't interested."

"How d'you know?" She parried. "He's divorced."

168

"He doesn't like you."

She snapped the lipstick closed and put it back in her bag. "Since when does that mean anything between a man and a woman? Sexual attraction is often covered by aggression." Her tone was light, flirtatious. "Fuseli knew all about sexual innuendo, didn't he? Those erotic drawings, with the weird hairstyles and the overly muscled men." She laughed "You have to admit he had a vivid imagination. *The Nightmare* was a tour de force. And Fuseli knew it, look how many versions he painted." She paused, then launched in, full sail. "I have to ask you, as we're old friends and colleagues, *do* you know where the painting is?" When he didn't respond, she pressed him. "Come clean, Louis! You used to know everything that went on in the business."

"I *used* to, years ago, not anymore."

"But you still have contacts. Anthony Hallett's still your partner and a friend. You knew his wife and he knew yours. You socialised together, here - in this house - I heard all about it, your fantastic parties." She didn't notice the flicker of hatred in Willes's eyes at the mention of the dealer. "You don't want to lose a golden opportunity, do you? Not when *we* - you and I - could make a deal for the Fuseli and share the commission. I have collectors who would crawl, bare assed, through fire, for that painting."

"I'd like to see that," Willes said, Je-Yun moving around the room silently, closing curtains, locking windows. And listening.

"Seriously, you could make a killing, Louis. I mean, it would only be fair, after all, you're the one with the knowledge, you deserve to be rewarded."

"You're wrong, I don't know anything --"

"Shit!" she snapped, all pretense of manners gone. "Just tell me if the fucking picture is up for sale!"

In the hallway outside a grandfather clock sounded, the Westminster chimes announcing eleven o'clock, Willes listening then glancing back to Ronnie.

"Two hours and fifteen minutes."

"Huh?"

"It took you two hours and fifteen minutes to get around to asking me." He chuckled, Je-Yun refilling the glass of water on the table beside him and glancing up when Gus walked in.

Obviously unsettled, he brought the cold night with him as he moved over to the fire and warmed his hands for several moments before turning to Willes.

"John Cummings has been murdered --"

"Murdered? What the fuck!" Ronnie exclaimed, shocked. "Who killed him?"

"The police don't know, his body's just been found." Gus was staring at Willes. "It was messy, Cummings was butchered."

As Ronnie scrabbled in her bag for her mobile, Willes leaned forward in his seat, peering at Gus.

"What else?" His eyes, rheumy and weary, were suddenly brilliant with excitement.

Gus watched him, wondering how much he knew, and how much he was hiding. "It wasn't just a murder."

"Tell me the rest!" The old man demanded.

"John Cummings had been keeping the Fuseli in his home--"

"And?"

"The killer took the painting."

London
December 1782

My dear Johann,

I apologise for my exceedingly late reply to your letter. I have no excuse which absolves me, only that I have been much perturbed of late. Mystified, troubled... As you know, I intended to paint Anna Landolt's portrait, and indeed have done so. Yet it is not to stand as a loving tribute to my adored - more a memento, some painted epitaph which I sought as a sick man would seek an antidote to poison.

*For she **has** poisoned me, do not doubt it. Her face has imprinted itself on all others. When I sketch, I sketch her. When I paint, I paint her, the images so many that a crowd of Anna Landolts occupy by waking hours.*

And now my sleep.

Or should I say, my longed for sleep... Never before in my life have I found rest elusive, yet now as the darkness falls I dread its yawning hours. She comes to me, not as a lover, and yet I long to possess her, more so than when I was in love. I ache to feel her body under my own, to see the longing, even fear, in her face, to know myself the possessor of her and also the aggressor. The hatred has changed form, is now erotic: as corrosive and burning as fever, as intense as the gasping of breath of a falling man.

I am not mad, I trust myself in this, though you might judge me otherwise. After a month of this unrelenting torment, I now attempt to sleep with candles beside my bed to hold the dark at bay and sometimes - in the border between wakefulness and sleep - the drapes around my bed shift and I sense a figure beside me. There is warmth there, the bedclothes humped, or an imprint from where a body has lain.

Is this the Mara, the devil of death and desire? If so, I believe it would have Anna Landolt's face. She comes to suffocate me in my sleep! And I will have none of it. So I have begun her exorcism. Yes, my dear Johann, I have decided on a course of action to rid myself of this poison, to scrape her image from my mind, the longing from my body, and the torment from my soul.

The fables we heard as we grew up we considered merely stories, yet I tell you there is a nub of truth to all these fairytales; for every monster must find its victim and every victim match themselves to their particular ghoul.

I am painting a work that has exercised my imagination for many weeks. It will have no explanation for those who will view it when completed; nor will I offer any elucidation myself. Instead London will see in paint what I endure in sleep. I am using pigment and oils to destroy this madness and free myself. What irony it is that my painting will be created on the <u>reverse</u> of Anna Landolt's portrait?

172

For I dare not make the female in the picture resemble her, nor the other figure resemble myself. Instead it will be an image of the unexplained, of night terrors - from which so many have suffered. As I have. As you have. As perhaps one in every tenth person on the street would admit. For sleep is not always a place of rest and safety; it harbours shadow creatures attuned to the dark; ghosts, demons, and spirits of folk lore. And in the corners of the night hours linger the smoky longings we suppress or deny when awake. There is no society, no morals, in sleep. We dream alone and in our dreams we may kill and seduce without censure.

The sketch for the picture is completed and tomorrow I begin to paint. There is light in the image, yet the darkness surrounds it and would snuff it out, had it the power to do so. As I would extinguish her.

My dear friend, forgive these frantic outpourings. Perhaps I will create a tremendous painting and establish a reputation by doing so. Perhaps London will laud me for my imagination, when in truth they would be applauding a man's worst instincts. Only one matter is certain - what demon I will create on this canvas has already created the monster in myself.

Your loving friend,
Henry

TWENTY THREE

Graybrooke Lodge
Hampshire

Ronnie slumped back into her seat and looked over to Willes. "Did *you* know about Cummings?"

"*What*! How could I know?" He asked, raising his eyebrows. "Gus has only just found out, so how the hell would I know?"

"You just don't seem shocked."

"I wasn't close to John Cummings --"

"He was murdered! The painting's gone!" She snapped, turning to Gus. "Who told you?"

"It doesn't matter who told me."

"So why hide it?"

"Did I say I was hiding it?" Gus responded. "I don't have to tell you anything."

She folded her arms, looking from Willes to Gus, her expression suspicious. "It is true?"

"What?"

"*That Cummings is dead!*" She demanded. "I mean, you could have made it all up."

Sighing, Gus stared at her. "Why would I?"

"It just seems very convenient that the painting's been stolen and *you're* the first to hear about it."

"But I'm not the first. The Swiss Police are handling the murder, it's common knowledge in Zurich, by now the news will have circulated around the art world. I'll bet money that most of the dealers in London know. It's all over the internet." He pointed to her mobile. "Why don't you ring Edward Leigh, or ask Anthony Hallett? You two were always on such good terms."

The barb found its mark, Ronnie getting to her feet and facing Gus. "Does it matter to you who I fuck?"

"No, only who you fuck over." He retorted, Willes laughing.

"Well, it looks like there's no reason for you to stay any longer, Ronnie." He said, with mock sadness "It's been a wasted visit for you. As I told you on the phone, I knew nothing about the Fuseli painting, and now" he shrugged "God knows who has it, but they wanted it badly enough to kill for it. If I were you, I'd keep well out of this mess."

"Good advice."

Immediately she rounded on Gus. ""*Good advice?*" Really? So you two are just looking out for me, hey? Just being English gentlemen. Hah! I don't know what's going on here, but something is. Nothing about this adds up." Angry, she moved towards the door, then turned, her gaze fixing on Je-Yun. "Get me a cab, will you? I'm not staying in this frigging mausoleum another minute."

Quarter of an hour passed, Ronnie waiting in the hall, and asking Je-Yun three times if he had ordered the taxi. Three times he told her he had, but it was delayed by the weather. Fog was coming down, making visibility difficult and the roads treacherous.

"Christ," Willes said, overhearing the exchange, "I hope the driver can get here. I don't want that bloody woman staying overnight." He looked at Gus quizzically. "By the way, who *did* tell you about Cummings?"

I imagine you would like to know, Gus thought, his suspicions roused. Or do you know already?

"Perhaps I saw it on the internet."

"Perhaps you did. But you didn't, did you?" Willes replied, waving one hand dismissively. "Ah, keep your secrets, more people should keep secrets. Too many people blab about everything these day, bleeding all over the place, victims of everything, especially themselves." He sighed nostalgically. "In the old days so much was hidden. Maybe too much, but then again, life had more *bite* to it. Secrecy should be made compulsory."

"You know, Ronnie Gilchrist has a point," Gus said, changing the subject. "You *didn't* look shocked to hear about Cummings's murder."

"So what? So he died! I'm going to die soon, what's it to me?"

"But he didn't die of natural causes, he was *murdered*. There's a difference --"

"Cancer is pretty brutal!" Willes snapped, Gus nodding.

"I know, but murder is deliberate. Someone killed Cummings and stole the painting. We both know about men who are hired to 'steal by order'. They're paid well for the risk - but they **never** kill. They're thieves and thugs, but not murderers. They never go that far."

"Maybe this one was an exception."

Gus shook his head. "Nah, they usually watch for a while, plan; then break in when they're sure they've worked out the security system and the staff timetables. But they never - *never* - strike when there's someone at home."

"So the burglar slipped up --"

"You don't 'slip up' if a mistake could be the difference between a few years, or life in jail." Gus persisted. "The thief was hired to go to Zurich. There he would have watched Cummings, memorised his routine, when he got up, when he went out, and when he was at home. He would have ensured an easy theft, with no complications."

Willes shrugged. "So your point is?"

"Did he *mean* to kill Cummings*?* "

"Why would he!"

"Maybe he was paid for stealing the painting *and* killing John Cummings?"

Willes blew out his cheeks: "I say it was a mistake."

"I say it wasn't."

"And you're an expert, are you?" Willes asked, his tone combative. "Perhaps your little running mate, Jimmy Gold, has educated you in the world of crime?"

"You're saying that the art world isn't criminal?" Gus countered, incredulous. "We both know that's not true. We've both been cheated and had our reputations tainted. But this is *murder*. An art dealer was killed for a painting --"

"How d'you know that for sure?"

"Because if John Cummings had surprised the thief he would have been no match for him. Cummings was a small man, he could have been overpowered easily to allow the thief make his getaway. Instead he was killed and his corpse displayed for shock value."

"So it was deliberate?"

"Yes, it had to be. Hold on" Gus put up his hands to prevent Willes interrupting him "just forget Cummings for a minute, what about the painting? Don't you care that it's been stolen? You've been obsessed by Fuseli for years, you're desperate to finish his biography - yet you seemed indifferent when you heard that the painting's disappeared."

Sighing, Willes reached for his glass of water, glancing over to the window. "See if the fog is getting thicker will you? We can't have that flaming woman in the house any longer."

Curious as to why his questions were being ignored, Gus moved to the window, held back the curtain, and looked out. The driveway was barely visible, a dense fog building, the light from the window extending only a couple of feet. Without street lamps, along narrow circuitous lanes, the journey would be impossible.

"The taxi won't get through this, not on these roads."

"Well she can't bloody stay here!"

"She'll have to," Gus replied, his mobile ringing again. Eager to avoid being overheard, and knowing that Je-Yun was safely upstairs, he headed for the kitchen before answering.

"Hello?"

To his surprise, it was Jimmy Gold, his voice high pitched, urgent. "Gus! Can you hear me?"

"Yes, are you alright?"

"I found out something --"

"John Cummings has been murdered."

"Yeah, but there's more... and it's important...." Jimmy paused, talking to someone who had called his name, loud music in the background and distant laughing. **"Gus! Can you hear me?"**

"Yes, tell me what you found out --"

"It's about Louis Willes ..... **hello**! Can you hear me?"

"Yes, I can hear you, Jimmy! Where are you?"

"Still in Berlin... Jesus, this connection's terrible!" The line was breaking up, then coming back. "... it's something about Willes that you should know..." the connection dropped again. **"Can you hear me?"**

"Yes, yes! Go on - what about Willes?"

The line crackled.

"Fucking phone!" Jimmy snapped, "I can't hear you..." his voice was angry, frustrated, the background noise growing louder as he called out: "Hold on! I'll ring you back!"

But he didn't. Gus waited for a couple of minutes, then tried Jimmy's number. It was turned off. Surprised, he tried again, with the same result. Finally, he turned and was about to leave the kitchen when he saw Je-Yun standing in the doorway, watching him.

For an instant the two men stared at each other, Je-Yun the first to speak. "Do you need something, Mr. Egan?"

"Did the taxi arrive for Ms. Gilchrist?"

"I rang the company again and was told that there is a delay because of the fog, and as it is increasing it may not be possible for a taxi to get to Graybrooke tonight." He glanced towards the counter top. "Mr.

Willes has asked for some more coffee, may I make you another cup?"

Gus nodded, watching Je-Yun as he moved from the fridge back to the counter, measured out the coffee, and then started the machine. His hands were immaculate, the nails short, the fingers without jewellery. There was only a thin gold band around his wrist, as fine as a thread of cotton.

"Do you visit your family often?"

Je-Yun was opening the fridge door, his figure obliterated for an instant, only the top of his head showing. "My family in Korea?"

"Yes. Do you see them often?"

"I have only a brother and he lives in Germany." Je-Yun replied, closing the fridge door and moving back to the counter. His head averted, he laid out a tray with two cups on it.

Gus raised his eyebrows. "Ms. Gilchrist didn't want any coffee?"

Je-Yun turned, a teaspoon in his right hand, his black eyes steady. For a fleeting instant he seemed unnatural, his appearance pristine, his skin clean-shaven, the cheekbones and jawline as smooth as the limb of a child. The effect was both fascinating and perturbing, Gus watching as Je-Yun turned away and then placed a china sugar bowl on the tray beside the two cups.

"Ms. Gilchrist is anxious to leave." He said simply. "I understand, but it will not be an inconvenience for her to stay overnight. There are plenty of bedrooms."

"How many?"

"Ten," Je-Yun replied promptly. "Only two are occupied on a permanent basis. Mr. Willes and mine, there is always room for guests."

"Do you have many guests here?"

181

"Not since Mr. Willes became ill," the Korean replied, the coffee machine behind him gurling, the aroma starting to build in the kitchen. "Before then, I believe there were some visitors."

"Art dealers?" Gus asked. "Perhaps I know them."

"Mr. Anthony Hallett used to come. He and his wife are old friends of Mr. Willes."

Gus thought of what Willes had told him about Hallett, and wondered if Je-Yun was testing him to see how much he knew, or if he was unaware of his employer's hatred of the dealer.

"They came here often?"

"Apparently they were frequent visitors when Mrs. Willes was alive, so Mr. Willes tells me," Je-Yun paused, glancing over to the coffee percolating, then back to Gus. "Did you know her?"

"Mrs. Willes? No, why would I?"

"Being in the art world, I wondered if you had met her in the past."

Gus shook his head. "No, never. Actually I only just heard about her death. That she died in a car accident."

"It was long before my time," Je-Yun replied, "but although she's been deceased for many years Mr. Willes speaks of her often. More so lately." To Gus's surprise, Je-Yun folded his arms and leaned against the counter, his voice lowered. "Over the last few weeks Mr. Willes has developed some strange fancies. No doubt caused by the medication."

"What kind of 'fancies?'"

"He dreams of his late wife and at times believes he can see her." The words sounded an alarm as Je-Yun continued. "In my religion, and in much of Korea, such matters are accepted. For many people, they are a normal part of life."

"To see the dead?"

"They might be real visions, or hallucinations. '*A hope metamorphosized into reality*'. It is not for me to judge."

"What does Dr Richards say about it?"

Je-Yun smiled absently. "Dr Richards is always very busy and dismisses such matters as imagination."

Surprised by the sudden and unexpected confidences, Gus encouraged Je-Yun to talk further. At the same time he was wondering if he was being manipulated, remembering the woman and the keys - now resting in his back pocket. If it *had* been staged what better way to make it look convincing than to bring up the subject of the dead Mrs. Willes.

"Do you believe in such things, Mr. Egan?"

"What things?"

"Mr. Willes believing that he can see his late wife. Or the dead coming back to life."

Gus thought of the woman he had seen in the wood. Was the question an idle one? Or was the Korean taunting him?

"Some places lend themselves to the paranormal." Gus replied, keeping his tone casual. "It's dark here, remote, and tonight it's foggy, which makes Graybrooke Lodge the ideal setting for ghost sightings."

Je-Yun nodded. "The house is beautiful, but very old, and like all such places it creaks and shifts at night.

Gus had heard the shufflings himself, but dismissed them. Many buildings of long standing had sounds and sighs. Uneven floorboards, drafty attics, and damp, underground cellars developed a language of their own, the quiet of night making it all the more audible. Add to that the spirit of a dead woman and the ghosts of five patients who had apparently perished in the same location and who knew what Louis Willes really heard or saw?

And what had *he* seen? Gus thought. A vision? Or a clever hoax? His hand moved to his back pocket, feeling the reassuring outline of the keys as Je-Yun poured the coffee into two cups.

"The gardener comes tomorrow," he said. "When my employer takes his afternoon nap I'm sure Mr. Parker would be pleased to show you around the grounds. There's the lake, which must have been beautiful once, but is now dried up, the derelict ice house, and a copse. You may have noticed it." Je-Yun paused. "Apparently it was Mrs. Willes's favourite place. It was manicured and orderly then. She used to hold summer dinner parties there, and musical evenings. My employer wanted to have her buried there –"

"*Buried*?" Gus repeated, taken aback.

"Sadly it was not allowed. There were objections."

"Surely not by neighbours - you don't have any."

"I don't know who objected, only that it was forbidden for the grounds to be disturbed." Je-Yun moved to the door with the tray, pausing to look back to Gus. "Are you ready?"

"For what?"

"Coffee," Je-Yun replied, "what else?"

Still in the hall, Ronnie was berating the taxi company, her voice high pitched. She was keen to leave, wearing her coat, her suitcase beside her, her handbag tucked under her arm as she paced the floor.

"You have to send someone!"

There was a murmur at the other end of the line.

"God damn it! I'm not staying here!" She replied furiously. "Look, tell the cabbie I'll pay him extra…." She listened to the reply and then responded. "I'll dou-

ble his fee! Just get him here. *I need to leave.* What?…
Yes, of course I've been invited to stay!..." She paused
again, "*What did you say?... The fog could last a day!
Or more!...* Aren't there any other cab companies?"
When the answer was in the negative, she swore,
clicked off her mobile and stormed back into the sitting
room to confront Louis Willes. "Seems I have to stay
here because of your stinking weather."

Surly, she glanced at the tray Je-Yun had brought
in and reaching for a cup.

"You said you did not want any coffee, madam"
Je-Yun said quietly. "These are for Mr. Willes and
Mr. Egan –"

"Well I *do* want a coffee! Is that too much to ask?"
she snapped, sitting down.

The old man was sipping from his cup, watching
her. Gus had a fleeting impression of a stoat sizing up
a potential victim.

"Do you play bridge?"

"Do I *what*?" Ronnie snapped.

"What about gin rummy? Wasn't it created in
New York? A nice American game."

She turned to Gus and raised her eyebrows. "What
about a nice English game? Croquet on the lawn? The
weather's perfect for it."

"The fog's nobody's fault." He replied, watching
Je-Yun return with a third cup of coffee. "We'll have
to make the best of it. You're lucky you got any mobile
connection in this weather --"

"What's the weather got to do with phones!"

"Everything." Willes replied. "You do realise we
could end up marooned here? But never mind, Ronnie,
we could talk about John Cummings being murdered,"

he said mischievously. "You like to gamble, should we lay bets as to who the killer is?"

"Is that supposed to be funny?"

He ignored the comment and continued. "It has to be someone who's ruthless." Willes paused, thoughtful. "Now, who wants the Fuseli enough to kill for it?"

"What about you? Would you?" She responded. "I mean, not now, you're out of the game now, but *would* you have killed for the Fuseli?"

"Kill for a painting?"

She leaned towards him. "Not any old painting, the newly found Fuseli. The one painted by the artist you worship. The one that will break all records when it's sold."

"At auction?"

"No one with a head for business would let the auction houses get their cut. No, you'd have to sell it privately. So, who'd be *your* buyer of choice? I mean, if you'd killed to get it, who would you sell it to?"

He thought for a moment, Gus watching him, Je-Yun standing beside his employer's chair.

"*Me? Sell it?*" Willes asked, chuckling. "No, I'd keep it."

"Hide it away?"

"Naturally."

She was eager, alert. "Where?"

"Somewhere no one would look." Willes replied, his voice cold. "Somewhere no one would *dare* to look."

She pretended alarm. "You're scaring me, Louis! Where is this hiding place and why would no one dare to look there?"

He held her gaze, locked into it. "Because, my dear lady, they wouldn't be able to live with what they saw."

186

TWENTY FOUR

Dover Street,
London W1

As Gus had predicted, the news of the murder of John Cummings flooded the art world, dealers passing the gossip from gallery to gallery like a baker handing out hot pies. Always accompanied by a myriad rumours, Cummings had been a shadowy, divisive figure and the killing seemed to cement his enigma. Distant colleagues - for who was *not* distant from Cummings? - either declared their suspicion of the man or pretended intimacy. Everyone had heard of his machinations. Or had they? Everyone had known of his convoluted and strategic dealings. Or did they? And although the full extent of his connections could only be guessed at, there wasn't a dealer in London who could resist speculating.

"We all guessed he had the Fuseli," Edward Leigh said, glancing over to his partner. "Did you know?"

"No one knew, we *supposed*." The pug-faced Hallett replied, "Cummings was always a great admirer of Fuseli, even more so when that painting was discovered --"

"The painting that's now been *stolen*."

"Yes, indeed, the painting that's now been stolen. Poor Cummings" he said, the mellifluous voice lowered in respect. "What a tragedy. I didn't know him well, but it was terrible to die as he did. Such a sordid end. If I'm in Zurich I may go to the funeral."

"When is it?"

"The body's in storage until they find out who killed him. Only then can they have him buried. That's what I heard, and of course there will be a coroner's report done in Zurich."

Edward's right hand was toying with his beard, tweaking at a stray hair beneath his bottom lip.

"Why don't you go to a barber? Get that thing of yours…" Anthony waved a finger at Edward's chin "… trimmed properly."

"I could say the same for your tongue. A few inches off that won't hurt anyone." Edward retorted, and saw, with no little satisfaction, that he had rattled his partner. "What about Cummings's relatives? Won't his father want the body flown home?"

"To London, yes, possibly. If it does get returned to London I'll definitely go to the funeral." Anthony said magnanimously, then leaned forward in his seat. "You did know that he was gay?"

"John Cummings? Doesn't surprise me. Is that why he never married again?"

"I suppose so. It makes you wonder - what if he was killed by a lover? Perhaps someone who seduced him."

"*Do* men seduce men?"

"How naïve you are! Of course they do." Anthony replied, giving Edward a sidelong glance. "And if it was a rent boy --"

"Do they have rent boys in Zurich?"

"I would think so."

"You know a lot about it," Edward replied, still fiddling with his beard and changing the subject. "I wonder if Ronnie Gilchrist has heard the news."

He glanced over to Anthony. Did he know she was visiting Louis Willes? Or that she had wanted to go into partnership with *him* in order to sell the Fuseli? Or perhaps the abrasive American was playing one off against the other? Edward sighed. That would be typical of her. And if she *was* setting them against each other, her ex-lover Anthony Hallett would have a head start.

"Crazy woman," Edward continued. "I wouldn't put it past her to kill Cummings herself for that Fuseli. If she thought she could get away with it. After all, it would set her up for life --"

"Or jailed for life." Anthony laughed, tapping Edward on the knee. "You must be joking! The poor girl isn't up to it. She's talks tough, but she's not that ruthless."

"So who is *that* ruthless?" Edward countered. "You tell me, *who is*? And what was the motive? Was Cummings murdered to get the Fuseli? Or was it personal? Some kind of revenge?"

Anthony sighed, shaking his head. "It's dangerous to gossip, of course, but there *is* another rumour going around."

"Why do *I* never hear these rumours!" Edward snorted.

"You don't socialise enough."

"Is that what you call sleeping with other men's wives?"

"What if..." Anthony ignored the slur, his voice low as he continued "...it was one of his Russian oligarchs? Or someone from the UAE? If they'd discovered Cummings had the painting in his possession they might have sent someone to steal it."

"And kill Cummings at the same time?" Edward asked. Frowning. "Why?"

"Perhaps he didn't intend to kill, but Cummings surprised him --"

Edward shook his head. "No, I don't believe that. These crooks are paid to steal. They're professionals, they do all the time. They aren't equal opportunity thieves, they're specialists."

Anthony paused, pondering. It took almost a minute before he spoke again. "But why *would* anyone kill John Cummings?"

"You tell me."

"Perhaps there's more to it." Anthony mused. "What if the painting is more important than anyone knows?"

"It's by Fuseli, so obviously it's valuable."

"True" Anthony nodded, warming to his theme. "Many paintings are valuable, but people don't kill for them. And they say the murder was brutal."

Edward grimaced with annoyance. "How do *you* know so much about it? I only saw what was on the news and the internet."

"Remember I have a place in Zurich," Anthony replied smugly, moving on. "Perhaps you're right, perhaps Cummings wasn't killed by accident. I mean, the thief didn't panic, did he? He took his time. Gossip is that Cummings's body was *displayed* on an easel. The same easel where the Fuseli had been. Perhaps whoever did it was making a point."

"What point?"

"That the painting's dangerous --"

"Bull shit!"

"Why? It's been bad luck from the moment it was found. Some even say it's..." he laughed mockingly "...cursed."

Edward didn't reply, but he remembered what he had seen before when they had talked of the Fuseli, the fleeting image that had played on his mind for days afterwards. He had slept fretfully, dreaming of it, unable to shake the image.

"Alright," Edward responded finally, "I consider your theory, that the painting was stolen not merely for its value, but for some *particular* reason. If that's true, who would know what the reason was?"

"The person that hired someone to steal it --"

Edward nodded. "Or someone with insider knowledge about Henry Fuseli?"

"Which applies to at least ten dealers I could name!" Anthony interrupted him. "But I agree that the person who wanted the painting stolen would have checked their facts. They were spending good money, breaking the law, they didn't want to be conned by a fake. They would have demanded proof as to where it came from. Who it had belonged to. Its provenance -- "

Edward waved the words aside. "So now they've got hold of it, what next? They've got their Fuseli - and a dead dealer." He shook his head. "I'm not convinced that's what they were paying for, and it certainly wouldn't be what they expected."

Anthony leaned forward. *"What if the wrong person stole the painting?"*

"Say that again."

"Maybe there were *two* people after it, one professional, the other an amateur. That's why the theft was botched and Cummings was killed." Suddenly Anthony paused, glancing behind him. "Did you feel that?"

"What?"

"It must have been a draft" the dealer said, smiling uncertainly, "but just for a moment it felt like someone was walking over my grave."

Ealing, London

To avoid the heavy onslaught of November rain, Caroline pulled her hood and ran up the steps of the library, colliding with a middle aged man who was coming down at the same time. Almost losing his footing, Caroline grabbed the man's sleeve, apologising as she helped him upright. Annoyed, he jerked his arm free and moved on, chuntering to himself as Caroline continued into the library. The warmth was welcome, steamy after the chill outside, as she shook off her coat and ruffled her fringe, wiping her sleeve across her forehead to dry it.

"Oh, my God, what are *you* doing here?" A man said suddenly, lowering his voice when several people turned. "I was just thinking about you."

"Liar!" She kissed him on the cheek. "Actually I've been thinking about you, Mike, thinking that you were just the man I needed --"

"I've been waiting for years to hear you say that." He replied, his tone light although the words were heart felt.

For several years he *had* hoped that he might have a chance with her, but on the few occasions Mike Owen had gathered enough courage to ask her out, Caroline had been busy. Or she had said she was busy. Both in their early thirties they had pursued their own relationships, but Mike had still hoped to date the elusive Caroline Lever. Then the day came when he had seen her walking down Regents Street with a good looking man and his confidence had plummeted. Fortune had not gifted Mike Owen with great beauty, nor had she been over generous with talent.

"You're staring at me."

He blinked, nodded. "I was, yes."

"You always stare at me when I come in here. It's weird, but it's cute too." She grinned. "I need your help. I need a brilliant librarian." Her manner changed as she pulled out a piece of paper, sodden around the edges. "Oh, shit, look at that! It was in my bag and *still* got soaked."

"What is it?" Mike asked, taking it from her and reading: "'*Register of Nurses*.' What d'you want that for?"

"I want to track a relative of mine." Caroline explained. "And after all my searching, I've finally found one. She's not alive. She's dead - they're all dead in my family - but I really want to know about her."

"Even though she's dead?"

Tucking her short hair behind her ears, Caroline challenged him. "It's all right for you. You have a huge family --"

"There are only six of us."

"-- there are *none* of us, and I want to find out about my great aunt. Miriam Levy she was called."

He thought for an instant. "You said Miriam *Levy,* not Lever."

"Our name was altered, only my great aunt kept kosher." Caroline explained, hurrying on. "Miriam was declared Missing, Presumed Dead in the war, but I discovered that some people who were *presumed* dead actually turned up later. They'd gone abroad during the conflict, and as there was no death record in this country they were declared deceased. Hang on, I've got the details somewhere…"

As she reached in her bag, Mike guided her to the back of the library. It was emptied of people, the dilapidated antique shelves heavy with reference books, the labels faded, whilst others had been renewed, brightly optimistic amongst their dated peers. And next to the grand old shelves were the cheap metal rows, sporting paperbacks, a torn poster of a bestseller mended haphazardly with sellotape.

"… I joined an Ancestry thing but they were hopeless," Caroline said dismissively. "Honestly it's a rip off, they didn't find anything except Miriam's name. Then I discovered this Nurses Register and I was wondering if I could find out more here. I mean, libraries have records, don't they?"

"I doubt we'd have anything about nursing records or history. Not specific to individuals anyway." He could see her disappointment and hurried on. "But let me have a look, see if I can help."

Smiling, she pointed to the list, her voice animated. "It says Miriam Levy was the Sister at a private clinic, and that it was closed down."

"Why?"

"I don't know," Caroline shrugged. "But the doctor who ran it was *'removed from the medical register.'*"

Mike raised his eyebrows. "He was struck off*?"*

"Yeah.... why do they do that?"

"A few reasons." Mike stared at the name, scrawled in Caroline's sloping handwriting, *Addison Franckel.* "Let's look him up --"

"I have done, there's nothing about him apart from his name and the fact that he was struck off. Is there some other way we could find out?"

"Where was the clinic?"

"No record of that either. Just said it was in England." She jutted out her chin; he knew the look, the stubborn determination he admired but found daunting at the same time. Short hair, short stature, short temper, with a pretty face that mesmerised him. "I tried ringing the Royal College of Nursing but they didn't have any more information - not from so long ago," Caroline continued, talking quickly "and anyway many wartime records were destroyed. Then I trailed through the birth and death records at General Register Office and *www. recordsearch.co.uk* - again nothing."

Mike frowned, re-reading the copy of the register. "Hang on a minute, this doesn't make sense. Look at the list, all the nurses have the name of the hospital they worked at written next to their names. But with your relative it says *St Edward's Hospital, London, 1939 - 42*, and then there's another entry for *1942* - but the name of that hospital's been crossed out."

"Maybe it wasn't NHS but a private clinic?"

"But they're listed too. See" he pointed at three other nurses names, "the private clinics are registered for *these* nurses. So why not for Miriam Levy?"

Caroline shrugged. "Perhaps the place doesn't exist anymore?"

"But it existed at one time, so there should be some record. If only we knew where it had been situated in England." He glanced at her enquiringly. "What kind of doctor was this Addison Franckel? I know you said he was stuck off, but he was practicing once and he can't have just disappeared. There must be some record of him. What was his discipline?"

"Huh?" Caroline asked, moving her damp fringe away from her forehead.

"Was he a GP? Specialist?"

"No idea, and I've exhausted my research." Her mood darkened. "Maybe there was nothing to find. I just hoped I might be onto something when I found Miriam, but it seems Addison Franckel evaporated and took her with him."

"People don't disappear --"

"Apparently they did in wartime."

"Some might have done, but clinics don't vanish. That's can't happen." He raised his eyebrows. "They're big premises, they have equipment, consulting rooms, nursing staff, wards - there *must* be some record of the place."

"Well, I don't think I'll find it without more information. There just isn't enough to give me a lead." Caroline sighed. "To be honest, I was probably fooling myself. You know, I even daydreamed that Miriam didn't die in the war. That she went abroad instead, got married and had a family. That there were relatives out there somewhere, and if I could just find the path she took, I could find them." She smiled, ruefully. "It would have meant so much to me, just to think I wasn't alone."

There is a time in the life of a man when he is presented with an opportunity to impress a woman. That time had finally come for Mike Owen and he was not going to let the chance escape him. It was one thing to admire Caroline Lever, quite another to make an impression that might lift him from the friend zone into date material. The family of six to which Caroline had referred consisted of his parents and three siblings, a sister and two brothers. None of the Owen offspring had been brilliant, except for one, the eldest, Malcolm, who had qualified as a doctor, then as a consultant at St Edward Hospital. The same hospital where Miriam Levy had once nursed.

"You know something, Caroline?" Mark said smoothly "I might just know someone who can help."

TWENTY FIVE

East London

There was no fog in the capital, just drizzle, and a thin and bitter wind coming from the River Thames. No one had noticed the elderly woman in a raincoat, her head covered with a scarf, her walking slow and measured as she moved to the back of a café and sat down at a small corner table. The cold from the outside, meeting the warmth from the interior, had caused the inevitable condensation, the lights from passing traffic and winter shop windows smearing into stained glass patterns between the threading of water streamers.

Taking off her gloves and headscarf, Ella Fairchild glanced around. Perhaps it was due to the weather, or the time, but there were only a few customers. Two weary businessmen, a girl with a baby in a pushchair, and a family of four, the father checking his mobile repeatedly as his children grizzled about the menu. They wanted a burger, they said, or fish and chips. It was a horrible place, they went on, and they wanted to go home. Then the youngest - a girl of around five - started crying, one of her brothers jabbing her with his elbow.

Children, Ella thought, never changed. They wanted attention, and cheap food. Her gaze settled on the waitress who was approaching her table. It was relaxing to be served, in fact that was why she came to the café, to avoid queueing and standing, waiting in line. Something that was difficult at her age.

"How are you today, Mrs. Fairchild?" the girl asked, nose ring, pink hair, one arm a sleeve tattoo. "Here on your own?"

"I am, my dear," she replied, "but not for long. I'm meeting someone."

"Hot date?"

She paused, then realised what the girl meant and smiled. "No, just a business meeting. We'll have a pot of tea for one now, and order food when he comes."

The little girl had stopped whining at the next table, her two brothers piling into plates of egg and chips, the father answering another phone call, one of his cuffs trailing in ketchup. Ella wondered if he was a single parent, and how such a thing would have been unthinkable when she was young. Then again, it had been wartime, most of the men were away fighting. Many didn't return to become parents. Single or not.

Startled by the chair being pulled out from under the table, Ella glanced up. She recognised the man from the description he had given her '...*eighty one, five feet nine, grey, bearded, wearing jeans and hoodie...*' He hadn't mentioned that his face was the colour of the belly of a dead fish, that his hands shook, and his nails were bitten down. One of the thinnest men Ella had ever seen, he moved stiffly, like a clockwork toy she had once had as a child.

"Freddy Wilson?" She asked, her tone more abrasive than she had intended.

He nodded. "Yeah, so I'm here, what d'you want?"

"As I said in my message, I want to talk about your father, Addison Franckel."

"It'll cost you."

"Excuse me?"

"I'm not giving you anything for nothing" he replied, looking around "and anyway, how do I know you are who you say you are? Maybe someone sent a little old lady to con me."

"We're of a similar age --"

"That's all we have in common."

"My name is Mrs. Ella Fairchild, just as you were told. I'm not deceiving you, Mr. Wilson, only seeking some information about your father, who ran the Addison Franckel Clinic --"

"Yeah, yeah." He rubbed his jaw with the palm of his left hand.

"You know about the place?"

He shook his head. "No. Yeah. Well, to be honest until the other day I'd forgotten about it. It was a long time ago. No one mentioned it for years, decades. Then someone sent me some anonymous messages." He shrugged. "I don't have them now though, because I don't have my bloody phone anymore. Some bastard stole it --"

"What did the messages say?" Ella interrupted, studying him. The information her contact had given her about Freddy Wilson was accurate. He was drugged out, an addict who had bummed his way around London for the last two decades. A man without focus or plans. Willing to do anything - or sell anything - for money.

"Mr. Wilson," she urged him "please tell me what the messages said."

"I don't remember much about my father." His eyes were sly, the eyebrows sparse. "But I can be *persuaded* to remember."

Ella saw the waitress approach and smiled at her. The girl had seen Wilson arrive and was worried.

"Are you Ok?"

"Fine, dear," Ella replied, nodding to underline her words and reassure her. "We'd like two rolls, please. Chicken would be nice, and some more tea." She glanced over to the raddled man sitting opposite. "Is there anything else you'd like?"

"Nah."

He was jiggling his left leg under the table, his hands clenching and unclenching, the waitress giving him a sidelong look before she left. Druggie, she thought, an old, dirty druggie. Or maybe he was too old for the drugs now, but still on the booze. Either way, an addict… And all the time she was preparing the rolls she kept glancing over, watching the mismatched couple, before finally returning to the table with the food.

"You sure you don't need anything, Mrs. Fairchild?"

"No, we're fine for now, dear. Thank you." After waiting until the girl moved off, Ella returned to the previous conversation. "*What did the messages say?*"

Wilson leaned towards her over the table, the smell of body odour pungent, his tone bullying. "Why d'you want to know?"

And then Ella Fairchild, refined old lady that she was, reverted to her earlier years when she had run a successful business with her late husband. A time when she had been proficient, and tough.

"Mr. Wilson, *if* we can do business we can only do it on my terms." She put up her hands to preventing him interrupting. "I have the opportunity to make a great deal of money, and I will be willing to be generous to those who have helped me. I do not intend to *persuade* you in any way, either verbally or financially. However, if you want to have money in the near future, I would suggest that you help me now --"

"For nothing?"

She picked up her handbag as though preparing to leave, Freddy Wilson gripping her wrist. "I didn't say I wouldn't help!"

Imperious, she shook off his hand. "Perhaps you can't. After all, Mr. Wilson, how do I know that you have any information that could be of benefit to me? I've asked you three times to tell me who contacted you and I'm still waiting for an answer."

He sighed, picking at the bread roll again. "I don't know. The texts came out of the blue. No name, nothing like that."

"And what did they say?"

"That you wanted information about my father." He replied, his leg still jiggling under the table. "Look, I'm not asking for much, just need a bit of cash to see me over --"

"Did you live with your father at the clinic?"

" -- Nah! I was with my mother in Berlin. He left us when I was in my late teens..." Wilson paused, eyes narrowed as he gazed out of the window. For several seconds he stared blindly, wiping the condensation off with his left hand, the lights outside coming into focus. "I started drinking when he dumped my mother, then got into drugs." He continued to stare out of the window as it started to steam up again. "There was all this talk about my father being disgraced, struck off in England. They said he was arrested --"

"Arrested?"

"So they said." Wilson sighed. "They said he was a right bastard. I could have told them that. He was a liar... I remember now, how much he used to lie. Yeah, it's all coming back to me, he was --"

"He was a practicing psychiatrist in Berlin, wasn't he?"

Wilson paused, struggling to remember. His eyes would clear, focus, and then cloud over, the life going out of them. But his leg never stopped jiggling, the chicken roll reduced to a snowfall of breadcrumbs on the table between them.

"My memory's fucked up... has been for years." He gazed out of the window again, concentrating. She could tell he was straining to remember, his leg slowly paused its jiggling, his head tipped to one side. Silent, Ella watched him, waited whilst he sifted through the past; through confusion to reality. And she watched as he remembered. "My mother committed suicide after she realised he wasn't coming back."

"I'm sorry."

He shrugged, but his voice had lost its metallic edge. "They'd been rich and she couldn't take the shame, people talking, sneering at her... at *us*. No one wanted to know us... I lost my friends because of it." He paused, frowned, remembered. "...You know, I tried to find him, that's why I came to England. I tried hard, but I couldn't find him, because the fucker had changed his name -- "

"He was originally called Otto Weiner, wasn't he?"

Wilson's eyes flickered, colour coming into the drooping cheeks. Colour and anger. "Yes! Yes, he *was* called Otto Weiner! And I was his son, Fritz Weiner --"

"And you changed your name to Freddy Wilson."

"Well, I didn't want to keep the name Weiner, did I?" His face hardened, suspicion coming into his eyes. "What d'you want!"

"Your father abandoned you and his disgrace drove your mother to suicide --"

"And you care?" he replied, his tone contemptuous. "The hell you do! What's in it for you? Nah, don't bother to answer, you'll only lie. *Everyone lies*. You want to know all about my father? Then pay me for it, or fuck off now."

Taking some banknotes out of her bag, Ella placed them on the table and laid her right hand over them. From the counter the girl was watching the interaction, Ella keeping her voice low.

"Do you have any of your father's belongings?"

"No."

"No patients' notes? Nothing from his practice in Berlin?"

"No!" Wilson snapped. "The police took everything and we didn't want any of it back."

"Do you know if your father made any tapes? Did he film any of his patients?"

Wilson stared at her. *"Film them?"* He shook his head, but the action was uncertain.

"You said your father was arrested in England --"

"Maybe it was Berlin." He shook his head impatiently. "Jesus, I can't remember! I don't *want* to think about it!" He paused, scrambling for recall. "Wait, maybe I *do* remember. Yeah, my father was arrested in

England. I was still in Germany then and I heard that he was caught doing something unethical…"

"Unethical? What did he do?"

Wilson shook his head. "I don't know! No one told me what he did! I can't remember."

"You must remember! It's important. He ruined your life and your mother's. You can't have forgotten --"

"Don't tell me what I can't do!" Wilson snapped. "I could have lived like him. I was going be a doctor. Yeah, that's funny isn't it, when you look at me now. I was in my first year of studying when my father left Berlin, and it all fell apart after that, and then there was the scandal and my mother killed herself…" He slammed his fists down on the table, Ella glancing over to the waitress and shaking her head to prevent the girl intervening. "I could have lived like him! A liar, a cheat - but I defied him. *I chose to be nothing.* To forget, to drink, fuck my life up with drugs to wipe it all out - and I've done just that. Until now."

Suddenly he reached out, trying to grab the money, Ella pulling it back towards her.

"Not just yet, Mr. Wilson. I'm buying, and you're selling. So let's get down to business – what do you know about the Incubus Tapes?"

TWENTY SIX

Graybrooke Lodge
Hampshire

The text came up on Gus's mobile. It was short and precise.

> *I need to speak with you. My name is Paul Shore. My grandmother was called Elizabeth Shore, and she was at the Franckel Clinic at the same time as your grandfather, George Lyman. Both died there.*

In the sitting room beyond Gus could hear Ronnie Gilchrist talking, her voice irritated as Louis Willes insisted that they play cards. No matter how much she denied having any skill, or interest, Willes persisted. She was an unwanted guest in his house, he said, it was the least she could do. The pain medication was working, Gus thought, remembering how he would react himself, the torment having ceased and a temporary euphoria taking over.

Gus glanced back to the text, typing his reply:

I was told you would get in touch. Who contacted you?

> *I don't know. Someone sent an anonymous message a few days ago, together with your details. Do you know who it is?*

No.

> *May we have a conversation? I will call you, or send you my phone number. Whichever you prefer. Perhaps we could talk later?*

He was polite, Gus thought. Old fashioned.

After a pause, he replied:

Send me your number. What do you want from me?

> *Justice, Mr. Egan. I want justice for my relative, just as you must do. I was a coward before, but now there are a few of us and there's always safety in numbers.*

Do you know Ella Fairchild?

> *I do, and I know about Miriam Levy, the Sister at Addison Franckel's Clinic. In fact, I remember hearing a great deal about Sister Levy, she was a heroine. Let me know when you want us to talk, Mr. Egan.*

Thoughtful, Gus moved back into the sitting room, Willes having dismissed the idea of cards and regarding Ronnie Gilchrist with resignation as she struggled with her mobile.

"It was working a moment ago and now I can't get *any* connection! Damn this God forsaken place, don't you have any decent service?"

"It's intermittent. You have to keep trying." Gus answered her.

"What about a landline? Don't tell me you don't have a landline here."

"We do. But it's out of service --

"Out of service!"

" -- and has been for three weeks. People tend to rely on their mobiles."

"How the fuck can they if there's no connection!" She blasted back, Gus sanguine.

"It happens in the countryside."

"Yeah, I gathered that!" She snapped, jerking her head towards the window. "How's the fog?"

"Getting thicker."

"Of course it is."

After trying her mobile again, Ronnie tossed it into her bag and glanced over to Willes.

"The whole trip has been a waste of time, and I'm tired. Could someone show me to my room?" At once Je-Yun stepped forward, Ronnie's voice demanding. "Is the bed aired? It needs to be. This place is damp, I doubt I'll get any sleep."

"Give her a hot water bottle," Willes told the Korean. "And if she needs a sleeping tablet, give her one of mine --"

"You should never take someone else's medication" Ronnie retorted "a pill that suits one person could kill another."

"Then give her two." The old man replied, Ronnie angered as she followed Je-Yun out of the room. When the door closed behind them, Willes looked over to Gus. "This has been quite a night. One dealer dead and another stranded. Ronnie is exhausting, isn't she? Such a sensationalist." He paused, then asked. "Does she know the history of this place?"

"What history?"

"That there was a clinic here once. Didn't you tell her?"

"Why would I? There was no reason to." Gus replied, surprised that the topic had been raised. "Besides, what could I tell her? You hardly knew anything about the place or Addison Franckel - that's what you told me anyway."

"When you *interrogated* me!" Willes snorted. "You hadn't been here five minutes before you tackled me on the subject. Then gave me some cock and bull story about a shrink and five dead patients --"

"And a journalist."

"-- the journalist probably deserved it," Willes said dryly. "So *did* your anonymous caller contact you again?"

"You have a good memory."

"I'm not deaf, nor dead!" Willes snorted. "Who *wouldn't* remember something so bloody weird? I don't understand anything that's going on."

"Neither do I."

Willes's eyes narrowed. "So you *haven't* been contacted again?"

The lie was automatic. "No."

"I just wondered…" Willes replied, Gus noticing his shoulders relax. "It seems like Addison Franckel is doomed to be forgotten and buried."

"Along with his patients."

"If there were any."

"And the journalist."

Willes looked at Gus, smiling. "You know I don't think I believe you. You're a clever, thorough man. The type to track down facts. The kind that digs and digs until they uncover the remains."

"I'm a researcher, not an archaeologist."

Willes rose to his feet, wincing with the effort as he straightened up. For several seconds he rested his hand on a table to steady himself then moved to the door and paused.

"I should have mentioned it before," he said "don't wander around outside at night. The grounds are overgrown in places and full of old bones."

Maida Vale, London

Entering the road where she lived, Ella Fairchild nodded to young man walking his dog. Usually they would stop and exchange a few words, but this time Ella moved on, eager to be home. Her expression was composed, her face betraying nothing of her rapid heartbeat as she rested momentarily against a gate post.

If she had been liable for a heart attack it would have already happened, she reasoned. After all, that was how it had gone with her late husband, intense stress which had resulted in his falling, legs crumpled, at her feet. At first she had thought he was playing a trick, always a joker, but there was no dupe, no hoax, his lips the colour of damsons by the time the ambulance arrived. He had only been fifty nine and they had just booked a holiday to Copenhagen, which never happened, instead Ella had given the plane tickets to her daughter and son in law. She didn't remember if they had gone.

It had been a long time ago, and had only come to mind because now she was shaken by the meeting she had just had with Freddy Wilson. Her own 'intense stress' which had reminded Ella of her age, her vulnerability, her unwelcome and resented frailty.

After meeting his son, the hatred Ella Fairchild had felt for Addison Franckel had quadrupled, although his cruelty and neglect had not come as a surprise. Her mind kept replaying the image of Wilson's dirty hands crumbling the bread roll, the white dough becoming brain-matter grey, his voice alternating between aggression and self-pity.

Ella's father had told her what he had learnt about Franckel and had described him physically; portly, fashionably dressed, with a thin moustache that was popular in the 1940's. Apparently he had spoken eloquently and without any trace of a German accent, claiming that he had been born in Austria and left the country when Hitler had come to power. Such had been Franckel's hatred of the tyrant he had dedicated his psychiatric practice to the treatment of shell shocked soldiers.

That was what her grandfather had told her father, and *that* was what was passed on to her, together with a warning not to repeat it. It was private information about her family, he had said, and as such it was to remain within the family. Ah, but that had been a long time ago, Ella thought, and if she had lacked courage before she was about to make up for it.

Slowly she began to walk again, moving under the street lamps, now lighted, now in shadow, as she glanced into the windows of the houses as she passed. Once, many years earlier when she had been young, she had glimpsed the lives inside and longed for the same, the passage of time bringing her own family. And then she had wondered - when safe and settled - how many passing lonely girls had envied her.

It was all so fast, she thought, a lifetime seeming to last as long as the fall from a ladder. You were up and then you were down, waiting only for the inevitable end. Ella paused again. She was scared, but prepared, even for the likes of Freddy Wilson. Even for the jumble of names and characters that were falling on her life like flecks of soot from a long deserted chimney; a myriad smudges of humanity thrown together.

People like Gus Egan, a man she was unsure of, yet tied to by their anonymous contact. That unknown person who was moving everyone around in his personal game of punto banco. But this time she wouldn't falter. Whoever, or whatever, tried to scare her off *this* time would fail and she would persist. After all, how many elderly widows got an opportunity to challenge the authorities? To upturn an eighty year old scandal?

Sliding her key into the front door, she turned the lock and entered, flicking on the hall lamp. The bulb lighted, then blew, Ella left standing in the hallway in darkness as a figure made its way towards her down the stairs.

TWENTY SEVEN

Graybrooke Lodge
Hampshire

Without getting undressed, Ronnie Gilchrist slid onto the lumpen antique bed, flicking away the heavy drapes which surrounded it, and huddling under the covers. Her mood had plunged with the realisation that she was unexpectedly isolated and had no contact with the outside world. No mobile phone, and stuck in a remote house with three men, two of whom she suspected since the news had come through about the death of John Cummings. She didn't believe they were murderers, but Ronnie knew both had had a dark history within the art world, with valid reasons to want revenge.

Her feet reached for the hot water bottle under the blankets, the rubber burning her skin as she kicked it to one side. Who had rubber water bottles these days? She wondered petulantly. And who lived in house that needed an army of workmen to make it comfortable?

Or even safe. The staircase looked unstable, and the door of her room hadn't shut until she had jammed a chair under the handle… Calm down, she told herself. Everyone joked about Louis Willes's mothy old house, it had been falling apart for decades. And why *shouldn't* Gus Egan be there? He was doing the research for the Fuseli book. And if the old man had hired some Korean as his assistant cum nursemaid, what of it?

What of it? Ronnie asked herself incredulously. They were in the middle of the English countryside, why would a Korean come to work in somewhere so remote? Was he really looking after Willes? Or here for another reason?…Restless, Ronnie sat up, an iridescent moon shining its slow light through a gap in the curtains. Uneasy, she slid out of bed, putting on her outdoor coat, then trying her mobile again. There was no signal.

Surely the landline was working? She thought, suspecting Gus's account of it being out of order. No one left a phone line that long before repairing it, even in England. Silently, she moved to the door and listened, there was no sound of movement from the floor below where Willes had his room, Je-Yun's alongside. Cautious, she walked into the passageway. Only Gus Egan was on the same floor as she was, and there was no light shining out from under his door.

In the downstairs hall the clock sounded its Westminster Chimes, Ronnie surprised that it was already two o clock in the morning as she crept towards the staircase. The lack of light hampered her but she didn't turn on the torch on her mobile until she reached the hall downstairs, making her way towards Willes's study and moving over to his desk. Hopefully she picked up the landline phone and listened. For an instant she thought she heard a dial tone, but then realising it was dead, replaced the receiver on its cradle and moved towards the window.

Holding back the curtain she looked out. The fog was dense, like an animal's hide, her gaze then falling on the mess of papers on the desk beside her. Obviously Willes had made copious notes, print outs from the internet lying alongside old photographs, time charts and maps. Curious, she moved gingerly around the room in the semi darkness, the trophies overhead throwing gothic shadows, the vast reproduction of Fuseli's *Nightmare* suddenly lit by her torch, the Incubus staring out malevolently from the canvas.

"Ugly bastard," Ronnie said under her breath, her attention moving back to the desk, her hands flicking through the mess of papers. Newspaper articles and essays in Apollo magazine had been highlighted in yellow, others in bilious green, Ronnie suddenly noticing the edge of a paper poking out from underneath the deepest pile. Intrigued, she pulled it out. The name John Cummings was written on it. Then crossed out. Another name added alongside, with the words - '*confirm with Edward Leigh.*'

"*Edward Leigh?*" she repeated under her breath. "So what's that sneaky old goat been up to?"

Hastily, Ronnie pushed aside more of the papers, finding a leather notebook which had been hidden between a periodical and an old fashioned blotter. Tucking the mobile under her chin at an angle, she shone the torchlight on the writing pad. Ronnie was just preparing to read it when she heard a shuffling sound and turned to see a woman standing at the window, watching her from the garden outside.

Startled, Ronnie dropped the torch, then bent down to retrieve it, her hands shaking. But when she glanced back to the window the woman had gone. Unnerved, Ronnie backed away then ran from the room, leaving the notebook behind and making for the hall. She was heading for the stairs when she heard noises coming from above, and unwilling to be caught, looked for a place to hide. As she did so, the looming statue of *The Dying Gaul* was suddenly highlighted. Someone had obviously woken and turned on a light upstairs, which was now throwing illumination down the stairwell. Breathing fast, Ronnie slid behind a wooden screen, listening for the sound of a toilet cistern flushing, followed by silence when the person returned to their room.

Instead, several moments later, she heard footsteps move across the landing and then slowly descend the staircase. Her gaze moved back to the library. In her panic she had left the door open. Would someone notice that? Would someone see the papers had been moved?... Jesus, she thought helplessly, where did she leave the notebook? She had dropped it when she had seen the woman thorough the window.

Her heart beating rapidly, Ronnie tried to reason with herself. She couldn't have seen the woman. What would anyone be doing wandering in the garden at two in the morning? And how *could* she had been standing there one moment and gone the next?... Confused, Ronnie tried to settle her nerves. It had just been an illusion, the fog causing a pattern on the window pane. She hadn't *really* seen a person, just her own image distorted in the torchlight.

Yes, that was it! Ronnie told herself, she had been startled by her *own* image, her imagination heightened by the atmosphere at Graybrooke. She was jumping at shadows, all the talk of John Cummings's murder had unnerved her. That was all it was, just nerves, in the morning the fog would be gone and she would leave. All she had to do was to get back to her room and wait the night out. That was all.

In that moment she heard the footsteps arrive at the bottom of the stairs and shrank further behind the screen as someone paused only feet away from her. Ronnie could hear their steady breathing and knew it wasn't Louis Willes. It was obviously a younger man. So was it Je-Yun, or Gus Egan? Or maybe someone she didn't even know was in the house?

The precariousness of her situation hit home. She had invited herself to Graybrooke to make a deal, but that had been *before* the news of John Cummings's murder. Both Louis Willes and Gus Egan hated the art world *and* the dealers - who was to say they weren't involved, working together? After all, Willes hadn't seemed shocked by Cummings's death, and it was more than a little suspicious that Gus Egan been the first to get the news.

Afraid, she watched through the slats of the screen, a hand suddenly coming around the edge and drawing it back.

"Ronnie, what *are* you doing?" Gus asked, amused. "I thought I heard someone moving about."

"I couldn't sleep." She blundered.

"I doubt I could, hiding behind a screen." He glanced towards the library and the opened door. "Did you find what you were looking for?"

"I wasn't looking for anything!" She snapped, stepping forward, and trying to regaining her composure. "I was just startled by something I thought I saw… This place is fucking spooky."

"Especially if you don't turn the lights on." Gus replied, moving into the library. For an instant Ronnie hesitated then followed, watching as Gus bent down to pick up the notebook she had dropped. "So you *were* looking for something?"

"I told you, I couldn't sleep so wandered around." She shrugged, trying to lighten the atmosphere, her voice shrill. "Ok, you got me, I *was* snooping!"

"What d'you want to know?" Gus asked. "Tell me, it'll save us both a lot of time if I understand what you came for."

"I came to talk to Louis Willes about the Fuseli painting."

"And now you're looking for something particular? Or do you usually snoop around peoples' houses when you're a guest?"

"*I didn't intend to stay here!* I wouldn't be here now if it weren't for the fog. I swear to God if I stay any longer I'll *really* start seeing things." She noticed a shift in Gus's expression. "What is it? *Is* this place haunted?"

"Why ask that, Ronnie? What did you see?"

"I didn't say I *saw* anything, just that I *thought* I saw something."

"And what did you *think* you saw?"

"There was a woman in the garden, she was looking at me through the window. I was startled and when I looked back, she'd disappeared." Smiling unconvincingly, Ronnie pulled her coat around her. "The fog is thick out there, I couldn't see clearly, I must have imagined it." She laughed jaggedly "I mean, why would a woman be wandering around at night?"

"What did she look like?"

"*'What did she look like*?'" Ronnie repeated, her tone suspicious. "Why? Have you seen something?" She moved closer towards him, studying his face. "You have, haven't you! Shit, so there *is* a ghost here. Who is it?" Intrigued, she pressed for details. "Is it his wife? You know, Ava Willes. Does she haunt the old man? Well, they said her death was suspicious --"

"There's no ghost here, Ronnie." He interrupted her. "You imagined it."

"So why did you ask what she looked like?"

"I was curious," Gus replied, studying the notebook he had picked up off the library floor. "You won't find anything in this, just some old reference notes."

"Really? Well, did you know that Willes is talking to Edward Leigh? That *has* to be about the Fuseli." Her voice was peevish. "That frigging dealer's always trying to get one over --"

"And you're not?"

She shrugged. "Sure I am, I don't deny it, but this trip has been a dud. The painting's not up for sale. Nor ever will be now."

"How d'you know that?"

"Hired thieves don't usually return the goods they steal –"

"Thieves hired to order don't usually butcher dealers."

She blinked, her tone wavering. "It's scary hearing that Cummings has been murdered... The business is ruthless, got some grubby people in it, but murder's something else."

"You worried?"

"Nah," she said, her tone dismissive. "I just want to get home, away from this place." She seemed suddenly anxious. "I had nothing to do with it, you know?"

Wrong footed, Gus frowned. "Nothing to do with what?"

She hurried on." I don't deny I wanted the Fuseli, but I had nothing to do with John Cummings being killed."

"Who said you did?"

"I just wanted to make that clear," Ronnie blustered, unnerved by Gus Egan's cool manner, her anxiety rising. "Besides, I wasn't the only one interested. Many dealers wanted the painting, Edward Leigh, Anthony Hallett, others in New York, and it's hard to guess how many in the UAE. Christ knows where the Fuseli is now…" She let the words hang, wondering if he would pick up on them. When he didn't, she continued. "I just hope the killer thought it was worth it."

"That depends on who he stole it for, doesn't it?"

Maida Vale
London

Alarmed, the cleaner came hurrying down the stairs into the hallway below where Ella Fairchild stood rigid in what appeared to be shock. "Are you alright?" she asked, putting her arm around her. "You look like you're going to pass out!"

"You startled me, that's all." Ella replied, glancing up. "The light bulb went and I wasn't expecting you today, so when I saw a figure on the stairs…."

"Oh, I'm sorry, it's just that I came because I was worried. I hadn't heard from you in two days and you didn't answer the phone. I'm so sorry to have given you a shock, Mrs. Fairchild." Guiding Ella into the kitchen beyond, the woman turned on the kettle then took a seat next to her employer. "I'll put a new bulb in the lamp, don't worry." She reassured her, staring at her face. "You're getting some colour back now, thank goodness. Why didn't you answer my messages?"

"I've been busy," Ella replied, taking off her coat, her hands still shaking.

"You shouldn't have been out in this weather --"

"I'm not an infant, Maggie!" She retorted more sharply than she meant, then rested her hand on the woman's arm. "Forgive me, I didn't meant to snap. Sometimes I just need to get out of the house, need to see people." She smiled, watching as the cleaner stood up and began to make tea. Carefully she placed the tea leaves in the china pot, then laid out two cups and saucers, and a separate milk jug. All the meticulous, old fashioned rituals of another time; a time when Ella had been secure, never imagining encounters with the likes of Freddy Wilson. His hands had been so dirty, she thought, the nails bitten down to the quick. The son of a doctor, meant to follow his father's footsteps, but ending up broken, feral.

"Addicts don't usually live long, do they, Maggie?"

She was openly surprised. *"Addicts?* You mean drug addicts?"

"I suppose so, or alcoholics. I thought that usually an alcoholic's organs failed with cirrhosis. Or a drug addict overdosed…. I didn't think they could live to be old."

Puzzled, Maggie poured the tea, handing one cup to her employer and regaining her seat at the kitchen table. "Why would you ask that?"

"Oh, I don't know, when you have a lot of time on your hands it's amazing where you mind leads you." Ella replied, composed again. "You start thinking in a different way, well, I do anyway. When I was younger my husband thought for me - that was pretty much the way things were back then - but I loved him and was more than willing to let him be the master of the home. Then you're widowed and realise that all those responsibilities you ducked before have to be faced. So you face them and you learn." She sipped the tea. "My widowed friends did the same - but then they *stopped* learning. Became old ladies, dipping in and out of the past like they're ducking for apples. But the apples are rotting now, and the game's long over…." She sighed, smiling at Maggie. "I don't want to get like them."

"You used to run a business with your husband." Maggie offered, not sure that she understood. "Do you miss it?"

"Oh, no! That's not it." Ella shook her head. "I meant that now I want to be *brave*."

She paused, wondering how much courage she actually had. When she had returned home she had thought someone had come to attack her, or warn her off, as they had done before, decades earlier. She had felt the same slack terror, the sense of being helpless, and had wanted to surrender. Yet there had been no threat, merely a false alarm, Ella angered with herself and promising that if - or when - she was threatened again, she would stand her ground.

An hour late Maggie left, Ella going into her sitting room to look for the book she had been reading the night before. Not finding it, she realised she had taken it upstairs and decided she would retire for the night. Drawing the downstairs curtains, she double locked the front door and checked that the back exit was secured, before pulling down the blinds in the kitchen. The house was safe, she told herself, relieved that Maggie had replaced the bulb in the hall lamp and deciding to leave it on for the night.

Once upstairs Ella continued the search for her book, then stopped in her tracks when she noticed the door of her dressing room ajar. It was opened a few inches, the black interior like the mouth of a cave.

"Who's there?"

Her voice sounded weak, pitiful, and she coughed, repeating the words as she moved forward and pushed the door open. Inside the clothes had been torn from their hangers, shoes with their heels broken, jumpers ripped, Ella staring at the shelf of books which had been emptied, their contents pulled onto the floor.

And in the middle of the chaos lay an empty cardboard box. The same box in which she had stored the patients notes, entrusted to her by her father, in 1984.

Graybrooke Lodge
Hampshire

It was just past two thirty in the morning when Gus paused outside Ronnie Gilchrist's room, and listened. There was a lamp burning, he could see the muted glow under the door, but that didn't surprise him. She was frightened, certainly not going to lie in the dark waiting for morning, and unlikely leave her room again. Silently, he moved downstairs into Willes's library, replacing the notepad under the blotter where the historian had hidden it. Willes had a habit of hiding things, just as he would leave hairs laid over the door locks and cabinets, checking them in the morning to see if anyone had tampered with them overnight. It was something Gus had noticed when he first came to work at Graybrooke, one of the many trip wires set by his employer to test him. Was it due to his age? Gus had wondered, or some paranoia set off by professional betrayals?

When his eyes had adjusted to the semi darkness, Gus moved over to the window. Ronnie Gilchrist had obviously seen s*omething*, badly shaken, but quick to discount it. Perhaps *too* quick. Standing before the window, Gus looked out, but there was little to see, the fog making visibility impossible beyond eighteen inches. Still staring into the furred air, he took the keys out of his pocket, glancing at the label marked *Addison Franckel.* The psychiatrist who had disappeared, as much a ghost as the woman Ronnie had seen.

Was it a hoax? Or was the place truly haunted?... He considered the options. A hoax would need clever organization, but Je-Yun could arrange something like that; it was obvious he was devoted to Willes, more than capable of employing a woman to appear suddenly and catch the unwary off guard. The question was *why* would they want to trick him? Gus had never believed Willes's apparent ignorance of Addison Franckel, had doubted his denials from the start. The house was well known in the art world, famed for its past hospitality - surely someone had looked into its background?

Willes was a historian, and a man used to uncovering the past didn't ignore the memoir of his own home. He couldn't have lived for decades without catching some whiff of scandal; some noxious odour from history. Yet one thing was for certain, he wasn't going to confide. Instead Gus would have to uncover the mystery himself. For his grandfather, and for the other victims, he needed to know the story. And he *had* to find the tapes.

Glancing away from the window, Gus checked his mobile. The connection was still down, then he looked over to the reproduction of Fuseli's *Nightmare* above Willes's desk, his gaze resting on the Incubus figure. What had been recorded on The Incubus Tapes? What did they show to make the authorities destroy them? What was so horrendous to necessitate the obliteration of Addison Franckel and the clinic he had founded? And what tied together Graybrooke Lodge, the tapes, and the murder of John Cummings?

Gus looked at the keys in his hand, then glanced back to the window. There was no woman standing there. Instead a limp moon filtered through the fog in murky patches, the garden forbidding, only visible for a short space before disappearing into the quick sand of darkness.

Making his way into the hallway Gus paused to listen for anyone stirring. Only when he was sure that everyone was settled in their rooms, did he open the door and then close it noiselessly behind him.

TWENTY EIGHT

**Highgate,
London**

Taking laundry out of the drier, Ziva turned to look at her son, Mark unpacking his school bag onto the kitchen table.

"Are you going to do your homework?"

"Yeah... I'll do it after dinner," he said, pulling a face. "Something weird happened today."

"Like what?"

Mark handed her his sports gear, with the inevitable grass stains. "A friend of my Dad's stopped me --"

Ziva paused, turning to him. "Stopped you?"

"He was at the gates when school finished. He said he was called Grant something."

"I don't know anyone called Grant."

"He said he was a friend of Dad's." Mark continued, helping himself to some orange juice out of the fridge. "Said that they went to school together."

229

"I've never heard your father mention anyone by that name," Ziva said, suspicious. "What did he look like?"

"You know, old."

"Same age as your father?" she replied, smiling. "I'll be sure to tell him that. Was he tall?"

"Average."

"Fat?"

"Average."

"Did he have a hump?"

Laughing, Mark shook his head. "He was just ordinary, but he had an accent. Not that I noticed it at first, only when he talked some more. Not like we heard when we were in France, but it was some kind of accent. Or he could have been putting it on."

Lifting the newly dried sheets out of the drier, Ziva gestured for her son to take the corners and together they folded them, her curiosity heightened. "So what did this 'Grant' want? To see your Dad?"

"He gave me a message for him --"

"Can you tell me?"

" -- yes, sure. He said that he was '*sorry about the dealer*.'"

"'Sorry about the dealer'?" Ziva repeated. "Which dealer?"

Mark had opened a packet of crisps and was eating them hurriedly, Ziva sighing. "I'm making dinner, you can wait another twenty minutes."

"I can't" he grumbled "we had sports and I'm starving. Ben got a cut lip and said he got it fighting one of the older boys."

Ziva returned to the previous topic. "This 'Grant' said to tell your father that he was '*sorry about the dealer?*'"

Mark nodded. "And then he asked if I'd like a lift home."

Pausing, Ziva stared at her son. "You never --"

"'*Accept lifts from strangers.*' I know, Mum, that's why I walked home." He replied calmly. "And when I said no he was fine about it, didn't press me to go with him or anything."

"Did you see his car?"

"No," Mark replied, chewing some more crips before continuing. "It was busy, there were people around, loads of cars at the gates."

Ziva kept her voice nonchalant. "Perhaps I should pick you up tomorrow?"

"Why? You want everyone to laugh at me!" Mark responded heatedly. "I walked home with Ben and the man didn't follow us. Honestly, Mum! I shouldn't have told you --"

"Yes, you should, it could be important - and besides he gave you a message for your father. You've got to pass that on."

"You don't believe it, do you?"

She paused. "*What?*"

"You think he was a pervert --"

"I didn't say that!"

" -- but he wasn't! He was just a man wearing a suit. He looked like he worked in an office somewhere." Mark was becoming surly. "I wasn't abducted."

"Well, that's good, I've got a chicken in the oven and I don't want to waste it." Ziva replied, lightening the atmosphere. "Tell your Dad about it at the week-end. He said he'll be here on Sunday afternoon--"

"That's great. He can meet Grant then."

"*What?*"

"Grant said he was coming over."

"He did?" Ziva asked, puzzled. "How did he know your father would be with us on Sunday? Did you tell him?"

Mark shrugged. "He said that he knew Dad was in London at the weekends, and not in Hampshire."

The words rang an alarm bell. "He said *Hampshire*? You're sure?"

"Yes!"

"And you didn't tell him your father was working in Hampshire?"

"I didn't have to tell him, he knew," Mark replied. "Said that he had our address here in London and that he'd call by at the weekend. Then he said he had Dad's mobile number and he'd check the time with him."

Uneasy, Ziva shook her head. "Think carefully, Mark. Are you *sure* you didn't tell him where your father worked?"

"No, I didn't tell him! And I knew I shouldn't have said anything!" He said shortly. "Grant said not to tell you --"

"He said *what?"* she reacted, her voice sharp.

" -- he said to keep quiet because you were always worried." Mark replied, on the defensive. "I didn't do anything wrong! He just gave me a message for Dad. He was OK, honestly. And he was right - you *do* worry too much."

Some stranger had criticised her, planted a bitter little pill into Mark's head, and the fact that he had risen to the man's defense made Ziva all the more eager to defuse the situation. So instead of talking about it any further she looked at the homework Mark had to do and then listened to his step by step recall of the football game.

And all the time she was thinking about some stranger called Grant. A name she didn't know and doubted was genuine. Of course, it *could* have been innocent, Ziva told herself. The man *could* have been one of Gus's old school friends. Or he might have been involved in the art world, which was why he had said he was 'sorry about the dealer' - but she doubted it. She doubted any stranger approaching a boy and giving that child an enigmatic message. Because if he *really* had Gus's mobile number and knew his comings and goings he could have contacted him directly; doing what any normal man would have done. Instead he had approached his son, knowing it would seem strange at best, and a threat at worst.

One thing she knew for certain. 'Grant 'wasn't a friend to any of them.

London
July 1782

My dear friend, Johann

Your congratulations were effusive, surely you of all people do not imagine that I believe your sentiments? Our friendship is long standing, without deceit, yet you would write to praise me and my work! 'The Nightmare' is a triumph indeed. Of that there is no doubting, yet you seem to have forgotten its inception, the reason it was painted, and, most importantly, what it represents. Or rather, what it hides. It is rewarding to be feted and admired in London, and even courted by the great and worthy Joshua Reynolds, yet at what deceptive price? If it were known the bitter kernel inside the creation who would then truly admire?

You will admonish me, rightly so, for did I not suggest that this work might make my name?... I see this letter is brim full with questions. Yet my life mirrors it. I am a composite of queries, of interrogations, of questionings, and the esteem this painting has brought to me only finds me asking more. Doubting more. Fearing more.

As you are in Germany again, I wonder if you have heard the rumours of the strange happenings around 'The Nightmare?' If you have, forgive me repeating them, if not, allow me to enlighten you. The Incubus within 'The Nightmare' has caused great distress amongst a number of female viewers to the Royal Academy; there are incidences of fainting, mature ladies even coming accompanied by a nurse. And yet they still attend! Doctors, psychiatrists and lecturers in the paranormal chunter amongst themselves, seeing meanings that never even approach the reality. They believe the work signals the end of formal academic painting and gives free rein to the imagination, the much vaulted 'subconscious.'

Such is the power, the magnetic force of 'The Nightmare'. 'These are not my words - I would not dare to put the laurel wreath on my own head, I am reporting only what is being said in London.

It might even be considered amusing to read of women fainting or accompanied by nurses - one imagines to catch them as they fall! Yet there are other happenings that are darker and lack anything of the ridiculous. When the painting was first exhibited a watchman reported that, on locking up for the night, the Incubus figure had vanished. Left the painting and moved about the room, stalking the poor man, tracking him, until half maddened, he escaped. Shaken and confounded, he left his post and would not enter the Academy again.

Dear Johann, there is more - although this account was first met with derision, footprints were reported appearing on the gallery floor! Footprints not of a human, more of some creature the size of a canine.

I laughed when I was told, yet soon curbed my levity. Other incidents were reported within days. The sounds of movement coming from the gallery when it was secured for the night, the doors locked to deter intruders. Then there was the sighting of a light from the window after all the lamps had been extinguished. Who lit them? ... Perhaps you believe - as I first did - that such events were staged by those who would create ever more interest around the work. The paranormal, the devilish, are irresistible to many, and are driving hundreds of people to stand, open mouthed, before 'The Nightmare' never once realising what earthly depravity it represents, what personal, sickly longings of my own.

Then questions began - who is the sitter for the Incubus? If the face did not belong to a living man, then how could I draw such a creature from my imagination? Was I the insane painter so beloved in literature? Or was I complicit in the legend, as fast growing as mould, that swamped 'The Nightmare.' A gifted painter, or a clever opportunist?

I never shared with you 'how' I created this painting, only my reasons for doing so. It was laughably simple at first. The woman was my revenge on Anna Landolt; the horse some cack-handed and blatant stallion of the night. The obscenity was denied by many, yet welcomed by the psychologists who relish picking over a man's brain to claim insight whilst waving his dirty laundry at the world. As for the Incubus, there everything changed. He came to me in a dream, the very nightmare he represented.

*Whilst I had I wanted the ghoul to be **my** own inner self, he became his **own** self.*

Yes, Johann, I understand what I am writing and do not exaggerate. The goblin grew under my paintbrush, his fur flowed from it, his body becoming weighty as I created his shape, even seeming to distort the canvas at times. A being made from pigment, a creature as easily destroyed as made. Yet I did <u>not</u> destroy the Incubus. I could not, for I had committed myself and needed to complete the work to expunge what had poisoned me.

Exhausted by the speed at which I was painting, I would fall into a doze in the studio, only to be awakened by the sensation of something behind me, or the feeling of fur brushing against my cheek. When I opened my eyes in terror it was looking at me, staring out from the canvas with blind eyes, for I would not give it sight. I could not - for if it was granted vision, it would be able to see me and co-habit with the world.

So I worked on, painted the background, the details, all the time the ghoul blindly waiting. Waiting. I wanted to finish, I wanted it to be completed, yet I could not bring myself to paint the demon's eyes.

Many times I began; I mixed the pigment, drew the outline of the eye sockets, coated my brush with the colour - yet I could not, <u>would not</u>, continue. To give it sight was to give it life. I was trapped within a snare of my own making. For if it remained unfinished, I would never rinse the pollution from my system.

It was a Sunday morning when I decided it could be avoided no longer. I chose the morning for its daylight, so much at odds with the darkness of the painting; I chose the morning for the sound of the church bells bringing God into the studio from which He seemed to have shrunk for so long. I chose morning, bird song, sunlight to dispel the evil, and in that sunlight I began to paint the eyes of the Incubus. Timidly I coloured in the sockets, the flesh around, the lumpen forehead and the bulbous brows. Then I paused.

The sun was still shining when I finally mixed the burnt umber with linseed oil and laid in the pupils of the Incubus. The eyes looked back at me, blank, the colour of gutter water, lacking the highlight which brought reality. It was such a tiny morsel of lead white; a flick of paint; hardly bigger than a grain of rice, and yet when I placed it the Incubus came into being. It did not move, yet I felt it shudder; it did not speak, yet I heard it murmur; it did not blink, yet its gaze focused; and for one moment - believe me as I write the truth - I heard it breathe...

What have I done? What have I brought into the world? What image of my own evil have I freed so I might liberate myself?

I did not return to the studio, yet put the painting in the hands of my agent and you know all that followed. Except for one matter ~ that of the night watchman. The man who was driven insane by his experience. Yet there was more to that story. Whilst London eulogised 'The Nightmare' the porter was discovered dead in his bed in Bedlam Hospital, having died of suffocation by persons unknown...

My dear friend, I wish you would come to London again. I would show you what the city offers now that my pockets jangle with coins and I am never refused entrance to the theatre or the most fashionable salons! Grant me your kind company soon and allow me to repay you for your patience and sound judgement.

> *With affection,*
> *Henry*

TWENTY NINE

Berlin,
Germany.

Left handed, Jimmy was struggling to write; his note-pad balanced on his thigh, one leg crossed over the other, his bony knee sticking up like the spindly mast of a tug boat. It was breezy, the city bench wet from recent rain, as he reached for the mobile ringing in his pocket.

It was not the person he expected. "*Ziva*? Hi, I've just been trying to get hold of Gus --"

"You're not the only one. I've been trying all morning, Jimmy, but no luck. When did you last speak to him?"

"Yesterday."

"Same here. Since last night I can't get through, and I need talk to him urgently."

He caught the anxiety in her voice; happy to ride in as the knight in shining armour because he was in love with Ziva. Had been for years, even hoping when she and Gus split up that he might have a chance. But what would a woman like Ziva want with a scrawny opportunist, with a criminal record? She was out of his league, but she never made him feel that way. Always welcoming, accepting him as a friend and Mark's 'uncle.' There *were* some conditions when he visited - don't mention jail, or bring any iffy girlfriends, don't smoke weed, and never around Mark - otherwise he was taken in like the affectionate runt of the litter.

"Is there something wrong, Ziva?"

"I think so…I got a bad feeling...Where are you?"

"Berlin." Jimmy replied, "I'm working for Gus and have some information for him. Are you ok?"

She hesitated, then told him about Mark. How he had been accosted by some stranger and asked to pass an enigmatic message onto Gus - *'tell him I'm sorry about the dealer.'"*

The reply was out of Jimmy's mouth before he had chance to check it. "Did he mean John Cummings?"

"Who's John Cummings?"

Cursing himself, Jimmy tried to sound nonchalant. "Oh, just a dealer in Zurich --"

"Stop lying, I know you too well! What's the hell's going on? Nothing's made any sense since Gus went to work for Louis Willes." She stopped, changing tack. "Who's John Cummings? And why should Gus be *'sorry about him'*?"

Jimmy picked his words as carefully as a man juggling hand grenades. "Cummings was an important dealer, with far reaching - and some say dubious - contacts. When the new Fuseli painting was discovered everyone wanted to get their hands on it. John Cummings kept it hidden at his home in Zurich --"

"And?"

" -- he was murdered yesterday --"

"Christ."

" -- and the killer stole the painting."

Ziva took in a breath. "Does this have anything to do with Louis Willes?"

There was a pause on the line.

"**Jimmy!** Come on, tell me, you have to. This involves my family. Some bastard approached my child. He knew everything about us! He knew Gus was working in Hampshire and that he was coming to see us *this* weekend."

"Ziva, calm down --"

"The man had Gus's address and mobile number!"

"A lot of people have Gus's work number --"

"But they don't have his timetable and they don't accost my son at his school!" Her voice was raised, but she knew she won't be heard. Not with the noise coming from Mark's bedroom, the over-excited playing of computer games with his friends. "And now you've just told me an art dealer has been murdered - and neither of us can get hold of Gus. What if something's happened him?"

"That's a leap!"

"You think so?" She retorted "When Gus took this commission he was told it could be dangerous, but he made light of it, thought Willes was exaggerating. Well, maybe he wasn't. Maybe it *is* dangerous. What did Gus tell you about the job?"

Put on the spot, Jimmy wavered. "He asked me to find out details about Fuseli when he was in Germany, and he wanted to know about his grandfather."

"What else?"

"Nothing --"

"I don't believe you!" She snapped. "And don't tell me you didn't know about the anonymous messages."

Jimmy sighed wearily. "Yeah, I know."

"Did he ask you find out who was sending them?"

"Gus tried to, I tried to, but they can't be traced."

He could tell that Ziva was struggling to connect the pieces. "Have you uncovered anything about Addison Franckel?"

"*Franckel*?" he replied, surprised and wondering how much Gus to told her, and how much he had held back.

"I know some." She admitted. "I know he was a psychiatrist who disappeared during the war and left no trace. But it sounds ridiculous. I mean, how *could* he and his clinic simply disappear?"

"The authorities *made* it disappear --"

"*'The authorities*?'" She repeated, alert. "What does that mean, Jimmy? Which authorities?"

"The government, the police, the medical profession - apparently they banded together and suppressed it."

"Why would they do that unless they were covering something up?" Her voice was interrogative. "What was it?"

"Come on, Ziva, I don't know! If I did, I'd tell you."

"No, I don't think you would." She replied bluntly. "I think you'd wait for Gus to explain. But I can't get hold of Gus, so I'm asking *you*. The house where Louis Willes lives was once Franckel's Clinic, wasn't it? The same place where five patients died, one of them being Gus's grandfather."

"You know all about it?"

"No, I don't, Jimmy. I don't know *how* the authorities managed to bury the story. Or why was it so important that they *needed* to bury it." She persisted. "What was done there?"

"Ziva --"

"What happened to Addison Franckel? Did he disappear, or die? Why were there so many deaths?"

Jimmy didn't mention the journalist who had supposedly committed suicide. Or the Incubus Tapes.

"I'm helping Gus to find answers."

"Is he in danger?"

"Ziva, don't jump to conclusions just because you can't get him on his mobile! Gus is out in the sticks; you know how often they lose the signal there. This isn't the first time it's happened." Jimmy was calming her and calming himself at the same time. "Don't let your imagination run away with you. Anyway, I'm coming back to London tonight."

"Was that planned?" She asked. "Or are you coming back now because you're worried about what's going on?"

"It was planned, kiddo, the flight was already booked." Jimmy replied, trying to lighten the atmosphere.

Her voice was steady when she spoke again. "What part does the painting play in all this? Louis Willes is writing about Fuseli, he hired Gus to do the research." She was trying to fathom it out. "Does Fuseli tie in with Addison Franckel somehow?"

"Gus knows what he's doing."

"What *is* he doing, Jimmy?"

"He's trying to discover what went on in Franckel's Clinic --"

"The elusive Franckel's Clinic! *Is any of it true?*" She persisted, confused. "I mean, *was* there ever a clinic?"

"Yeah, and Gus grandfather was one of Franckel's patients there."

"And he died?"

"Yeah."

"Why did he die? *How* did he die?"

"I don't know, I couldn't find a record of his death."

"What about Franckel?"

"Same, no death registered."

"Ok, so just tell me this" she said calmly "*why* was Addison Franckel struck off?"

There was a pause on the line, Jimmy grimacing. Shit, he thought, why hadn't Gus confided in her? But he knew why - telling her as little as possible would have been his way of protecting his family. It had been the murder of John Cummings and the stranger accosting Mark that had accelerated the situation. Dangerously.

"Why was Franckel struck off?" Ziva repeated.

"Ask Gus, he'll explain. He'll be back in contact before you know it."

"And if he isn't?" She countered. "**Don't do this, Jimmy**! I'm scared. I need to know what's going on."

"Gus wouldn't want --"

"Don't tell me what *he* wants! I know what *I* want. And I *want* to know the truth." She retorted. "Whatever it is, I have to know. Don't you understand, Jimmy? This is my man, and my child, and if anything happens to them because you didn't trust me, then God help you."

Graybrooke Lodge
Hampshire

The moon was listless, smothered by the fog, Gus relying on the weather to conceal him as he lighted his way. It would have been easier on a clear night, but he knew it might be the only time he would have chance to search. As he walked, Willes's word resounded in his ears:

> "...don't wander around outside at night.
> The garden is overgrown in places and full of
> old bones."

Had it been genuine advice? Or a warning? And what kind of bones had the historian been referring to? Animal bones? Dog bones, human bones? Or the bones of the dead patients - including those of his grandfather?... Slow in the fog, Gus made his way down the lawn and crossed into the spinney. He had decided that if the woman appeared again he would challenge her and take a photograph as proof. Ghosts never came out well, he thought wryly, especially in a fog, but a human being could be exposed easily enough.

Passing on through the trees he heard branches creaking, a shuffling of winter leaves underfoot, and a fox barking shrilly, calling for a mate. Of the woman there was no sign. Gus's thoughts turned to John Cummings, and Jimmy on the phone talking about something he had tell him concerning Willes... A sudden dip in the ground made Gus stumble. His hand went out to steady himself, catching hold of a fence covered in barbed wire. The blades dug into his palm, drawing blood, Gus swearing and wrapping his handkerchief around the cut before continuing. This time, with more caution.

Yet as he moved further on he realised he was walking on ground that felt less springy, more solid under his feet. Bending down, he scraped at the earth, finding - a few inches below the surface - what seemed to be broken concrete. Was this the foundation of the wards that had once belonged to the Franckel Clinic? Or the operating theatre Ella Fairchild had spoken about?

In the distance Gus could hear dogs barking, the sound muffled by the fog. He must, he reasoned, be well away from the house and even further away from the lane that led into town. Had he really walked that far already? Pausing, he glanced back. The mist had become so dense he couldn't see Graybrooke and for an instant considered turning round. But when would he get another chance to search the grounds? He had been working with Willes for over two weeks, both knowing the historian's condition was terminal and that at any moment the Fuseli book might be abandoned. Or Willes might suddenly collapse, the pain too difficult to manage, morphine inducing a coma.

Time was short for Louis Willes, and precariously short for Gus. His mind made up, he continued. This time he walked straight ahead, without detouring to the left or the right, ensuring that at least he could find his way back to Graybrooke when he finally retraced his steps.

In the instant he made the decision, his foot knocked against a broken piece of paving stone, Gus looking down at a dilapidated pathway, much of it concealed. Uncertain where it led, he followed it, walking slowly over the uneven stones as the atmosphere became oppressive in the darkness. The fog was swirling quickly, shuffling around him, the torchlight barely able to make any impression on the intense gloom, Gus putting out his right hand blindly. To his astonishment, he felt an obstruction in front of him and ran his hands over it. It was a wall. With a door... Shining the torch-light onto it, he pushed the door open just as he heard a gunshot crack over his head, the crows woken from their nests and flying upwards into the blind night.

Shaken, he called out. **"Stop!** Don't shoot!"

Another gunshot shattered the air around him, Gus ducking through the door and moving for cover against the inside wall. Breathing heavily he listened, waited for another shot, or someone calling out. Surely it was a mistake? No one could have been firing at him deliberately, he told himself. It must have been a poacher, out hunting for rabbits or foxes... Listening in the darkness, he waited for several minutes before turning his torch back on, shining it around the confined chamber in which he had taken shelter. The Ice House, he thought, remembering what he had been told, the beam of torchlight moving over the bare stone walls, the freezing dampness dropping the temperature below zero, the floor moist, grey stone.

It was a grim place, Gus thought, wondering when it would be safe to leave when he suddenly saw the door swing forward and slam shut, trapping him inside.

WEEK THREE

THIRTY

Maida Vale
London

Shaken, realising that someone had burgled her house, Ella Fairchild backed away from the ruined clothes taken from her closet and thrown on the floor with the discarded box. Who did something like that? She asked herself, incredulous. And how did they know about the notes she had kept hidden for so long? The notes on Addison Franckel's patients. No one knew about them. She had never mentioned them to anyone - except Gus Egan.

Instinct told her he hadn't broken into her house, but someone had. Had it been someone Egan had confided in? Someone who had come into her home looking for the files of long dead people? And why? Shaken by the loud ringing of the doorbell below, Ella Fairchild pulled back the bedroom curtain, glancing down towards her front door. The outer security light had come on, illuminating the man standing below. His head was balding, a tonsure of pink skin surrounded by a neat fringe of grey, his glasses catching the light as he glanced up. Alarmed, she stepped back, the doorbell ringing again, a muted voice coming through the letter box.

"Hello, Mrs Fairchild? My name is Paul Shore and we have a mutual acquaintance, Mr Gus Egan. I wondered if we could have a talk. I won't take up much of your time."

He paused, looked around the street, then rang the bell again, Ella buttoning her cardigan, and glancing in the bedroom mirror.

Well, should we answer it, or not? She thought, *addressing her reflection. You said you weren't going to back down, that you wanted to be a heroine. Well, this is your chance....*Reality made her waver. ... *But it could be the burglar... If I open the door it could mean danger... I should ignore it.*

The bell rang again. Politely, almost apologetically, as if to say that it didn't want to become an annoyance, but it would keep ringing until it was answered.

Slowly moving downstairs, Ella kept the safety chain on as she opened the door a few inches. "Hello? Can I help you?"

Paul Shore smiled pleasantly, with a slightest incline of his head.

"Please excuse my arriving unannounced at this late hour, but it is a matter of importance that concerns us both. My grandmother died at Addison Franckel's Clinic and I believe both of us have suffered grievously from the loss of our relatives."

The words had their effect. Sliding the safety chain back, Ella opened the door, showing the elderly and unassuming Paul Shore into the sitting room and turning on the gas fire. The room was chilled, the heat welcome as she offered him a seat.

"Forgive my wariness, you see I was robbed earlier this evening --"

His eyebrows rose, his precise, quiet voice concerned. "Are you alright?"

"Oh yes, fortunately I wasn't at home," Ella replied.

"Was anything valuable taken?"

"Yes, actually there was. A selection of Addison Franckel's notes on his patients. Not all of them, of course, but some that had been given to me by my late father for safe keeping. They *had* been safe since 1984, but they were stolen today." Her right hand went to her forehead for an instant as though to calm herself. "It must have been in the early evening when I was out. I keep wondering how anyone even knew I had them, and why they went to the trouble of stealing them."

"Are you sure you're alright?"

She nodded, then changed the subject. "I'm making some tea." Carefully she got to her feet. "I'm sure that would be welcome for both of us. It's rather cold in here but the fire should warm it up soon."

He moved to rise, but she shook her head. "No, stay where you are, I can manage. Besides, why should you help me? It would seem that there is little difference in our ages."

As it happened Paul Shore was five years older than Ella, but his sprightliness and upright posture had barely changed for forty years. He had found children rewarding to teach, whilst being relieved to be free of them after three in the afternoon. Patiently he waited for Ella to return, sitting before the gas fire, his suit pressed, shoes shined, smiling when she re-entered with the tea. If he had suffered much grief or trauma in his life it was not obvious in his appearance, and after they had talked pleasantries for several minutes he turned the conversation round to the reason for his visit.

"I want Addison Franckel to be exposed." He said frankly. "Have you seen the tapes?"

Surprised, Ella laid down her cup and saucer before answering. "You are very direct."

"Sadly, we are of an age to act quickly when so much of life has already passed and little is guaranteed to follow. I am a widower with no relatives and therefore no responsibilities." He smiled, his glasses bordered with gold, mimicking the gilded rims of the tea cups. "*Have* you seen the tapes?"

"Have you?" She countered.

"Excuse me, I was presuming too much, asking such an important question and expecting you to confide on such a short acquaintance. Please let me reassure you, Mrs Fairchild, I have not come to pry into your private family matters, neither have I come here empty handed. I have done some of my own research, however it is not very impressive, I'm afraid. As we both know the authorities did not encourage curiosity in the 1940's --"

"Not in the 1980's either, when I tried to find out what had been going on. I was warned off in no uncertain terms, and when I went to my local MP he was defensive and dismissive." She paused. "I hate to admit it, but I was scared off."

He nodded in agreement. "We all were."

"But not now?"

"Old age makes some people reckless."

She smiled. "You do not seem reckless."

"Nor do you, but we are both worried about what happened to the people we loved."

"Is it true that five people died?"

"There were others."

"Others? Who else are you talking about?"

"There was a patient called Mrs Ruby Hodge. She died at the clinic in 1944. When I tried to pursue the matter with her great nephew he said he wanted nothing to do with it. He lives in Holland and had no interest in his aunt's past --"

"Didn't he know that five patients had died under Addison Franckel's treatment?"

"Five we know of." He sighed. "Of course, I am aware of Mr Egan's grandfather, George Lyman, I know of your relative, Peter Opie, Mrs Hodge – the lady I just spoke of - and my own grandmother, Elizabeth Shore. There was also a soldier called Lance Carter, transferred from Spike Island - as was George Lyman. Captain Carter was an officer, much decorated for bravery. He'd been injured from shrapnel and invalided home from France, but when he recovered and returned to the fighting he underwent a total mental collapse. Shell shock, like my grandmother. That was when he was sent to the Franckel Clinic."

Ella sighed. "Five deaths left unsolved."

"Six."

"Six?"

"Don't forget the journalist, Ted MacNeice." Paul replied. "He was as much a victim as the patients."

"I didn't know anything about him until Gus Egan mentioned him the other day."

"Mr MacNeice's records seem - like Addison Franckel and so much else concerning these events - to have disappeared. I couldn't discover much, only that

Mr MacNeice was an Irishman working as a journalist in London. He committed suicide in 1944, just after Addison Franckel went missing --"

"Franckel was listed as '*missing*?'"

"Actually he wasn't listed as anything." Paul shook his head. "It was very thorough, wasn't it?"

"I'm sorry," Ella said, baffled, "I don't understand. *What* was very thorough?"

"The way everything was suppressed. So many lies, so many contradictory accounts. They scared us into staying quiet, didn't they?" He smiled, gentile, old school. "And now here we are, at the end of our lives, trying to make up for our cowardliness when we were young... Excuse me, I was speaking for myself, not criticising your actions."

"It's true, I *was* frightened off. But that was then."

"And now you wish the history of the clinic to become public knowledge, and for Addison Franckel to be exposed?"

"Indeed I do. Just as you do." Ella paused, studying him. "May I ask why you came here tonight, of all nights? I've never been burgled before and I never answer the door to strangers, particularly so late. There must be some reason you wanted to talk now."

Paul lowered his head, clasping his hands together. "A bad conscience forced me here. I should have done more earlier, and suddenly it was unbearable. I *had* to talk to someone about what we'd kept secret for so long. We colluded with them, you see. Indirectly we allowed the authorities to bury Franckel and everything that happened at Graybrooke Lodge." He looked up, apologetic. "I shouldn't have come, it was selfish of me --"

"No, no, it wasn't." Ella replied. "It's good to know that I'm not alone now, and neither are you. We have each other for support, and we have Gus Egan. We *need* him, Mr Shore, he's much younger than we are, and more resourceful. If we'd had a man like him in the 1940's everything could have been different." She sighed, clicked her tongue. "I admit I had my reservations about Mr Egan. He was reluctant to get involved, but now he's committed because of his grandfather."

"I haven't met him yet. What kind of a man is he?"

"Outspoken, blunt, and he seems tough, if you know what I mean." She paused before continuing. "Does he know you're here?"

"No. I contacted him yesterday. We agreed to speak, but I haven't heard back from him yet." Paul smiled. It didn't matter, the gesture said, implying at the same time that he considered it rude. "Mr Egan was introduced to me by a third party --"

"The same way we were all introduced." Ella replied, interrupting. "Any idea who this anonymous contact is?"

"None, but they're obviously determined that we should join forces."

Ella paused before speaking again. "I wonder what their motives are? D'you think they lost someone at the clinic? A patient we don't know about?"

"It's possible."

"Or then again," her shrewd brain shifted into gear "they might be using us for their own ends. I mean, we're presuming they want to expose Franckel in the name of justice, but perhaps they want to know what we discover and make sure we don't tell anyone."

Unnerved, Paul leaned back in his chair. "I don't think I understand."

"If they wanted to expose Franckel they would have to have a genuine reason to do so. Especially after so long."

"Meaning?"

"*The tapes*, Mr Shore. What if they want the tapes. And what if they believe we can find them?"

"Why would they think that?"

"Because we're the last surviving relatives of the patients who died whilst under the 'care' of Addison Frankel. The last people who have memories, information of that time. Perhaps that's why we were brought together. Perhaps they hope we can uncover, or remember, something that would lead them to the tapes."

"But we don't where they are!"

"No, we don't, but a man like Gus Egan could find them. He's a researcher. A man with contacts. And he has his own reason for revenge. Wouldn't that be the perfect person to choose?"

Thoughtful, Paul nodded. "Have you seen the tapes?"

"No," Ella replied, with a slight shake of her head. "Have you?"

"No."

"Do you know what's on them?"

"No," Paul said, sighing. "All I know is that they were supposedly destroyed at the same time that Franckel and the clinic disappeared." Paul reached into his jacket pocket and brought out a small, leather bound notebook, opening it and reading a name: "*Miss Miriam Levy* - she was the Head Sister at the Franckel Clinic, have you heard of her?"

"I certainly have," Ella replied "my grandfather told my father that she was a heroine. For what reason, I don't fully know."

Paul glanced away, remembering. "My grandmother, Elizabeth Shore, served in wartime. Most people don't realise that there were women in the forces who suffered from shell shock as badly as the men. My poor grandmother was one of them. She came home and was treated for a nervous breakdown, night terrors, what they call PTSD now, then she was sent to London, from where she was transferred to Addison Franckel's Clinic. Do you know the place?"

"Only from what I've heard. I've never been there."

He drew out two small black and white photographs. One of a young woman and the other of a large building set in a verdant, capacious landscape.

Taking the first image offered to her, Ella asked: "Is this your grandmother?"

"No, that's Miriam Levy. Obviously she was not on nursing duty as she's in civilian clothes."

"She was beautiful," Ella said honestly "a striking woman."

"You know she was in love with Addison Franckel?"

The words came into the room like a cold draft. "But I thought you said she was a heroine."

"She was indeed," Paul replied, finishing his tea and glancing back to the gas fire. "She was in love with Franckel, which was why it was all the more difficult for her to betray him when she discovered what he was. She talked to my grandmother about it, that's how I know."

"She told you?" Ella said, surprised. "But you'd only have been a boy back then."

"You don't understand, Mrs Fairchild, my grandmother liked to talk, to gossip, to laugh. She loved my visits, even more than seeing my parents. Older people can find it easier to communicate with children, she certainly did." He was tapping his knee with the other photograph. "She said that she'd watched Miriam and Franckel together in the garden. She smiled when she said it. Romance always made her giddy, and she wanted Miriam to marry the doctor and be happy.... She was recovering at that point, even talked about coming home...." His voice wavered. "That was the last time my grandmother ever spoke about happiness. Soon after that she changed. She became dark, thin, angry. Hunched up in her bed, gibbering about the war and her dreams and how there was something wrong in the clinic."

"Did she tell you what?"

"No, she wasn't coherent by that time. She would grab my hand and tell me to warn Miriam Levy, '*...tell her to leave him, that man is wicked...*' she'd said; '*... tell her to run away from here....*' But Miriam didn't leave. Instead she was caught trying to smuggle my grandmother out of the clinic in the back of Addison Franckel's car." He stared at the photograph again. "The following week my parents told me that my grandmother had suffered a fatal heart attack and when they went to the clinic to speak to Franckel he said that Miriam Levy had left and returned to London."

"Were your parents given your grandmother's possessions after she died?"

Paul turned to look at her, his eyes unreadable. "There were none."

"*No possessions*?" Ella said, aghast. "What about her personal affects? Her clothes? Her toiletries?"

"Gone."

"Where?"

"Franckel said they had been burned because my grandmother had contracted a contagious disease --"

"What!" Ella said, leaning towards him. "How could that have been possible?"

"He said she became infected whilst she was serving overseas, some parasite which had gone undetected for years. Until it finally affected her brain and led to her fatal heart attack." He paused, handing the other photograph to Ella. "That's the clinic. It used to be called Reid Hall, but now not even the name remains."

Ella studied the black and white image. "Does it still look like this?"

"The main house does. It hasn't altered very much at all, but the extensions, the wards, theatre, and all the outbuildings, were completely demolished. Not a trace left of any of it." He sighed, taking a breath in deep. "The grounds were - *are* – expansive. The lake has dried up, but the wood is still there and the Ice House --"

"How do you know this?"

"I went there a month ago." Paul confessed. "I drove down the lane, made certain there was no one about, and then wandered around the grounds. It was trespassing, I know, but I had to revisit the place, had to see it again. I took the path at the boundary, between the property and the brook --"

"Graybrooke Lodge," Ella murmured.

"Yes, it was called that before Franckel named it Reid Hall. That's why it returned to its rightful name afterwards. The path was very overgrown, but still there, running through the wood and alongside the Ice House." He paused, uneasy. "I stood there for a while, looking at it and remembering... When my grandmother was nearing the end, she was confused, rambling. She would say that they put difficult patients in there to teach them a lesson."

"Patients?" Ella asked in a whisper. "They punished the patients?"

"Oh yes," he answered. "My grandmother told me it wasn't the dark or the cold of the Ice House that was so frightening, it was because they were never alone in there."

THIRTY

Ealing,
London.

Grabbing a towel, Caroline wrapped it around her wet hair and reached for her mobile, then recognising the number, answered eagerly:

"Hi, Mike! Any news?"

"Indeed there is, I've got something for you --"

"Hang on a minute, I have to let the cat in." She interrupted his flow, sliding open the kitchen window and standing back to let a large feline enter. "You're soaked, wet through like me," she said, then turned her attention back to Mike Owen. "Sorry, sorry, what were you saying?"

"I'm found out something about your great aunt."

"You genius!"

He flushed at the other end of the line, continuing triumphantly. "My brother's a consultant at St Edward hospital, where --"

"*Miriam was a nurse!*" Caroline said, briskly rubbing her hair with the towel.

" -- and he pulled a few strings for me, asked the woman in Records to dig around for some Personnel information for him. He wasn't sure there would be anything dating back to when your great aunt was working there, but we're in luck, there's a brief entry about her time at St Edward's. She was working on the Men's Surgical Ward and previously she had worked in the Psychiatric Department."

"*Psychiatric?* That's interesting. Thanks, Mike," Caroline said, genuinely pleased. "What else did your brother find out?"

"This bit is rather strange, but an entry in your aunt's records included a newspaper cutting. Apparently there was a connection between Miriam and a man who had once been a patient at St Edward's." Mike looked at the notes he had made, reading through the scattering of words and doodles. "He'd been admitted after a fight and came in to have a face wound stitched --"

"*A fight?* If he was admitted it must have been bad. What did the medical report say?"

"I don't have any more on that," Mike replied with some disappointment in his voice. "But I have the date; July 7th 1941, and his name, Ted MacNeice. Apparently he had been the victim of an 'unprovoked attack' in the East End and the police were called. They interviewed him, but for some reason he didn't want to press charges, even though the injury was severe." Mike squinted at his notes, trying to decipher what he had written. "Hang on a minute, I can't make out this bit."

"Why was there a newspaper cutting of Ted Mac-Neice's attack put into Miriam's Personnel file?"

"Probably because they were married."

"What!" Caroline stopped rubbing her hair and sat down. "So she *did* get married. What else did the newspaper say?"

"'*...Mr MacNeice was admitted with a
serious head injury but was expected to make
a full recovery. The police commented that
it was the third attack in the area within
the last week. There is no evidence that the
attacks were related. Mr MacNeice
had no comment to make...*'"

"Perhaps there are medical notes for him?"

"Tried that - and also tried my brother's patience - but there were no notes on Ted MacNeice. St Edward's don't keep all the records from so far back."

"But at least I could look for a marriage certificate now," Caroline replied. "Did it say anything about why Miriam left St Edward's?"

"No, sorry."

"Anything about where she went afterwards?"

Mike shuffled through his notes again.

"Oh shit, you're not going to believe this, I've given you everything in the wrong order!" He was impatient with himself, anxious he might look stupid in her eyes. "Just a minute, Caroline, I'll get it organised." There was a scuffling of papers down the line before he spoke again. "Ok, I've got it sorted, here we go. There's a note that Miriam had been working at a private clinic --"

"Yes, yes, I know! *Where?*"

"Hampshire."

"Whereabouts?"

"Don't have an address."

"I don't suppose you know what it was called?"

"I do indeed!" Mike's voice was jubilant. *"Reid House."*

"Do you know that you're amazing?" Caroline replied. "No one else could find all this out, but you did! I can search for the place now I have a name."

"Er, no, you can't."

"What?"

"I already tried to find it, but it doesn't exist any longer." Mike explained. "There's no record of it anywhere."

"There has to be *some* record! A clinic can't vanish."

"Seems like this one did."

"Who ran it?"

"Again, no details. Just that it was a private clinic, but no information about the owner." His voice wavered. "Sorry, I tried, but I couldn't do more."

She rushed to console him. "No, no, you did brilliantly! Honestly, Mike, you did a great job."

"At least you know a bit more about your great aunt."

"I do, but I'm not stopping now."

"No, I didn't imagine you would."

She was thinking quickly, running over what she had heard. "Miriam Levy got married, and at one time worked in the Psychiatric Ward at St Edward's."

"Yeah."

"Well, it can't be that difficult to find out where there was once a private clinic called Reid Hall in Hampshire. Even in wartime, a clinic couldn't just pop up and then evaporate into thin air. People in the area would know about it."

"They might, or they might not. Depends if it was in a town, or in the country. If it was the latter, not many people would know. And in wartime, people wouldn't be interested --"

"Unless they worked there. Or they were patients." Caroline said optimistically. "It's worth a shot. I know it could be a dead end, but I have to see what else I can dig up."

"I'm more than willing to help, you know." Mike replied, desperate to keep their connection. "If you want me, just give me shout. I'm always here."

Graybrooke Lodge
Hampshire

The night crawled on, Ronnie having returned to her room, jamming a chair under the door handle to prevent anyone entering and then trying, repeatedly and unsuccessfully, to get a mobile signal. Hungry, she longed to go to the kitchen for food, but didn't dare, instead lying down on the bed, fully dressed, thinking about the murdered John Cummings.

People had always talked about the dealer, admiring and despising him in equal measure. Envy motivated much of the gossip, but Ronnie knew that Cummings had been greedy and reckless. Perhaps he had believed his father and brother would use their legal clout to protect him from danger, but obviously Cummings had spun the wheel once too often, and in the wrong company.

He was dead and the Fuseli was gone... Her thoughts shifted back to Zurich, to the house of John Cummings, glacially perfect in amongst the winter slopes. Wealth oozed from the fittings like sap from a cut tree, the swimming pool ludicrously large for such a tiny man. Or perhaps Cummings didn't think of himself as tiny. In the water, when he was not obliged to stand beside other men, he might have thought of himself as a marine titan, transformed by weightlessness and underground lights.

Her visit had been brief and had taken place many years earlier, Cummings polite but leaking dislike, all of her attempts at a collaboration repelled. It was difficult for a female dealer, even a handsome woman who had the advantage of looks to attract interest. Determined, Ronnie had employed the tricks of the other dealers, whilst adding her own sensual slant. It had worked well with the likes of Anthony Hallett and Edward Leigh - the former a lover, the latter a sometime ally - but what none of them knew was that Ronnie Gilchrist was struggling. To be more precise, she was teetering on the edge of bankruptcy.

Which was why the Fuseli had been of such importance to her. If Ronnie could have got hold of the painting and convinced Edward Leigh - or Louis Willes - to stump up finance to buy it with her, then it could have been sold privately for a hefty sum. Alone she could not possibly raise enough to buy it herself, but with an ally it might have been possible.

Sighing, she covered her eyes with her arm as she lay on the bed. What was the point of even thinking about it? The painting was gone, and the person who had it had been prepared to murder to get it... A soft noise from below disturbed her, Ronnie turning off the lamp and moving over to the window. The curtain was heavy in her hand as she pulled it aside, glancing down into the colourless fog below. One by one, she could see the outer lights coming on as someone left the house and moved down the steps towards the garden. She couldn't recognise the figure in the fog, but consoled herself with the thought that ghosts didn't activate searchlights. Yet someone was moving about, Ronnie thought, watching as the lights went out one by one, consumed by the muffled darkness.

Curious, she stayed at the window and continued to watch, a couple of minutes passing before the lights came on again. Which mean only one thing - someone was moving *back* to the house. A moment later Ronnie heard the sound of the front door opening.

Uneasy, she checked her bedroom door was still locked, the chair jammed under the handle, and thought of John Cummings. Someone had killed the dealer. For a painting. A painting *she* had wanted. And now she was marooned in a remote house with three men, with no means to get help.

Stop dramatising, she calmed herself, stop letting your mind play tricks on you... Nervous, she stood by the bedroom door uncertain of what to next. If there *was* a allegiance between Gus Egan and Louis Willes, an alliance concerning the Fuseli, she wanted to know. She had come all the way from New York to the backwoods of Hampshire and wasn't about to go home empty handed.

Taking off her shoes, Ronnie crept on to the upper landing, seeing a figure enter the front door and then lock it behind them. In the semi darkness she couldn't see the person clearly and it was only when they reached the middle of the staircase that Je-Yun became visible. He was moving soundlessly in his muffled shoes, walking past her hiding place, Ronnie watching him approach Willes's bedroom and enter.

She could hear the faintest murmur of voices and turned to go back to her room, then paused. If she listened to their conversation what might she hear? But then again, if they found her listening, what might they do? Ronnie hesitated. This was England, she reassured herself, they weren't murderers. No, but they weren't friends either. How could she be sure exactly *what* they were? She was stranded and the fog didn't look like it was going to clear soon. If she was sensible she would simply stay in her room and wait it out, but her curiosity egged her on.

Nervously, Ronnie moved to the door of Louis Willes's bedroom and listened, the old man the first to speak.

"Have you done it?"

"I have, Mr Willes."

"Leave the light on by the bed, I can't sleep," Willes replied, "You think she'll come?"

Ronnie tensed, was he talking about her?

"I don't know, perhaps," the Korean replied. "Are you afraid?"

"Not of the dead, only the living. I need my medication now. And perhaps a little more to help me sleep… My wife slept badly before she died. Did I ever tell you how much she loved the Fuseli painting?"

"You did, sir."

"She adored it. Was fascinated by *The Nightmare*. She used to laugh at the Incubus in the picture, say how comically ugly he was, throw paper darts at it when we had guests and a few too many to drink. If you look carefully you can see indentations in the canvas… I was always interested in Fuseli, but it was Ava that fed the obsession." Willes laughed softly. "She said the house wanted the picture. Did I tell you that Addison Franckel hung it over his desk."

Still listening, Ronnie frowned. Who was hell was Addison Franckel?

"Here you are," Je-Yun continued, apparently passing Willes his medication. "Drink that and you'll rest."

"Are the lights on in the garden?"

"They're automatic. They come on when someone sets them off."

"You've checked them?"

"I have," Je-Yun replied calmly, "all the way to the boundary, past the Ice House and the wood. The lights will activate if she comes tonight."

Willes's voice was stricken. "And if she does? *What will I do*?"

"What you always do. Ring the bell, and I'll come immediately."

"And Gus Egan?"

"He's sleeping elsewhere... Just get your rest now, sir. When the fog lifts everything will return to normal."

Moving quickly, Ronnie ducked back out of sight, Je-Yun leaving his employer's room and moving along the corridor to his own. After several minutes she could hear music playing softly, lamplight coming through the gap under the door. Who had Willes been talking about? His dead wife? And all the talk about the painting and some man she had never heard of. Addison Franckel wasn't a dealer she knew. She was also wondering about the Korean's statement that Gus was '*sleeping elsewhere*.' Was that true? Ronnie thought, frowning. When she last saw him he had seemed settled in for the night, and besides where could he go in

273

the fog? No one could reach Graybrooke, nor leave it. *So where was Gus Egan sleeping tonight?*

There had been something in his tone of voice, something off kilter, and she wondered again what Je-Yun had been doing in the grounds. Still carrying her shoes, Ronnie crept downstairs and out of the front door. Only then did she slip her shoes back on, and without know why she did it, started walking in the direction she had seen the garden lights turning on.

And then off.

Maida Vale
London

"It's me," the voice said "Freddy Wilson."

Surprised, Ella glanced over to Paul Shore, her expression alerting him. "*Freddy Wilson*" she mouthed, before turning her attention back to the caller. "I didn't expect to hear from you again after our last meeting."

"Yeah, well, I've been thinking. And thanks for that, it was *exactly* what I didn't want," his voice was hard around the edges, a rough sleeper's voice. "What d'you want to know about my father? I told you, I don't remember much."

"The tapes, Mr Wilson, what do you know about the tapes?"

"*Tapes?*" he paused, she could tell that he was thinking, wondering how much the information was worth. "What tapes?"

"Films your father made. I know they were some, I've seen patients' notes where it was recorded on their files that he filmed them." She paused. "Did he film his patients in Berlin?"

"I don't remember."

"Try. It's important."

"Who the fuck d'you think you are?" Wilson asked aggressively.

"I may remind you that it was *you* that called *me.* Which means you believe you have something to sell." She thought of the burglary. "When our mutual contact put us in touch, did he give you my address by any chance?"

"Nah. Just your phone number. He always texted. I had a phone then, before it was stolen --"

"You told me that before. So you've no contact with him without a phone?"

"I've got a replacement."

"That was lucky."

"Yeah, well I've always been lucky," Wilson retorted sarcastically. "You know something? I think my father *did* take photographs in Berlin."

Ella leaned forward in her seat. "He took photographs of his German patients? Did the images survive?"

"Dunno. The Berlin police took everything."

"Everything?"

"Everything, It was all taken --"

"But the police might still have some of it?"

"From back then?" He laughed, the sound bitter. "You're too late, it's old history. No one cared then and no one cares now." He paused again, toying with her. "But you know, there might be something worth looking at. My mother had a close friend in Berlin and she took some of our stuff for safe keeping, only after my mother killed herself I never went to pick it up. She might have kept it, stored it. I doubt it, but you never know."

"Can you give me her name and address?"

"I don't know if she's still there, or if she's still alive, but her family might live there now." His voice wavered. "Who knows? She was called Helga something... If I remember I'll text you the name and address. But don't bank on it. My memory's not what it was --"

"Try, please."

"*'Try, please.'*" He mimicked her. "You know you'll have to pay for anything I do remember?"

"I understand."

"It's the past, over and done with. All that matters to me is my father's dead."

"When did he die?"

"Eh?"

"I asked when he died."

Wilson was confused, blundering. "Everyone dies."

"You had communication with him when he came to England?"

"No! I told you, he left us –"

"But if you weren't in touch how did you find out your father was dead?"

There was a long hesitation. "I heard."

"Heard? Did you hear, or were you notified as his next of kin?" Ella persisted. "Who informed you that your father had died? He'd been disgraced, struck off the medical register, everything about him suppressed by the authorities. Both Otto Weiner in Germany and Addison Franckel in England had disappeared from the face of the earth. Isn't that right? You said you'd been looking for him, but you didn't find him. Yet someone knew who *you* were --"

"No one knew who I was!" He shouted. "I told no one!"

"-- but they found you, didn't they? Even living rough, with no job, no home, they knew who you were. And if they knew you, they knew what had happened to your father." She paused, her voice steady. "I'll pay you for the information, Mr Wilson. Just tell me *who* told you that your father was dead?"

Graybrooke Lodge
Hampshire

Stumbling on the uneven pathway, Ronnie dropped her mobile, cursing as it landed on the ground in front of her. She had turned its torch on and the light shone upwards into the fog, illuminating the small, domed building in front of her. To Ronnie it seemed like some English folly, a little goblin's house, distanced from the main property, hump- backed as though bending under the weight of the fog.

Just as Je-Yun had said, the security lights had come on one by one as she had moved down the lawn, only ending their scrutiny when she had entered the wood and relied on her mobile to light her way. And all the time - breathing rapidly and chilled by the cold - Ronnie had believed herself watched, unnerved by the memory of the woman she had seen standing at the library window.

Bending down to pick up her mobile she heard the sound of voices. Male voices. One calm, the other angry. Voices she recognised as belonging to Je-Yun and Gus Egan.

"What the fuck are you playing at!"

"Mr Egan, I did not lock you in there. No one did. The door swung closed and jammed." The Korean explained. "It happened once before. That's why rocks were placed in front of it --"

"Which aren't there now."

"I don't know why," Je-Yun replied calmly, "I'll ask Mr Parker if he moved them--"

"Oh, I would. And perhaps the gardener will explain *why* he moved them. Maybe he was building a rockery. Or perhaps it was the *gardener* who wanted to lock me in there?"

Concealed by the fog, Ronnie continued to listen.

"Mr Egan, you're mistaken --"

"Don't patronise me, I know it was no fucking mistake!" Gus snapped, adding. "And how lucky it was that you should come long now. Why is that?"

"I came because of the dog," Je-Yun pointed to the animal at his feet, Louis Willes's terrier spinning round in circles, its tail wagging. "She told me something was wrong. She came to my room barking. She wouldn't stop, so I followed her. It was the dog that lead me here."

"Bullshit! Someone closed that door on me deliberately." Gus said, enraged. "It's too heavy to swing closed. You think I'm a fool?"

"But who would *want* to lock you in?" Je-Yun asked, his tone placatory. "Luckily I found you, because if you had stayed there all night, it would have been dangerous –"

"In what way?"

"For your *health,* Mr Egan. You might well have become hypothermic."

Pushing him aside, Gus walked off, the Korean following. "Didn't Mr Willes warn you that these grounds can be dangerous for a stranger? There are all kinds of hidden traps for the unwary."

Gus turned on him. "Was it you shooting?"

"*Shooting?*"

"Someone was out here with a gun. They were shooting - you must have heard it. It scattered the crows. They shot once, then again. And the firing was close to me. *Too* close, that was why I took shelter." His voice was hard, the sarcasm lethal. "Perhaps it was the gardener keeping the fox numbers down? Or maybe it was a poacher? You could keep a lot of rabbits fresh in that Ice House."

Unperturbed, Je-Yun answered him. "We don't have poachers around here. Perhaps it was a car back firing?"

"Of course, because it's the perfect night for a bloody drive." Angry, Gus moved on, the Korean continuing to follow him, Ronnie remaining hidden and watching them both.

"Why *did* you go into the grounds, Mr Egan? Whatever made you wander around at night? In a dense fog?"

"I needed some air."

"The garden has air."

"I needed a different kind of air."

"What were you looking for?"

Gus stopped short, turning to Je-Yun. His figure was swaddled in the fog, his grey clothing melting into the mist around him.

"I was looking for a ghost."

"Were you successful?"

"Oh yes," Gus replied, "there's no shortage of phantoms here."

THIRTY ONE

Berlin

Fish scale grey, without the iridescence; just *dead* fish scale grey, the concrete street and buildings in unison, the sky morose, the sun gone early, even for winter. Having tried to contact Gus again, and failing, Jimmy decided that he would return to London. His investigations had petered out - apart from the latest revelation about Louis Willes. And that *was* a revelation. Not only that, but the *means* by which the news had been delivered.

Who the hell would have expected *Freddy Wilson* to have contacted him? The son of Addison Franckel texting him out of the blue. If it *was* Freddy Wilson. Could just as easily been someone pretending to be him. Someone who had caught wind of Jimmy's investigating, someone who had watched him asking questions and moving around Berlin. It wasn't as unlikely as it sounded, Jimmy knew that only too well. People were often watched; wives, husbands, lovers, business colleagues, and people who asked questions about disgraced psychiatrists who had disappeared.

Whistling under his breath, Jimmy walked on, glancing into a shop window and then clicking his tongue at the price of a pair of trainers. Germany was expensive, the hotel bill inflated, the service sullen. But then again, Jimmy couldn't complain, the food and surroundings might have been average, but the bed had been perfect. As perfect as the woman in it, and the time they had spent there.

He smiled to himself, walking on, turning up the collar of his jacket. Should have brought some warmer clothing, but what the hell, he was going home and the forecast said the weather was mild in England. Foggy in parts, but mild. He knew all about the foggy part since it had been hampering his communication with Gus. No signal in Hampshire. And when he had tried the landline at Graybrooke Lodge that had been out of order too. How did people live like that? He wondered. No proper services, no shops within reach, it was like the 18th century. Creepy, Jimmy thought; time locked, suspended.

He didn't like things being held up, or old fashioned. Didn't like anything slow: slow talking, slow walking, slow thinking. No, that wasn't for Jimmy Gold. It was true he had been a bit too hasty in the past, too greedy, too fly, a spell in prison teaching him keep moving - but with his eyes open. He did a soft shoe shuffle and smiled to himself. Yes, Jimmy thought, fast was good. Especially when you were digging into scandals from the past. Speed was how you kept alert, speed gave you a chance to outrun anything. Unless you were John Cummings.

Feeling a tap on the shoulder, Jimmy turned and smiled. He had wondered if he would see Lily again before he left Germany and hugged her.

"You didn't leave your number --"

"**I got the job!**" she said excitedly, waving a piece of paper around her head, a couple of passersby glancing over. "I actually got the bloody job! And I wasn't the prettiest girl there."

"Don't believe it, you must have stunned them." He kissed her, feeling her nose cold against his skin. "You're freezing."

"Yeah. But I don't feel it, I'm too happy. We need to celebrate."

He wavered, "I can't. I'm going back to London. Flight at ten."

"That's hours away!" She said, pulling a face. "Oh, come on, we could have a couple of drinks and *then* you could leave for the airport." She stroked his cheek, her red hair vibrant against the grey concrete that surrounded them. "Jimmy, come on, please….." Then she drew back, disappointed. "You don't want to spend time with me?"

"That's not fair! I've just *got* to leave, I'm expected back and my flight's booked." He paused, studying her face, the brilliant bright eyes, the upturned mouth. "Ok, we'll have one drink - two at the most - but I *have* to leave at eight thirty. No later."

She leaned against him, snuggling. "You sure about that?"

"Yeah, I'm sure. Don't make me miss my flight, Lily." She moved away, laughing as he ran after her. "I'm warning you, don't make me miss my flight!"

THIRTY TWO

Graybrooke Lodge
Hampshire

In silence, Gus walked on, Je-Yun following him through the fog. At times uncertain of the way Gus would pause, the Korean then taking the lead and moving confidently ahead. He had the impression that if he had tried to linger in the grounds Je-Yun would have remained by his side, accompanying him for as long as he remained there. In Gus's pockets were the keys he had yet to use. The keys that had belonged to Addison Franckel; the keys that had been delivered to him in a way he had yet to understand.

When the Ice House door had closed on him he hadn't immediately panicked. Instead he had searched for a lock, thinking that perhaps Franckel's keys could be used to escape. But there had been no lock, nothing in the solid stone door to offer a release, Gus shivering, an ice draft coming from under the door. And it was then that he wondered if he had been deliberately trapped, and if he was going to be left there. If he was even expected to die there. Because who would know? The building was a long way from the main house, in deserted grounds that no one visited, with no one in earshot, and the winter cold slowly seeping into his body. He would have lasted a few days, no longer…

In silence, the two men walked on, Gus herded back to the house like a recalcitrant dog. What neither of them knew was that Ronnie Gilchrist was following. She had escaped the worst of the brambles and broken masonry, but the hem of her coat was torn, her shoes scraped and her gloves shredded from holding back thorn bushes.

And as Ronnie followed them, taking care to keep enough distance to ensure she was not heard nor seen, her gaze fixed on the men's silhouettes in the fog, the rough path underfoot ending as they reached the wood. The overhang of interlocking branches made the fog thicker there, the snap of breaking twigs exploding like firecrackers, Ronnie pausing momentarily. She wanted to rest, but was afraid of losing contact, her breath catching in her throat as the men suddenly disappeared.

Silence fell, the fog seeming to have swallowed them, Ronnie panicking as she spun round, peering into the greyness that surrounded her, straining to catch a glimpse of the men. The fog seemed to enclose her, blank out vision and sound, Ronnie seeing the blurred outline of a figure standing a few feet away.

Her immediate relief was replaced by fear. The figure did not move, but remained, silent, watching her. The outline was too slight for a man, Ronnie could see that, realising in same instant who it was. The woman that had watched her through the library window.

Frightened. Ronnie shouted at the top of her voice, loudly, repeatedly, calling for help, the sound of footsteps approaching fast.

"*Ronnie?*" Gus said, taken aback. "What are you doing out here --"

She cut him off, turning to Je-Yun. "*Who is she?*"

"Who are you talking about?"

"*That woman!*" Ronnie cried out, pointing behind her. "There's a woman standing just there. She's following me. **Who is she?**" Her voice rose frantically, panicked. "Get me out of here! Get me out of this fucking place!"

"It's the fog," Je-Yun said calmly. "It plays tricks with your eyes --"

Gus cut him off. "Just get us back to the house! We'll follow you.

Nodding, Je-Yun took the lead. It took almost ten minutes to return to Graybrooke, Ronnie stumbling alongside Gus, finally breaking into a run when she saw the house. Once inside, she threw off her coat and faced Je-Yun, her hands on her hips, her face bloodless.

"*Who is she*? And don't give me any bullshit, there *was* a woman out there, the same woman I saw through the library window." She spun round on Gus. "*You've* seen her as well, haven't you? Don't deny it, this place is haunted."

"Ronnie, it's the fog –"

"Liar!" She shook her head, badly frightened, then moved over to the staircase and was about to mount the first step, when the Korean blocked her way.

"Where are you going?"

"To talk to your employer."

"Mr Willes is seriously ill. He cannot be disturbed."

"Why not? His guests are well and truly disturbed." She shot a look at Gus. "I want to know what's going on here! I want to know who that woman is, and why Louis Willes isn't bothered about the murder of John Cummings. To be honest, he looked like he *already* knew. And so did you, Gus."

"You're wrong --"

"Am I? So how did you get the news first? And don't give me that guff about the internet!" Her voice rose. "I want the truth! And *you* can get out of my fucking way!"

Thwarted, she tried to push past Je-Yun, but he stood his ground. "Ms Gilchrist, please be reasonable. You are upset, but we are all stranded here at present and must make the best of it. As soon as the fog lifts, you will be able to leave --"

"Aren't you going to tell me who she is?" Ronnie said, exasperated. "Is it Ava, the wife of Louis Willes?"

"There is no ghost --"

"**Don't lie to me!** I heard you talking to the old man earlier. I heard him say '*... You think she'll come?*' And then he said he wasn't afraid of the dead." She stared at Je-Yun defiantly. "He was talking about his late wife, wasn't he?"

"You misheard --"

"**I did not!** And I didn't mistake what I saw either! I saw a woman and she wasn't a living woman." Her voice began to calmed, its tone malicious. "I heard Louis Willes talking about his wife. How she loved the Fuseli painting of *The Nightmare.* You can bet *that* got my attention. I mean, isn't that what we're all caught up in? The Fuseli book, the picture, the murder of John Cummings." Her voice became shrill. "*What's the con-*

nection? There **must** be one, some link between Ava Willes, Fuseli, and this place."

"Ms Gilchrist --"

She put up her hands to silence him. "Willes was talking about the lights in the garden, and you told him that they would turn on *'if she comes tonight.'*"

"It was a private conversation," Je-Yun said coldly. "Mr Willes imagines things."

"Really?" Ronnie countered. "Did he imagine the past too? He was talking about his wife and their life together in some detail. How he had always been interested in Fuseli, but it was her that *'fed the obsession.'* And that *'... the house wanted it too.....'*" Ronnie gave Je-Yun a baffled look. "*The house wanted the painting*? What does that even fucking mean!"

"It was a private conversation --"

"You keep saying that! But it's not an answer, is it?" Ronnie challenged him. "Does it all revolve about the painting? Willes has spent years of his life working on the Fuseli book, but I think there's more to it."

"Ms Gilchrist --"

"I haven't finished!" Ronnie snapped. "And then I heard Willes said something else. That *'... Addison Franckel hung it over his desk...'*" She saw Gus react and turned on him. "Who the hell was Addison Franckel? Was he an art dealer who once lived here?" Gus didn't reply, Ronnie pushing him. "Come on, tell me! Because if you're keeping secrets for Louis Willes, I'd be careful, because I'm not sure he means you well."

"I've had enough of this," Gus replied, unnerved by the mention of Franckel. "I'm going to bed --"

"You're lucky if you make between the sheets tonight." Ronnie responded. "If I were you, I'd watch your back. Earlier I overheard Willes ask where you

289

were, and Je-Yun replied that you were *'sleeping elsewhere.'*" She looked from one man to the other, anger making her reckless. "And then I find that you'd been locked in the Ice House --"

"It was an accident" Je-Yun said steadily "the door swung closed."

"Of course it did!" She replied, turning to Gus. "And it was very lucky that Je-Yun found you there with the help of a psychic dog, wasn't it? But ask yourself this - did he find you *before* he realised I was watching him? Or *after?*" She snatched up her coat and bag, staring at the Korean. "Don't worry, I won't disturb your employer tonight. I'll let him rest - you just make sure I do the same."

Maida Vale
London

It wasn't a course of action Ella Fairchild would have taken at any other time of her life, but this *wasn't* at any other time and she needed information. The burglary had unnerved her, her home suddenly invaded, under threat, and she was dreading the night. It was one thing to be courageous, but quite another to be fearless alone. So the unexpected arrival of the fastidious and polite Paul Shore had been a comfort, his presence welcome as he listened to her recount the conversation she had just had with Freddy Wilson.

"Are you sure he doesn't have your address?"

"He says not."

"But how can you be certain?" Paul replied, "I was given your details and he's being directed by the same contact that put us in touch."

"True, but Freddy Wilson isn't related to one of Franckel's patients, he's his son."

"All the more reason to keep him at arm's length." Paul replied. "Have you met him?"

"Oh yes." She said dryly. "A sly man, greedy for money, would betray his father without giving it a second thought. But he's a long time addict and his memory's bad. When you talk to him you can't work out what he remembers and what he's just made up to please you in order to get paid."

"So why were we put in touch with him, of all people?"

"Because we *all* want revenge." Ella replied. "We want it for our relatives; I suppose Freddy Wilson wants it for his mother's suicide and his own dismal life. Thing is, he won't tell me how he found out his father was dead. He admitted searching for him, but won't tell me who gave him the news. He said he *'just heard it.'* Now honestly, does that sound likely?" Reaching for the teapot she frowned as she touched the side. "It's cold, I'll make us some more tea. Or would you prefer a brandy? I think I would." It was coming up for one thirty in the morning, a long night ahead, Ella hesitating before she spoke again. "You'd be welcome to stay here, Paul."

He shuffled his feet. "Oh, I don't think --"

"There's a guest bedroom with its own bathroom. It would be no trouble and I'd like the company."

"But you don't know who I am."

"You don't who I am," she replied, deftly. "For all you know *I* could be running the whole charade. After all, who would suspect an old woman?" Smiling, she rose to her feet. "I'll get the brandy."

Left alone in the sitting room, Paul's looked about him. There was a dated oil portrait, a collection of Imari china, and a new laptop in pride of place on a walnut sideboard. It was obviously expensive, pert in its red casing, as flippant as a poppy in a field of thistles. Paul had never been interested in such things, teaching in the traditional way, the slow infiltration of computers eventually becoming one of the reasons he retired at sixty five.

"You're admiring my new laptop," Ella said, returning to the room and handing Paul a glass of brandy. "A costly extravagance, but necessary --"

"How did he find us?"

She was wrong footed by the unexpected change of topic. *"Pardon?"*

Paul repeated the question. "How did our contact find us? He *must* have a list of the patients that attended Franckel's clinic and tracked down their surviving family members with it." He stared at her intently. *"But how did he get hold of the list?"*

The question was a good one. "I don't know."

"I was told that everything was destroyed."

"Who told you that?"

"The police. I went to see them back in 1960's. I said I believed that there had been medical abuse - 'maltreatment' they called it then. When they asked me for details I told them about Addison Franckel and his clinic and was immediately informed that the clinic had been closed and that *'everything had been attended to.'* When I asked by whom, I was threatened."

"How?"

"Apparently my accusations were slanderous and I was told – advised - that I should forget the matter." He sipped the brandy, felt the warmth down his throat, the lingering afterglow, and smiled. "I haven't drunk brandy for many years. Not since I was married."

Regaining her seat, Ella returned the smile. "Are you still married?"

"No. Sadly a widower now. No children, no family at all - I imagine that was your next question." He sipped the drink again. "This is all rather wonderful, you know. I should feel guilty for even admitting it, but my life has been a colourless experience and this *adventure* - could it be called such? - has made me grieve for all the times I avoided taking a risk for the sake of a quiet life."

The feeling wasn't new to her. "Have you heard from our contact lately?"

"No, not for several days."

"I suppose we just have to wait for them to get back in touch." She paused, her thoughts returning to the previous subject. "Who told Freddy Wilson that his father was dead? That's was all I asked him. It was a simple question, but he overreacted. Why would he do that? I even offered him money to tell me, but he refused and ended the call. *Why*?" She glanced over to Paul.

He shrugged. "I don't know. Is it important?"

"I think it might be," she replied, continuing. "What if he was *afraid* to tell me? So scared that even money couldn't persuade him to talk. He'd kept quiet for decades, but then he was contacted out of the blue and the past got dredged up - together with all the old reminders of *why* he had wasted his life. And then he suddenly saw a way to make money. He's a greedy man. When you talk to him his speech veers from confusion to rage; the past and the present get mixed, and then his anger makes him aggressive, reckless." She paused, thinking. "A man like that is a menace to people wanting to keep a secret."

"You think he's in danger?"

She shrugged, "Maybe, but one thing's for certain, forgetting is no longer an option for Freddy Wilson."

THIRTY THREE

Graybrooke Lodge
Hampshire

Morning came in cold, the thick press of fog clinging to the house, Gus sleeping for an hour or so then waking, trying his mobile and finding there was still no signal. All night Ronnie Gilchrist's words had resonated in his head. When Willes had asked Je-Yun where Gus was, he had replied that he was '...*sleeping elsewhere..*'

That meant only one thing – that he had trapped Gus deliberately. If Willes did not expect to see him in the morning it would be easy to explain; Gus had slept elsewhere and was running late. And perhaps when he didn't reemerge later, Je-Yun would say that Gus had returned to London.

And how long would it have been before he was found in that freezing tomb? Asleep, or dead? Another thought followed on. Would Je-Yun *ever* have released him if Ronnie hadn't been wandering the grounds? Or would he *still* be locked in the darkness without light and no escape? Shouting for help, hammering on a stone door, Graybrooke deaf and peaceful in the distance... Unnerved, Gus moved into the bathroom, splashing his face with water. Stop it, he told himself, he was becoming paranoid. He had misread the situation, let his imagination escalate. As for the gunshots, it probably had been a poacher, there had been no one shooting at *him*. The door of the Ice House had swung closed by accident and Ronnie Gilchrist had misheard a private conversation...

That's what he told himself at four am. By five, he no longer believed it. At six, he gave up on any chance of sleep, dressing, and going down to the kitchen. He was braced for a confrontation, Je-Yun coming up behind him.

"You have injured your hand, Mr Egan, please allow me to tend it to."

Without resisting, Gus watched as he unwrapped the bloodied handkerchief, frowning as he saw Gus's lacerated palm.

"The grounds here are very dangerous, too overgrown to wander in safely. Especially at night and in bad weather." He was cleaning the wound, putting antiseptic on it. "Ms Gilchrist is a highly strung lady."

"Perhaps she has reason to be."

"I imagine that she feels cut off, isolated out here with us." Gus noted the use of the word 'us', an obvious ploy to make them feel allies. "And being an American makes it more difficult. England is a complicated country, I felt the same when I first came here, and Graybrooke is remote, gloomy in winter. It must feel very strange to her."

Gus kept watching as his hand was bandaged, as neatly as a someone wrapping a Christmas present, the gauze interlocking in precise strips, the remainder tied around his wrist above his watch.

"How does that feel?"

"Fine," Gus replied, "Are you going to run me a bath now?"

Je-Yun's eyes flickered. "Please do not believe what Ms Gilchrist said, she was eavesdropping and could not have heard our conversation with any accuracy." He moved to the counter and began to make coffee, Gus watching.

"So she was lying about all of it? Even the talk of Ava Willes, the Fuseli painting, and Addison Franckel? Isn't it odd that when I spoke to your employer about him, he claimed to know nothing? And yet he knew Franckel hung a copy of *The Nightmare* over his desk." Gus paused, glancing towards the kitchen window. "What were you doing outside last night?"

Je-Yun reached into the fridge for milk. "I told you, the dog alerted me."

"Does she do that a lot? I mean, does she tell you when there are other things happening?" Gus asked wryly. "Like ghosts women appearing and disappearing?"

"Sometimes animals see more than we do."

Exasperated by the enigmatic reply, Gus changed tack. "I've been wanting to ask this for a while - how did you come to work for Mr Willes?"

"As I said before, he hired me from a London agency."

"For a position in Hampshire?"

"They find employees for situations worldwide."

"But not in Korea?"

"I wish I could settle your doubts," Je-Yun replied, "you seem hostile towards me and suspicious of Mr

Willes. However I put it down to our American visitor. You must admit that the house has been disturbed since Ms Gilchrist arrived."

"Oh, it was disturbed long before then," Gus answered. "Look, I'm just interested in doing the research for the book --"

"And yet you were in the garden last night searching for something." Je-Yun replied calmly. "It would be so much easier if you would tell me what you're looking for, possibly I could help you," he glanced at Gus's bandaged hand "or at least prevent any more night time injuries. Mr Willes would be most unsettled to hear what's going on."

"What *is* going on?"

"You tell me, Mr Egan. It's obvious that you didn't want anyone to know what you were doing last night, so why the secrecy?"

Gus poured himself a cup of coffee and moved to the door, then paused. "I don't have to answer to the hired help. You just stuck to your job, and I'll stick to mine."

As though he was waiting for him, Louis Willes was in the hallway, leaning on a cane.

"Sleep well?" He asked, jerking his head towards the library. "No time to lose, we've a book to finish. Thank God that bloody American woman hasn't put in an appearance yet." He had been given his medication, his attitude sprightly, pain free. "Fog's still here, can't see a bloody thing outside. Little dog won't venture more than a few feet to relieve itself."

"She seemed very active last night."

Willes ignored the comment, moving towards his desk and sitting down, *The Nightmare* looming behind him. "Did you do the research on Fuseli in Germany?"

298

"I did. He was there from 1779 to 1780, met up with his friend Johann Lavater and completed a sketch design for some of his Shakespeare illustrations." Gus reached for his notes. "It was at the time he was heart-broken over Anna Landolt."

"Women should be avoid at all costs," Willes said darkly, then laughed. "You know that Ronnie Gilchrist has a thing for you? Her reputation is pure paprika. There are a few dealers in New York who admire her abilities, but word is that she got where she is horizontally."

Gus glanced over to the old man, his head crowned by the image of the Incubus behind him, the affect unpleasant.

"Je-Yun was saying that your late wife was a great admirer of Fuseli, that she encouraged your interest in the artist." He was feeling his way, inching along. "Addison Franckel had a copy of *The Nightmare* too and apparently hung it just where you've hung yours."

If he was expecting some confession, he was disappointed.

"Well, why not?" Willes replied, "It's the only wall space big enough, and it gets the light from the window--"

"How did Je-Yun know?"

"*What?*"

"That Addison Franckel had the same painting and hung it in the same place?"

"You're obsessed with that dead shrink!" Willes replied, almost amused.

"But don't you think it's strange that a Korean, who only moved to England a few years ago, knew all about the interior layout of this place in the 1940's?"

"Maybe he saw a photograph."

299

"You have photographs of Graybrooke Lodge at that time?"

"Maybe."

"Can I see them?"

"If I can find them. Unlike you, I don't have a passion for the last resident, or for his furnishings --"

The words came out of Gus's mouth before he could check them. "Is it the *same* painting?"

In silence, Willes studied him across the room, his balding head and sloped shoulders hunched over the desk, the Incubus behind him. For a moment Gus wavered, the fog outside muffling the light and making the room oppressive. He had a sudden and unexpected impression of Louis Willes as a younger man, full fleshed, holding court before his admirers who had come to play homage to their mentor, whilst the Incubus looked on. The painting glowered down from its frame, enveloping Willes and the photograph of his late wife on his desk, the sudden entry of Ronnie Gilchrist breaking the spell.

"I've got a signal!" she said triumphantly, waving her phone at Gus, then turning to Willes. "The forecast said the fog should clear today --"

"Then you can leave, and we can take down the bunting."

"You're a shit, Louis." She glanced over to Gus, her expression challenging. "Did you sleep well?"

"Better than expected."

"So how long exactly do we continue to play this game?"

Willes let his reading glasses slide down his nose, glancing over to her. "*Game?* What game?"

"Pretending that everything is normal here, when anyone can see it's not." She took in a breath, exhaling loudly. "When I get back home --"

"You'll send flowers and a thank you note," Willes said mockingly. "Dear God, you're so hysterical, Ronnie, all worked up over a little fog and no mobile signal. You've had a bad case of the Robinson Crusoes, feeling abandoned. What *did* you think was going to happen to you here? Gang rape? Or perhaps a meeting with the killer of John Cummings? The way you've been acting it's almost as though you think it's one of *us*." His eyes were flint like. "My apologies, but life is very dull here. And *my* life - what is left of it - is not to be wasted listening to someone who talks like a fortune cookie. That is what they call them in the U-S-A, isn't it?"

She flinched. "You're despicable --"

"I'm also busy," Willes replied, "so if you'd leave us to work, that would be appreciated. Have a look round the house, open some more doors, snoop a little, it will kill time. Oh, but stay out of the grounds, Ronnie. Things become dangerous when you can't see where you're going."

THIRTY FOUR

"Gus, thank God!" Ziva said, her voice relieved over the phone line. "When I couldn't get hold of you I was beginning to panic --"

"Signal's bad out here; it's back on now, but unreliable. The fog doesn't help." Gus replied, moving into his bedroom and closing the door, then locking it. Automatically he kept his voice low. "You sound upset, what's happened?"

"Something that's troubled me." She then told him about the stranger who had approached their son, Gus's voice anxious. "Is Mark alright?"

"He's fine," she reassured him "he refused the man's offer of a lift --"

"I should think he bloody did!"

" -- and he's at home now. In his room with Ben playing video games *again*. They're carrying on from yesterday and the noise is deafening." She took in a breath, releasing it slowly. "Jesus, I was *so* scared. I rang Jimmy when I couldn't get hold of you."

"I want you to keep Mark home from school."

"I can't do that! He won't agree to staying home." She paused, then asked. "What about Sunday when this man said he was coming to see you. What do we do?"

"I'm going to call the police. In the meantime get a friend to stay with you. I don't think you're in danger, this is just a threat. A way to make sure that I realise they're serious."

"Why didn't you tell me what was going on?" Ziva said, irritated. "You could have prepared me --"

"For what? I didn't know this was going to happen, and I didn't want to frighten you for no reason. I thought that if I did what they wanted that would be the end of it." He rubbed the back of his neck to loosen the tension in his muscles. "I can't get out of it, Ziva, I have to do what they ask."

"'They.'" She repeated, "Jimmy told me *they* were the authorities --"

"Jimmy has a big mouth."

"Jimmy has a big heart too, and he knew I was scared." She sighed. "I pressurised him into telling me what was going on. And he did - but only up to a point, because he didn't want to break a confidence."

"It's Ok," Gus said, calm again. "I'm glad you called him."

"I wasn't trying to cause problems between you two --"

"You didn't, I overreacted. Just tell me what else Jimmy said."

"He told me that they've got you over a barrel. But he didn't - *wouldn't* - say why. So you tell me, Gus. Don't lie to me, don't try and protect your family, because ignorance is not our best defence. I need facts, and I need them now."

It was no time to hold back. "Addison Franckel was involved in some unethical treatment. And he was making tapes of his patients."

"Filming abuse?"

"I don't know."

"Violence?"

"I don't know –"

"You don't know?"

"No, I don't, because I haven't seen them!" Gus replied shortly. "They were destroyed by the authorities. No one would ever talk about Franckel, or The Incubus Tapes."

"Incubus? Is that where the connection with Fuseli comes in?"

"It must be, but I haven't worked out *how*." Gus admitted. "I'm treading carefully here, Ziva, but I know I'm being watched."

"Who's watching you?"

"Willes, via his assistant. I don't know who to trust, and this place is so isolated." He paused, listening for anyone moving outside his room. When he was certain there was no one there, he continued. "Louis Willes is hiding something, I know that much. His assistant? God knows what he's up to. He's devoted to his employer, perhaps too much, they seem like confidantes. There was something else that bothered me. When I told Willes about the murder of John Cummings he was sanguine. A killing that has upturned the art world seemed trivial to him. He must know that the dealers will be running scared --"

"Why would they be?"

"Because they'll be wondering how someone got to John Cummings. He was the man who had body-guards, extreme 24 hour security, the man who was

305

overtly protected, with handpicked staff. A man who kept himself remote, but never alone. So how did they get to him? Why did they kill him? For the painting?... That's what the dealers will be asking themselves, and wondering who else has been involved with the Fuseli. Who else might be in danger."

"Does anyone know who the owner is?"

"Obviously Cummings knew. Who knows if he told anyone else. He was notoriously secret, hid all his dealings and only confided in his brother and father."

"So ask them. Maybe they know."

"Maybe they do," Gus agreed, "but then again, maybe it would be better if they *didn't* know. Cummings handled that painting and got killed for his trouble..." He sighed. "None of this makes sense, Ziva. Thieves are hired to 'steal to order', but murder? No, that's not the way it goes."

There was interference on the line, Ziva raising her voice. "So what's special about this picture that it's causing all the turmoil?"

"It was the last version of *The Nightmare* that Fuseli painted. It's considered to be the best one and because it's such a huge find every dealer and collector wants it."

She knew the next question to ask. "Does it have a genuine provenance?"

"As genuine as it gets. *Too* genuine. Fakes, good ones, always come with a great provenance. As reliable as a reference from someone who got fired."

"But this Fuseli's checked out?"

"Enough for John Cummings, and he knew the business."

"How did Cummings get hold of it in the first place?"

Gus kept his voice lowered. "Usual way, I suppose. He would have been approached by the seller's agent. They'd know Cummings had all the contacts to get them the best price."

"I know it's getting loads of attention, but d'you think it's a genuine Fuseli? Forget all the PR, the provenance, the fact that someone was murdered in order to get hold of it. *Is it genuine*?"

"It's a forgery." Gus said firmly. "I've thought that from the start. No proof, just a feeling. But if I'm right it means that John Cummings died for nothing."

There was a sudden distortion on the line, the mobile signal fading in and out. "Take care of yourself, Gus!" Ziva shouted. "And don't forget to ring Jimmy!"

Whilst he still had a signal, Gus put in a hurried call, praying that Andy Fields would pick up on his private line. A police detective in the East End, they had known each other for years, Gus sometimes asking for information when he was a dealer, trying to check out one of the many ex-cons and thieves employed in the demi monde of the art world. A place where once he been an unsuspecting victim. Later, when he was fighting the accusation of dealing in fakes, Gus had turned to Andy Fields, and it had been Andy who had put Gus in touch with another detective. A man knowledgeable about the trading - importing and exporting - of forgeries. His advice had been sound and had, after a torturous few months, ultimately cleared Gus. The help Andy had given when Gus had been facing a jail sentence had never been forgotten.

Unwilling to explain his situation over voice mail, Gus left a short message asking for Andy to call back, and only fifteen minutes later Andy Fields replied, his rasping voice reverberating down the line.

"Christ, Gus, I haven't heard from you for a while! How are you, we should meet up."

"We should, and we will."

"I gather this isn't a social call. You in trouble?" He said with a kind of grim humour. "Again?"

"I'm in a situation I can't get out of --"

"Art dealing?"

"Indirectly, but this is worse, it's involved my family." Gus replied, keeping his voice lowered as he explained about Louis Willes, Graybrooke Lodge and the newly discovered painting.

In silence Andy listened, waiting for Gus to finish before replying. "And you've no idea who the anonymous contact is?"

"None."

"You tried to trace him?"

"Yes, no luck."

"And you've not met up with him?"

"No. But my son has –"

"How come?"

"He stopped Mark outside his school, saying he was an old school friend of mine. Apparently he intends to visit my ex-wife's home this weekend, when I'll be there."

"How does he know that?"

"There's only one way he would. He's been watching."

"So what does he want?"

"Information on Addison Franckel and his clinic. Justice for five dead patients. I told him to go to the police if he was talking about murder and he said that the authorities suppressed everything in the 1940's and would do the same now."

"Tell him to fuck off."

"I can't do that."

"Why?"

"My grandfather was one of the patients who died."

Andy took in a breath, his voice abrupt when he spoke again. "You *do* know that patients sometimes die in hospitals?"

"This is no joke."

"I'm not laughing. How d'you know if this shrink did anything unethical?"

"He made tapes of his patients. They were seen by the powers that be and then Addison Franckel disappeared. We can't even find a record of his death."

"Who's 'we?'"

"I'm talking to relatives of the dead patients. We were introduced to each other by this anonymous contact. Oh, and I've got Jimmy Gold helping me."

There was a snort of laughter down the line. "*Jimmy Gold*! Bloody hell, how is that little runt? Still going straight?"

"Like the MI."

"More like a scenic railway. Crafty little bugger." Andy replied, laughing. "But if he's working for you, good luck. He'll ferret out any secrets --"

"He's uncovering stuff already." Gus agreed, continuing. "As for the tapes. Copies survived, and I'm supposed to find them."

"*If* they still exist. And if they do, what do they want them for?"

"To expose Franckel."

"He's dead."

"But his followers aren't! There are psychiatrists in Germany and Switzerland who are now using his methods."

"What *are* his methods?"

"I don't know until I see the tapes."

"So you're supposed to do *what* exactly?"

"It seems I'm the appointed grave robber to dig up the past *and* the dead." Gus's voice was bitter. "Meanwhile my family is being threatened to make me take them seriously. Come on, Andy! There has to be a way I can protect them."

There was a long pause on the line. "The trouble is that unless there's an actual physical assault, the police can't do anything. Threats are nasty, but usually harmless."

"The man accosted my son!"

"But he didn't harm him."

"I have to wait until he does? Jesus, what the fuck is you talking about!"

"Does anyone have a grudge against you?"

"No." Gus replied. "Not that I know of. But interestingly enough, the dealer who had possession of the Fuseli painting was murdered two days ago --"

"Murdered?"

"In Zurich. The Swiss police are handling it. John Cummings was killed and the picture was stolen."

"You think it's all interlinked?"

"Yes, and I'm getting nervous." Gus admitted. "I'm worried about my family. I *have* to protect them, there has to be *something* you can do."

"I can't act on a threat. You said this 'Grant' was coming to see you on Sunday?"

"That's what he told my son."

"He probably won't turn up. He might just have said it to unsettle you." Andy replied, his voice serious. "If it was me, I'd get my family out of the house and wait for him alone --"

"That's just what I plan to do."

"Frankly, I don't think he'll appear. People who threaten are usually cowards, they like tugging at the victim's strings but won't risk getting tied up." He sighed down the line. "You're in a bit of a mess..."

"I know."

"… got yourself mixed up in something you'd do well to get out of."

"I can't, until I find the bloody tapes."

"And when you do, what happens next?"

"They'll leave me alone." Gus retorted.

"You really think so?"

"My only purpose is to find the tapes --"

"But you said one of the patients that died was your grandfather. They'll know that you'll want to find out what happened to him."

"That's true."

"And if there *were* any murders committed, or you uncovered something sinister, they won't want you walking around with that knowledge, Gus. Not after it was suppressed for so long. It's a hell of a secret for someone to expose --"

"Which is why my family is being targeted to keep me in line?"

"Yes, it looks like that. You said that everything about this doctor was suppressed, and that anyone asking questions was warned off."

"In the 1940's *and* again in the 1980's." Gus replied. "And the journalist who did try to investigate Franckel and his clinic supposedly committed 'suicide'"

"Whoa! When was that?"

"In 1945. His name was Ted MacNeice."

Gus knew Andy Fields would be making a note of the name. "I can have a look around, see if I can find anything on him."

"Yeah, do that for me, would you?"

"No problem.... You're in a bit of a mess, aren't you?"

"You're right there. This bastard knows *everything* about me, Andy. My family, my past. He even knows about the allegations of forgery --"

"So maybe he works in the art world?"

"Maybe he does."

Andy was silent for a moment. "Be careful. You need to watch your back."

"Watch my back?" Gus echoed. "John Cummings had 24 hour security, but look what happened to him."

Berlin
Germany

Calling the number on Jimmy Gold's mobile, she waited, hearing it ring out and then finally answered.

"Hello!" a voice said urgently. "*Jimmy!* Thanks for getting back to me --"

"It's not Mr. Gold," a woman replied in perfect English, "this is Nurse Fischer. Are you Gus Egan?"

She could hear his hesitancy down the line, the familiar reaction. He had heard the word 'nurse' and had realised that if she was using Jimmy Gold's phone it couldn't be good.

"Yes, I'm Gus Egan. Where's Jimmy?"

"I'm calling from the Alexianer St Hedwig Hospital in Berlin. Do you know a Mr. Jimmy Gold?"

"*Yes!* Yes, I know him. Is he alright?"

"You're listed as his first contact --"

"Is he injured?"

"I'm afraid that Mr. Gold was hit by a car earlier today. He sustained a serious head injury and has been placed in a coma to reduce the swelling in his brain." She was being professional to avoid a panicked reaction, knowing that traumatised people responded in two ways; dazed, or confrontational.

"What happened?"

"Does Mr. Gold have family we can contact?"

"No, no one. I'm the closest he has to family. How bad is he? Is he going to be alright?"

"The doctor will speak with you shortly --"

He interrupted her. "I need to see him."

"The doctor --"

"Not the doctor! *I need to see Jimmy*!"

"The doctor will explain the situation, Mr. Egan. Please try to be calm --"

"How did it happen?"

"I have a contact number for the police officer who was at the scene."

The nurse sensed that he had guessed the answer, but Gus asked it anyway. "Was it a hit and run?"

"I'm afraid so."

"Were there witnesses?"

"The police will be able to tell you that, Mr. Egan, I don't know." She was remaining professional. "I'll text you the name and contact number of the officer who will be in touch. The doctor will try to phone you within the hour. Is this the best number to call you on?"

"Yes, yes…" There was a momentary pause. "Tell me about Jimmy, how bad is he?"

"The doctor will explain --"

"You said he was in a coma."

"He is, it was decided that in Mr. Gold's critical condition it was the best treatment."

"Critical? He's critical?... Could he die?"

"Mr. Egan," she said calmly "Talk to the doctor, I can't tell you anymore. He's the best person to advise you regarding Mr. Gold."

Ealing
London

Planning the route on her Satnav, Caroline Lever then checked the weather forecast. Apparently there had been a heavy fog, but it was supposed to lift after midday, the afternoon and evening promising to be clear. The journey to Damerham, Hampshire, was approximately ninety miles, and expected to take two, maybe three, hours - even in a fifteen year old Renault. Plenty of time to reach there by early afternoon, Caroline thought, if she set off late morning.

The information that Mike had relayed, courtesy of his brother, had stated that Miriam Levy had once been a psychiatric nurse. So although she had later chosen to work on Men's Surgical wards, Caroline had wondered if the elusive *Reid Hall* might have been the private psychiatric clinic where her great aunt had once nursed. The lateral thinking had paid off, and searching for *psychiatric clinics* in records dating back to 1939 she had uncovered Reid Hall, which had then become The Addison Franckel's Clinic, a psychiatric hospital in Hampshire which had been active in wartime, specialising in shell shock. But when Caroline looked for information on the owner, there was only a listing of his name - Addison Franckel.

How likely was it that there had been more than one private clinic in the area? Caroline asked herself, certain that it was the clinic where Miriam had once worked. It was certainly worth a trip to find out if the place still existed. If not as a clinic, as a private house. If it did, perhaps there she could discover more about her relative. As for Ted MaNiece, Caroline had not uncovered anything more than Mike had told her - that he had been an Irishman from Dublin, who had apparently committed suicide.

Packing a small holdall in case she decided to stay overnight, Caroline left London, making good time and crossing the border to Hampshire two hours later. Finding Damerham was more difficult. It was not on the Satnav and when she finally found the place it wasn't large enough to call a village. Book-ended by the green lands of the New Forrest, its main street sported a couple of pubs, an old cinema, and a few well-kept cottages bordering a village pond with a broken bridge.

Parking, Caroline typed the name *Reid Hall* into the Satnav, knowing it was unlikely to be listed. As she expected, there was no entry and grabbing her coat she got out of the car and entered the nearest pub. A couple of regulars looked up as she walked in, nodding at her, curious as Caroline moved over to the bar.

"Hello, can I get a coffee? Black, no sugar."

The landlord was pleasant, welcoming. "My pleasure. Haven't seen you here before."

"I haven't been here before. Drove from London this morning." Caroline replied, glancing through the window. "I heard that you'd had a heavy fog, but it's not bad now."

The barman slid the cup of coffee across to her, taking Caroline's offered money and handing her the change.

"It was a real stinker, you couldn't see more than eighteen inches in front of you. No one went out, terrible for business." He smiled, then became inquisitive. "You have relatives living here?"

"No, it's work. I'm looking for a particular building. I'm doing a research project for an architect." Caroline had prepared her story earlier, unwilling to go into her family history and the obvious questions that would arise. "There was a clinic here once. Is that right?" She took a sip of coffee. "A place called Reid Hall."

The landlord shrugged. "Must have been long before my time. Rings no bells with me. A clinic, you say?"

"Yes, it was in wartime and owned by a doctor called..." she paused, reached for her mobile and checked the name. "…. Addison Franckel. Sound familiar?"

"Nah," he said, calling over to an elderly man sitting alone in the snug. "Seth, *Seth!*"

His customer was warming himself in front of the fire, logs banked high, giving an ochre glow to both him and the grey-muzzled Labrador at his feet. Glancing up when he heard his name he nodded to the landlord and shuffled over.

"What is it?"

"This young lady's come to Damerham looking for a place that was once a..." he glanced at Caroline "…. did you say clinic?"

She nodded. "Yeah, psychiatric clinic."

"*'Psychiatric clinic'*?" He raised his eyebrows. "You know anything about that, Seth?"

The old man stared at Caroline suspiciously. "I've never heard of it. And what would we want with a place like that?"

"It was to treat soldiers with shell shock."

"Nah, not here! You've got the wrong village."

The landlord wasn't accepting the denial. "You *must* have heard of it, Seth. You and your family have lived here all your lives."

"That's the point I'm making!" The old man retorted, his voice raised. "I'd know of a place like that, wouldn't I? Doctors, clinics, psychiatrists, you think we wouldn't know? You're daft if you think that."

"She wasn't insulting you" the landlord said, trying to placate him. "She's a stranger with a job to do. Try and help the young lady. Think back, see if something comes to mind."

"As I said, the doctor's name was Addison Franckel." Caroline added hopefully.

"I don't know that name."

"Does *Reid Hall* sound familiar? That was what the property was called. I mean" she persisted "it *was* here. It's on the records that it existed. Are there any houses big enough to have been used as a private clinic? Any properties that still exist that could have been used for that purpose?"

"Only Graybrooke Lodge," the landlord said thoughtfully. "Now that's a great mausoleum of a house. It's a private home now, owned by some writer who keeps himself to himself, but I daresay it would have been big enough for a clinic with the house and the grounds --"

"It's not the place you're looking for!" The old man interrupted. "You've got the wrong idea, Miss, there was never a clinic in Damerham. Not in wartime, nor any other time. Just private houses. And most of them are long gone." His voice was curt, adamant. "If I were you I wouldn't go bothering Mr Willes at Graybrooke Lodge. Be's dying, they say, and doesn't need nosy Londoners poking around."

"I wasn't going to --"

Before Caroline could finish the sentence Seth got to his feet and headed for the exit, his dog following, the surprised barman watching them leave before turning back to Caroline.

"Well, sorry about that, miss. Old people get that way sometimes. He's not usually so bad tempered, but at ninety he's entitled to speak his mind. Trouble is, you can never tell which way they'll go, nice or nasty." He shrugged his shoulders. "Don't let it bother you. You've come here for a reason, it would be a waste of time and petrol not to see it through."

She smiled gratefully. "Can *you* tell me where Graybrooke Lodge is?"

He pulled a dusty paper napkin towards him on the bar, drawing out the directions, and then handing it to Caroline with a nod. "Mind the last turning before you get to the gates. It's very sharp and the lane's narrow there. Go on," he said, encouraging her "I hope you find what you're looking for. Oh, and remember if you're staying over in Damerham, you can always get a room here. Reasonable rates, off season."

Graybrooke Lodge
Hampshire.

Numbed by the news of Jimmy's accident, Gus walked into the library and stood before the window overlooking the drive. It was his fault. He had placed Jimmy Gold in danger, and it didn't matter than he had underestimated the threat, he *should* have anticipated it. Instead he had sent his best friend on a job that had resulted in him lying in a coma in a Berlin hospital.

If it had been an genuine accident it would have been tragic, but to know that someone had driven a car, a crushing machine of steel and glass into that wiry, hyper-active body, was unbearable. Did they back up and run over him afterwards? Or did the first impact send him up into the air like a flesh kite, only to return, landing broken on German concrete?

Gus knew it had been deliberate. It wasn't an accident. Not some driver panicked by what they had done and driving off. Even before the nurse had told him, he had known. And yet he hadn't expected it - and the thought shamed him. His family had been threatened and he had taken that seriously, but had never worried for Jimmy. His friend knew his way around, he was fly, he was street wise, he was worldly - and now he was fighting for his life.

Since early morning Gus had been working alongside Louis Willes, the historian motivated, eager to write. With surprise, Gus had noticed how quickly he could type, his large bony hands moving over the computer keyboard with alacrity, his bespectacled eyes fixed on the screen. His work had a curious rhythm to it; a few minutes of reading his notes, a scrabble of editing, then the frantic typing. When coffee had been brought to him, Je-Yun had left it beside him on his desk, Willes brushing him away and allowing the drink to go cold. Several times he had looked up and demanded information from Gus - *did you get the dates of the Germany trip made by Fuseli? When were the first Shakespeare illustrations sent for printing?....* and Gus had answered, wondering if Willes had been testing him, or if the compulsion to complete the book reminded him of the little time he had left.

Around three the activity had subsided, Willes's tiring as the pain medication wore off. His limitations had irked him, his sense of helplessness palpable as he fought Je-Yun's advice to rest.

"'*Rest*'? You stupid bugger!" Willes had roared. "I don't need rest, I need energy." He had glanced over to Gus. "You take drugs?"

"No. Why?"

"I just thought if you used that cocaine stuff it might help me out."

Gus hadn't been able to tell if he was serious or not, but only fifteen minutes later Willes had been forced to retire to his bedroom, and almost immediately after that Gus had got the call from Berlin.

And now he was standing by the library window, the fog finally lifting, the heavy grey muffler transformed into a silken mist. He had decided he would leave for London to stay with Ziva and his son. It was Friday, usually he would have left for the weekend already, only the weather delaying him. He then wondered if he should go to Berlin to see Jimmy, deciding to wait until he had spoken to the doctor.

His mobile sounded abruptly, a text message arriving.

I heard about Jimmy Gold, I'm sorry, but you see how we are all in danger?

Gus replied immediately. He had waited two days for a message and had been frustrated by the lack of contact:

*I heard what happened. You stay away from my family, you bastard. God help you if you go near them again. You deal with **me**, you hear? You don't involve them.*

The answer came within seconds.

I have not injured your family. I was merely making a connection.

Gus texted back.

*You accosted my son, and scared my ex-wife. You've got my mobile, contact **me**, not them!*

Again, a reply.

I did not harm your son, I merely said I would call by at the weekend. Surely that can't be perceived as a threat?

Gus's hands were shaking as he texted back:

Make sure you come, because I'll be waiting for you. I want to meet my 'old school friend.' And I want to know if it was you that attacked Jimmy.

There was a longer pause before the reply came.

Perhaps it would be unwise of me to call by. You seem angry, and you might even contact the police in the hopes of setting a trap for me.

No, perhaps we'll meet another time, when you're not so stressed. Just remember one thing, Mr. Egan, when you find the tapes and give them to me, your part in this is over. You'll never hear from me again.

That is what you want, isn't it?

And there the message ended.

Frustrated, Gus threw his mobile across the desk, realising he had acted stupidly. He should have played along, encouraged the man, agreed to meet up, not panicked him.

"Well, you're in a hell of a mood," Ronnie said from the doorway, "the fog's cleared now. I've rung for a cab and they say they'll send someone." She walked over to him. "I don't envy you staying here --"

"Have you spoken to any of the London dealers?"

"What?"

"Jesus, just answer the bloody question, will you!" He snapped. "Have you talked to Edward Leigh or Anthony Hallett?"

She was taken aback by his anger. "I spoke to Anthony first thing this morning. He was really upset about Cummings being murdered, seemed to think that anyone involved was under threat --"

"Was *he* involved?"

"No more than the rest of us." She replied. "We all wanted the Fuseli --"

"You're lying."

She flushed. *"You have some nerve!"*

"What was Anthony Hallett so upset about? The death of a colleague? I doubt it." Gus continued. "Mind you, he's always been greedy. Perhaps greedy enough to do something rash. Or was it his partner?"

"What are you talking about?" She said sharply. "Anthony didn't kill John Cummings!"

"I didn't mean that," Gus replied, "I just want to know who's involved in all of this mess. Who's got an interest in the Fuseli."

"Half the dealers in London –"

322

"No, Ronnie, only a few would be capable of raising enough money to buy it, and then gamble that they could sell it on for a profit. Did Anthony Hallett want it?"

"He was interested at first, but realised that the money Cummings would ask for it would probably be out of his league."

"Edward Leigh?"

She clicked her tongue. "Edward is too gutless to go all out."

"Yes, he is. But you wanted to do a deal *with* him, didn't you?" Gus countered. "Did he agree to it? Perhaps it was his idea to come here and try to pump Willes for information?"

"You think Edward would suggest that?" She replied, raising her eyebrows. "Hardly. He wouldn't want me get ahead of the game --"

"But he was willing to work with you? *How* exactly? Neither of you have the funds to buy the Fuseli if it had ever come up for sale, so were you intending to pool resources?" He paused, smiling. "But of course *you* wanted to see if there was a quicker way and came here direct."

"You know the art world, don't act like a outraged virgin!"

Gus was inching his way along. "What I don't understand is that Anthony Hallett - your sometime lover - is supposed to be a friend of Louis Willes. So why wasn't it Hallett who approached him first?"

"How would I know? Maybe I'm wrong, perhaps he didn't want the Fuseli --"

"Well, that's not true, is it, Ronnie? You **all** wanted it." Gus paused, thinking back. "Doesn't Hallett have a holiday home in Zurich?"

She flinched, it was barely perceptible, but Gus caught it. "Well, doesn't he?" When she didn't respond, he laughed. "Don't deny it! It must have been the perfect love nest for you - and all the others."

Folding her arms, she stared at him. "What are you getting at?"

"The truth." Gus replied. "Where was the Fuseli originally found?"

"Germany."

"Who was selling it?"

"No one knows, it was an anonymous seller."

"Based where?"

"Berlin." She sighed. "You know all of this, it's common knowledge."

"And the Fuseli was sent from Berlin to Zurich for John Cummings to deal with?"

She sighed. "Yeah."

"Who were the transporters?"

"How the hell would I know!"

"You told us a story about the painting having some mishap on its journey --"

"But I don't know who was hauling it!" She snorted. "Why does it matter?"

"Ronnie, you are either very stupid or very cunning. I can't decide which, just as I can't decide if you're involved with Louis Willes in some way, and if the two of you are actually working together."

"So his dislike of me is just to cover his admiration?" She asked, her tone sarcastic. "You really think we've been putting on a show for you? Why would we do that?"

"You tell me."

"Why go to all that trouble just for you? You're doing research for a frigging book, that's the only reason you're here. You're not a dealer anymore, you've been out of the game for a while now. Or maybe you think you've found a way back in?" She tilted her head to one side. "Is that it? So maybe I should ask *you* the same question - are you in league with Louis Willes?"

He smiled slowly. "But I didn't know you were coming here, did I? Whereas you could have been plotting your trip beforehand."

"To do *what?*" She paused, wiggled her index finger at her temple. "You want to get out of here before you lose your mind. It would be so easy. This place is creepy, like the people in it. Think of your career, Gus, and your health. All this stress can't be good for you. Remember how sick you were before? You don't want that to happen again, do you?"

He studied her with contempt.

"You think you and your running mates caused my cancer? You think you have the power? You managed to close my gallery, ruin my reputation, and you and your cronies nearly got me jailed - but you didn't succeed, did you? You tried, but you failed." He looked at her, his expression scornful. "You really *are* a ridiculous woman, Ronnie. You believe that you're better than a lowly researcher, but you really should appreciate my profession, because I find out things people try to hide. You think I don't know about your business? You're holding on by your finger nails, and one push, just one teeny little push, and you'll plummet into bankruptcy --"

"You bastard!"

" -- and if I have any way of helping to make that happen, Ronnie, I will. You trod on my neck, now I get to tread on yours." He paused, then added. "And if you *are* involved with the Fuseli, watch out. John Cummings might not be the only dealer that wished he had never set eyes on that painting."

THIRTY FIVE

Maida Vale
London

Hearing the shower running in the guest bathroom, Ella moved into the adjacent bedroom, hurriedly taking Paul Shore's wallet out of the inside jacket pocket and glancing at the identification. Paul Shore, dob 7.07.35. She was surprised that he was older than her and impressed that he had kept himself in such good health; but she was even more impressed that he was *exactly* who he had claimed to be. Replacing the driver's license in the wallet, Ella noticed a photograph of a woman in middle age, a little overweight, but sweet faced, laughing as she struggling to hold a large cat. A happy woman, Ella thought, not fashionable or elegant, but likeable.

The shower still running, Ella tucked the wallet back into the jacket pocket, then checked the trouser pockets. There was nothing of any note; just car keys, two door keys, a handkerchief, and a little brass figure of a goblin that had to be over fifty years old. Then, as silently as she had entered the room, Ella left, as quickly as her legs allowed. Old age, she thought with resignation, was embarrassing. Retracing her steps back to her own bedroom she stared into the closet. The empty cardboard box was still in the middle of the floor and frowning, she nudged it with her foot, then picked up the phone and tapped out a number.

Gus answered immediately. "Hello?"

"I wonder if I could have a word with you, Mr. Egan?"

"Of course. What is it?"

"It's about Freddy Wilson. He contacted me --"

"When?"

"Last night."

"Just out of the blue?"

"We'd already had a meeting a few days ago--"

His voice became cool. "I wish you'd told me, Mrs. Fairchild."

She batted back a response. "I would have done, Mr. Egan, had your mobile been turned on."

"It was bad weather here and I couldn't get a signal." Gus explained, "So you met Freddy Wilson in person?"

"Yes. He's a nasty old man who hated his father. And still does, but his mind's raddled and his memory's intermittent."

"He made the initial contact?"

"Yes."

"To suggest a meeting?"

"No, I suggested that. In a public place. I was perfectly safe. Well, I thought so, but I've been robbed, Mr. Egan. Nothing to trouble the police, we don't want to involve them. I wasn't home and I wasn't hurt, but the patients' notes that my father left me have been taken. Stolen from my bedroom closet - and I'm wondering who knew they were there."

He picked up the inference immediately. "You think I told someone?"

"No, no...I don't."

"You're right, I didn't. So who else knew about them?"

"No one." She replied. "And anyway, who would want them?"

"Who knows? But obviously someone does. What was the outcome of your meeting with Wilson?"

"Very little. He said that the German police had taken all of Addison Franckel's notes - sorry, I mean Otto Weiner, as he was then. Freddy Wilson also said that his wife –"

"Freddy Wilson's married?"

" – no, I meant his mother, Elise. Apparently she passed some information to a neighbour. He said that when he remembered her details he'd pass them on to me."

"Did he?"

"No, when he phoned last night he was rambling. Drunk, incoherent. Then I asked him again how he had found out his father had died."

Surprised, Gus asked: "Why's that important?"

"Because Freddy Wilson is an addict, who's been drifting around London for decades, homeless, unnoticed. And yet *someone* knew his identity and knew how to find him."

"I see what you mean... And he wouldn't say who?"

"That's the point, Mr. Egan. When I asked he reacted very badly. He seemed afraid." She took in a breath before continuing. "Paul Shore came to see me last night --"

"*Paul Shore*? We haven't spoken yet."

"I know, he told me."

"And he arrived out of the blue?"

"He was given my address –"

"And then you got burgled?"

"Oh, it's not Mr. Shore," she said emphatically. "That would be too obvious, and besides he didn't know about the patients' notes until I told him they had been stolen. We decided that if I told the police about the robbery, I'd have to explain what was taken - and then they'll ask questions and it would all come out. If they suppressed everything before, they might do it again." She hurried on. "I can't risk that! This time we can't be stopped."

"Someone's trying to stop me."

"*What?*"

"My son was accosted and my colleague was the victim of a hit and run yesterday in Berlin --"

"Oh, dear God."

" – just after he had told me that Freddy Wilson had contacted *him* with important information."

"*Freddy Wilson*?" She repeated, confounded.

"Yes. Unless it was someone pretending to be Franckel's son."

"But how could Freddy Wilson know your colleague?" Ella asked, bewildered. "I didn't know you were working with someone, so how could he? What did your colleague tell you?"

"Jimmy didn't have time to tell me anything," Gus replied. "We lost contact and the next I heard he was in hospital in a coma, where he still is, and where his doctor thinks he might stay for a long time… Obviously whatever Jimmy found out was the reason he was stopped."

There was a long pause because she spoke again. "Is your son all right?"

"For now, but I want to get my family out of London."

Silence fell between them, Ella the first to speak. "I never thought it would get so dangerous."

"Didn't you? But you tried to warn me off." His voice was cool. "You were the first person who got in touch with me. The first person I talked to about any of this. I remember that I asked you about the tapes and you denied ever seeing them."

"I haven't seen them." Ella replied. "But I did ask Freddy Wilson about them --"

Gus interrupted her. "You *must* know something! Your father told you all about the tapes, so don't tell me that you have no idea what's on them, or what happened to them."

"*I don't!*"

"I don't believe you!" Gus snapped, "I think you're hiding something. Have you been contacted again?"

"No, I've had no messages, and neither has Paul Shore --"

"The good Samaritan, who turned up just when you needed him." Gus said sardonically "How much do you know about Mr. Shore?"

"His grandmother died at Franckel's clinic. He visited her there often –"

"Has he seen the tapes?"

"No!" She replied, her tone abrupt. "He's as much in the dark as we are. But he did tell me about two other patients who died - Ruby Hodge and Lance Carter.

Miss Hodge's relative wants nothing to do with it, and there are no surviving relatives for Captain Carter."

"Then we need to know more about the journalist," Gus said, changing the subject. "Perhaps Ted MacNeice found something out before he died. I've got the police looking into it --"

She reacted strongly, her voice hostile down the line. *"We don't want the police involved!"*

"He's a friend of mine, and frankly Mrs. Fairchild, I don't care what you want." Gus retorted. "I need to protect my family."

Shaken, Ella ended the call. She found Gus Egan rude, abrasive, and wished she was dealing with someone else. At the same time she could sympathise with his dilemma, then reminded herself that *her* family had suffered. Hadn't her grandfather died at Franckel's Clinic? Gus Egan didn't have a monopoly on grief.

"May I come in?" A voice asked, tapping lightly on the door.

"Yes, of course." Ella replied, Paul entering, fully dressed, his hair still damp from the shower.

"I heard you talking, you sounded upset."

"I was speaking to Gus Egan. I'm afraid he's a man who always unnerves me. Apparently a colleague of his has been injured by a hit and run driver. He believes it was deliberate."

Shocked, Paul stared at her. "Is he dead?"

"No, in a coma."

"Where was this?"

"Berlin," Ella replied, "I don't know what he was doing there, but Mr. Egan is very upset, especially as his family have also been threatened." She moved to the door, Paul following as she made her way downstairs. "Maggie, my daily, will be arriving soon. She'll be happy to make you breakfast --"

"Actually I must be on my way, Mrs. Fairchild," Paul replied. "You've been so kind and I can't impose on you longer."

"Surely you don't have to rush off?"

"I truly wish I didn't have to, but I have an appointment." He picked up his coat and moved to the front door. "I'll call you later. Thank you again."

Surprised, she waved him goodbye from the window, watching him walk down the street and turn at the corner. He walked more like an ex-soldier than a teacher, back straight, his balding head exposed under the unforgiving winter sun. The perfect gentleman. Certainly a comfort to have around after the burglary... and yet he had left very quickly. Perhaps he had noticed that his wallet had been opened, or that his pockets had been searched. Or perhaps he was reacting to the news he had just heard. About Gus Egan's colleague.

"'Is he dead?'"

'Is he dead?' Was it her imagination or had she noticed a nuance of hope in the words?... No, Ella told herself, she was being foolish, it was an innocent question that anyone would ask. It was perfectly normal. And yet it seemed off kilter, and she wondered - for an uncomfortable moment - if she had confided in the wrong person.

Graybrooke Lodge
Hampshire

After calling Ziva, Gus went into the library looking for Louis Willes. His computer was humming, music turned on, a fresh cup of coffee still sporting steam, his tartan dressing gown hanging slovenly over the back of his chair - but there was no sign of Willes. Apparently, his rest completed, his earlier vigour had returned, the slam of a door followed by a hoop of jubilation announcing his entrance.

"The bitch has gone!" he said, flopping into his chair, his long thin legs stretched out underneath the desk, his mood affable. "I think Je-Yun puts something in my food."

"You think he's poisoning you?"

"Jesus, you're insane!" Willes bellowed. "I mean, I think he gives me herbs or some Asian pep me up, which it does. And being rid of that woman is a bonus. Blood sucker. Did she really think she could come here and bleed a dying man dry?" He leaned forwards, matchstick arms folded. "Even if I've had the Fuseli I'd have set it on fire rather than let her get it." He paused, giving Gus a sidelong look. "Did you hear about Anthony Hallett?"

"What about him?"

"Apparently he's invested money in a property previously owned by John Cummings and he's shitting himself because he's now been drawn into the murder investigation." Willes laughed roundly. "Serve him right, his luck's been too good for too long, karma had to get him some time. The Zurich police are '*going to interview him*' about his finances out there, and his property dealings. Dear, dear, poor Anthony."

"So Hallett had a connection to John Cummings?"

"He did."

"Seems like all roads lead back to Zurich --"

"And the Fuseli." Willes finished the sentence. "Can you imagine the PR stunt I could pull off if I had that painting? We could reveal it at the book launch. Now *that* would be real revenge on the business...." He trailed off. "... if I'm around that long."

"It's something to aim for. Especially if you *do* have the Fuseli."

"I don't!" Willes said empathically, "I wish I did, but really I don't."

"Ok, if you say so." Gus changed the subject. "I need to go home a day earlier this week --"

"*Well, you can't!* I need you, even more now. We have to get this book done and time's passing."

"I'll be back Monday." Gus retorted. "What's the problem? I go home every Friday, that was our agreement. This is just a day early, that's all. And I can work at home."

"I want you here!"

"Sorry about that, but I'm leaving tonight."

"If you do, don't come back!" Willes replied, his voice raised. "I mean it, if you go, you can't come back here. No more snooping around Graybrooke, it'll be off limits to you. You think I don't know what you've been up to? Creeping about, looking around the library, at my notes, my private possessions. Oh yes, I know all about it. And I know how you've been searching the grounds --"

Gus stared at him, his voice cold. "You know a lot, but you haven't asked me *why*. That seems odd. You know all about what I've been doing, but you don't you ask me *why* I've been doing it."

Willes paused. "I know why."

"Tell me."

"It's about Addison Franckel."

"Addison Franckel?'" Who's that?' Gus smiled mockingly, mimicking Willes. " '*I don't know much about him, except that he used to live here.*' That's roughly what you told me when I arrived. I knew you were lying then."

Willes shrugged. "I mean what I say - you leave and that's it. You don't come back."

"I have a family that needs me --"

"*Alive.*" Willes said, seeing Gus flinch. "You think I don't have every room in this place filmed? Every word recorded? It was something I set in place years ago. That's how I found out about Anthony Hallett and my wife - and many other things." His eyes narrowed. "Ronnie Gilchrist has sticky fingers. I've got her on tape stealing two pieces of silver. Not thirty, her bag wasn't big enough."

"What the hell are you playing at! It's illegal to film and record people without their knowledge –"

"But I've just told you." Willes replied wryly.

"What's your bloody game!" Gus snapped. "What's going on here?"

Willes laid down his whisky glass and regarded Gus steadily. "You're not leaving tomorrow. Or on Friday. In fact, you're not leaving here at all."

Gus laughed. "Really? You can't stop me."

"You're wrong about that." Willes replied. "Was it very cold in the Ice House?" He asked, watching Gus's face for a reaction. "I thought it would teach you a lesson, stop your wanderings. I *hoped* it would, but it didn't. Which told me a lot about the kind of man you are. And then you got the call about Jimmy Gold."

"*Who are you?*" Gus asked, moving towards him.

"Don't jump to the wrong conclusion!" Willes put up his hands. "It wasn't my doing. I just listened to the call, I didn't organise a hit and run. My interest extends to being a voyeur, not a criminal… Mr. Gold's a bit of a character, isn't he? Perfect terrier to root things out for you --"

"If you heard all my calls you know why I need to be with my family."

Willes clicked his tongue. "You're divorced, you don't even live with them. They don't need you --"

"Fuck off, Willes!" Gus snapped, moving to the door, the old man calling after him.

"Don't leave, or you'll regret it --"

"How d'you work that out?"

"Because we both know that you have to find those tapes - and I'm the only one who can help you do that. Leave Graybrooke, you lose."

THIRTY SIX

Following the directions she had been given and trying to decipher the sketch, Caroline Lever headed for Graybrooke Lodge, missing the first turning and doubling back. At Graybrooke Cottages she paused, then realised she was mistaken and drove on further. The fog had lifted, the afternoon cold but clear, the trees shimmying off the remaining leaves with every gust of wind, the lane mushy under the car wheels. As directed, she took care at the turning, the lane serpentine as she finally reached her destination.

The rusted iron gates were open, the old Volvo under the oak tree, a Peugeot parked by the front entrance, and facing her the remarkable, blasted, and weathered house. It was obviously in need of renovation, and seemed defiant, as though embarrassed by its loss of fortune. As she parked, Caroline noticed lamps turned on in several of the downstairs rooms and many outside lights lining the driveway. Obviously well pro-

tected from burglars, she thought, picking up her handbag and moving to the entrance.

Hopeful, Caroline rang the bell; perhaps here she
would discover more about her relative. Waiting several seconds she rang again, taken aback when the door
opened and Je-Yun welcomed her.

"Good afternoon, may I help you?"

"My name's Caroline Lever, I came…" she fal-
tered, suddenly unsure. "… I came to find out about a
member of my family. She worked here once, a long
time ago."

"This is a private residence, Miss."

"I know it is now," Caroline interjected, "but I'm
talking about when it was a clinic, called Reid Hall. It
was owned by a doctor called Addison --"

"*Franckel.*"

Startled, she looked over to Gus who had just
materialised beside Je-Yun.

"Yes, that's right!" She said, smiling. "Addison
Franckel."

Gus stood back to let her enter. "Come in, please.
Have you come by car?"

"I parked over there, is that alright?" Caroline
asked. "Let me know if it isn't and I'll move it. I drove
from Ealing, luckily missed the fog. I hear it was really
bad --" She stopped short when she came face to face
with the sculpture of the *Dying Gaul*. "Oh, that's quite
something, isn't it? I heard that the present owner was
an art historian. Is that you?"

"No, I'm a researcher, Gus Egan." He extended
his hand, Caroline shaking it, relieved by the welcome.
"Louis Willes is the historian and the owner of the
house. He's seriously ill and resting, but we can talk in

the sitting room." Glancing over to Je-Yun, he added. "Perhaps we could have some tea?"

Unaware of the resentment between the two men, Caroline followed Gus. On the window ledge sat the little terrier, barking as she approached it.

"I wouldn't, she doesn't like women."

"I can see that." Caroline said wryly. "I've just realised that I should have notified you before I came, not just arrived on your doorstep. But I couldn't find any contact details and came on spec." She was talking fast, her nervousness obvious, smiling at Je-Yun as he returned with the tea. Carefully he set it down on a low table between two sofas, then nodded briefly and left the room.

Immediately Gus turned to her. "So you're trying to find a relative?"

"My *only* relative. I don't have any living family. I joined one of those Legacy things and drew a blank, except for one person that I hope to find some trace of." She rummaged in her bag and brought out the notes she had made. "You see, I did a bit of detective work and there was only one clinic in Hampshire that had been operational in the war. *Here.* Well, I *think* it was this house." She hurried on, "I looked at a couple of others on the way, but to be honest, this is the only one big enough."

"You're right. The clinic *was* here."

Caroline smiled. "I knew it! And yet when I asked an old man in the village, he was adamant there had **never** been a clinic. Said he would have known because his family had always lived in Damerham and he'd been here for decades. He even seemed insulted to think there had been a place for people with mental problems. Or suffering from shell shock." She sighed with irritation. "But he *must* have known about it--"

"Before it gets too dark, let me show you the gardens." Gus said suddenly, "Mr. Willes is very proud of them." He ushered her outside, Caroline surprised but following him, Gus turning to explain when they left the house. "Look, I'm sorry to rush you like that, but people don't talk about the Franckel clinic. It's off limits here, a subject that shouldn't be mentioned."

"Why?"

"It's a long story." Gus said. "I'll willingly share what I know, but in return I'd be grateful if you'd tell me about your relative."

She was baffled. *"Why would you want to know about her?"*

"I'll explain later, but not now. Now I just want you to tell me your relative's name."

"Miriam Levy." She could see that the name resonated with him and became nervous. "What's going on?"

"Nothing to worry about. Let's just say that you're not the only person trying to find out about Miriam Levy."

"Are you the police?"

"No, I told you, I'm a researcher." Gus replied, walking alongside her as they crossed the lawn, moving further away from the house. "What relation was Miriam Levy to you?"

"My great aunt."

"You said your name was Lever --"

"My grandfather changed it from Levy. Miriam kept the original family name."

"What do you know about her?"

"Not that much. Together with a friend of mine, we discovered that she worked at St Edward's Hospital in London, in the Psychiatric Department first, then moved over to Men's Surgical." Turning up the collar of her coat against the chill, she shivered. "It said in the records --"

"What records?"

"There's a Registry of Nurses, Miriam was listed on that. It said she went to work in a private clinic after St Edward's, but didn't specify where, only that it was somewhere in Hampshire. So I guessed that perhaps she had returned to psychiatric nursing and then looked up the clinics that specialised in that field. Which brought me here."

She waited for his response, but Gus Egan remained emotionless. "Did you find out anything else about Miriam?"

"Only that she was married to an Irishman called Ted MacNeice."

Abruptly Gus stopped walking. And in that instant Caroline became nervous. She wondered who he was, what she was doing, and if she had been reckless coming to Graybrooke alone. "Maybe I should leave and come back another time --"

"You're safe, don't worry, you're in no danger." Gus reassured her. "Just tell me everything you know about Miriam. And then, when this is all over --"

"When *what* is all over?" She said, her tone insistent. "I don't understand --"

"Just trust me."

"*I don't even know you!*"

"Take a leap of faith, Miss Lever, and listen. You want to know about your relative - for my own reasons, so do I. But you have to keep everything we say confidential. Don't repeat a word to anyone."

"But --"

"The police are looking into Ted MacNeice at this moment. I asked them to. He is not a criminal, neither was your relative, but they were involved in a scandal which has been covered up for decades. And now people are trying to expose it."

She was staring at him, openly suspicious. "What did Miriam have to do with it?"

"She was the Nursing Sister at Addison Franckel's Clinic. Franckel was disgraced and struck off, he then disappeared and anyone trying to investigate him or his treatments was silenced. Ted MacNeice - who you've just told me was married to Miriam Levy - tried to find out what was going on. He failed and he died."

"He died?"

"Apparently he committed suicide."

She stared at him, stunned. "He killed himself?"

"Maybe. Or maybe he was murdered because he wouldn't stop digging... *Now* do you realise why I want you to keep quiet?"

It took Caroline a moment to find her voice, her tone uneven when she answered. "Look, I don't understand any of this, or why Miriam was involved --"

"I imagine that she told her husband about the clinic. He was a journalist, so naturally he'd investigate it - with disastrous consequences."

"There's a record of his death?"

"Yes. Like I said, it was listed as a suicide."

"I couldn't find any death certificate for Miriam. She went missing in the war and was presumed dead. But I hoped that she might turn up. People did. They went missing or moved overseas. Quite a few people declared dead turned up later…." She was talking too much and too fast, gazing blankly over the garden. "I just wanted to know what happened to her. If she *had* survived, made a new life, had children…" Pausing, she turned to Gus. "*Did* she have any children?"

"Not that I know of. Her husband died in 1945."

Subdued, Caroline nodded. "I still don't understand. Why did you want me out of the house?"

"Everything in there is recorded and filmed."

She glanced over to shoulder at Graybrooke. "Are you joking?"

"No, it's no joke, believe me."

"And that's because of the Franckel Clinic?" She asked, hurrying on. "What happened here? I mean, that man in the pub pretended it never even existed."

"They've been pretending that for nearly eighty years."

"So why is someone digging it up now?" She asked, curiosity turning to impatience. "You have to tell me what's going on! I need to know what happened to Miriam."

"That's what I'm trying to discover." Gus took out his mobile and paused. "Give me your number so I can contact you…"

She hesitated.

"… Fine, I'll give you my number." He entered it into her mobile and handed the phone back to her.

"What happens now?"

"You leave and forget you came here."

"I'm not going anywhere! I wanted to trace my relative and I will. I *need* to find her." Caroline hesitated, embarrassed. "I was hoping I could find some family I could visit, share holidays with. You know the kind of thing, TV Christmas adverts…. It was a fanta-

sy." She paused, all levity gone. "I never expected to find something bad… it *is* bad, isn't it?"

"Very," Gus agreed "and I suspect that it's going to get a lot worse."

She paused, shaking her head. "I gave myself away, didn't I? Walking in and announcing why I'd come here --"

"Which is exactly why you can't stay." Gus replied. "Keep in touch with me via phone, but for now, just go. Trust me**, go."**

Nervous, Caroline returned to her car, grinding the gears as she tried to reverse. The winter light was fading, dusk already turning the house into a gloomy monolith, the grounds a daguerreotype of looming shapes and winter trees. Finally managing to turn the car round, she flicked the headlights onto full beam, illuminating the burly form of Gus Egan, standing in the doorway as he watched her leave.

London
1786

My dear friend Johann,

I am beyond pleased to know that you are coming to London and we will see each other again after four long years; time in which we have both been much engaged, that pretty vixen Fame rewarding our efforts as she should, for we have courted her assiduously!

Again, I must protest at your praise regarding my translation of your brilliant volume on physiognomy, which is the success it was surely intended - and deserves - to be. My translations do not end there! I have been assisting Mr. William Cowper in his translation of Homer. As for my painting? You ask. I am still working on the commission for publisher John Boydell's Shakespeare Gallery. So much industry and so many opportunities. Where did all this begin? Where will it end? I hope it will continue for as many years as I am able to invent and produce.

And yet I remain known primarily as the creator of 'The Nightmare.' Do not misinterpret my confusion for ingratitude. The painting made my name known in London to those that now court and raise me up, the generous Joshua Reynolds as good a mentor as any Renaissance cardinal. As for our mutual friend, Joseph Johnson, he has a copy of the picture and praises me often at his weekly dinners enjoyed by many of London's leading thinkers and writers. If you recall I sold 'The Nightmare' for twenty guineas - would I had waited longer for its value to quadruple! And yet if I say I was saddened to see it leave my studio, I would be a liar.

And here I must check myself! I am not the fanciful man I was when besotted by Anna Landolt. I am a city gentleman with the girth to prove such, and aside from being an admired and prosperous artist - 'The Nightmare' is now famous enough to be lampooned! - I am become what is known on the streets as a 'ladies man.'

I seem always to be able to shock you, dear Johann, for I am now much changed from the poor Swiss dolt of my youth. You may have heard some talk of Mary Wollstonecraft, a vigorous woman 'of the feminist persuasion.' Which, translated, means a female eager and willing to pursue and run to ground any male on whom she has set her sights. Her brain is most admirable, and she is most passionate, and yet I do not wish to have another shadow walk alongside my own. Clever women are to be admired, yet not seduced. In love, they become barnacles.

And here I would introduce you to a young woman I have met, who might - ah, I wonder as I trace these words - _might_ prove to be the true love I have sought so long. We met at the Society of Artists; she is pretty, witty, too occupied with fashion, yet the elaborate coiling of her hair I find enthralling. I imagine the Minotaur wishing to remain in the labyrinth if it was as alluringly seductive as Miss Sophia Rawlings's coiffure. She *has become my model, chaperoned by a crone with the face of a stewed apple, and yet looks kindly on our romance, allowing Sophia rather more freedom that her father would choose for her. I was set on this Miss Rawlings to become my wife and was duly prepared to ask her father for her hand in marriage when some other matter halted me.*

Last night I woke to find a shadow over my bed. It was above me and though I could not make out its face nor features, yet I could hear its breathing, long, slow breaths that blew fetid air upon my cheeks and dribble on my lips. I could not move, Johann, it was as before - years ago - and I had hoped that I had exorcised it. The painting did so. It did so. I knew peace, and sleep, and waking without glimpsed memories of dreams I would sweat to recall. She was gone from me, and with her leaving went that black ghoul I had created and burdened with my own carnality.

The Incubus I painted I freed to titillate and taunt its viewers, to make clever men ponder on the brain, and clerics ponder the life beyond death. As you well know, I blamed myself for the death of the nightwatchman... Certainly the painting turned him mad... And though I had no direct hand in it, for many years I believed it was the ghoul I had created that had murdered him.

You cannot mock me more than I have mocked myself. When I woke this morning I threw back the covers and searched the room, looked beneath the bed like a whimpering child, and then upturned cupboards, thrashing curtains manically with my hands to drive out the malignant shadow. By nine this morning I was calm again, telling myself it was but a flicker of my old tormenting night terrors. That the imagination I val-

ued, and others did also, had perhaps rattled its cage enough to loosen the lock and free itself.

You see how I talk? Such madness... I remained placid until eleven, when I dressed and left the house. The sun was shining, Piccadilly pretty with women and children, carriages with shiny horses, and boys calling the news from corners stands. London, with its winter sky freckled with clouds the colour of farm milk, and the bells of St Martins chiming the hour.

She called my name. Yes, she called me... 'Henry Fuseli, is that you?'... and I turned and Anna Landolt stood before me. White hat with blonde feathers to match her hair, lace collar tied with jade green ribbon, and a cameo at her throat. And I knew then why I had dreamed as I had, and I knew that if I spoke to her, if I engaged with her, reset the compass on that ugly journey, I would never be free again.

So I did not reply and turned away, walking towards Piccadilly knowing she would be confused, so embarrassed she might flush, even in the winter chill.... Her appearance, I do not lie, unmanned me. Had one of the passing carriage horses kicked me in my gut the injury would have been no less. My brain simmered with the heat of unrest and remembered passion, my palms sweated, my collar tightening like a hangman's noose, the drop opening beneath my feet as I staggered and leaned against a wall to prevent myself falling....

That was several hours ago, my friend, and I dread the coming night. I dread the shadows lengthening, the darkness creeping towards my bed, the windows turning black and sightless. Already there are candles lit about the home, my housekeeper remonstrates, warning of fire and admonishing my lavishness, but no one - besides you - could understand this fear.

*Believe me, I will **not** be a wearisome companion on your visit, that much I promise you! London awaits you as I do, and you will see much to enjoy here. How happy I am to think my true and trusted friend will be here within the week.... I bid you a joyous and safe journey, and long to see your handsome face, hear your voice, and laugh at your clever wit..*

Until then, I remain your loving friend,
Henry.

WEEK FOUR

THIRTY SEVEN

Graybrooke Lodge
Hampshire

"I want you to go to your parents' house with Mark --"

"*What?* I thought you were coming back to London today," Ziva interrupted him. "What's changed?"

Gus was walking away from the house, down the lawn towards the wood. The fog had disappeared, the grounds in brilliant winter clarity, the bare branches of the trees a ribcage against the sky. The garden was the only place he could talk without being overheard, and as he walked Gus could sense that he was being watched. By Je-Yun? Possibly, the Korean was certainly in league with his employer, Gus thought, pausing beside the Ice House and jingling Franckel's keys in his hand as his attention turned back to Ziva.

"I have to stay here. Please, don't argue, Ziva, just go with Mark and stay at your parents' house." He gave her no time to interrupt. "Willes *is* involved with the clinic, Franckel, the tapes - and I need to know that you and Mark are safe. Go to your parents' house, when this is over, I'll come for you."

"Are you serious?" she responded, "Just leave. Get out of there –"

"I can't. Willes has insisted that I stay –"

"He can't!"

"*He can!* Because if I leave, he'll bar me from the property. Then I'll have no chance of finding the tapes."

He could hear the confusion in her voice. *"So he knows where they are?"*

"No, I don't think he does," Gus replied, "but he must believe they're here, otherwise there's no point in keeping me at Graybrooke. He wants me to find them."

"So now *Willes* wants the tapes*?"* Ziva asked, baffled. "Since when?"

"Since he's realised that they would create massive publicity for his book."

"But *how* did he find out about them? You said before that he denied knowing anything about Franckel."

Gus looked towards the house from the safety of the garden. "I'm ringing from outside because Louis Willes has the house rigged, every conversation is recorded and everything's filmed. He heard my conversations with you, Jimmy, and Andy Fields. In fact everyone I spoke to -- which means that he must know about the anonymous messages."

"Especially if he's sending them."

"I wondered about that too," Gus admitted, "but then I realised it couldn't be Willes. When some of the calls and texts came through he was under sedation or too sick to leave his bed."

"Maybe someone is doing it for him? What about his assistant?"

"Je-Yun? Could be, but then again that would be too obvious, and Willes is not obvious." Gus looked at the keys he was holding and then glanced towards the Ice House. "I rang the police and told Andy Fields about the man who approached Mark. He said they can't do anything about threats, they can only act if there's a physical attack. When the anonymous contact got in touch later I lost my temper and he backed off, scared that I'd put the police onto him."

"If you scared him off, why do we need to leave London?"

"Because I haven't done what he wants yet, and because I can't risk my family. The man who approached Mark knew your address and my routine - that's why you have to leave London." Gus kept his voice steady. "Think of what's just happened, Jimmy was going to tell me something important, but before he could he was hit by a car. He's in a coma and the doctor said his condition was worsening and that the next 24 hours were critical… I'm not going to risk you!"

"But you're risking yourself –"

"I have to, but I must get you somewhere safe." His voice wavered. "You think I don't want to get in the car now and come to get you? I do, but I *can't,* because it's only by finding the fucking tapes that I can finish this." He lowered his voice, calming himself. "Just get Mark and go to your parents, Ziva. Be safe, please."

"And what about you? You worry about Jimmy, you worry about us, but you're in danger too." Her voice was urgent. "Don't let anything happened to you, Gus. Please, don't. I nearly lost you once before, I *can't* lose you now."

Dover Street
London W1

Slumped in his desk chair, Anthony Hallett stared ahead, the noise of the London street outside and the expensive chink of the gallery doorbell below passing unnoticed. Absentmindedly, he hummed under his breath and fiddled with his cuff links, the gold edges buffed, sliding fluidly between his fingers. Sensations were important in life, he mused, flesh, food, the smell of an autumn fire and a landscape... He stopped at the word landscape. Switzerland was famous for its landscapes, its views, the summer iron slopes that metamorphosized in winter to accommodate the hue of the skis. The sapphire skies, with their Impressionist clouds, all the fluff of a Monet shifting over the macaroon chalets of tourists, or people who had cheated their way up the slopes to take residence there.

Yes, he told the Swiss police, he had known and done a few deals with John Cummings, but they had never been friends. Acquaintances, no more.

"Mr. Cummings was a very private man." He had said on the overseas link, his pug-like countenance not flattered by the computer screen. "In fact, I had not seen him for over eighteen months."

"Yet you bought a house from him, sir." The officer had replied, his face morose.

"No, Mr. Cummings put me in touch with someone who was selling a home. I didn't buy that one, but I bought another that Mr. Cummings had recommended to me."

"Did Mr. Cummings take a commission?"

Anthony had shifted in his seat at the question. "It's only normal in business --"

"How much, sir?"

"Twenty five per cent."

"That seems a great deal of money, sir," the officer had continued. "Would you say that Mr. Cummings was greedy in his dealings?"

"I would say he was a businessman," Anthony had replied, sweating.

"Did you share your clients?"

"Never." The reply was a little sharp, Anthony remembering how John Cummings had made it clear he did not see him as any threat. "Mr. Cummings had his clients and I have mine."

"And you don't know of anyone who would wish him harm?"

"No, I do not."

"None of his clients were engaged in any nefarious activities?"

"Not that I know of."

"None with criminal records?"

Anthony had felt a streamer of sweat trickle down his back towards his buttocks and changed position in his chair. "I wouldn't know. As I have told you, we were not colleagues and did not share clients information."

"And yet Mr. Cummings helped you purchase a property --"

"As I explained, it was merely an introduction."

" -- and you visited him a month ago, on the 3rd October." The officer had continued, reading from his notes. "That's not what you said earlier, sir, when you said you hadn't seen him for over eighteen months."

"I forgot," Anthony had replied blithely, his bass voice affable. "I was visiting Switzerland and meeting up with friends when, on a whim, I called by to see Mr. Cummings. He was not at home. That was why I said

I hadn't seen him for over eighteen months. I hadn't *seen* him." Anthony had shrugged, as though it was of no matter that the officer had not understood him. "Forgive me, I should have explained myself more clearly."

The call had ended soon after, but the policeman's expression was that of a man who was not convinced, and Anthony knew that he would be back. He would return and come with more questions, more collated information. It might take him a while to discover it, but he would persist - because that was his job. His duty to find the murderer of a reclusive art dealer and then expose his clients and associates. And all the while John Cummings's father and brother would flex their legal muscles and make demands, the glacial house with its vast swimming pool remaining empty, the secret storage room cordoned off, the press transfixed by the theft of the painting. After all, Fuseli was Swiss born, the story was about one of their own.

Everyone knew the painting of 'The Nightmare'. Many homes in Switzerland had a copy, many restaurants too, the image having become something of an emblem. So whilst there might prove to be little sympathy for John Cummings's death, the Swiss wanted to know who had thought the painting worth stealing. And who had dared to taunt their peaceful, neutral country by murdering to possess it.

Maida Vale
London

It was not a feeling Ella Fairchild enjoyed; the uncomfortable suspicion that she had been duped. That the well-spoken and convincing Paul Shore might

360

not have been what he seemed. Irritated with herself, she took care as she bent down to gather up the two remaining documents which had been tipped out of the box and left scattered during the burglary. The writing was well preserved, only a few pages where the ink had faded. Why he had taken some and left others was a mystery, Ella thought, but then again, wasn't everything concerning Addison Franckel?

All morning she had hoped that Paul Shore would ring her, but she heard nothing from him and her unease grew. Perhaps she was too old, too slow witted, to continue. Her home had been invaded, she was vulnerable, if she were sensible she would stop now. After all, the events had taken place nearly eighty years ago, was she that vain to want to be remembered as some kind of heroine? Standing up against the authorities to expose the past?

How foolish it seemed suddenly, her amateur attempts at sleuthing an embarrassment, her clumsy searching of Paul Shore's wallet making her blush. Guilt had prompted her to act, and revenge had kept her focused, her thoughts turning back to Paul Shore.

'Are you sure he doesn't have your address?'

Wasn't that what he had asked her, planting a maggot of doubt into her brain? Making her wonder if Freddy Wilson *did* know where she lived. Or if *he* had even been the burglar. She dismissed the idea immediately; Freddy Wilson wasn't capable of organizing a break in. He was barely able to speak coherently.

Downstairs she could hear the phone ring and moved out onto the landing, looking down to see Maggie answer it in the hall below.

"Hello, if you hold on a moment I'll get her for you." She looked up the stairwell, smiling as she spotted Ella. "Call for you, Mrs. Fairchild."

"Who is it?"

"He didn't say his name, just that you were waiting to hear from him."

Graybrooke Lodge
Hampshire

The text was acerbic:

> *I hope we can communicate pleasantly, Mr. Egan. Our last conversation was unnecessarily aggressive on your part. You must see this from my point of view, three weeks have passed and the tapes have not been found - why is that?*

Gus replied at once:

> *I need more time.*

Back came the answer:

> *Willes hasn't got much time left and neither have you. Find those tapes and all this will be over. Life will resume as if nothing had ever happened.*

Gus replied:

> *What d'you intend to do with the tapes?*

Reply:

> *That doesn't concern you. And don't think You can outsmart me. If you find them - then decide to withhold them from me -I will visit your family.*

What if someone gets to you first?

Aren't you worried that you might end up like

Jimmy Gold?

> *I have a long reach, Mr. Egan, don't under-
> estimate me. Get on with it - for your
> own good.*

I'm the only person who has a chance of finding
those tapes. Harm me, and you've lost.

There was a pause before the reply:

> *Watch your back. You're right to be wary of
> me; but perhaps you should also ask your-
> self if everyone at Graybrooke is wishing
> you well?*
>
> *Goodbye for now, my friend.*

Suspicious, Gus glanced over to Willes who was
hunched over his computer, concentrating. He had
been working intently for most of the day, clicking his
fingers at Gus when he wanted information, asking for
the research he had uncovered, then brushing Je-Yun
away when he suggested he take a rest. The historian
was pushing himself on, invigorated by the thought of
the 'Incubus Tapes' and what their discovery would
mean. *Triumph*, his chance to cock a snoot at the art
world. And how the press would love it, would clam-
mer around Graybrooke, would write reams of dross
and psychoanalytical interpretations, and regard Willes
as some conduit of Fuseli's, some interpreter of his
most lauded work.

"Have you never wondered what's on the tapes?"
Gus said suddenly, Willes looking up, his glasses sliding down the bridge of his nose.

"Don't you know?"

"How could I? I haven't seen them." Gus replied.
"But it can't be good."

"You don't know that."

363

"The Government and the Police don't suppress information and force people to keep quiet for no reason."

Willes waved the words away with his hand. "Pah! That was in the 1940's, this is the 21st Century. Franckel was a shrink, they're all crazy, but whatever he did his methods will have been long superseded, out of fashion by now."

"Depends on what they were." Gus turned back to his laptop, then glanced over to Willes again. "You think Dr Richards can keep you alive long enough to finish your book?"

"*What!*"

"I saw him here this morning, he's visiting daily now, isn't he? Has he given you an updated prognosis?"

"Same one as before," Willes replied coldly, "a few weeks. Or a few months if I'm lucky. You want me dead?"

"Why would I? You pay me very well. Besides, as you've made very clear, I need to be with the owner of Graybrooke in order to have access and find the tapes. They *are* here, aren't they?"

"I believe so," Willes replied, bending down to stroke the head of the little terrier that was sitting beside his desk. "Je-Yun has promised that he will look after her when I'm gone --"

Gus ignored the comment. "You hired me for a reason, didn't you? I mean, apart from my work."

"I thought we might have a great deal in common, Mr. Egan. We both want to get our revenge on the art world, and I want to see the likes of Anthony Hallett destroyed. Which he will be."

"How can you be so sure?"

"Life appears to be random and yet little happens by chance. If we are clever, we plan our existences whenever we are able. Misfortune, sickness, natural disasters and betrayal we cannot control, but our revenge, *that* we can strategise."

"What about death?"

"Our own? Or others?"

"My colleague is in a Berlin hospital because someone tried to kill him." Gus continued, his voice even. "And you know what's strange? In our last conversation Jimmy told me that Freddy Wilson had contacted him, and that Wilson had some information about *you.*"

Unmoved, Willes shrugged. "Who's Kenny --"

"*Freddy.*"

" -- who's Freddy Wilson?"

"Addison Franckel's son." Gus replied. "And I've been thinking. How on earth did Freddy Wilson know how to contact Jimmy Gold? He didn't know Jimmy, he didn't know he'd be in Berlin, yet somehow he *did* know. And then I remembered what you told me - that you record all the calls made in this house. So that was how Freddy Wilson found my colleague - *through you.*"

Sighing expansively, Willes leaned back in his seat. "So now this Freddy Wilson is a killer?"

"I didn't say that. I said he was in touch with Jimmy because of you. And he told Jimmy something about you which he didn't have time to tell me." Gus was staring at the old man. "What was it?"

"I was asking him for answers --"

"*Asking him for answers*?' A minute ago you denied even knowing him!" Gus said, exasperated. "Can't you tell the truth about anything? You swore you knew nothing about Addison Franckel and yet you contacted *his son*? How?"

Willes rolled his eyes. "Wilson approached me."

"What, out of the blue?"

"Yes. He knew his father's clinic had once been here, it wasn't difficult for him to get in touch."

"Your answers are very well prepared."

"The truth needs no preparation."

Incredulously, Gus shook his head. "Jimmy said he had something on you - what was it?"

"Freddy Wilson's a bullshitter, he says anything, does anything, for money --"

"You're using me to find those tapes because you know I'm in no position to refuse - but you won't give me any help. Time's short, Willes, for both of us. I need some answers."

"I'm tired. Later."

"No, now!" Gus said, the door opening and Je-Yun walking in.

"It's time for Mr. Willes to rest --"

"No, I don't think it is." Gus cut him off. "I'm guessing that you've just watched the exchange between us, so you know what's going on. Perhaps this is the opportunity to ask if *you* know where the tapes are."

"No, Mr. Egan, I do not." Je-Yun replied levelly. "I've looked for them since we became aware of their existence, but found nothing."

"This is a big property, with grounds," Gus said, turning back to Willes. "There are numerous places to hide something. You could hire a dozen men to search, so why don't you? Why are you now leaving it all to me?"

"I don't want other people involved."

"Still keeping secrets? Aren't you worried that if I do find these tapes I won't hand them over?"

"Who else would you give them to?"

Gus laughed sardonically. "Come on, Willes, don't play fucking games! You know about all the anonymous messages I've been getting. Someone else wants the tapes and he's threatening my family, so who d'you think is going to get them?"

Willes took off his glass, his voice threatening. "You *have* to give them to me. They belong to me. They're on my property."

"Possession being nine tenths of the law?" Gus countered, knowing he might be endangering himself by suggesting he could withhold the tapes. "What if the authorities come after *you*?"

"I'm an old man, dying of cancer, what can they do to me?"

"What they did to John Cummings."

Willes blinked, wrong footed. "What makes you think the powers-that-be killed him?"

"Well, why not? The journalist that was trying to work out what happened in the 1940's was probably murdered. What's to say that someone eighty years later wouldn't meet the same end? You shouldn't dismiss the possibility without watching the tapes, without knowing *why* they caused such turmoil." Gus could see that he had rattled Willes and pressed his advantage. "You've gone to a lot of trouble, I'll give you that. Jerking me around, trying to confuse me, to get me wondering what was real and what was imagined. And all against the backdrop of that painting." He pointed to *The Nightmare* behind Willes's desk. "I admit that it was a clever trick with the woman appearing and disappearing. I was supposed to think she was the ghost of your dead wife, wasn't I? All those rumours about her death, all the gossip," he was provoking Willes, banking on the fact that he would remain safe as long as he was needed. "It *was* a car accident, wasn't it?"

"You're on thin ice, Mr. Egan."

"I've been sliding around ever since I got here, Mr. Willes."

"I don't know what you think you saw, but it wasn't any party trick of mine," the historian replied, his confidence shaken.

"But you admitted that you see your dead wife --"

"I get confused!"

" -- that makes two of us," Gus retorted. "Be honest for once, just tell me why Freddy Wilson got in touch."

"He wanted money."

"For what?"

"The tapes. He wants me to buy them from him."

This time it was Gus that was wrong footed. *"Freddy Wilson has the tapes?"*

"He said he had *some* tapes and he's trying to get money for them. He said that he'd made contact with their neighbour when the family had lived in Berlin. She'd held onto a package that had been left with her --"

"After all this time?"

"She's old. She put it away for safekeeping, and forgot about it."

"Until Freddy Wilson got in touch?"

"That's what he told me!" Willes snapped. "I don't know how true it is."

"Did you meet with him?"

"No, it was over the phone." Willes replied brusquely. "He was almost incoherent, his thoughts wandering all over the place. He's old, maybe he's senile, or he's cooked his brains, who knows?" Much as he blustered, the historian's arrogance was faltering, his gaze moving over to Je-Yun. "I need my medication and some pain relief."

Immediately Je-Yun responded. "I'll help you to your room" he said, raising Willes to his feet, the cord of his tartan dressing gown trailing on the floor as the historian looked back to Gus.

"It wasn't a trick. If you saw someone it was either my wife or one of the patients who died here." Willes said bleakly. "This house is damp with blood. Can't you feel it? Many have, that's why I used to invite mediums to come here, they could sense the darkness. Some of our guests could too, and Ava was as fascinated by Addison Franckel - as she was with Fuseli." He gestured to the picture of *The Nightmare*. "You're right, it *did* belong to him. When the place was closed they destroyed the outer buildings and razed them to the ground. The furniture was sold off, apart from a few big pieces and that painting." He gave Gus a sly, sidelong glance. "I know what you're thinking, and yes, that was the first place I looked for the tapes. I thought perhaps they had been hidden behind the canvas or even in the frame, but there was nothing. It's a reproduction, no more than that. This conversation is over --"

"Tell me one thing," Gus said, holding Willes's gaze. "Where can I find Freddy Wilson?"

"Just wait for it to go dark, Mr. Egan, that's when all the vermin comes out."

"I really must apologise for rushing off earlier, but I'd forgotten an important meeting I had planned and had to leave in a hurry." Paul Shore sounded remorseful, genuinely apologetic. "You must think me very rude."

Ella wasn't sure what she thought, her voice cool.

"You seemed perturbed after my call from Gus Egan when he told me about his colleague being the victim of a hit and run. In fact, you seemed taken aback, almost as though you were *disappointed* that he'd survived." She glanced over to her daily, Maggie moving into the sitting room and turning on the vacuum.

"Nothing could be further from the truth!" Paul retorted. "I was just... shaken."

"But you always knew it could become dangerous. We've spoken about it often, we agreed to continue anyway."

"It's not that, it's just that my niece is in Berlin at the moment. It just seemed such an awful co-incidence."

"*Your niece?*" Ella echoed.

"Yes, Lily was visiting Berlin for an audition, and she told me the other day that she had met up with an Englishman who had been talking about Addison Franckel --"

"Are you telling me that she met up with Jimmy Gold?"

"Yes! And that's what startled me. That was why I hurried off. I had to ring her, you see. She was really upset about the hit and run. She was saying that she'd been approached and threatened herself and told to forget what she'd heard --"

Ella was struggling to keep up. "What *Jimmy Gold* told her?"

"Yes! But there was more to it than that. You see Lily had been rather foolish, asking around about Franckel herself, and she'd even visited his old surgery --"

"Why, in God's Name, would she do that?"

"Boredom."

"*Boredom!*"

"She's very naïve and said it gave her something to do whilst she was hanging around. Lily knows that we're trying to uncover everything about Addison Franckel and she wanted to surprise me. You know what young people are like. She thought it was exciting until she heard about the hit and run, and then almost immediately afterwards someone threatened her --"

Ella was incredulous. "Why, in God's name, did you get her involved?"

"*I didn't intend to!* She came to visit me before she went to Berlin and saw my notes on Addison Franckel and asked questions --"

Irate, Ella snapped back at him. "Why weren't you more careful?"

"It was a mistake! I was careless! She just saw my notes and asked me about it --"

"And you told her?"

"Not much."

"'*Not much*' you say? It was enough, Paul, obviously more than enough to get her into trouble. Where is she now?"

"That's the point," he replied "I haven't heard from Lily since yesterday and her phone is turned off. D'you think she's in danger?"

"What do you think?" Ella asked coldly. "Did she tell you who approached her?"

"What?"

"You said someone approached and threatened your niece in Berlin, *who*?"

"She didn't say, just some man. I told her to come home straight away, but she said she had to go to another audition and that she would be back tomorrow. She said not to worry…" His voice fell. "But I *am* worried. I don't know what to do."

"I'm expecting a call from Gus Egan. He needs to know about all of this.*" Her tone hardened. *"I can't believe you would be so stupid*! You know we were threatened before. You know we were terrified into keeping silent. You know what happened to Ted MacNeice."

"I didn't mean for Lily to read my notes --"

Too angry to listen to excuses, Ella interrupted him. "We were told to keep quiet! To wait until the time was right. **It was all spelt out for us**." Her voice rose. "If you ruin this --"

"I never thought Lily would get involved!"

"*But she is!* And now she's missing, and she's heard all about Addison Franckel. We both know how dangerous that is." Her voice was accusatory, unflinching. "So tell me, Paul - no lies, no fudging the issue – what *else* did you tell her?"

THIRTY EIGHT

Damerham
Hampshire

Hungry and cold, Caroline decided that before she set off for London she would call by the pub. Welcomed by the landlord and taking a seat by the fire, she ordered a steak and mushroom pie which arrived with a pyramid of chips teetering on a white ceramic plate the size of a carving platter. Watching her eat, the landlord leaned on the bar, obviously pleased to have company before the regulars arrived.

"Did you find Graybrooke Lodge?"

She nodded. "Yes, I did…. This is good," she gestured to the plate. "And there's plenty of it."

"My wife thinks you should feed people well. No silly kiddy portions. So, was Graybrooke the place you wanted?"

Caroline sighed, shaking her head. "No. Someone had given me the wrong information. I hate it when that happens, it such a waste of time. I suppose it's because it was all such a long time ago."

He nodded, polishing some glasses. "Nearly eighty years. The world's changed since then. Who could remember what things were like so long ago? I mean Seth - the old fellow you met earlier - he was so angry when he came back, grumbled on and on about it."

"Why was he angry?" Caroline asked, dabbing her mouth with a paper napkin.

"He said that there was never a madhouse here." The landlord continued. "Said he didn't like to hear rumours like that, that it wasn't fair for Londoners to come snooping and spreading gossip."

"I was only looking at a building," Caroline replied, feeling the warmth of the fire on her legs. "As I say, it was for an architect --"

"Yes, but it's stirred things up."

"How? I meant no harm."

"Whether you did, or you didn't, it's caused some, Miss," he went on, leaning further across the bar. "If you ask me, it's brought back some old memories, you know what I mean? Scuffed up some old secrets."

Unsettled, Caroline turned back to her food, eating more quickly. It would only take a few minutes longer before she could leave. Don't look nervous, she told herself, just act naturally. But the chips were beginning to taste like rotting wood and the gravy was congealing into an oil slick.

"If the fog comes down again --"

Caroline nodded and rose to her feet. "You're right, I should make a move. If it does get foggy it will be difficult driving back in the dark." She moved over to the bar, opening her bag. "What do I owe you?"

She paid him cash, smiling a goodbye and moving out into the early winter darkness. The car keys were already in her hand as she slid into the driver's seat and turned on the ignition. The engine struggled, tried to turn over, but failed. She tried again. Same result. Finally, uneasy, Caroline walked back into the pub, the landlord glancing over as she entered.

"Problems?"

"I'm afraid my car won't start. Where's the nearest garage?"

"That would be Graham Falmer's place. But he's closed now and will be until morning."

Feigning nonchalance, Caroline shrugged. "Looks like I'll be staying in Damerham longer than I thought. Can I get a room for the night?"

"You'll have your pick of rooms, Miss" he replied, smiling and handing her a wooden key. "This is the nicest. Room 6, overlooks the garden at the back. Bathroom along the corridor."

The bathroom sported a dark green suite, the curtains Regency striped, the floor mock marble. It was dismal and depressing, Caroline returning to her room and slumping onto the divan. Apparently there had been a sale on Regency striped fabric, because the bedroom curtains and bedspread were of the same material, the television pushed to one side of the window under a corner shelf.

Bored, the time passing slowly, Caroline wandered downstairs, two regulars eyeing her with interest, the old man from before scowling from his place by the fire as the landlord turned to her.

"Everything alright with your room?"

"Very nice," Caroline replied, launching into the lie. "But I need to stretch my legs. You know what it's like, sitting too long in a car when you're driving." She looked towards the door. "I think I'll get some air before it gets dark."

He nodded encouragement. "You'll not have long, Miss, but at least you'll see what's left of the roses. The red ones bloom until Christmas here."

Knowing she could be seen through the window, Caroline dawdled around the flower beds then walked down to the end of the lawn, moving behind a row of conifers and ringing Gus.

Immediately he picked up. "I'll call you back." He was true to his word and a few moment later, her mobile rang. "Are you on your way home?"

"No," she whispered. "My car wouldn't start and I had to take a room at the pub --"

"What d'you mean, your car wouldn't start? Have you had trouble with it before?"

"Never. It's just dead, the battery's flat." She said, hurrying on. "I don't know anything about cars, so I have to wait until morning when I can ring the garage and get someone out."

"I can't help you, sorry. If I leave Graybrooke, I can't get back in –"

"What?"

"It's complicated." Gus said shortly. "You've no choice, you'll have to wait until morning."

"I'm nervous." She said, feeling the chill as the daylight faded. "And I'm not usually the nervous type."

"Has anyone said anything to you?"

"The landlord said I'd '*stirred things up.* '"

"Like how?"

"Talking about the clinic. Apparently the old man from earlier had been grumbling about me." She shivered in the cold. "Am I in any danger here?"

"I'd rather you were back in London." Gus replied, then added. "I've found out something else about your relative. Something I should have told you earlier. Miriam was having an affair with Addison Franckel. She was in love with him --"

"But she was married to Ted MacNeice!"

"Yes, she was, and Franckel was also married. He had a wife in Berlin that he'd deserted years earlier."

There was a lull before Caroline spoke again. "You said Franckel was disgraced, struck off the Medical Register. Why?"

"His methods were unethical."

"In what way?"

"I'm not sure."

"He was a psychiatrist in the war" Caroline said tentatively, "so he'd be treating soldiers, men suffering from shell shock?"

"That was some of it."

"What else?"

"Not all the patients were men, there were women who had PTSD too, and others that suffered from night terrors, hallucinations --"

"What happened to them?"

There was a long pause before he answered her. "Five patients died under the care of Addison Franckel. My grandfather was one of them --"

"Your grandfather?" She was obviously shaken. "God Almighty, was Miriam involved?"

"Not as you think. I don't know how much your relative knew at first. She probably thought of Franckel as some Messiah figure, saving souls in wartime. But as time went on she must have found out what he was doing because she attempted to get one patient, Elizabeth

Shore, away from the clinic. She hid her in Franckel's car, but it was stopped before they could get away --"

"What happened?"

" -- Elizabeth Shore died a week later from a supposed heart attack and her relatives were told by Franckel that Miriam had returned to London."

"But there's no record of her working at any other hospital or clinic! There's no listing after this place." Caroline replied, unnerved. "Franckel would have seen what she did as a betrayal, wouldn't he? She was his lover, he would have trusted her and then found out that she turned against him. Jesus..."

"It would have put her in a difficult situation –"

"*Difficult?*" She glanced around the garden to check that she was still alone. "Was Addison Franckel dangerous?"

"Yes," Gus admitted, "but I don't know to what extent."

"If it's true that patients died her, and Miriam found out, she would have been terrified. Why didn't she leave?"

"Perhaps she couldn't."

Repeatedly turning to look behind her, Caroline continued, firing questions at Gus. "What did Franckel do to the patients? *Why* did they die?"

"His treatments are secret," Gus answered, "but whatever he did, he filmed it."

"*What d'you mean?*"

"Franckel called them The Incubus Tapes. Apparently they were so disturbing that the Government and the police stepped in and suppressed them. Word is that all the tapes he made were destroyed - but some survived."

"Where?"

"At Graybrooke." Gus replied. "I wasn't joking when I told you that it's serious. My colleague was the victim of a hit and run. He's in Berlin, in a coma. And my family's been threatened - all because of these tapes. The tapes I have to find."

She was flustered, trying to organise her thoughts.

"The patients who died - where did they end up? I mean, where are they buried? You must have their names! Their death certificates!"

"Everything was destroyed –"

"So how did you know that your grandfather was one of Franckel's patients?" her tone had shifted, become mistrustful.

"I was told that he was. That's all I can say at the moment." Gus sighed. "Yes, it's sounds suspicious, doesn't it? But believe me, the less you know, the better."

"So nothing's left of the clinic?"

"Nothing. The operating theatre, the wards, the medical records, the equipment - all of it was obliterated. Until now no one even dared to talk about the clinic."

"So who's digging it up?"

"Someone who's planned its exposure for a long time. As soon as I came to work for Louis Willes I was contacted anonymously –"

"By the same person who told you about your grandfather?"

"Yes. I was told about the clinic and then manipulated into doing what they wanted. Someone is prepared to go to any lengths to get the tapes and expose Addison Franckel. They've done their research thoroughly, and got the relatives of the murdered patients - myself included - all working together."

"You *want* to do this?"

"No, I don't want to do it!" Gus retorted. "I didn't want to get involved until I found out that my grandfather was one of the victims. Since then I've been searching for the tapes."

"Knowing it's dangerous?"

He laughed bitterly. "I didn't have a choice! But now I don't *want* a choice. I want to find out what happened. I want to know what Franckel did, and most of all, I want to find those tapes."

There was pause before Caroline spoke again. "Why are they called The Incubus Tapes?"

"Franckel admired a painting by Fuseli, called *The Nightmare*. It depicts a sleeping woman and an Incubus, it's a psychological, creepy piece that was a scandal when it was first exhibited. There have always been rumours about it, and gossip around the death of a nightwatchman who was unhinged by what he saw when he was guarding the painting. Or maybe I should say what he *thought* he saw."

Caroline was listening. "Which was?"

"The man was declared insane --"

"What did he see?"

"He claimed that the Incubus came out of the painting and attacked him. The guard lost his mind and was admitted to Bedlam. Soon after he was found smothered in his sleep, by person or persons unknown."

"Was he murdered?"

"It was 1789, who knows?" Gus replied. "The picture created massive interest when it was first exhibited. Some people were afraid of it. Many believed it was haunted."

She clicked her tongue. "Oh, come on!"

"I'm not saying I believe it, I'm just telling you its history. But what *is* interesting is that Addison Franckel owned a copy of The Nightmare and hung it at Graybrooke. Where it still is."

Her eyebrows rose. "The same painting?"

"The same one." Gus agreed. "And I'm sure the tapes are somehow related to that picture."

"How could they be?"

"Franckel was a psychiatrist like Freud, and both men had a copy of The Nightmare in their consulting rooms. Many believed that the picture represented the dream state. That Fuseli was depicting sleep paralysis, when the sleeper can't move and feels something sitting on his chest. Perhaps the tapes show something along those lines --"

"*You can't believe that!*" Caroline said scornfully. "It's fantasy, not reality."

"How d'you what's real or not?" Gus countered. "The man who owns Graybrooke is writing a biography on Fuseli. He has the painting - the *same* painting that belonged to Addison Franckel - hanging in his study now. Louis Willes is dying and knows it, tormented by his past. His wife died in a suspicious car accident, he claims to see her ghost, and I've witnessed things in that house that are inexplicable. So frankly my personal reality has become blurred." He paused, then asked: "D'you know about the Fuseli painting that's just been found?"

"No, what about it?"

"Allegedly it's the last version that Fuseli painted of The Nightmare and, as such, would be worth a fortune. It was 'discovered' in Berlin, moved to Zurich, and stored by a London dealer there called John Cummings. He was murdered at his home a week ago. His killer stole the painting."

Disturbed, Caroline glanced behind her, looking back to the pub. Through a window she could see the landlord laughing with a middle aged couple, the old man still sitting beside the fire. She felt threatened and wanted to leave, to drive away from Damerham and never come back.

"The tapes and the murder of this dealer…" she said, anxiously "… is it all connected?"

"Yes, I just have to prove it. The police couldn't find anything on Ted MacNeice. I spoke to my contact and he was surprised to discover that the journalist's history had been wiped --"

"But I saw a newspaper cutting about him! It was in Miriam's notes."

"Have you still got it?"

"No… a friend of mine found it, but I doubt he could get access to it again. It was in Miriam's personnel file." Caroline shivered, her gaze still fixed on the drinkers inside the pub, the warm lighting spilling out into the chilled garden. "Could there be bodies at Graybrooke? The patients who died at the clinic, could they be buried there?"

"I doubt it," Gus replied. "The authorities would have ensured they were properly buried."

"How d'you know that?"

"Because they couldn't risk them being found at a later date. It would be a worldwide scandal. No one could suppress evidence of murder. Bodies would lead to questions and questions to autopsies. So no, I don't think the victims are at Graybrooke --"

Caroline interrupted him. "But Miriam might be. She betrayed Franckel. He could have killed her for that and then covered it up. Didn't you say he told people she had gone back to London? What if Miriam Levy never left Graybrooke?... *What if she's still there?*"

THIRTY NINE

When he walked back into the house Gus found Willes seated at his desk, white gilled, head bent over his laptop.

Beside him was Je-Yun, obviously anxious. "You need to rest, sir. Your blood pressure is too high --"

Willes pushed him aside with his left arm, the Korean almost losing his balance. "I have to finish this book and your bleating in my ear is not helping! Why are you holding me up? Is it deliberate? Have you no idea the pressure I'm under to get this fucking thing finished?" Hearing Gus enter, he glanced over to him, his tone fierce. "And where the hell have you been?"

"In the garden. And I'm going back there after I get a stronger torch. It's getting dark."

Willes tensed. "Did you find something?"

"Why? Did you plant something for me to find?" Gus countered, Je-Yun watching the interplay between the men. "I need Freddy Wilson's contact details."

"I don't have them." Willes retorted. "As I told you, he just said he would call by sometime."

"Nothing specific?"

"He didn't sound like a man who was specific about anything," Willes riposted. "The book's almost finished, I'm just doing some last minute editing and adding your notes for the preface, then it's done."

"No reason for me to stay here then."

"*You're not going anywhere!* Besides, I need you to check the Bibliography - I wouldn't want Ronnie Gilchrist accusing me of plagiarism again."

"Have you heard from her?"

"No, apart from some message about how she wasn't involved with anything to do with John Cummings. I never thought she was, Cummings was too rarified for her." Willes said dismissively, changing the subject. "I spoke to my publishers and explained that because there was a chance I might drop dead, it would be wise to get the book out asap. It's publication should coincide with the news of the Fuseli theft --"

"And John Cummings's murder." Gus finished for him. "No one's been arrested yet."

"Which is why the likes of Ronnie Gilchrist, Edward Leigh, and the bastard Anthony Hallett are all so twitchy."

Gus studied the old man. "I thought you were waiting for me to find the tapes before you went public with the book? Why the sudden rush?"

"It's not sudden. You'll find the tapes any day now --"

"What if I don't?" Gus countered. "That would really bugger up your plans, wouldn't it? What if you and my anonymous contact are wrong. Maybe there are no tapes. Maybe they never were. Maybe it's a hoax."

"The tapes exist!" Willes snapped, pushing aside his laptop. "They're on the grounds. Or in the house. Somewhere on this property, where they've been hidden for eighty years."

"Who hid them?"

"What?"

"Who made a copy of the tapes eighty years ago?"

"How the hell would I know!"

"You see, I have a problem here." Gus said drily. "You keep saying that you know nothing about Franckel or the tapes, and then later it comes out that you know *plenty.*" He paused, returning to his previous query. "So if you *do* know who hid them, tell me. Because that might help me find them."

Without replying, Willes turned his attention back to his laptop, whilst Gus went upstairs. In his room he lay down on the bed and stared upwards, his gaze moving over the ceiling looking for some spy hole, or a random wire that might indicate some listening device. He doubted Willes would have invested in the most expensive equipment - or that his paranoia would have allowed him to hire some stranger to install it – and instead had relied on Je-Yun.

Unwilling to phone Ziva unless he was out of the house, Gus reached for his laptop and began to work again. His mind moved into its usual routine, a researcher, meticulous with detail, precise at checking and re-checking facts, of making order out of chaos, and filling in blanks.

So he went back to the basics. First he typed the dealers names:

Ronnie Gilchrist
Edward Leigh
Anthony Hallett
John Cummings - *murdered*

and then he listed the patients surviving relatives:

Paul Shore
Ella Fairchild
myself

Then the names of the dead patients:

Elizabeth Shore - *grandmother of*
Paul Shore
George Lyman - *my grandfather*
Peter Opie - *Ella Fairchild's grandfather*
(Ruby Hodge - *relative refused to be*
involved)
(Lance Carter - *no living relatives)*

Whistle blowers:

Miriam Levy - *missing/presumed dead*
Ted MacNeice - *suicide/murder?*
Jimmy Gold - *hit and run/attempted murder*

Relatives of Franckel:

Freddy Wilson, son

Relatives of Clinic Nursing Staff:

Caroline Lever

Outsiders:

Anonymous contact.
Lily Shore - *niece of Paul Shore* - *MISSING*

And lastly, Graybrooke residents, past and present.

Addison Franckel
Ava Willes - *died in car accident*
Louis Willes
Je-Yun

Gus studied the names on the screen, remembering what he knew of each; how Ella Fairchild and Paul Shore were eager to expose Franckel.

"…. *Paul seems very keen to make amends to his grandmother*," Ella Fairchild had told him the previous day. "*But why he was stupid enough to involve - albeit accidentally - his niece is beyond me.*"

And why was his niece in Berlin at the same time as Jimmy? Gus thought? It was suspicious What was the chance of them meeting up like that? How likely was it that Jimmy would be indiscreet, sharing information about Franckel? It was true that Jimmy *could* be careless when he was drinking, or trying to impress a woman, but would he have been *that* careless?… Gus stared at the names on the screen. He needed to find out more about Lily Shore. If she was *really* missing, or if she had been setting Jimmy up. Or possibly even involved in the hit and run.

Slowly Gus's gaze travelled down the list again, pausing at *John Cummings*. He still trusted his first instinct, that the murder had been a mistake. Gus knew what the press and the London dealers believed, that the brutality of the killing and the way the body had been displayed was deliberate, intended to frighten, but he still doubted it. Still believed that the painting was the focus and that John Cummings had been killed by accident.

His gaze moved to the name *Anthony Hallett*. How convenient that Hallett had a property in Zurich where the Fuseli had been stored. How the dealer would have longed to get possession of the painting. But what lengths would he have gone to. Murder? No, Gus knew Hallett, he was greedy but not murderous. Nor was his partner, Edward Leigh. As for Ronnie

Gilchrist - it was true that she wanted the Fuseli, but she was easily scared, had been jumping at shadows at Graybrooke. A woman desperate to save her business, yes, but with the stomach for murder? Unlikely. And she hadn't the money to hire someone.

Gus glanced away from the laptop, thinking of the painting. Everything came back to the painting. Always the painting. *The Nightmare* with its Incubus. So what *was* its connection to the tapes? What did they show? Franckel's deviance? His treatments? But why name them after the Incubus?... Gus glanced at the name *Freddy Wilson*. A junkie with a grudge, willing to sell anything. Was he lying to Louis Willes when he said he had tapes from Franckel's clinic in Berlin? Maybe. You could never trust an addict, and according to Ella Fairchild and Willes, he was borderline senile, his memory erratic. Long term addiction would do that, Gus thought, addiction and age. Which brought him back to Willes...

He knew that the historian wasn't the anonymous contact, and nether was Je-Yun. Gus had investigated the Korean and discovered, to his surprise, that everything about his past concurred with the version he had been given. So perhaps it *had* been an accident when he had locked Gus in the Ice House. Or maybe Willes had been lying when he said it was deliberate, to teach him a lesson. Maybe the little terrier *had* brought Je-Yun to the rescue, and maybe - just maybe - Ava Willes *did* haunt Graybrooke. Maybe everything was what it seemed - but Gus doubted it.

From below he heard Willes calling for Je-Yun, his voice loud enough to be heard over the music sounding out from the study below. Willes always played Beethoven at high volume, then the Beatles, then Frank

Sinatra, songs dotted through the decades like music notes on paper. Had he danced with his wife to Sinatra? Had he impressed his guests in the illuminated grounds, the wood hung with lanterns, a dinner served under the trees at midnight to the echo of Beethoven. Had he played Beethoven when he discovered that Ava was sleeping with Anthony Hallett? And when his wife died, did Willes sit looking out of the window towards the Ice House and imagine a woman approaching through the fast growing vegetation that would soon turn the spinney into a gnarled knot of shuffling, shifting trees?

Frustrated by the numerous unanswered questions, Gus snatched up the torch and was about to leave the house when his mobile rang. Recognising Caroline Lever's number he answered her immediately.

"Please tell me you're back in London."

"I am indeed. The garage fixed the car first thing this morning, it was something trivial - but I'll be honest, it spooked me last night. I thought someone had tampered with the car so I couldn't leave." Gus had thought the same, but didn't say it, Caroline continuing. "I'm ringing because I remembered something, and I've got to tell you about it. Last night I was going to my room when the landlord stopped me. The pub had got really busy and he pointed someone out to me who was sitting in a corner, away from everyone else. It was a sordid old guy, bearded, and apparently he'd been causing a bit of trouble. He was drunk, a stranger, and he was talking about Addison Franckel --"

This was news. "Did you get a name?"

"No, the barman didn't know him and obviously wanted him out, because he didn't like the look of him. But he knew I'd been talking about Franckel and tipped me off." She paused on the line. "I went over to have a word with the man, but he was senile, I think, and when I mentioned Addison Franckel he told me to piss off. The landlord threw him out then, and..."

"*And?*"

"... I followed him."

"That was stupid."

"*I know!* I didn't think. Anyway, that's not the point, when I got outside he'd already made his way down the road, really unsteady on his feet, then he suddenly dropped out of sight. It made me wonder where he'd gone. He was really drunk, so I wondered if he's passed out and was going to sleep it off in a field. Anyway, I walked a bit further but I couldn't find any trace of him." She hurried on before Gus could interrupt. "Then suddenly he reappeared, walking ahead of me. So I kept following him. We went down several lanes, and I was just thinking that it was a waste of time idea when he stopped. He looked round – he didn't see me because I'd ducked behind a hedge - and then he went behind a wall and a few moments later drove out in a car."

"*He was driving?*"

"Yes! Dead drunk and driving. And more than that, it was an expensive car. A Mercedes." She paused. "That's why I had to let you know. I mean, how did a man, who looked like he was destitute, have a car like that?"

"And why did he hide the car?"

"Exactly." Caroline agreed. "He must have parked it well away from the pub to make sure no one saw him." She sighed, frustrated. "If only I'd been driving I could have followed him."

"Thank God you didn't."

"D'you know who is he?"

"No idea, but I'm glad you told me."

"Whilst I was driving home I kept thinking about him." She said, musing. "He must have gone to Damerham on purpose. It's off the beaten track, people don't go there unless it's for a reason."

"That's true."

"I'm glad I'm away from there."

"Just make sure you *stay* away. I'll let you know what I find out."

"Before you go" she said hurriedly. "I know *why* you have to stay there, but be careful. Watch your back.""

"Believe me, I will."

"Whatever's hidden at Graybrooke, whatever Addison Franckel did," Caroline's voice was serious "was hidden for a reason."

"All the more reason to expose it –"

She cut him off. "But maybe it's something no one **needs** to know. What if it was something terrible, something that should be forgotten. And if it was that bad, truly bad, couldn't you *keep* it a secret?"

Surprised, he took a moment to reply. "Are you worried about your relative? The part Miriam played?"

"No!" she said briskly. "I'm just uneasy, *really* uneasy. Everything about Graybrooke, everything you've told me about Addison Franckel scares me... I've never had much of an imagination, but the atmosphere around that property is unhealthy, the air seems rank. I don't know what's on those tapes, but even the thought of them frightens me. The situation could really be dangerous."

"It could," he agreed "but leave it to me now. I'll be fine."

"And if you find Miriam —"

"I'll tell you. I promise, I'll tell you."

After reassuring her again, Gus ended the conversation and headed out into the grounds. This time there was a full moon as he made his way down the lawns, making for the rough meadow before the Ice House. He looked about, trying to remember the route he had taken before; but the fog had been disorientating, sending him in difficult directions, then making him double back. This time he could see his way by torchlight, the moon also helping to light his way.

A few yards on Gus stopped, and then stamped his feet on the earth. The ground was hard. He moved further along, and repeated the action. Again just compacted earth. But he remembered that *somewhere* he had felt the ground change and realised that it was further on, Gus moving ahead and then coming across the dip where he had stumbled before. He remembered the barbed wire on the fence and how he had grabbed it to steady himself, shining the torch towards it and seeing the dark marking of his own blood.

This was the place, he thought. And when he had been here before someone had been firing a gun… Hurriedly, he moved on, shining the torch light before him and then saw the dilapidated pathway, the stones broken, some upturned… Bending down, he scraped at the earth with the knife had brought with him, digging under the surface until he revealed what appeared to be rubble. Encouraged, he dug further, then used his bare hands, dragging away the debris to expose a ruined wall, evidence of the outbuildings which had once belonged to the clinic.

Staring at the rubble Gus sighed. So there *had* been outbuildings, there *had* been a clinic, however much people tried to deny it, or bury it. And then he remembered Ella Fairchild telling him what Paul Shore had told her.

> '...When my grandmother was nearing the end, she was confused, rambling, she would say that they put difficult patients in the Ice House to teach them a lesson. My grandmother told me it wasn't the dark, or the cold that was so frightening, it was because they were never alone in there....'

Brushing the dirt off his hands, Gus rose to his feet. The atmosphere was oppressive, watchful, as he walked towards the Ice House. He thought of Ava Willes, bracing himself for her appearance as he propped open the door of the Ice House with several weighty stones to prevent it swinging closed. Standing at the entrance, he shone the light inside, running the beam over the floor and walls, tensed, waiting at any moment for a touch on his shoulder.

Breathing fast, he pointed the torch upwards. The figure was so indistinct that Gus could not decipher at first, moving further inside and then shining the full beam on the ceiling above. The Incubus startled him, its outline scratched into the stone, crouching malevolently, its eyes fixed, unblinking as it stared down at the shaken man below.

FORTY

Quickly Gus ran his hands over the damp walls of the Ice House, certain that he about to find some hiding place. Some secret alcove hiding the tapes. One by one he tapped at the stones, pressing each of them to see if any were loose. None were. But surely, he thought, this was where the tapes were hidden. Crouching down on his haunches, he then checked the floor, brushing aside the dead leaves that had blown in when he had opened the door. And all the time he searched he kept looking over to the entrance where the rocks were holding the door open, a breeze from the garden shuffling the trees overhead.

Using his penknife, he tried to loosen the deep flags in the floor, to prise them apart, but they were fixed in place, and after a while Gus realised that there was nothing concealed there. Thwarted, he glanced up at the Incubus on the ceiling high above him, staring into the malevolent face, and then dragged a weighty stone from outside and placed it directly below the image. Standing on the boulder, Gus reached up and gripped the stone bearing the Incubus image, trying to turn it, or lever it loose. But hard as he tried, it didn't move, and as he gave it one last effort a violent wind blew against the door, overturning the rocks that were holding it open.

Jumping down, Gus ran out of the Ice House, the door slamming closed behind him. His hands shaking, he stood outside, knowing how easily he could have become trapped. He had hoped that the tapes were hidden there, but he had been wrong. Frustrated, his gaze rested on the blank stone door without a handle or lock, then reached into his pocket to pull out the keys labelled *Addison Franckel*. They had to work somewhere. They had to be important. They opened a door, a desk, or a vault, and when he found the lock they fitted he would find the tapes.

He was certain they were not in the house, where they would have been discovered by residents, or during removals, decorating or laying flooring. No, not in the house, but in the gardens, somewhere amongst the rubble of the demolished outbuildings. In amongst the wards and the operating theatre that had been flattened long ago, pressed deep into the ground, opportunistic seeds creating a barrier of vegetation under decades of falling rain.

Thinking of the woman who had materialised in the fog, Gus glanced at the keys again. Had it been Ava Willes? The chatelaine of Graybrooke, the woman who had deceived her husband and died suspiciously? Perhaps she had a right to haunt the place, Gus thought, glancing around him and beginning to walk towards the wood. He wondered fleetingly if he was trying to call her out, a man who had never believed in the paranormal seeking help beyond any reality he understood.

Determined, he moved on through the trees, the winter grass high, crusted with frost. Above his head the early moon remained sullen behind clouds, the light veiled as he came to a partially concealed wall bordering the brook that gave the house its name. The wall was aged, much of it below ground; many of its stones scored with scratches and furred with lichen. Walking its length slowly, Gus searched for almost an hour, at times holding back branches that overhung it, then suddenly he stopped, his gaze falling on an image carved into a dilapidated cornerstone. The image of an incubus.

His eyes locked onto the symbol. The same as the one in the Ice House, and he began to search the wall below the sculpture, feeling for any loose edges or indentations, whilst the Incubus watched him. He felt its eyes follow his progress and kept his face averted as he began to dig at the base of the wall, scratching away at the soil with his knife and hands. It took effort, the wind gathering around him, its sound becoming a hoarse chuckling as the earth finally loosened under his frantic digging. The soil piled up in mounds, the wind intensifying, blowing the earth upwards, the dirt making circles around him as he uncovered what looked to be a trapdoor. With a lock on it.

Urgently reaching for the keys in his pocket, Gus tried the first one. It slid into the lock, but it did not turn. Then he tried the second. This time the key turned without effort; as though it had been in regular use; as though someone had used it that very day, Gus lifting the trapdoor and looking down into the mouldering space below.

Maida Vale
London

Have you heard from Paul Shore today?
His niece is missing in Berlin. Germa-
ny seems
To be unhealthy for her and for Jimmy Gold.
Why? Because Gus Egan can't keep his side
of the bargain.
All he had to do was find the tapes…

Ella Fairchild read the message twice. Something did not ring true. Not the undercurrent of a threat
against Gus Egan, or the apparent smugness about
Jimmy Gold's condition. No, it was something else
and Ella couldn't place it. She read the message again,
thinking of Paul Shore. He had seemed to be a friend
to her, apologising endlessly for his niece's involvement and insisting that he would do anything to expose
Franckel -- because that was what they had all come
together to achieve, wasn't it? Despite the danger to
any of them.

"Have you received any message from your
niece?" Ella had asked him earlier. "Any communication at all?"

"Not a word."

"Perhaps her disappearance isn't connected to
Franckel --"

"*'Isn't connected?'*" He had repeated, aghast.
"Addison Franckel was born in Berlin! She was threatened by a man in Berlin --"

"Have you reported it to the police there?"

"They didn't seem concerned. You can't file a
missing person's report for 48 hours. Unless they're

398

a suicide risk, or in danger - and although Lily was threatened, she wasn't physically assaulted." Paul had replied, changing the subject. "If only Gus Egan could find those tapes. Why is it taking so long? When he finds them, all this will be done with."

"*Will it?*" Ella had countered. "You don't know that. We don't know whose been contacting us all this time. Maybe *they're* guilty of injuring Jimmy Gold and threatening your niece. Or.." she said idly "…maybe they aren't."

"What d'you mean? Who else could it be?"

"What if there are *two people* wanting the tapes? For two different reasons?" Ella's voice had been composed. "Our contact seemed surprised when he heard about Jimmy Gold --"

"He was trying to make himself look innocent!"

"What if he *was* innocent?"

"He threatened Gus Egan's family!"

"In *England.* And yet somehow he managed to get over to Berlin, injure Jimmy Gold and threaten your niece?" She had paused, shaking her head. "It doesn't gel. I'm sorry, but just doesn't feel right."

It *didn't* feel right, Ella thought again after Paul Shore had left, pouring herself a drink and sitting at the kitchen table. Think back, she told herself, think back over everything people have said. *Think* and remember everything you were told.

Her mind retracked events, the anonymous messages, the burglary and stealing of the patients' notes, the meeting with Freddy Wilson, and the conversations with Paul Shore. He had told her so much about the clinic and Miriam Levy, even more than Gus Egan had known … Ella paused, why *hadn't* Egan found the tapes? Or had he, and was now withholding them? She was surprised by her own suspicions, Gus Egan was the one they relied upon. They had to trust him… She gazed into her wine glass, forcing her memory, shifting through dozens of conversations - and then finally it came back to her.

On the night of the burglary Paul Shore had visited her home for the first time. They had talked for a long while, forming a bond because of their shared experiences, quickly at ease with one another. Mostly they had talked about Franckel, comparing what they knew, then they had chatted briefly about their pasts, their lives, and their families.

And that was when Paul Shore had said:

"'…. I'm sadly a widower now. No children, no family at all…'"

No family at all.

Not even a niece in Berlin.

Graybrooke Lodge
Hampshire.

His mobile ringing on the passenger seat next to him, Dr Richards drove up to the front doors and parked, answering the phone and taking several messages from his secretary before getting out of the car. Having been caught in an earlier rainstorm his tweed jacket was sodden along the shoulders, steaming gently as Je-Yun admitted him into the warm entrance hall.

"Damn it!" The doctor said as his glasses clouded up. Cleaning them hurriedly with a handkerchief, he listened to the latest report from Je-Yun.

"Mr. Willes is not sleeping more than an hour at a time. He cannot seem to rest."

"That's not good." Dr Richards put his glasses back on, blinking behind the lens. "Did you give him the sedative?"

"It's no longer having any effect. My employer is exhausted, overworked, and emotional. Whatever I suggest, he will not rest, because he's afraid of lying in bed unable to sleep. I had hoped that finishing the book would calm him --"

"He's finished it?"

Je-Yun nodded. "Yesterday, and apart from completing the bibliography, it's complete. Mr. Willes wishes to send it to his publisher this week."

"It's odd" Dr Richards said, glancing up the stairs as though expecting to see his patient appear "but sometimes people who are terminally ill let go when they've accomplished what they set out to do. Is Mr. Willes eating and drinking?"

"Not eating, drinking little."

"Is he in pain?"

"Last night, but not this morning. I gave him his medication at eight thirty." Je-Yun explained. "But when he woke an hour ago he was restless and then he collapsed. He was very disturbed and muttering about his late wife, becoming seriously agitated. Which is why I called you."

"Right thing to do." Dr Richards murmured. "You know, many terminal patients do that as they approach the end. They speak about their relatives, spouses, all kinds of regrets and memories come back." He heard his mobile ring and clicked it over to answerphone, continuing to talk: "I can remember coming to this house when Ava Willes was alive. I was young then, not long been in practice, and they were a glamorous couple. Visitors coming up from London at the week-ends and articles in newspapers."

Je-Yun encouraged the recall. "Mrs. Willes died in a car accident, I believe."

"Yes, she did." The doctor nodded sadly. "She did indeed. It was on that damn hairpin bend on the lane. You know the place, it's a death trap. I told the council that something should be done, but nothing ever was. We're too remote here, you see, that's what comes of being in the country." He sighed, remembering. "I was on call that night and found her at the wheel. She was dead."

"Was Mr. Willes with her?"

"Yes, he was in the passenger seat. He always said it should have been him that died, not her. But survivors always say that." Dr Richards paused, thinking. "Between us, if it *had* been him driving the accident would have happened long before that night. Louis Willes is a fine writer, but he was a reckless driver. Everyone breathed a sigh of relief when his license was taken away after he failed the sight test." Again, the doctor sighed, his thoughts coming back to the present. "I've had his latest blood results through and it's not good. I think at this point the best we can do for Mr. Willes is to keep him comfortable, his body free from pain, and his mind at peace. We're very near the end now."

Alexianer St Hedwig Hospital
Berlin

The first sound Jimmy recognised was the venti-lator, breathing for him: 'In, out, in, out,' to the rhythm 'Left, right, left, right'. He tried to move his leg, won-dering how he could march, then heard a scrape on the floor as the screen was pulled back from his bedside. 'Left, right, left, right. In, out, in, out.'

You should have moved faster. *I didn't see the car coming…* Jimmy stirred. Car, what car? *The car that hit me… So I'm alive? My bloody arm and leg hurt.* No one could march with a leg like that… *You don't have to march*, Jimmy consoled himself, as he fought the sedation and confusion. *It's ok, you're alive.*

He had been hit by a car. It had come out from nowhere, straight towards him. Didn't have a chance, and the girl with him… the girl with him, who was that? *Lily,* she was called Lily. What happened to her?.. Jimmy moved his leg, wincing, the bleeping of the machine speeding up. He could see his heart monitor, up and down, up and down, and then blip, blip. What did that mean?

Come on, Jimmy, you've seen it in films a hundred times, he told himself. You'll be fine, any minute now and a nurse comes in….

"Mr. Gold?"

He said yes, only it didn't sound like yes. More a wheezy grunt, but she was pleased. Never seen a woman so pleased hearing a man grunt before. And then he reached out his hand and gripped her arm.

"Gus."

It came out like 'Goose' and the nurse ignored it, thinking he was confused. Only he wasn't, and he repeated it, more clearly.

"Gus…Egan. Call him."

The nurse didn't respond, and after her attempts to calm him failed, Jimmy tried to heave himself up in the bed, demanding his mobile.

"Mr. Gold, calm down --

"*Give me my fucking phone*!" He shouted, the words blurred but the meaning clear. "Phone! *Please….*"

His side was bleeding again, his leg like a raw shank of beef under the plaster cast, the nurse startled as he snatched the mobile from her hand and pressed the entry **Gus Egan.**

"Gus."

"Jimmy! Thank God, you're alright."

"Are you at Graybrooke?" He was struggling, struggling hard to make his voice clear, the nurse hovering at the bedside. "Gus! Are there now?"

"Yes --"

He cut him off immediately. "*Willes told Freddy Wilson his father was dead.* He knows <u>everything</u> about Franckel and his son. Get out!" His strength was fading as he struggled to talk. "Willes planned it. He used you to find the tapes. Once you do, you're not needed." He was sweating with the effort. "Get out, Gus, before it's too late."

FORTY ONE

Unsteady, he stumbled out of the taxi, fishing deep into his pocket to find some money, without adding a tip. Disgusted, the cabbie moved off, then paused a little further down the lane, opening all the windows to let out the stink of booze and body odour. Why a filthy old man would be welcomed by the likes of Louis Willes was a mystery; all muffled up against the cold in an old Army greatcoat, his hands ingrained with dirt when he had handed the driver his fee.

The afternoon light was fading, the rain beginning as the stranger staggered up the steps towards the front door and rang the bell, then leaned against the lintel for support. An instant later Je-Yun greeted him, showing him into the sitting room where Louis Willes was seated. The pain of the cancer, lack of sleep, and minimal food intake had reduced him within forty hours, the thinness barely disguised by the tartan dressing gown hanging loosely over his slackened clothes.

Indicating that his visitor should sit, Willes leaned forward to study him. "What a pitiful creature you are." He said, relishing his malice. "What exactly *do* you want from me, Mr. Wilson?"

He mumbled something incoherent, Je-Yun pouring a double whisky and handing it to him, Wilson's hands wrapping around the glass to steady their shaking.

"Has he found the tapes yet?"

"Mr. Egan is trying very hard," Willes replied, "isn't he, Je-Yun?"

The Korean nodded. "He is, sir."

"I want my cut. My father owes me that much. I've earned it." Wilson said, downing the whisky and holding it out for a refill, Je-Yun obliging. "You promised me that when Egan found the tapes I'd get half of what you'd sell them for."

Willes wasn't going to sell the tapes, instead he was going use them to promote his book. But Freddy Wilson didn't need to know that. All Willes had to do was to placate him until the book came out. Jolly him along with enough booze to keep him sodden, pliable, his usefulness long over. Had Wilson been sober and clean Willes might have felt pity, but instead he looked at the destitute man before him and wondered why he hadn't exposed his father already. And then he remembered that Wilson didn't have the tapes. He might *pretend* that he had some films which Addison Franckel had taken in his Berlin practice, but he was lying. Just trying to hook Willes's interest, or wheedle more money out of him. Addicts were always easy to manipulate, greedy addicts with a grievance even more so.

"Are you using?"

Wilson looked at him, frowning. *"What?"*

"Drugs. I don't want drugs in my house."

"I only use them now and again." Wilson replied, his tone truculent, the lie ready under his tongue. "Yeah, only now and again." He stared at the historian, his expression mirthful. "You said you were sick, you weren't lying. You look like you're about to peg out."

Amused, Willes studied him in return, Freddy Wilson's lined face, hollow at the temples, his eyes pouchy, the veins raised on his scrawny neck and arms. No trouble finding somewhere to inject, Willes thought, wondering what Freddy Wilson would have looked like as a young man. Son of a wealthy psychiatrist in Berlin with the world smiling on him. Then ruined by his father's disgrace, reduced to a transient with no fixed abode, with only a thirst for revenge and a greed for money keeping him breathing.

"If you would show Mr. Wilson to his room," Willes said, terminating the conversation and watching Je-Yun approach. "Perhaps we should have dinner early today. Whilst our guest is still conscious," he whispered. "… Yes, a little before seven would be good."

Grounds of Graybrooke Lodge

Unnerved by Jimmy's call and remembering what he had said, Gus stared down at the open trapdoor.

"Willes planned it all. He used you to find the tapes. Once you do, you're not needed…Get out, Gus, before it's too late."

So Louis Willes *had* organised everything. Gus found it hard to believe, knowing that the texts and messages had come when the historian was either occupied or sedated. Could he have asked someone to send them? Like Je-Yun? Gus shook his head, no, it *wasn't* Willes, it couldn't be. The contact had accosted his son and Mark had not described him as an old man or an Asian.

'He used you to find the tapes Once-you-do, you're not needed...'

Gus stared down into the open trapdoor. Was Jimmy right? Finding the tapes would put him in danger? How much danger? It was true that Willes wanted the tapes, but only to promote his book. *Or was he involved with the theft and killing of John Cummings?* Gus tried to imagine it; could Willes's desire for revenge have really driven him to murder? No, it was too much, far too much for a man who was terminally ill. Unless Willes had plotted everything *beforehand,* whilst he was still capable.

The moonlight was muffled by rain clouds, the chimney stacks alien minarets silhouetted against the ebonised sky as Gus glanced towards the house. Behind him he could hear the trees in the wood beyond shifting in the growing wind and hurriedly knelt down and propped open the trapdoor, reaching into the space below. It was several feet in depth, filled with soil, his hands feeling around and realising that it extended horizontally for some distance. Taking a tree branch, he pushed it into the space, the earth mouldy, reeking of rotting vegetation and dampness as he leaned forward, pushing the branch along as far as it would go. Finally it stopped, its progress halted by some hard object, Gus scrabbling at the earth and finally uncovering a tin cash box.

Reaching for the keys, he tried to open it with the smallest, but the lock resisted several attempts, sliding in but not turning. Then suddenly from the house came the loud of loud music, lights turned on upstairs, Gus glancing around startled. Again, he tried the lock, shaking the box with frustration, then levering it open with his knife and shining the torch onto the contents. Two small, sealed, circular tin cannisters, obviously 16mm film, had been wrapped in a soiled towel, mostly disintegrated over the passing of time. He had found The Incubus Tapes.

The music from the house had reached a deafening volume, Beethoven sending the rooks from the night trees, the grounds illuminated as the outer lights came on. Hurriedly Gus slid the cannisters into his jacket pocket, then reached back into the hole to see if there were others, digging out the soil until it was piled around him. He dug without pause, his arms aching, expecting at any moment to feel a tap on his shoulder or a blow to the head; and then he felt the hard outline of another object and scrambled to loosen it.

Immediately he drew it from the earth, he dropped it, recoiling as he realised he was looking at a human leg bone. His gaze turned back to the house, watching for anyone to come out as he scrambled for his mobile and called the police. But before the call connected, he cancelled it. The police had suppressed everything before, would they again? Gus looked back to the open trapdoor and then the house, waiting for the outer lights to warn him someone was approaching, knowing that if the lights came on he would have a couple of minutes leeway before they would reach him.

Taking off his coat, he spread it on the ground next to him and reached back into the hole. He had hoped he would be wrong, but he uncovered the other bones quickly, his hands and sleeves grimy with soil, his breathing rapid as he lifted out the remains that had been laid there nearly eighty years before. Then he placed the tapes alongside the bones and rolled the coat into a bundle.

Still watching for the outside lights to come on as a warning, he closed the trapdoor and then covered it over with the mounds of earth. Then he scuffed the ground until there was no sign of the opening, or that the earth had even been disturbed. Finally, he gathered a few broken stones from the wall and placed them haphazardly as though they had fallen, the rain heavy as he rolled up his jacket with its grim cargo and headed back to Graybrooke.

He was holding the bundle tightly against him as he skirted the garden lights, a reading lamp coming on in one of the downstairs rooms. Ducking out of sight, Gus avoided the house and made for the garages off the driveway. Expecting at any moment to be discovered, he leaned down and slid the bundle under the spare wheel in the boot of his car.

He had just closed the lid when he heard a voice behind him.

"Dinner will be served at any moment," Je-Yun said, glancing at the open boot. "May I help you with anything?"

"I was looking for the spare charger for my mobile." Gus replied, taking it out and smiling. "And here it is."

"If I may say, you look a little dishevelled."

"I've been searching the grounds."

"Did you find anything?"

"Not what I was looking for," Gus answered, clicking the automatic lock on his car and following

410

Je-Yun into the house. "I need to have a chat with Mr. Willes."

"Dinner --"

"Can wait," Gus interrupted him, moving into the sitting room, Willes looking him up and down as he entered.

"You're very dirty. Did you have an eventful time?"

"Do you have an old school projector?"

Willes jerked up in his seat. *"You found the tapes!"*

Gus shook his head. "No, but whilst I was out there digging, I wondered if - when I *do* find them - we have a way of watching them. You know, like a family gathering." He studied Willes. "You seem very chipper tonight. Is that because you've finished the book? How does that feel after so long, finally completing your *epitaph*."

Willes's expression hardened. "I'm not dead yet!"

"No, you're not, are you?" Gus replied. "In fact, I'd say you've got a little while left. But I appreciate the acting, trying to convince everyone you're about to die. Putting the pressure on me to find the tapes, to help out an 'old man about to meet his Maker--'"

"You bastard!"

"The acting's not working anymore." Gus said coldly. "I haven't found the tapes, but I know where they are --"

"Where?"

"What will you do when I tell you?" Gus asked. "I mean, I've served my purpose then, haven't I?"

Willes rolled his eyes, his voice strident. "What are you fucking talking about?"

"You. I'm talking about you. About how you planned everything."

411

"I'm a dying man --"

"Which is quite an alibi," Gus replied. "You knew about Addison Franckel, you've been in contact with his son, you knew the history of this place. How long have you been plotting? Staying silent until you finished the book and then – when you got the tapes – you'd get full exposure and publicity. Worldwide attention for you, and a chance to get your revenge on the art world. That Fuseli is a fake, isn't it?"

"Really?" Willes said, his eyebrows raised.

"I suspected it from the beginning, but I couldn't prove it. *You* were the anonymous seller, giving a forgery to John Cummings, knowing everyone in the business would want the Fuseli. And of course Cummings would grab at the chance to do the deal, thinking of the commission he could get. I suppose you posed as a Russian oligarch or a collector from the UAE --"

"You've lost your mind!"

Gus ignored him and continued. "It went perfectly, didn't it? Cummings took the bait and kept the Fuseli at his home. Naturally he wouldn't press too hard to know the identity of the anonymous seller, he was too interested in going through his address book of collectors, looking for the richest buyer. But then it all came unstuck - or did you hope it would? Because someone else wanted the painting. And they were prepared to steal it --"

"You're talking like an imbecile!"

" -- but the thief was never supposed to murder Cummings, was he?"

"How the fuck would I know!" Willes shouted, "I just gave Cummings the painting to sell--"

"But someone *did* steal it. And they killed Cummings at the same time. The poor greedy bastard died for a fake."

"Big deal, Cummings was a fake himself." Willes replied nonchalantly. "I wonder how long it will be before the new owner discovers it's a forgery."

"Who *is* the new owner?"

"Anthony Hallett," Willes replied triumphantly, reaching for the glass of water beside him and taking a drink. "I told you when you first came here what that bastard had done, how he'd used my wife. How he'd made me look a fool. Well, now he's ruined."

"How d'you know it was Hallett who ordered the theft?"

"I made *sure* it was Hallett." Willes replied. "A word here, a word there in the right ears - and Ronnie Gilchrist has *big* ears."

"I heard she was trying to do a deal with Edward Leigh –"

"Edward Leigh wouldn't risk his arse or his gallery!" Willes said scornfully. "No, Ronnie Gilchrist was Hallett's ex-lover and desperate to impress him and do a deal to save her business. I knew Hallett would hire someone to steal the painting so he could cut Cummings out and sell it on anonymously for a fortune. After all, Hallett knew Cummings's house, he has a place in Zurich himself. It was easy for him to set it all up."

Gus shook his head. "So Cummings *was* killed by mistake?"

"He was supposed to be away, but it turns out he was at home when the thief broke in. The man bungled it, panicked, and then tried to make it look like an intentional killing --"

"John Cummings died for a fake." Gus repeated. "How does that make you feel?"

"Ask Anthony Hallett, he was the one who hired the incompetent who turned a theft into a murder. And now Hallett's been arrested in Zurich. He's destroyed - which is exactly what he deserved, and exactly what I've planned for decades. *But I had nothing to do with the murder of John Cummings!"* Willes roared, leaning forward in his seat, her hands gripping the arms of the chair. "I was going to wait until Cummings sold the painting and then expose it as a fake --"

"Why did you choose the Fuseli painting?"

"I knew a forger down on his luck, needing money. I knew he'd do a painting so like Fuseli it would be accepted. He's very careful – I paid him to be careful – he ground his own paints, reused an old canvas, made his own primer and varnish. Clever sod. When I saw it I knew it was good enough to fool everyone. Remember, it wasn't a copy of a *known* Fuseli, but apparently his last version of The Nightmare. Which no one had ever seen."

"And you're sure the forger won't talk?"

"If he did a quarter of London's dealers would be in trouble. No, he'll keep quiet." Willes tilted his head to one side. "Of course I picked Fuseli! What kind of a question is that? I've been writing a bloody book about him for decades! A 'newly discovered' version of *The Nightmare* was the perfect choice. The picture's famous, enigmatic, media friendly, and this place" he waved an arm around the room "has a relevant history --"

"Because of Addison Franckel." Gus interrupted. "You knew about Franckel all along, didn't you? You lied to me, hooked me in because of my grandfather --"

Willes sighed. "What the hell are you talking about now?"

"*Stop lying!* You can't claim ignorance. You told me that everything that happened in this house was recorded, or filmed. That's how you always knew what was going on. I thought for a while that it wasn't you - but now I realise that it couldn't have been anyone else. You arranged all those anonymous texts --"

Willes was staring at him, baffled. "I wasn't the one that sent those!"

"Was it Je-Yun?"

"Jesus," Willes laughed softly to himself. "You really thought it was me?"

"It *wasn't* you?"

"No! I wanted to piss on the art world, that's true. Show them up for the money-grabbing liars they are. Nothing else --"

"Then tell me, why d'you want the Incubus Tapes?"

"Why d'you think? It would make a hell of a splash along with my book being published and the Fuseli being exposed as a fake." Willes paused before continuing, his voice adamant. "*I didn't send the messages.* I didn't kill Cummings. I didn't threaten your family. Or drive a car into Jimmy Gold."

"Jimmy told me that you were in touch with Franckel's son, that it was *you* who informed him of his father's death. So how did you know Franckel was dead? There's no record of it --"

"Nothing on paper anyway." Willes replied slyly "but I knew. There's always someone who lets something slip. When we first came here no one would talk about Franckel. Everyone was scared to mention him, but even the authorities can't keep their hands over peoples' mouths forever." He sighed. "In the 1970's we had a plumber, he'd lived around here all his life, and one day he told me about when he'd been a kid. He was here when the Addison Franckel scandal broke and he'd hidden in the garden and spied on the people who came to the clinic. He'd watched them demolish the outbuildings, and then he saw Franckel being taken away."

"Alive?"

"He didn't think so. Said he was beaten up, covered in blood." Willes replied. "When I pressed him he suddenly clammed up, said he'd just been a kid and probably imagined it all. Then he swore he'd been lying. Like everyone else around here, he was terrified."

"Who came for Franckel?"

"He said it was a group of men." Willes replied, shrugging. "And that's all I know. Really, that's *all* I know." He leaned forward in his chair, staring over Gus's shoulder. "Isn't that right?"

Surprised, Gus turned round to see an elderly man walk into the sitting room. His thinness was disguised by an expensive jacket and trousers, his hair combed away from his face, his beard trimmed. Scrubbed hands and trimmed nails appeared groomed, but the veins were knotted and raised, blue tinted against the white cuffs.

Confused, Gus looked from the stranger to Willes.

"Allow me to introduce you to Addison Franckel's son, Mr. Freddy Wilson, who - it has to be admitted - has scrubbed up rather well. You smell better too." Intrigued, Willes studied the man before him. "You didn't look, or sound, like this an hour ago. Why the disguise?"

Ignoring the question, Wilson turned to Gus. "Can I have the tapes?"

"*What?* I don't have them."

"Yes, you do." Wilson replied, eyes flinty. "I saw you running back from the garden holding a bundle, all wrapped up. You were hiding it, using the back way through the garage, taking care that no one would see you. It had to be the tapes -- "

Willes turned to Gus. "You bastard!" he said, reluctantly amused. "So you *did* find them?"

Wilson repeated the question. "Can I have the tapes, please?"

"I don't have them."

"I don't believe you."

"There are three men in this room and two are liars. I'm not one of them." Gus replied, playing for time. "Why d'you want the tapes anyway?"

"I have my reasons. Better reasons that anyone else involved in this —"

"Were *you* the one who sent all those anonymous messages?"

Freddy Wilson moved over to the drinks on the sideboard and poured himself a triple whisky before replying. "Yeah, I sent them." His voice was clear, not at all confused, nothing like the addict he had seemed before. "Give me the tapes --"

"You threatened my family and attacked my colleague."

"No, I didn't do that," Wilson replied, aggression just below the surface, his left hand gripping the whisky glass so tightly that the tips of his fingers splayed. "Why would I?"

"Why? I don't know. You tell me what you're up to." Gus replied, remembering what Caroline had told him earlier: "You came here by car, didn't you?"

"Did I? To be honest, I arrived by taxi - but my car's parked nearby."

"What is all this!" Willes was irritated, baffled. "Why the big act? Why let everyone think you're some crazy bastard, living rough?"

"Because it kept me alive." Gus moved over and refilled his glass, Wilson smiling sarcastically. "Should I say thank you?"

"Not to him," the historian snorted, "It's my bloody whisky!"

Unperturbed, Wilson continued. "I was safe because no one cares about an addict. Most of the time they leave you alone. They watch you, but they leave you alone. I'm old, they must have been expecting me to die long ago. But I didn't, because I've waited to get hold of those tapes."

Gus wasn't convinced. "Why didn't you look for them earlier?"

"How could I? I needed the perfect time. Which is now."

"Now? Seems like you've been plotting for a long time."

"Decades."

"That's a lot of hate to hold onto."

"It kept me alive."

"So if you didn't threaten my family and injure Jimmy Gold, who did?"

"Take your pick, Mr. Egan," Wilson replied, some of his malice surfacing. "I had a lot of time to work this out. You think I didn't plan *everything*? You think you're the only one who can do research?" His thin face turned from Gus to Willes and back again. "Have you never wondered about the people you're trusting? The people you're helping? What about Ella Fairchild, Caroline Lever?"

"What about them?"

"Are *they* who they seem? Fairchild said she was burgled, but was she? Or was she lying to get you on her side? Is Caroline Lever the poor orphan she makes out? Or perhaps everyone is using you because of your grandfather. That debt of honour you thought you owed him." Wilson finished his drink before continuing. "Guilt does that to you, doesn't it? Poor George Lyman - you *had* to find out what happened to him, didn't you? I mean, he was your grandfather. *Or was he?*"

"What are talking about!" Gus snapped, angered. "Of course he was my grandfather."

"If you say so. But what about Paul Shore? Is he who he says he is?"

"His niece is missing --"

"*Is she?* Or perhaps she lives in Berlin and drives a car."

Gus stared at him: "Are you telling me she was the driver of the car that hit Jimmy?"

"Perhaps. Or perhaps she works for me. Or perhaps for the people who don't want anyone asking any more questions about Addison Franckel."

"But *you're* asking questions."

"Yes, but I want revenge at any price. I want the tapes exposed. If it costs me my life, I don't care. It's been a shit life and I've no intention of holding onto it after I've done what I set out to do. I just want everyone to know what my father was. What he *truly* was and what he did." Wilson paused, looking around him, pulling out a packet of cigarettes and lighting one.

"Smoke makes me cough," Willes said, waving his hand extravagantly. "If you want to kill yourself, be my guest, but I'm holding on for as long as I can."

"Too scared to die?" Wilson asked. "You know, my father loved that Fuseli painting you admire so much. He used to stare at the copy he had in his consulting rooms in Berlin. Yes, he had one there as well. Or maybe it was the one you have... He said that Fuseli was a demon, that he had 'impregnated' the picture. *The Semen Demon...* " Wilson laughed bitterly. "My father found it exciting; he was always stimulated by fear, he loved to experience it and feel it, and cause it. He believed you could make the emotion real." Wilson fell silent for a moment, then studied the historian. "The people who admire Fuseli's painting are always similar, goblins who feel out of place, ghouls that repel love."

"Speak for yourself, I was happily married --"

"Your wife cheated on you with the man you've now destroyed." Wilson retorted, inhaling and then exhaling the smoke languidly. "But that wasn't enough, was it? Be honest, you hear her and see her sometimes, don't you?" He asked, looking at Willes, his hostile eyes steady, his face scored with deep Marionette lines; tragic and sly by turns. "She died in a car accident, taking the turn too quickly on the bend out there. Isn't that right? Well, they found her in driver's seat anyway."

Gus glanced at Louis Willes, the old man's expression ferocious. *"What the hell are you suggesting?"*

"You were driving, weren't you? You crashed the car, then swapped seats. Getting rid of an unfaithful wife with no questions asked." Wilson smiled, thin lipped, cruel. "Everyone knows that you were always a dangerous driver, and clever enough to pull off a stunt like that on an unlit country road --"

"You lying bastard!"

Silent, Gus watched the blood drain from the historian's face, his hand shaking, reaching for his glass of water as Wilson continued.

"No wonder you think she haunts this place. But she isn't the only one. *Everything* haunts Graybrooke. My father, the patients who died here, and your wife. She waits for you, like my father waits for me."

"Get out!"

"'*Get out?*'" Wilson queried. Peevishly amused. "But we haven't watched the tapes yet," he turned to Gus. "Stop lying and give them to me. After all, you want to see them, don't you? You couldn't do all this and miss the grand finale."

Out of the corner of his eye, Gus could see Je-Yun standing on the balcony above them, overlooking the sitting room, the Korean immobile, listening, as Wilson continued.

"They took my father away. They destroyed the clinic. They obliterated him to keep secret what had happened here. The authorities - the Government and the police - worked together to ensure no one talked about Addison Franckel. *Especially his son.* So I lived like a pig, someone no one wanted or cared about. Someone whose brain had become so scrambled they couldn't remember their father and what he'd done --"

"What *did* he do?" Gus asked.

"I don't know, until I see the tapes." He put out his hand. "Give them to me."

"And if I don't?"

"Don't tell me you think you're amongst friends, Mr. Egan?"

Gus knew he wasn't and hesitated. He had played for time, but had none left and remembered Jimmy's warning. How would he manage to leave Graybrooke, now he was cornered? Now he had found the tapes and was of no further use… He looked from one man to the other. The historian watching him from across the room, Je-Yun staring down from the mezzanine above, and the wiry, venal Freddy Wilson standing with his hand out.

"Just one thing" Gus said coldly "I want to see them before I hand them over --"

"*Hand them over*?" Willes repeated, incredulous. **"I'm keeping them!** They were found on my property and possession is nine tenths of the law."

"You want to take this to law?" Wilson asked mirthlessly. "Good luck with that. If the tapes are given to the authorities they'll disappear like they did before --"

"Not all of them." Gus interrupted. "And I want to know about the copies that survived, who made them?"

"Miriam Levy." Wilson replied. "She was the Nursing Sister at Franckel's clinic. But then you know that already, don't you? I'm not sure if she had copies made, or if she stole them from Franckel's clinic, but I'm guessing she hid the tapes because she wanted to make sure a record survived. Mind you, did *she* survive? Who knows? My father never forgave anyone who betrayed him." Wilson paused, looking into Gus's face, his voice resigned. "You *have* to give me the tapes now, Mr. Egan. You've really no other choice."

FORTY TWO

Walking ahead, Gus left the house with Freddy Wilson following, the two men entering the garage and pausing beside Gus's car. With the key in his hand, he was about to release the door locks when Wilson touched his shoulder.

"I'll do that."

"What if I said no?" Gus asked, his attention caught by the emergence of Je-Yun at the entrance of the garage. "Is he your back up?"

Wilson shrugged. "I'm hoping there isn't going to be any trouble."

"Well, that's some comfort," Gus replied, turning to Je-Yun. "Whose side are *you* on? I'm losing track."

"Mr. Willes sent me to help --"

Amused, Gus smiled. "To help *me*? Or *him*?" He pointed to Wilson. "Is your employer worried I'll attack him and run off with the tapes?" Gus looked around him. "I don't have my keys, and without a car I wouldn't have much of a chance, would I? Or maybe

I could end up like Jimmy Gold. I hear that bend at the end of the lane is a death trap."

Wilson sighed. "No one's threatening you, Mr. Egan, I just want the tapes." He clicked the button to release the automatic locking system, then turned back to Gus. "Get them out."

Reluctantly, Gus moved around the back of his car, Wilson following him as Je-Yun watched from the garage entrance. Lifting the lid of the boot, Gus reached in, taking out two film reels and then surreptitiously pushing his coat further under the spare wheel.

Impatient, Wilson put out his hand, Gus holding onto the tapes. "You don't even trust me to carry them?"

"I've waited too long to be cheated now."

Handing them over, Gus took back his car keys and slammed the boot closed - but not before Je-Yun had moved closer, his gaze locked on to Gus's car. "Were the tapes all you found?"

"I found a lot a lot of earth and some rocks, you want those too?" Gus replied, bluffing. "Be my guest and have a rummage in the boot, it's not been cleaned for six months."

Turning away, Je-Yun accompanied Wilson back into the house, Gus making sure his car was locked before he followed them into the sitting room. The armchair where Willes usually sat was empty, his strident voice calling out from the study, all three men entering to find the historian seated in front of a large, blank screen, another three chairs placed alongside him. A projector had already been set up, its lens pointing towards the screen like a cannon jutting out from a castle keep.

"You see, I've been ready for this show for quite a while." Willes gestured to the screen, then looked back to Gus. "You know how to run a projector?"

"I'll do it," Wilson interrupted. "It's 16 mm film, most people don't know how to set it up." He was holding the two reels in his hands, the steel cannisters aged, rusty around the rim.

"Are you sure?" Gus asked. "You wouldn't want to mess it up now --"

"My father had a projector in Berlin, he used to run his films on it. They were 16 mm --"

"Did you see them?"

Wilson shook his head abruptly. "We weren't allowed. My mother and I were forbidden. We just saw the machine and sometimes we used to hear it humming when he turned it on. But every time my father set it up he would come out of his consulting room and check that we weren't listening." Wilson was remembering, reliving it. "He would be angry, say that if he caught us spying he'd force us to watch everything and we wouldn't like it. And then maybe he would film *us* - and we wouldn't like that at all."

He stopped talking, pulling himself out of the memory and laying down the two cannisters beside the projector. In silence, Willes, Je-Yun and Gus watched as he picked up the first cannister and tried to open it. The sealing tape had been easy to sever, but time had rusted the threads along the lid, Wilson turning to Je-Yun.

"Get me a knife."

He did as he told, returning moments later with a blade and watching as Wilson carefully edged it around the rim to loosen it. His hands were trembling, sweat on his wasted face, as he struggled to open the can. Finally, in exasperation, he snatched up the second cannister and repeated the process. This time the lid unscrewed without effort, Wilson lifting the spool of film out and holding it to the light.

"I can't make it out!" He snapped, hurrying over to the projector and loading the 16mm film with quick, expert hands. Then, breathing heavily, he turned on the machine.

All four men stared at the screen. They saw the first blurred black and white images, then the blotching and spreading deterioration as the film disintegrated in front of them. Panicking, Wilson watched as the film ran on, the projector continuing to turn as he tried to stop it, the frames gobbled up one by one as the tape was erased. Hysterical, Wilson then turned on the lights, picking up the second cannister and prising it open. He was so desperate the knife slipped, the blade cutting into his thumb as the spool of film finally fell to the floor.

On his knees, Wilson scrambled for it, his hands with their raised veins, clutching the film reel as he held it up to the light, his voice barely human as he let out a scream of frustration.

"There's nothing left!" He wailed. "Nothing!"

"Give it to me. Something might be saved." Gus said, reaching out.

" 'Saved?' " Wilson held the film reel in front of him and shook it. "There's nothing left! **There's nothing left *to* fucking save!"** Hysterical, he struck out at Gus, then threw the reels across the room, Willes ducking out of the way.

"The famous Incubus Tapes" the historian said, his voice veering between anger and mockery. "After all this build up, and there's nothing to bloody see!"

Wilson was beside himself, turning on Gus. *"There are more*! There must be more! Go back!" he commanded him. **"Dig them up, there must be more!"**

"That's all there was. Two cannisters buried eighty years ago." Gus replied calmly. "Surely you thought that this might happen? After so long, you must have realised there was a chance the films would disintegrate."

Now mute, Wilson crumpled into his seat, ravaged, his composure gone, decades of waiting, of longing for revenge, deteriorating like the reels of film in front of him. A raddled old man sitting staring hopelessly at the mess around his feet.

"I could have made a fortune from those. I could have exposed the bastard and made a fucking fortune...." With the toe of his shoe he nudged one of the film reels. "Stupid bitch! Why didn't she hide them in a better place?"

In silence, Gus watched him, thinking of Miriam Levy, whose remains were lying in the boot of his car. He imagined how afraid she had been, knowing that Franckel would kill her for betraying him. She had been his lover, had worked alongside him, had known the layout of the clinic and chosen a hiding place underground, a place that would remain secret, locked up for decades. She hadn't known then that she would end up being laid to rest beside the tapes.

Gus didn't know that had come about either, but he knew that it had been Miriam Levy who had *guided* him to the tapes. Hidden deep under the ruins, under mounds of debris. It had not been the spirit of Ava Willes, but Miriam, waiting in the dark, amongst the trees, for someone to uncover the Incubus Tapes and find her bones.

Eighty years of waiting, alone, crumbling under the long press of earth, with the tapes lying beside her.

FORTY THREE

Pointing his walking stick at the film reels lying on the floor, Willes sighed and turned to Je-Yun. "Move that rubbish, will you? I don't want the dog to chew it and get sick." Then he glanced over to Gus, raising his eyebrows. "I should be disappointed, and I am, but I still have the publication of the book and exposure of the Fuseli fake to look forward to…. Did you know?"

"About what?"

"That the tapes were buggered."

"How could I?" Gus replied. "You saw them, they were sealed when Wilson took them from me… Where is he anyway?"

"He left. Walked out - didn't you say he had a car parked nearby?" Willes laughed. "All that planning came to nothing. Poor bastard was *living* for those tapes, Christ knows what he'll do now."

"He didn't ask you for anything?"

"Like what? A bed for the night?" Willes shook his head. "No, he was banking on those tapes. Literally banking on them --"

"But he wasn't poor, he was just acting poor. He drives a Mercedes and those clothes he was wearing were good quality." Gus replied. "So either he was already spending the money he was expecting to get, or he was being funded by someone."

"Not me," Willes said firmly. "A wise man knows when to *stop* asking questions, Mr. Egan."

Gus ignored the comment. "Was he right about your wife?"

"You never know when to stop, do you?"

"Graybrooke is a place that encourages questions. So many mysteries here. So many secrets, but then there aren't many secrets left for you, are there? Not that you'd admit to anyway." Gus sighed. "It's disappointing, I was looking forward to seeing the Incubus Tapes."

Willes pointed to the debris on the floor. "Have a good look before Je-Yun sweeps it up."

"What will he do?"

"*Who?*"

"Je-Yun. What will he do when you die?"

"Return to Korea, I suppose. Or Germany, where his brother lives." Willes replied. "I imagine you'll be leaving now. I mean, you've been paid for your work, the book's completed, and the longed for tapes have proved to be a pathetic anti-climax. No reason to stay, is there? You must be missing your family."

Gus looked around him. "This place should be knocked down. The whole house should be demolished, flattened on top of the ruins of Addison Franckel's Clinic so nothing remains, not even a memory." He moved to the door, then turned back. "But you'll never leave here. Alive or dead, you'll stay. You belong here, Willes, one more ghost. One more person silenced - because you *will* be silent when you're dead, silent and trapped, along with the tortured patients and your damaged wife."

"**Piss off, Egan!** Get out of here."

"With pleasure" he replied, "at least I can."

FORTY FOUR

Gus Egan's flat
London

".... I just want everyone to know what my father was. What he truly was and what he did. He said that Fuseli was a demon, that he had 'impregnated' the picture. He made a little joke about it, The Semen Demon... My father found 'The Nightmare' exciting; he was always stimulated by fear, he loved to experience it and feel it – and cause it. He wanted to create it, make it real..."

Gus remembered Freddy Wilson's words as he stared at the wall he was using as a makeshift screen, the images from The Incubus Tapes playing out before him.

When he had found the films at Graybrooke he had taken them back to his car and immediately swapped them for two *other* cannisters. He had bought them off the internet, taking care to ensure that they were authentic and had once held films from the 1940's. Cannisters Gus had hidden until he needed them. They had been easy to get hold of on eBay; old reels for film buffs, collected for decorative purposes, the tapes inside useless. Gus had planned the switch from the start, because he had never intended for either Louis Willes or Freddy Wilson to get hold of the Incubus Tapes. Instead he had wanted to know what Addison Franckel had done to his grandfather and the other patients who had died. Had wanted to see what the authorities had suppressed; what had been so disturbing that all evidence - including their creator - had been obliterated.

Something Gus had *not* expected to find was a small folded note, encased in a metal tube, taped to the inside of one of the genuine cannisters. The handwriting was uneven, jagged, and obviously written under pressure:

> *'My name is Barbara Todd, nurse and friend*
> *of Miriam Levy. She wanted to hide the tapes*
> *she stole from Addison Franckel and made*
> *me promise that if anything happened to her*
> *I would put the tapes with her body. **I saw***
> ***him kill her. I saw him bury her**... And*
> *I have kept my promise. God rest her soul.*
> *God help all who have suffered here.'*

Still holding the note in his hand, Gus had then watched what he would never forget, the tapes in showing the imperious figure of Addison Franckel striding through the wards where shell shocked soldiers were housed. Gus had researched the horrors of shell shock; the confusion, the tremors, impaired sight and hearing, hysteria, young men hiding under beds taking cover from imaginary gunfire, others hysterical, many with a blank, thousand-yard stare. And as Gus continued to watch the tapes he saw Franckel picking out individuals, having them taken to his private consulting rooms. There he injected them, Gus seeing the patient struggle against the gradual muscle paralysis, their limbs contorting, their eyes glaring out of their rigid faces.

And all the while Franckel was talking:

'*What is imperative is that we hold the patient in a state of shock. We then maximise that shock, that feeling, we hold them there, paralysed, so they cannot escape and the emotion becomes intensified...*'

The film ran on, then turned its focus onto a female patient, asleep, then waking abruptly from night terrors. She was screaming, begging for help, Franckel injecting her and locking her into her nightmare.

"*... She is unable to speak now, or beg for me to withdraw the drug that holds her paralysed. This woman fears the night, the dreams, not just of war but in her normal sleep. And her fear - you see it here - becomes **real** at the point at which the paralysis takes hold. It is no longer imagined, but **literal.** Of course the dosage must be gauged correctly or it could cause heart attacks and prove fatal...*"

Gus was staring at the images, barely breathing, sickened, but unable to turn away, watching the fear in the victim's eyes, their limbs moving, jerking, then finally paralysed.

Franckel was now standing beside a man and talking directly to camera.

"*I have discovered a means by which - through paralysis and the imposing of extreme stress - I can recreate and intensify trauma. And by doing so, can make **real** the **unreal.** What is most feared, is then cre-*"

435

ated. The Night Terrors are not imagined, nor dreamed, they are birthed..."

And then Gus saw something he could not understand. Could not comprehend, because it wasn't real, and yet he was seeing and hearing it. The sound of gunfire exploding in the consulting room as the paralysed patient 'heard' it. Lights glaring above the victim as though he actually was under fire and 'seeing' it. The consulting room alive with the recreation of war trauma.

*"...I have studied Night Terrors for many years and now I can prove they exist, not merely in imagination, but in a concrete form... You see, what we fear destroys us. Not merely mentally, but physically, when we birth the monsters of our own terror..." He paused again before concluding. "There is no weapon more lethal than fear. No opponent more ruthless than terror. To create physical terror is to control people and countries. To create **mental** terror has the potential to destroy man.'*

The film shuddered, flickered on Gus's wall then steadied, the film darkening as though the room itself had become night. Then another image took shape; that of a squatting creature, pressing down on a patient's paralysed body. And then Gus felt a sensation of touch against *his* shoulder, spinning round and seeing a shadow on the wall behind him bending down, a clicking sounding in his ear.

As quickly as it had appeared, it disappeared, Gus turning back to the screen and staring at the Incubus squirming on the chest of a female patient. It had the same eyes as in the Fuseli painting, the same ghoul that had taunted the artist now taunting a person suspended, paralysed in their own terror.

The reel of film then began crackling, black and white tape juddering, the volume echoing, distorted, but the fear was still clear, palpable. It seeped from the films, from the eyes of the paralysed soldiers and the stricken woman, and then Gus understood why the tapes had been considered so dangerous. To be able to immobilise soldiers, armies, with fear, to drive them to madness by making their terror into visible reality, would be a weapon that could topple governments and destroy countries. Something so potentially lethal that its very existence had been denied, and everything about it - and its creator - destroyed.

Everything.

Except the copy of the tapes Gus had just watched.

The tapes, and the remains of Miriam Levy.

-oOo-

When Gus returned to London he told Andy Fields what had happened and explained about the bones he had found.

"What?"

"Her name was Miriam Levy--"

"You have someone's remains in your car?" Andy asked. "What the hell are you up to?"

"I told you about Addison Franckel, you know as well as I do that the authorities suppressed everything as if nothing had ever happened. So what *do* I do, Andy? Who should I give the remains to? You? The coroner? And both of you will obviously ask me questions and I'll tell you the whole story and as soon as I mention Addison Franckel it will all be shut down again." Gus drew in a breath. "Just tell me what to do, and I'll do it."

"It's a crime to tamper with a dead body --"

"I didn't tamper with it, I found it buried with the tapes. She was murdered --"

"You don't know that for certain!" Andy replied. "You can't even be sure it was this Miriam Levy."

Having already decided not to disclose everything he knew, Gus made no reference to Barbara Todd's letter.

"Miriam Levy was Franckel's lover and his nursing assistant. When she found out what he was doing she tried to save a patient by smuggling them out of the clinic. She failed, but before she was killed --"

"Who killed her?"

"Addison Franckel."

"You have proof of that?"

"*She betrayed him!*" Gus retorted. "And as his son said, Franckel never forgave treachery. It was Miriam who had copies of the Incubus Tapes."

"*And she was buried with them?*" Andy raised his eyebrows. "Well, she didn't bury herself, did she? So who did? Who buried her?"

Again, Gus held back. "I don't know. It had to be someone who wanted to hide Miriam's body and ensure that the tapes survived."

"And who was that?"

"*I don't know.* I wish I did." He felt no guilt for lying. "If things had been investigated at the time we'd all know, just like we'd all know where the patients were buried, where Franckel ended up, and what happened to the journalist who was killed."

"You were lucky it wasn't you." Andy replied bluntly. "I can't let this slide --"

"I don't know why not, everyone did before."

Stung, the detective took a moment to reply. "What about these tapes, did you watch them?"

"I couldn't, they were ruined." Gus had meant to confide in Andy Fields, but suddenly it seemed foolish. An old friend might mention it to a colleague in the police, or let it slip that Gus Egan had the Incubus Tapes. And then what?

"You know that I have to take possession of the remains?" Andy said. "Go through the procedure."

"Just don't put her in storage and forget her. She deserves more than that. Miriam Levy has a relative, a great niece, she could organise a burial."

Caroline Lever did just that, at a London synagogue, Gus attending. It turned out that Paul Shore did *not* have a niece, but was a close friend of Lily's and regarded himself as her uncle, relieved when she re-emerged in London. He, like Ella Fairchild, was bitterly disappointed that the Incubus Tapes had been ruined, their destruction offering neither explanation, nor closure. Their mutual desire for justice unfulfilled, they took some comfort from the downfall of Freddy Wilson, his pretense having fooled both of them. At times Gus even wondered if they missed the anonymous texts, the messages, the excitement that had, briefly, ignited their lives.

Under the management of Dr Richards and the care of Je-Yun, Louis Willes relished his triumphant exposure of the Fuseli fake that had brought down Anthony Hallett. It was doubtful that he agonised over his actions, even though they had inadvertently caused the death of John Cummings. As for the murderous thief that Hallett had hired to steal the Fuseli, he was never caught, just slid like an eel into the thick sludge of the art world's underbelly. Gus heard, not long after, that Ronnie Gilchrist's business had been saved by a generous injection of cash from none other than Edward Leigh, now in full control of the gallery he had previously shared with Anthony Hallett.

Disturbed by what he had seen on the tapes, Gus confided in no one, although his relationship with Ziva became stronger and they talked of remarrying. He told himself that time would blur the memories, but he was wrong. It heightened his recall; brought the tapes into sharp focus, until they began to invade his dreams. At times he thought of destroying the tapes, but never did, seeing it as a betrayal of his grandfather and the other patients who had suffered. Time passed. He never told anyone that he had found the Incubus Tapes and kept them in a security box at a London bank until he could decide what to do with them.

It took over a year for Gus to come to terms with what he had seen, and another eighteen months until he no longer thought of the images he had watched. Or heard Addison Franckel's voice echoing through his dreams. Although he had longed to confide, as time passed he was relieved that he had never spoken to anyone about the tapes. He didn't want anyone else to see what he had, and in protecting them, protected himself.

And then, one morning in early March, he was on a flight to Munich, where he had been commissioned to undertake the research for another biographer. The journey was short and uneventful, Gus waiting for a taxi outside the airport when someone bumped into him. Apologising, the man then hurriedly walked on.

It was only later that Gus found the envelope which had been dropped into his pocket. Inside was a piece of paper, with the image of an incubus.

There was no note. There didn't need to be. The symbol of the incubus told Gus everything he needed to know. He was being followed, perhaps by people who suspected that he had possession of the tapes, or by the authorities who were waiting to see what he would do next.

Uneasy, Gus threw the envelope and its malignant image away.

And in the distance someone watched him go.

Putney, London
1822

My dear Johann,

Forgive this hasty reply, which must by needs be brief for I am again travelling.

*You asked me in your last letter if I had not become exhausted by the continued interest in 'The Nightmare' after so many years have passed. Well, I ask you in all honesty, how **could** I grow weary of such infatuation and fixation on the work?*

'Our ideas are the offspring of our senses. We are no more able to create the form of a being we have not seen, without retrospect to one we know. He whose fancy has conceived an idea must have composed it from actual existence..' There, my friend, you have just read the conclusion of my latest lecture!

*Only **we** know the truth of the painting's conception, and perhaps you - like myself - watch, with a mixture of incredulity and unease, how the Incubus still exerts its unwavering power.*

I sign off for now and wish you health and contentment, dear friend - and trust your dreams are not remembered.

With affection,
Henry

EPILOGUE

Louis Willes lived for another two months after fulfilling his revenge. Long enough to enjoy his triumph over the art world and to relish seeing Anthony Hallett jailed. Despite the combined forces of the Swiss and British police, John Cummings's murderer was never caught, and the forgery that was the indirect cause of his death was lost. Most likely destroyed. Or maybe in some secure vault or some unmarked storage locker.

The Nightmare, in its various versions, still holds a fascination for many; its meaning disputed endlessly by professionals, art lovers, and psychiatrists. Painted in 1781, Fuseli sold the work for £20 guineas. Now it is exhibited in the Detroit Institute of Arts, USA, and estimated to be worth £4,000,000.

It is still rumoured to be haunted.

Bibliography

Gothic Nightmares, Fuseli, Blake and the Imagination
Martin Myrone
Tate Publishing

Fuseli and the Modern Women: Fashion, Fantasy, Fetishism
Jonas Beyer, Mechthild Fend etc.
Publisher: Courtauld, October 2022

London: Hogarth Press and Institute of Psychoanalysis, 1931.

Andrei Pop, Sympathetic Spectators: Henry Fuseli's Nightmare and Emma Hamilton's Attitudes,
Art History vol. 34, issue 5, 2011

Spike Island: The Memory of a Military Hospital
Philip Hoare
Published by Fourth Estate, 2001

The Life and Writings of Henry Fuseli, Esq
John Knowles
Published by Henry Colburn and Richard Bentley, London, 1831

Printed in Great Britain
by Amazon